UNTIL PROVEN GUILTY

Christine McGuire

POCKET **STAR** BOOKS

New York   London   Toronto   Sydney   Tokyo   Singapore

This book is a work of fiction. Names, characters, places and incidents are products of the author's imagination or are used fictitiously. Any resemblance to actual events or locales or persons, living or dead, is entirely coincidental.

A Pocket Star Book published by
POCKET BOOKS, a division of Simon & Schuster Inc.
1230 Avenue of the Americas, New York, NY 10020

ISBN: 0-671-75012-7

First Pocket Books paperback printing January 1995

10 9 8 7 6 5 4 3

POCKET STAR BOOKS and colophon are registered trademarks of Simon & Schuster Inc.

Printed in the U.S.A.

*This novel is dedicated to prosecutors everywhere:
the true public defenders.*

Acknowledgments

With deep gratitude to Frederick Nolan,
without whom this novel would not have been
possible.

I would also like to express my thanks to my
literary agents,
Arthur and Richard Pine, for their support and
direction;
to my editor, Julie Rubenstein,
for helping shape the manuscript into the novel
it now is;
and to my family for their continued inspiration
and support.

Prologue

In Saigon, the Chinese street vendors sold little paper pills that you dropped into water and overnight they opened out to form a flower or a tree or a pagoda. That was how Lee felt from the moment he arrived: as if one of those paper pills was unfolding in slow-mo like a flower, a poison flower inside his brain, dark and dangerous and utterly evil. Every chance he got he prowled the sweaty streets, searching. He had no clear idea what it was he was looking for, yet he knew he would recognize it when he found it. It was as if he had always known he would find it. And know at once when he did.

He was assigned to the Military Information Office, based in a villa on the north side of the city. It was a milk run. All he had to do was brief the self-styled war correspondents. Most of them were old farts in their late fifties who hadn't heard a shot fired in anger since VJ Day. All they were interested in was filing some copy then getting back to the hotel and the booze and the Red Cross nurses dancing in their underwear; they wrote down whatever he told them. After that his time was his own.

The downtown area was a raucous glitter of gaudy neon, a bizarre movie set where the extras were hustlers, pimps, barflies, and grunts in civilian clothes; the soundtrack, the berserk roar of buses and cars and mopeds and jitneys; the location, a paved swamp where the fetid winds never blew away waste.

Around Tu Do Street there were half a hundred girlie bars with American names: Dallas, Chicago, Manhattan. Lee went down there all the time, soaking up the irresistible reek of squalor and debauchery. There was a place called La Bohème where the hostesses dressed in see-through dresses instead of leotards or swimsuits. There wasn't anything you couldn't have. There wasn't anything they wouldn't let you do. To get you interested they took hold of your hand and put it right there.

They had no shame. It was just something they did, like typing. What you like, Johnny? Tell me and I do it. *Something began to build up in him, an anticipation he could not define, a need he could not identify. He went with different girls, lots of them, but it was never any good.* Come on, baby, let me help you. *Then one Friday night he pushed into a bar in an alley off Tu Do Street and saw her.*

She was in a booth with a callow-looking kid of maybe twenty who was trying to get her to take a drink from a hip flask. She pulled away from him and he made a grab at her and missed. He flipped her the bird and turned back to his buddies. The girl eeled through the mob on the dance floor and as she looked up their eyes met. She was wearing a red one-piece cutaway bathing suit. All of them did now. She had a figure like a teenybopper. He grabbed her, digging his finger into her buttocks.

"What's your name?" he said. His voice felt thick in his throat.

"Kim," she said. She put her arms around his neck and pushed her crotch against his. The petals of the dark flower in his brain stirred.

"You buy me a drink, lover?"

"Sure," he told her. "What do you want, tea?"

A lot of the girls still drank what they called Saigon tea, a thimbleful of cold liquid that cost a couple of bucks and which they nursed long enough to make their pitch.

"You buy me a Coke?" she said in a little-girl-cute voice. "You buy me a Coke, lover?" Coke was three times the price of tea.

"You sure you don't want champagne?"

"No," she said, taking him seriously. "Coke okay."

The sweating bartender, who looked about a hundred and three but probably wasn't even forty years old, put the Coke and Lee's beer on the counter in front of them and whipped away the money.

"Is that your real name, Kim?"

"Sure. You like it, lover?"

Lee looked around. He didn't even know the name of the

place. They were all the same, the booths around the sweating walls crowded with shouting men and girls, everyone drunk or stoned or both, everywhere the stink of spilled beer and sweat, the dance floor a tiny space jammed solid with couples, practically screwing standing up.

"Yeah," he said. "I like it fine."

A big American got up out of one of the booths with his arm around one of the girls and they reeled off to the rear of the room where there was a doorway leading to the stairs. All the girls had "rooms"—little more than curtained cribs— above the bar. Lee slid into the vacated seat, pulling Kim in with him, his arm around her waist.

"How about this?" she said. She reached under the table and grabbed his penis, squeezing mechanically. The roaring in his ears grew louder. "You like this, lover? You want to make baby with me?"

Her body was lithe and firm and felt slightly moist to the touch. She had a wide mouth, good teeth, high cheekbones, glossy hair—the hair was an important part of a Vietnamese woman's grooming. You could tell which part of the country they came from by their hairstyle: the ones from the North cut it straight across at the waist, while those in the South did not. This one was from the North, a doll-like girl-child with fine features. He wondered if she had any Chinese blood. Some of them did.

"Not here," Lee said hoarsely. The pulse hammered in his head. "What about after work? I'll wait for you."

She leaned in close so that their cheeks touched. He felt the soft movement of her breath on the side of his face.

"You come upstairs with me now," she whispered. "I be nice to you, lover. I suck your cock till your balls drop off."

They all talked dirty, but somehow her particular childlike shamelessness excited him even more. He wanted to do it all with her. Now. Everything he had ever imagined.

"You want to come with me?" he asked her. "My place?"

"I can't leave here. Not allowed."

"I'll fix it. Who's your pimp?"

"Make no difference you talk with Dinh." She sounded upset, as if he might get her into trouble. She must be very new at this, he thought.

"That his name, Dinh?" Lee looked around the room. "Which one is he?"

"Over there. In the corner."

The man looked up, as though he had heard someone call his name. He was small and lithe, with a pockmarked face and dead eyes. He wore an expensive cream cotton double-breasted suit, a pale blue silk shirt, and two-tone shoes. He looked like a Cuban gangster. Lee jerked a thumb and the man came over warily. He watched Lee's hands, not his face.

"Got a problem, Jack?" His voice was flat and toneless, a strange mixture of Oriental and American. *"She giving you trouble?"*

"No trouble," Lee said. *"I want to take her back to my place."*

The pimp sucked in his breath through taut lips, as though Lee had suggested something obscene.

"You talking big bucks, Jack," he said. *"She's new. One of my best girls. Fresh off the farm. You know what I mean?"*

"How much?" Lee asked.

The dead snake eyes looked at him, speculating. *"Seven hundred fifty."* Ten Vietnamese piastres was a dollar.

"You crazy?"

"That's the arithmetic, Jack."

"I'll give you five. Tops."

"This is one expensive lady, Jack. Very desirable merchandise. Tell you what. I make you a deal. Seven hundred."

"Four fifty," Lee said. *"And next time it'll be four hundred."*

"Okay, okay, four fifty," the pimp said. *"What's your name, pal?"*

"Tom Bailey," Lee told him. *"Rifleman first class."*

"Okay, Tom. Let's see some dough."

Lee fished out his billfold, pretending not to see the look the pimp gave Kim. Pick him clean. He smiled to himself. You're out of luck tonight, Dinh, he thought, counting out the greasy bills. *"Four hundred, twenty, forty, fifty. Okay?"*

"Okay, Tom, you two have fun." Dinh leered.

On the street it was as sweatily humid as a New Orleans night. He flagged down a taxi and told the driver where he wanted to go. On Lam Son Square the street cowboys and pickpockets were as thick on the ground as sparrows. Men with thousand-yard stares sized up the whores in the red-light district. MPs in flak jackets and shiny white helmets counted their payoffs in alleys. Inside the cab Kim put her hand inside *his pants, her hair spilled over her face. Hey, cholo, you like that? Lust rose in his body like water filling a bottle. A roar filled his head, now, now, now. He couldn't speak, could hardly see or hear properly.*

He had the keys to a two-room shack on the western side of the city. It had been used as a store by some black marketeers. He had learned about it from reading prisoner interrogations at the Military Information Office where he worked, and appropriated the keys. Nobody knew about it but him. It had a bed and some chairs, a rudimentary bathroom, nothing by American standards but luxury to most Viets. He watched the movements of the girl's buttocks as she walked up the stairs ahead of him.

"This your place? You big rich guy, yes?" she said. She sounded happy, as if he was taking her someplace nice. The shutters were closed and the place had a musty smell, but he was conscious only of her, the soft whisper of her thighs rubbing together as she walked, the sharp vinegary scent of her skin. He tore off his shirt, kicked off his shoes, tossed his pants onto the chair. She stood in front of the window, her body outlined from the rear by a faint halo of moonlight, exactly like . . .

Lynda.

"Look at you! You know how estupid you lookin'? You really t'ink I was goin' to let you do it, hey? You really t'ink I let you anywhere *near* me? You t'ink you gonna satisfy any woman with that thing? I seen ababies with bigger dicks. I seen ashrimps bigger than that! You *pathetic*, you know that?"

The word echoed inside his head, pathetic, pathetic, pathetic. And as his mind filled with the memory of Lynda and his own shame, he felt himself shrinking, growing flaccid. God damn her, he thought, God damn that cheap bitch spic whore, would he never be able to forget what happened that night?

"Something wrong, baby?" *Now Kim was doing it. She was looking at him there. Dismay swept through him and then anger.*

"Nothing's wrong," he snapped. "Just wait . . ."

Kim reached out and tweaked his penis.

"You look funny," she said, and giggled. "Like shrimp."

The anger was like a bright explosion in his brain. Blindly, without thought, he hit her. She sprawled back on the bed, her laughing mouth suddenly a bright red blossom, naked fear in the dark eyes. He was across the room after her in one stride. He grabbed the front of the red bathing suit and ripped it off her body, pulling her half-upright as he did. She screamed and he hit her again, slapping her hard with his open hand. Again and again he hit her, shocking her into silence. She got loose and squirmed backwards into a corner, mewing in terror, bringing up her knees and wrapping her arms around her head in a fetal huddle.

"Get up!" he hissed, grabbing her by the hair and dragging her out of the corner.

"Don't hit me don't hit me ..." she screeched, her eyes squeezed tight shut, her blood-spattered face distorted with pain.

"On the bed!" he shouted. "Face down!"

She lay face down naked on the bed, shivering, whimpering. Inside his head the dark flower opened completely, spreading, blood red. The football-crowd roar filled his head. Now! Now! Now! Strength surged through him. He had never experienced such excitement, such power.

He tore his shirt into strips and tied Kim's wrists to the headboard of the bed, then tied her feet to the base so that she was stretched out face down in the shape of an X. In the drawer of the rickety table beside the bed was a K-bar knife he'd bought off a guy who was in the SEALs. It had an eight-inch blade, sharp enough to shave with. He took it out and sat naked astride her buttocks. He was big again now. She felt it and twisted her head around so she could see him. Then she saw the knife. Her dark eyes widened with apprehension, like an animal in a trap.

"Oh please," she mumbled through swollen lips. "Don't."

"You're frightened, Kim," he said. His voice was very soft. "You're sorry you laughed at me, aren't you?"

She nodded dumbly. He touched the inside of her thigh with the blade of the knife. When she flinched, he smiled.

"Please," she managed. "Please. I do anything you want. Anything. Don't hurt me."

"It won't hurt, Kim," he said. "I promise."

He knew exactly what he was going to do now. It was as if he had always known. And it was as if she knew, too. He took a strand of her long black hair in his left hand, and cut it off with one swift stroke of the blade. Then another, and another, oblivious to the soft sobs of the girl beneath him.

1

THE PHONE RANG AT 4:17 A.M.

Kathryn let the answering machine pick up the call, monitoring it without revealing her own presence.

"Ms. Mackay, this is County Communications," a terse female voice said. "We have a homicide at Shelter Island. Please contact County Comm as soon as possible."

"Damn it," Kathryn said, and rolled out of bed. She picked up her phone and dialed County Comm. The dispatcher told her the Sheriff's Department had requested her presence at the crime scene. At least it was nearby, Kathryn thought. Shelter Island was just down the hill from her condo in Espanola, a few miles east of the city of Santa Rita.

"Where exactly is the crime scene?" she asked.

"At the western end of the island," the dispatcher said. "You know where it is?"

"Near the lighthouse," Kathryn said. "Who's in charge down there?"

"Sergeant Forsyth, Sheriff's Department. The Crime Scene Investigation Unit will arrive momentarily."

"Okay. Please call the duty inspector from the DA's office and ask him to meet me at the scene. I'll be there in about fifteen minutes."

She cradled the phone and padded through the dark condo to the guest room, putting on a light in the hall as she did. She touched Ruth's shoulder in the darkness. "Ruth," she whispered, "wake up."

"Yuh, uh, what?"

"I just got called out."

"Wosstime?"

"Four twenty-five."

7

"Okay, okay. You need anything?"

"No," Kathryn said. "I'll be back as soon as I can. But just in case, can you take Emma to school if I don't make it?"

"Uhuh," Ruth mumbled, burrowing back into the pillow. During the two-week period when Kathryn was on call—an annual duty that fell to every member of the DA's staff— her neighbor Ruth Draper, who lived on the floor below, slept at her condo so there would be someone with Kathryn's six-year-old daughter Emma if she was called out. Tonight was the fifth time in ten days. Four more to go, she thought, as she headed for the bathroom.

The bright fluorescent light made her squinch up her eyes. God, she thought, I look like a corpse in a fright wig. She splashed cold water on her face to wake herself up. Back in the bedroom she dressed in jeans and a T-shirt, then started on her makeup: eyeshadow, blusher, mascara, lipstick, the works. She put on her earrings, slipped into a pair of tennis shoes and a jean jacket, picked up her purse and briefcase, and went down to the garage. It was still dark, silent and still. She hopped into the little red Mazda and backed out. The air outside was damp and cool. Driving down the hill she could see the intermittent flash from the lighthouse on Shelter Island. The streets were empty; as she turned left on Beach Avenue and took the bridge across to Shelter Island, it started to drizzle.

It wasn't really an island anymore. Years ago, the long sandy spit of land running parallel to the coast had been connected to the mainland by infilling: it was now a narrow peninsula sheltering the tear-shaped small-craft harbor of Laguna del Mar and the purpose-built Marina Village further east. There were fine white beaches on the ocean side. Turning on to the promenade, Kathryn saw flashing strobes up ahead, then police cars, parked askew the way they always seemed to be. A uniformed deputy flagged her down and she rolled down the window.

"Kathryn Mackay, DA's office," she said, showing her ID. Then she recognized the officer. "Oh, hi, Kennedy."

"Mornin', Ms. Mackay." Kennedy was tall, slim, and blond, maybe twenty-four or -five. He made a gesture with a flashlight. "You want to follow me, please?"

She eased the car along behind him and parked it where

he pointed her. She got out, locked the Mazda, clipped her ID to her jacket, and worked her way through a knot of locals gathered near the yellow police crime scene tape. They watched her speculatively as a bleary-eyed Channel Seven news reporter hurried over from the remote van when he saw her coming.

"Nothing now," she told him briskly and ducked under the tape held up by one of the cops. The Crime Scene Investigation team's white van was parked beside the road. A big man in deputy's uniform was shrugging into a yellow rain jacket. Kathryn smiled and tapped him on the shoulder.

"Hey, Sergeant," she said, "how many assistant DAs do you know who'll come out at four-thirty in the morning just to prepare you for trial?"

"G'wan, tell the truth, you came because I'm irresistible, right?" The big deputy grinned at her. His name was Mike Eastwood. He was a witness in a murder case Kathryn would be trying in a week's time. So far they had been unable to get together so she could prep him. "You want to talk to Forsyth? He's investigating officer."

"In a minute," Kathryn said. "What have we got?"

"Young woman, Hispanic. About twenty. Whoever did it carved her up pretty bad. Doc Nelson says it looks like it might have been done postmortem."

Dr. Morgan Nelson was the county pathologist; he was also one of Kathryn's favorite people.

"That's all he said?"

"Pretty much," Eastwood said. "Killed her someplace else, dumped her body here. Some kind of a freak, he thinks."

Kathryn didn't respond; Eastwood didn't expect an answer anyway.

"Who found her?"

"Guy who works night shifts, walking his dog. That's him over by the car."

The man standing by the police car, hands thrust into the pockets of his jacket, head down against the morning chill, was about thirty-five, short, powerfully built, with deep acne scars.

"You got his statement?"

"For what it's worth," Eastwood said laconically. "Which isn't much."

"What did Doc Nelson say about cause of death?"

"Strangulation. Says he can't fix time of death with any accuracy."

"I'd better take a look."

The naked body lay head down on a sloping dune, arms outflung, legs wide apart. A young woman, slender, small-breasted. Her mouth was wide open as if in a silent scream, her short, dark hair matted with sand, her skin as gray as the sea. The area around the groin was a mess of mutilated flesh. Kathryn suppressed a shiver.

"Why so little blood?" she asked Eastwood.

"Like I said, we figure she was killed someplace else then dumped here. Probably sometime after dark last night: too many people down here in the daytime for it to have been then."

"Why would he do that? Bring the body to such a public place?"

Eastwood shrugged eloquently. Kathryn looked around. The knot of local people had dispersed. Two cops were leaning against their prowl car drinking coffee from a thermos flask.

"I asked County Comm to send an inspector over," she said. "Could you call in and tell him to forget it?"

"Sure," Eastwood said. "Anything else?"

Kathryn shook her head. "I don't think there's much I can usefully do here," she said. "Unless you want me to stick around?"

"Na," Eastwood said. "G'wan back to bed."

"Nice thought," Kathryn said, and went back to her car. The Channel Seven reporter saw her and hurried over, the cameraman loping behind.

"Can you give us anything, Ms. Mackay?" She recognized the reporter: his name was Keleher.

"Nothing you don't already know, Bill," she said.

"Thirty seconds? Pretty please?"

She shrugged. Keleher set up the sound bite and she said the appropriate words in the stark shine of the camera light. A young Hispanic woman, so far unidentified, apparently strangled somewhere and brought here by her killer. Yes, there were mutilations. No, there was no clue yet as to the identity of the killer: the investigation had just begun. There would be a full statement after the autopsy.

"All right, you guys," Keleher said to the crew as they finished the sound bite. "Wrap it up and let's go home. There's nothing more here."

The callousness jarred on Kathryn, but she didn't protest. The dead girl on the beach was just another entry in the catalog of death and disaster the media shared daily with the cops. They even shared some of the same vocabulary: there were "good" murders and "bad" ones. From a media point of view, this was a good one: they could get a lot of copy off the murder of a young girl, dumped in a local beauty spot, her body savagely mutilated. For the cops, it looked like a bad one.

Dawn was streaking the sky over the mountains with fingers of palest salmon pink when Kathryn got back to Seaview Heights. The condo was silent and still. She tiptoed over to Emma's room and looked in; her daughter was fast asleep, one arm thrown carelessly back over her head, her long dark hair strewn on the pillow like seaweed. Kathryn turned to see Ruth peering sleepily at her from the bedroom doorway.

"Heard you come in," she said. She rubbed her eyes. "You going back to bed?"

Kathryn shook her head. "I might as well do some work. Maybe I can take a nap later."

"And maybe pigs can fly," Ruth muttered. "What did they call you out on?"

"Murder," Kathryn told her. "A messy one."

"Wanna tell me what happened?"

"Nothing much to tell. A man walking his dog found the body of a naked woman on the dunes at Shelter Island. She's Hispanic, about twenty. Strangled and then ... mutilated. Looks like a sex killing. That's all we know."

"Jeez," Ruth said. "You sure get the plums. You want some tea?"

Kathryn shook her head. "What I need is a shower. A long, hot shower."

She went through to the bathroom and stripped off her clothes, dropping them all in the hamper. She set the shower control for hot and stepped in, gasping out loud as the water beat down on her like a solid weight, surrendering to the welcome warmth. She stood in the cascading water for nearly fifteen minutes, trying not to think, not to remember. It was no good; no matter how hard she tried, she could still see the slender figure of the naked girl sprawled head down on the cold, wet sand beneath the stark crime scene lights, her sightless eyes staring at the uncaring stars, and a gaping wound where her groin had been.

2

KATHRYN USUALLY GOT UP AT FIVE-THIRTY, WHICH GAVE HER time to do the chores, make Emma's lunch—thank God, she loved cheese sandwiches—and get her own things together. While Emma got ready for school, Kathryn would do some work on her Toshiba laptop. At seven-forty they'd drive over to Donaldson's Bakery in the Laguna del Mar Mall. She'd grab a muffin and some tea for herself, a sugared morning bun for Emma, and eat as she drove one-handed to Emma's school on Lighthouse Drive. Today, however, because she had to go to the morgue, she'd asked her friend Ruth to take Emma in later.

"Awwww, Mommy," Emma protested. "You said we'd have breakfast." Her lower lip trembled.

"Emma, it's work. I can't help it."

"You said we could go for breakfast. Together."

"We'll go tomorrow."

"You promised. You said we'd go today!"

"Emma, don't," Kathryn said. "Just don't, okay? I really can't handle a tantrum right now."

"But you *said,* Mommy. And you know I like you to take me to school!"

"I'm sorry, sweetheart," Kathryn said, distractedly. "I can't. I just don't have time today. I'm really busy."

"You're always really busy!" Emma said, plonking herself down on a chair and staring at the floor. "Always always really really."

"Emma, we've talked about this so many times," Kathryn said. "I thought you understood."

"I just miss you, Mommy."

"Sweetheart, I'm not going to have a good time. I'd rather be with you than go to the morgue."

"Is that where you're going, to the morgue? Where they keep the dead people? Why do you have to go there?"

"It's . . ." Emma didn't really understand the concept of violent death and Kathryn wasn't anxious that she should. "It's something to do with work. I have to see one of the doctors. Now come on, give me a kiss and be nice." She put her arms around Emma and tried to hug her, but Emma held back.

"Can we go to Donaldson's tomorrow?"

"Sure," Kathryn said. "I promise."

"Okay." Emma's tone turned philosophical. "As long as you keep your promise this time." She put her arms around Kathryn's neck and kissed her and hugged her. She smelled of soap and shampoo. "Love you, Mommy."

"I love you, too, sweetheart," Kathryn said. "You be a good girl today, okay? Did you do your homework?"

Emma nodded and Kathryn reluctantly disentangled herself from her daughter's embrace. I'll make it up to her, she promised herself. I'll set some time aside especially for the two of us. And how many times had she said that before?

She read her notes again, sipping her tea. When she was finished, she got up and stretched her arms over her head, wishing she didn't feel so tired. Being on call—as she had been when the Shelter Island murder was called in—was a guarantee of two weeks without a good night's sleep. Anything that broke, you caught. Murder, rape, wife beating. Anything. For Kathryn, being on call posed all sorts of other problems; it meant she had to have someone in the house with Emma. Ruth was her standby; but there had been plenty of times Ruth couldn't make it, and Kathryn had to call on a friendly Espanola policewoman for help. The joys of single parenthood.

She drove over to the morgue, not looking forward to the hours ahead. Watching the pathologist at work was never easy. You always forgot: corpses are heavy, awkward, inert. The pathologist has to do what he does in spite of the chill resistance of the dead flesh, and he cannot do it gently. So you had to psyche yourself up to ignore the hard flat liquid sounds as he heaved the body around, the heavy thud of

limbs or head on the unyielding stainless steel table, the raw
ripe escaping stinks of the dead. It looked like uncaring
brutality and you had to keep reminding yourself it was not.
I ought to be used to it by now, Kathryn thought, but dispas-
sion wasn't the easiest thing to bring with you into the chill
atmosphere of the autopsy suite.

"All right, good morning, everyone."

Chief Assistant County Pathologist Erwin Waters was a
compactly built man of medium height who looked like everyone's favorite uncle. He had neat, regular features, brown
eyes with lots of laugh lines around them, and dark brown
hair hidden now beneath the surgical skullcap. He wore the
pathologist's green theater uniform, rubber boots, and
gloves. He looked up at his audience; the young deputy,
Ray Kennedy, who'd been at the scene, Sergeant Mike Eastwood, some other cops Kathryn didn't know by sight. She
was the only woman present.

"You know why we're here. We have a Jane Doe homicide victim, found at Shelter Island four days ago. Prior to
a full autopsy, we'll be conducting a rape kit to establish
whether the victim was sexually assaulted. I'll talk you
through it as we go. Any questions before we begin?"

No one spoke.

"All right," Waters said. "For those of you who haven't
seen one before, a rape kit examination is not dissimilar to
the examination conducted on a live rape victim by the Sexual Assault Response Team." He coughed to clear his throat
and went over to the gurney.

"You'll notice we put a special paper towel beneath the
body," he began. "Normally we'd comb the pubic hair using
a one-use comb. Here, the injuries around the genital area
preclude that part of the examination so we'll proceed with
the rest: what we'll be looking for here is dried and moist
secretions and foreign materials from the head, the hair, the
scalp, or the armpits. The towel will ensure none of the
foreign materials are lost. . . ."

The examination was itself a sort of rape, with every inch
of skin surface checked with a Wood's lamp for signs of
seminal fluid, the mouth clamped open for examination of
the oral cavity for injury and for swabbing, the legs thrust
rudely apart as the external genitalia were examined and
swabbed, the colposcope inserted into the vagina so the bin-

ocular microscope could photograph the inner walls. It was very hard to keep emotional distance as Dr. Waters heaved the body over, grunting with effort, to do the rectal swabs, two small ones for spermatozoa and a larger one for an enzyme phosphotoate test.

And as the poor sad lifeless thing on the table was thrown flopping this way and that until you almost wanted to shout *Let her alone, for God's sake!* the pathologist's voice droned on about fingernail scrapings and samples of head and pubic hair and blood and urine and saliva, and all you could think of was that this had once been someone's child, someone's friend, maybe someone's lover.

When it was over Kathryn drove downtown. Instead of going to her office, she went directly through the atrium to the Courts Building, walking briskly; it was nearly noon. She had promised to look in on a child molest trial being prosecuted by Laura Foster, one of the youngest members of the DA's staff. Dark-haired, slender, voluble and impulsive, Laura had a disingenuous manner that often misled defense attorneys into not taking her seriously. She was sort of a project of Kathryn's. She saw a lot of her younger self in Laura, and she wanted to be there in case she needed moral support.

Superior Two was on the east side of the building, facing Pacific. As Kathryn slid into a seat in the front row, Judge Calhoun gave her an almost imperceptible nod; a good judge missed nothing that went on in his court. She glanced around, trying to see the familiar courtroom the way a stranger might. All were pretty much alike: each had the same variegated wood strip paneling, twin light oak tables and swivel chairs, the lectern facing the judge and the court reporters, the state and national flags behind the carved wood bench, the judge's high-backed leather chair, the calendar on the wall from the Santa Rita Land Title Company.

Superior Two differed from all the others only in that the sectional bookcase was on the right-hand wall, the carved wooden Great Seal slightly off-center behind the bench, the jury box on the left. The jury—six men and six women, with two male and one female alternates—was watching Laura attentively as she questioned Janice Arnold. Kathryn glanced at the spectator section: apart from some relatives of the victim, the only other person present was Dave Berry, reporting for the *Gazette,* a steno pad on his knees. He saw her and nodded. Nobody from TV; Kathryn was surprised. She'd thought they'd be around like flies waiting to hear little Karen Arnold on the witness stand.

The woman in the witness box, Janice Arnold, was Karen's mother. The defendant, Ralph Arnold, was an uncle who lived four doors down from her. He had known Karen all her life, and was a trusted member of the family. As was often the case, the abuse had been going on some time before the mother, a divorcée, detected something amiss. The case haunted Kathryn; although all prosecutors tried hard not to become emotionally involved in the cases they were trying, it was hard not to empathize when the victim was an abused child. Perhaps it was because Karen Arnold looked a little like Emma, and because Karen had been a little over six years old when her uncle first began abusing her, that Kathryn had felt so strongly about it. When she and Laura had discussed tactics prior to the trial, Kathryn had put herself in Janice Arnold's place; she had no difficulty imagining how she would feel if it were her own daughter who had been victimized. I'd want to kill him, she thought. I'd forget everything I know about the law and justice and every man's right to a fair trial. I would want him dead. So she had played that part for Laura, showing her how to use the strength of the mother's loathing so the jury would know it and feel it and share it.

She watched now as Laura took Janice Arnold through her testimony, handling the woman carefully and sympathetically. She was getting better all the time, Kathryn thought. She was going to be a damned fine prosecutor. That didn't mean she wouldn't be glad to have someone out there rooting for her. Most of the prosecutors on the DA's staff were young, one or two of them just a year out of law school. District Attorney Hal Benton was a busy politician; while he was out there doing what he had to do, he expected his chief deputy and Kathryn to keep an eye on the younger prosecutors, and try to steer them clear of some of the traps set for them by the wily, experienced—and sometimes unprincipled—defense lawyers they came up against.

"I know this is very painful for you, Mrs. Arnold," Laura

said. "But please tell the jury exactly how you learned what had happened to Karen."

"It . . . it was almost by accident," Janice Arnold said. "I had no idea. Ralph was . . . family."

"Go on."

"I was going to see my mother. She lives in San Francisco. I asked Ralph if he would pick Karen up from school and look after her till I got back. Then I told Karen."

"And what was her reaction?"

"She told me . . . she didn't want to go to Uncle Ralph's house anymore. Because he would want to play the daddy game."

"The daddy game?"

"I didn't know what she was talking about," Janice Arnold said, her eyes filling with tears. "I asked her what she meant. She said it was a secret. I said, Is it so secret you can't even tell your mommy? And she started to cry, and she told me it . . . it was what all daddies did with their little girls."

"Did she tell you what that was, Mrs. Arnold?"

"Yes," the woman said. "She did. In very graphic detail."

"What did you do then?"

"I took her to our doctor. Our family doctor."

"And he examined Karen?"

"Yes. He said—"

"We'll be calling Dr. Lefkowitz to tell us that, Mrs. Arnold," Laura interrupted smoothly. "Just one more question. How old was your daughter at the time?"

"Six," Janice Arnold said. "She was six years old and he . . . he . . ." She hit the armrest of the chair slowly with a balled fist once, twice, three times.

"Thank you, Mrs. Arnold," Laura said.

She turned to face the jury, letting the words Janice Arnold had not spoken hang in the air for long silent seconds. Perfect, Kathryn thought.

"That's all I have, Your Honor," Laura said. She looked across at Kathryn and nodded to let her know she'd seen her.

"Mr. Slade?" Judge Calhoun looked at the defense attorney. Donald Slade was a senior member of the law firm of Burke, Hanson, Oppicelli and Slade, who contracted much of the county's public defender work. He was a neat, small man with a Sundance Kid mustache and receding dark blond hair. There was something actorish about his manner.

"Nothing at this time, Your Honor," Slade said.

"Very well," the judge said. "Thank you, Mrs. Arnold. You may step down."

As the witness stepped down, Laura came across and leaned over to talk to Kathryn.

"How's it going?" Kathryn said *sotto voce*.

"Pretty much the way we discussed," Laura said, keeping her head averted so the defense table couldn't see what she was saying. "What did you think of Mrs. Arnold?"

"Very strong. The jury never took their eyes off her."

"Slade's got me worried. A few halfhearted objections. He's hardly challenged me on anything."

"Probably saving it all for Karen."

Laura nodded. "Look at the time," she said. "My bet is Calhoun will recess now. We won't get to Karen until this afternoon."

"How is she?"

Laura shrugged. "She's eight years old, Kathryn. The waiting isn't making it any easier."

"Ms. Foster," Judge Calhoun said. "It's already twelve-fifteen. Unless you have any serious objection, I think we'll recess now."

"Yes, Your Honor," Laura said, turning to face the bench.

"I'll try to get back later," Kathryn whispered. She got up and slipped out of the courtroom as the judge turned to the jury and recessed for lunch. Part of her wished she could stay with Laura, part of her knew that if she did, it wouldn't be Laura's case. You had to let them go, give them the chance to win. Or lose. This was Laura's first big one; she was there because Kathryn had recommended she be given the opportunity. District Attorney Hal Benton hadn't been sure if Laura was ready to handle a child molest case yet. It was always touch and go how much reliance the jury would place on a child's testimony, he argued. Slade would make an issue out of the fact that Karen had remained silent for so long. And although they had moved for an early trial date, it was now more than seven months since the offense had come to light.

"She's ready, Hal," Kathryn had said. "She can do it."

She hoped she had been right, but there were never any

guarantees. Would Laura be able to get Karen to testify consistently with her initial statement? Would she be able to get the child to convey to the jury using the anatomically correct dolls exactly what had happened to her? Would Laura be able to take her gently through all the graphic details of her ordeal without leading her—Donald Slade would object strenuously to any help she might try to give the child—and cover every aspect of what had happened, without further traumatizing Karen by making her relive the experiences in public? Or would the defendant walk, as so many of them did, because the child couldn't convince twelve people on a jury?

Back in her office, Kathryn gave an exasperated sigh. She loved the law, but it was a damned inefficient machine, rather like an old clunker you could never be quite sure would get you to your destination. To love the law, her first boss had told her, was a little bit like masochism: the more you did, the more it hurt you. Well, she still loved it. She thought of Laura, bright and young and eager and hard-working, and said a little prayer that she would never let her integrity and idealism be blunted by the imperfections of the system. Too many attorneys did.

The next time she looked at the clock it was late afternoon, and the day had gotten away from her. The courts had closed. The judges would be hanging up their robes, looking forward to dinner, or a late game of golf and a glass of wine at the club. Down in the parking lot, jurors and witnesses, spectators and defense attorneys, headed for their cars, carefully avoiding one another. For an attorney or a witness to speak to a juror during a trial—even though court was adjourned, even out in the open in a parking lot—was to invite a defense motion for a mistrial.

Kathryn called Ruth to check that she'd picked up Emma from school as arranged, then stood by the window for a moment. Everyone was going home, but Kathryn's day was far from over. She would be back in court tomorrow, doing rebuttal on the Burke rape case. As well as her preparations for that, there were always upcoming cases to work on, witnesses to subpoena, examinations to prepare. Before they left for the night, the deputy DA's staff usually had an informal get-together in the conference room, checking with one another on the progress of their cases, offering advice here, sympathy there. She'd go over and see how Laura's case had gone, talk with the others awhile. The younger ones leaned on the senior attorneys for knowledge and counsel; sometimes their being there could prevent a case from going down the tubes. Old bones were for young teeth to sharpen on, she always told them.

She smiled at the analogy. She was thirty-nine. Hardly what you'd call old bones, although she had changed considerably from the wide-eyed kid who had gone straight from law school into the public defender's office in Kansas City. She was twenty-five then, starry-eyed. What she wanted to do was help young girls in trouble, runaways, exploited kids, battered wives, abandoned ones. She wanted them to know there was someone there for them, the way a deputy public defender named Melinda Gray had once been there for her. She never had a chance.

There was no room for specialization and even less for idealism in the PD's office. It was like working in the emergency room in a hospital: no matter how many lives you saved, no matter how many bodies you patched up or broken limbs you reset, there would always be more waiting, never any end to it. The name of the game was survival. Don't get me justice, lady, get me off.

There was no time for caring; she was too busy learning to use the law, bend the law, twist it on behalf of clients whose cases she took on because she had no choice, people she knew were guilty the minute she laid eyes on them: an endless parade of addicts, drunks, con artists, rapists, muggers, pimps, pushers, and thieves who made her want to spray the office with Lysol after they left.

She learned, all right. She learned to carry packs of Doublemint gum to damp down the liquor breath of the hungover flotsam the system washed into her office. She learned never to be alone with certain men or women. She learned never to wear jewelry or have anything valuable in her office. She learned about slum landlords and chop shops, repo men and bail bondsmen, sex offenders and substance abusers, old men who liked little boys, young men who liked old ladies, whores with pistols in their pocketbooks, and pimps with cutthroat razors up their sleeves. She learned how to cut a deal, how to discredit a witness, how to play a jury for sympathy. She learned how to spot the flaw in a hastily prepared prosecution, how to sense the uncertainty of an expert, how to cast doubt into a juror's mind.

And the cutesier tricks of defense technique: dropping a pencil or a file as the prosecution was about to make a crucial point, haggling over offers of proof, making a face of astonished outrage when a prosecution objection was sustained, sighing noisily when one of her own was overruled. Being as gutsy as the men, and making them respect her for it. She stuck it out for eighteen months, unwilling to give up or unwilling to admit she'd made a mistake, eighteen months of sheer hell before she gathered up the tattered remnants of her self-respect and quit. It seemed like a long time ago. She smiled again: the girl I used to be, she thought.

The phone rang and she grabbed it. The voice on the other end was that of her immediate boss, Hal Benton's chief deputy, "Mac" McCaskill.

"Walt Earheart just called," he said. "Two bums found a dead woman in Sedgewick Park. Been in the water about a week, maybe longer. Coroner says there are genital mutilations."

"Another one? Like the Shelter Island victim?"

"Apparently."

"Could be a copycat," Kathryn suggested. "The media made a big play of the injuries."

"Could be," Mac said laconically. "Alternatively, we could have a serial killer on our hands. We better talk. Come on over to my office."

"Mac, I've got plans . . ."

"Cancel them," McCaskill told her.

3

DISTRICT ATTORNEY HAL BENTON HAD THREE CHIEF DEPU-
ties: Neal McCaskill, in charge of operations; Norman Podnoretz, chief of inspectors, in charge of investigations; and
Ted Loomis, responsible for administration. McCaskill
pretty much ran the office on a day-to-day basis, assigning
cases, redeploying resources. In Benton's frequent absences,
he was effectively the county's district attorney, and he was
a good one.

His office was neat and functional; a couple of bookcases,
some framed diplomas on the walls, a potted plant. His chair
was behind the horizontal end of a T-shaped desk unit with
two chairs on either side of the table.

The door was open; Kathryn knocked and went in. Mac
was standing behind his desk looking at some photos with
Walt Earheart, lieutenant in charge of detectives in the Sheriff's Department.

"Come over here, take a look at these," Mac said as Kathryn came in. Spread on the desk were about twenty full-
color crime scene photographs.

"What are they?" Kathryn asked.

"Shelter Island victim on the left, Sedgewick Park on
the right."

A couple of general shots showed the crime scene location
in each case. The rest were eight-by-ten color close-ups.
Kathryn remembered the girl on the dunes, her mouth open
as if in a silent scream, her skin gray in the predawn light.
The starkly lit pictures were very graphic. The butchered
bodies looked pathetic, abandoned.

"This one's the Sedgewick Park victim?"

"Just got them rushed over from the lab," Earheart said.
"Thought you'd want to see them."

Kathryn made a face. "What does the pathologist say?"

"Preliminary findings on the new one indicate asphyxiation. The genital mutilation is similar in both cases. Same
or similar weapon," Earheart told her. Close to six feet tall

and weighing maybe two hundred and forty pounds, Earheart made the slender McCaskill in his dark, three-piece suit look austere and formal.

"So you think we've got a serial killer?"

Earheart's massive shoulders moved in a shrug. "We can't be certain until we get the autopsy findings. But two killings like this within a couple of weeks of each other, it sure as hell looks like it."

"No identification?"

"We're working on that."

"They did a rape kit on the Shelter Island victim this morning," Kathryn said. "I was up there."

Earheart looked up sharply. "They come up with anything?"

Kathryn shook her head. "No vaginal or anal trauma. No semen found."

"Great," Earheart said.

"Have we got anything else? I haven't even seen a Crime Scene Investigation report yet."

"I'll send the reports over," Earheart promised. "Not that you'll get much out of them. Okay, let's take the Shelter Island victim, you know the general picture, you were on call that night. An early morning walker found the body. Doc Nelson's protocol, as best I can recollect, said the victim was Hispanic, approximately twenty years old. He hasn't been able to fix time of death with any accuracy, but he's given us an educated guess: about two or three days. Cause of death was strangulation."

Kathryn picked up one of the photographs, studied it. "I remember wondering why there was so little blood," she said.

"Nelson figures she was probably killed someplace else," Earheart said. "The killer kept the body hidden, then dumped it on the beach where it would be found."

"Why would he do that?" As she voiced the question, she heard herself saying the same words to Sergeant Eastwood at the crime scene. Earheart's response was identical: he shrugged.

"Doc confirmed the mutilations had been inflicted postmortem, how long he wasn't able to say."

"You say the crime scene team didn't get anything?"

"Not so you'd notice. It's just sand and stones down there."

"What about the follow-up investigation?"

Earheart looked pained. "We did everything we could, Kathryn," he said. "Set up a pedestrian and vehicle survey, checked missing persons, videoed for a spot on *Crime Stoppers,* released a police artist's sketch to the media asking for information. We followed up seventy or eighty leads. And we ended up right back where we started, with a Jane Doe, an unknown perpetrator, and no physical evidence worth a damn."

"And now it looks like we've got another one," Kathryn murmured. She looked at the photographs taken in Sedgewick Park. The crime scene investigators had pulled the dead woman out of the lagoon and laid her on the reeds fringing the bank to take their photographs. "Similar cause of death, same mutilation of the genital area. Any sign of sexual assault?"

"Hard to tell. They'll do a rape kit, but the body has been in the water six or seven days. Any seminal fluid would have been washed away."

"So she was killed before the Shelter Island victim?"

"Looks like. Doc said he needs to do more tests before he can be sure."

"It's odd the killer picked such public places to dump the bodies. He'd be taking a great risk of being seen."

"Maybe he gets his rocks off that way," Earheart said. "Some of them do."

"A psycho," McCaskill said disgustedly. "A twenty-four-karat fruitcake. That's all we goddamned need."

"The question is, what are we dealing with here?" Kathryn said. "Someone who just flipped? Or has he done this before, someplace else?"

"We ran the Shelter Island killing through the CAL-ID computers in Sacramento to see if they had anything with a similar MO on file," Earheart said. "Zilch. We'll try again, of course. We'll try everything again. But I'd be lying to you if I told you I thought it would get us anywhere. This bastard isn't giving us a thing."

"What happens next, Mac?" Kathryn asked.

McCaskill massaged the bridge of his nose with thumb and forefinger.

"I'll tell you what happens next," he said, tiredly. "I think we're in for a goddamn media circus. The sheriff's already got reporters from four counties camping outside his office, not to mention people representing Hispanic and women's groups. As if that wasn't enough, he's been approached to appear on the Richard Sanchez show."

"Jake Gylam? On the Sanchez show?" Kathryn said, letting her surprise show. The sheriff was renowned for his lumbering lack of tact; the DA's inspectors said if being an asshole was a science, Gylam would be a Ph.D. "I hope you talked him out of it?"

"You know Jake," Earheart said expressionlessly. That was the other thing they said about Gylam: his jawbone wasn't connected to his brain.

"He said he'd do it," Mac guessed glumly.

"What he said was, and I quote, he 'would be happy to have the opportunity of assuring the public at large that we are not in a negative outcome situation,'" Earheart said. Kathryn suppressed a smile; Gylam's way with the English language was also something of a legend.

"Give me strength," McCaskill sighed. "Kathryn, what's your caseload like?"

"About the same as everyone else's, I imagine," Kathryn said. At any one time, most of the senior assistant DAs were handling between thirty and forty ongoing cases in various stages of preparation. "Why do you ask?"

"Hal thinks we're in for a media shitstorm," Mac replied. "And I agree. So Hal wants you on this full-time."

Kathryn raised her eyebrows. "Mac," she protested, "I'm a prosecutor, not a public relations exec."

"Nobody wants you to be," Mac said. "The plan is, we tell the media we're setting up a special investigation unit. It will be headed by Senior Trial Attorney Kathryn Mackay, who'll be in charge of a team concentrating exclusively on the investigation of these murders. How does that sound, Walt?"

Earheart smiled. "Like Scotch over ice."

"Kathryn?"

"Mac, do you know what you're asking me?" Kathryn said. "One, I'm closing on the Burke trial tomorrow; two, I've got the Broadwick trial coming up. I couldn't hand those over even if I wanted to. And on top of all that, I'm on call. No way can I devote full time to this, no matter what Hal says. I just can't."

"Okay, okay. You finish Burke, you do Broadwick, but other than those two, you're off trials until further notice. I'll reassign the rest of your cases."

Easier said than done, Kathryn thought, but she didn't say it. If that was how the DA and his chief deputy said it was going down, that was how it was going down.

"It doesn't look like I have a lot of choice, does it?" she said.

"In a word, no," Mac said, smiling to take the sting out of it.

"Fine," Kathryn said. "Just tell me this: Exactly how am I supposed to be a task force all on my own?"

"That's fair," Mac said. "Okay, how about if I gave you an inspector full time?"

"Oh, sure," Kathryn said. "Come on, Mac, you know what it's like around here—the inspectors are in worse shape than the prosecutors. Every one of them is up to his ass in alligators."

The DA's office had ten inspectors who worked either independently of or together with the Sheriff's Department, depending on circumstances. The Sheriff's Detective Bureau, headed by Earheart, had a complement of fifteen plus three CSI detectives and a property clerk. Patrol Division had over fifty more deputies. As Kathryn had pointed out, every one of them was on overload.

"I'll give you one anyway," McCaskill said doggedly. "Got any preferences?"

"Dave Granz."

"Why did I ask?" McCaskill said.

"Granz?" Earheart said, surprised. "Why him?"

"He's the best inspector in the DA's office," Kathryn told him.

"He's a damned maverick," Earheart rumbled.

"Maybe that's why he's so good," Kathryn replied defiantly.

"Look, look." McCaskill smiled. "You want Granz, you've got him. Walt, what about your people?"

"I can assign one man full-time," Earheart said. "That's all the manpower I can spare right now. If we get any kind of a lead, I'll review the situation."

"Who have you got in mind, Walt?" Kathryn asked.

"How about Jack Burrows?"

"Burrows," McCaskill said. "Sergeant, detective section?"

"That's the one."

"He's good." McCaskill nodded. "Kathryn, why don't you make him your coordinator? You'll need someone, and Jack's got the know-how."

"Fine by me."

"Okay, that does it. You think you can get started tomorrow?"

Kathryn smiled ruefully. "I'll get Granz on it first thing."

Earheart nodded. "Fine. Just tell him to go by the goddamned book, will you?"

"I'll tell him," Kathryn said. "Whether he'll take any notice is another matter."

4

NEXT MORNING WHEN KATHRYN GOT TO THE OFFICE DAVE Granz was waiting for her, drinking coffee from a plastic cup. He looked wan and hung over. He was wearing the same shirt he'd worn the preceding day and his clothes smelled of stale tobacco. She raised her eyebrows at him and he shrugged.

"Poker game," he said. "Went on longer than I expected."

All night, probably, Kathryn thought. Dave might be one of the most effective inspectors on the DA's staff, but there were times when he didn't have enough sense to come in out of the rain. An all-night diet of bourbon and Marlboros was no way to set yourself up for his kind of work.

"You'll need a shave before we go into court," she observed.

"You always were bossy in the mornings," he told her with a wry smile. "I miss it. Sometimes, anyway."

"Thanks for the sometimes."

"I think we were good for each other. Don't you?"

"Don't start that again."

"We could still work it out," he said. "I could change."

She had to smile at that one. Dave wasn't about to change his ways and he wasn't about to let anyone change them for him, as she knew from experience. Any woman who tried it would end up the same way as Dave's ex-wife Rita, forever torn between wanting him back and being glad he was out of her life.

"You got my message about the Sedgewick Park killing?" she said.

"Yeah. It was on the news. And Richard Sanchez."

"I missed that."

Richard Sanchez appeared on KKSU-TV with a topical report called *Here and Now* that immediately followed the nine o'clock news. He was the kind of reporter they described as tenacious, uncompromising, hard-nosed. The words were not used admiringly. Kathryn thought he was overrated.

"He did a real number on us. Another brutal murder, another Hispanic girl—he made a big play on that—what's the Sheriff's Department doing, why isn't it safe for young women to walk the streets of Santa Rita? Hell, you know his routine."

"I thought he was more interested in graft in Sacramento, that kind of thing."

"He's always big on anything with an Hispanic slant," Dave said. "This is right up his alley."

"You may be right. Apparently he's putting together some sort of special on the murders. Jake Gylam's agreed to appear."

"He'll get clobbered," Granz said, without sympathy. "Sanchez isn't asking him on so he can make the Sheriff's Department look good."

"Which reminds me. What are you working on at the moment, Dave?"

Granz grimaced. "You want a list?"

"I want you to take a look at the files on these two killings."

Dave looked at the ceiling. "Why me, O Lord?" he asked, spreading his hands theatrically.

"Spare me the comedy," Kathryn said, "and look, will you?"

"What's to look? Sheriff's Department hasn't got a single lead, from what I hear."

"Mac's assigned it to me. Us."

"I don't get it. We don't even have a suspect."

"Hal Benton's idea," Kathryn told him. "As of now, you and I are a special investigation unit, with Jack Burrows as coordinator. The idea is to impress the hell out of the media. Got any ideas for a name?"

"How about Batman and Robin?"

"Fun-ny," Kathryn said. "Listen, I want you to talk to Doc Nelson."

"Ah, Doctor Death," Dave said. "The old dreamboat himself."

In Santa Rita County, as in most of California, the sheriff was also *ex officio* coroner. The actual work was contracted out to a pathologist, in this case Dr. Morgan Nelson. The tabloids had once dubbed him Doctor Death, and the nickname had stuck. If it bothered Nelson he never showed it, but then, he wasn't the most demonstrative man Kathryn had ever met.

"What is it with you today, Dave?"

He moved his shoulder slightly. "You still go out with him?"

"I don't *go out* with him, Dave. We have dinner once in a while."

"He's married, isn't he?"

Kathryn shook her head in exasperation. Life was complicated enough without playing games like this first thing in the morning.

"Look, let's get off the subject of Morgan, okay?" she said. "He's a friend. I like him, and I'm going to go on liking him. End of story. Okay, Dave?"

Dave stared out of the window. She knew her friendship with Morgan Nelson bothered him. Perhaps because it was close, almost intimate; perhaps Dave felt excluded, perhaps he was jealous. Whatever the reason, he never missed an opportunity to snipe at the older man.

"I said, 'okay, Dave?' "

"Okay, sorry," Dave said, clearly unrepentant. "What do I ask him?"

"You know. Cause of death, weapon used, defense

wounds if any, tox results. Is it the same MO? Are we definitely dealing with a serial killer?"

Dave shrugged and ran a hand through his straw-blond hair. "This is urgent, I suppose?"

"No, no. Anytime in the next half hour will be fine."

"Ho ho. Have you got the crime scene reports?"

"Talk to Burrows. I'll—damn." The phone rang insistently. "Check with you later, okay?"

Granz gave her a signing-off gesture and went out, closing the door behind him. Kathryn picked up the phone.

"Kathryn Mackay?"

"Speaking."

"Hi. This is Richard Sanchez? KKSU?"

That familiarly mellifluous voice. What a coincidence, she thought. Like hell it was. "Yes, Mr. Sanchez. What can I do for you?"

"We've met, right? I seem to recall seeing you at the station once or twice."

"You've got a good memory." Or a good researcher, she thought.

"Look, I just talked to Hal Benton's office. They tell me you're in charge of some sort of special investigation unit looking into these two murders we've had."

"The unit was only formed yesterday, Mr. Sanchez. I haven't even read the reports yet. Try the Sheriff's Department."

"I want to talk to you, not the Sheriff. Listen, how about lunch?"

"Sounds like a nice idea," Kathryn said, keeping it vague.

"I'll pick you up. Twelve-thirty?"

"Today?" Kathryn didn't need to simulate surprise. "I'm sorry, I can't. I'm swamped, really. I'm in closing arguments on a rape case, and I've got a lot of—"

"Come on," he insisted, "be nice to the media."

"You're not being so nice to us."

"You mean on the show? I was making a point. You know the statistics on murder in this county? Three out of four victims are Hispanic."

"That's hardly the Sheriff's fault. Three out of four of the perpetrators are Hispanic, too."

"He's head of law enforcement. People get murdered, he takes the flak. We're just representing the public's disquiet."

"And selling advertising."

"Oh, spare me. We've all got bosses, they all want results. You have the DA on your back asking you for convictions. My boss wants ratings. Now, how about that lunch?"

"Look, I really am busy. This new unit—"

"That's what I want to talk to you about," he said. "Among other things. Come on, say yes. Just think what being seen with me will do for your image."

Kathryn smiled in spite of herself. "Lunch today, the cover of *Time* magazine tomorrow, is that it?"

"Guaranteed," he said. "You like Mexican food?"

"Not more than six times a week."

"Good. I'll pick you up. What time would be good for you?"

"Twelve forty-five?"

"You got it. Look, I've got to run. See you later, okay?"

Kathryn put the phone down. No such thing as a free lunch, she thought. What did Sanchez really want? She dialed an internal number that put her through to Hal Benton's office. His secretary answered.

"Oh, hi, Kathryn," she said. "Hal's in a meeting."

"That's a change," Kathryn said tartly. "Look on his calendar for me, Angela. See if he's got a ten-minute window anytime before lunch."

"Hold it a second. Mmmm . . . wait. How about twelve thirty-five?"

Kathryn looked at the clock. She had to be in court in about fifteen minutes. "Stevenson will probably recess around noon," she said, more to herself than Angela. "Okay, pencil me in."

"Done. Anything else?"

"Ask my secretary to put everything that comes in for me on hold. I'm going to be in court all day on Burke."

"Listen, good luck. Put him away. For all of us, Kathryn."

"I'll try."

The door opened and Dave Granz came back in. He'd freshened up in the basement locker rooms, changed his shirt, had a shave. He grinned at Kathryn.

"Who's a pretty boy, now?" he said.

"You look almost human," Kathryn told him, unable to resist smiling back. In his shambly, beach bum way Dave was a good-looking guy, and when he smiled that lopsided smile he brought the maternal instinct out in a lot of women. What was even nicer was that Dave didn't even know he was doing it.

"I talked to Jack Burrows," he said. "Going to meet with him later. You all set?"

"Just about," she replied, putting her briefcase on the desk and opening it. He watched her gravely.

"What?" she said, feeling the weight of his regard.

"Listen, Kathryn, I'm sorry. Bringing up . . . you know."

"Forget it."

"Don't you ever wish we could be like we were? You and me and Emma?"

"She was asking about you this morning," Kathryn said, ducking the question.

"How about we go to the beach one night after work, get pizza, what do you say?"

"Sure, sure," Kathryn said, abstractedly, leafing through the files she was going to need in court.

"You're not listening," Dave said.

"Sure I am," she said. "Go to the beach, get pizza. Sounds great."

"Okay, you win," Dave said. "Some other time, right?"

She looked up. Dave was smiling at her. She felt a twinge of conscience for keeping him at arm's length for so long. Emma did love being with him.

"You about ready to go?" she said.

He nodded. "I'm looking forward to seeing you take that NAACP hotshot apart."

Albert Blakely, defending Eric Burke on charges of rape, sodomy, and oral copulation, was an attorney on the staff of the National Association for the Advancement of Colored People out of Sacramento. They had decided to make the trial a cause.

"I'm not interested in Blakely," Kathryn said, gathering up her papers and folders. "It's Burke I want. I want him off the street and behind bars."

"You'll do it," Dave said. "He's as guilty as hell. You know it, I know it, and he knows it."

"More importantly, does the jury know it?" she asked. It wasn't as rhetorical a question as it sounded. Dave was a shrewd observer of jury behavior, and in such matters she trusted his judgment completely.

He raised one shoulder a couple of inches. "They're hard to read. I talked to Alice Hernandez. Her guess is they're maybe nine–three for guilty."

Alice Hernandez was the deputy from the Sheriff's Department on duty in Superior Court Three as bailiff. She was the only court officer allowed to talk to the jury.

"Then I've still got some work to do down there," Kathryn said. She was beginning to feel the tension that always took hold of her toward the end of a trial. Some cases were easier than others: you didn't get as emotionally involved. Others sucked you in, sometimes completely against your better judgment. Rape and child abuse cases were always the worst. It was almost impossible not to empathize with a battered child or a brutalized woman. She looked at the clock.

"Time to go do it," she told Granz.

"I'll make a couple of calls, grab a quick smoke. Meet you down there," he said, and went out of the office. Kathryn put the printout of the notes she had worked on the preceding night after Emma went to bed into her briefcase and snapped it shut decisively. She caught a glimpse of her face in the mirror: pale, serious, strained.

"Keep that breathless charm," she told her reflection, and headed for the courtroom.

5

THE COUNTY BUILDING WAS UGLY, AND THAT WAS ONLY ON the outside. On the inside, "ugly" would have been a compliment. Built of uncompromising gray concrete, it looked as if its main purpose was to withstand a nuclear attack. Five floors high, squat and square, it stood back from Pacific Street behind a two-acre parking lot flanked by a service facility for law enforcement vehicles. Kathryn hardly even saw it anymore. She was used to the wide stone-floored corridors, the flat white fluorescent light, the changing civic exhibitions of worthy local artists that no one ever seemed to look at, the sound of children's voices echoing from the high concrete ceilings.

Linking the County Building to the Courts Building was
an atrium, partly open to the sky, with concrete planters and
a couple of apathetic trees, where people could sit smoking
a cigarette over coffee or eat lunch. The annex beyond it
was a single-story hollow rectangle, with the courts around
its edges. The interior walls of its long, wide corridors were
lined with the same cedar paneling as the courtrooms. Severe, uncushioned benches were placed alongside the en-
trances to each court, with more beneath the floor-to-ceiling
exterior windows. At the end of each day, sunlight patterned
the floors of the empty corridors like a Mondrian painting.

Kathryn hurried through into the Courts Building, her
heels clacking on the stone floor. Today she was wearing a
dark gray suit with a white blouse, neat gold earrings, suede
shoes that exactly matched the shade of her suit. No law
said the senior trial attorney couldn't look attractive. She
always took time to make up properly: mascara, eyeshadow,
blusher, lipstick. The courtroom was a theater of sorts.

"Hi, Kathryn," someone called. She waved automatically,
so completely immersed in her own thoughts that she had
no idea who had spoken to her. At this time of day the
corridors were crowded with attorneys preparing for appearances, defendants checking the day's calendars to see where
their cases had been assigned, visitors seeking directions
from the volunteers by the main entrance, jurors registering
at the jury commissioner's office.

The jurors in the Burke case were already gathered outside Superior Three, some reading paperbacks or newspapers, others gossiping while they waited. She felt their eyes
on her as she pulled open the door and went inside.

"Hi, Alice," she said to Deputy Hernandez. "Hi, Janie."

Janie Welsh was the court reporter on the Burke case;
she belonged to the cadre who performed one of the most
crucial tasks in the judicial system: taking down every single
word that was spoken in every trial. It was arduous, demanding, anonymous, and indispensable work, yet few
judges showed them any consideration, despite the fact that
without them the system would simply cease to function.

Today Janie was wearing an ivory silk blouse and a cream
linen pleated skirt. She was a good-looking woman, Kathryn
thought; fine bones, a trim figure, blond hair fashionably
highlighted with gray—or was it gray highlighted with

blond? Janie was in her early forties. According to office gossip, she was having an affair with one of the Superior Court judges, Bill Calhoun. Dumb, Kathryn thought. Dumb on Janie's part—Calhoun had a wife and three kids. Dumber still on his: if the affair became public knowledge the revelation would sink Calhoun's impending elevation to the Appellate Court.

Kathryn took her seat at the prosecution table, opened up her briefcase, and immersed herself in the printout of the notes she had made before Emma woke up. About ten minutes later, Dave Granz slid into the chair next to her.

"The Sedgewick Park killing," he whispered. "I talked to Burrows. He gave me the reports by the cops who responded. Nothing there. Doc Nelson's people can't say for sure how long the victim's been dead—she might even have been killed before the one on Shelter Island, he can't tell. Jack says CSI got zilch at the crime scene so there's not much chance of the crime lab coming up with anything, either."

"What about CAL-ID?"

The acronym was shorthand for the California Department of Justice's Bureau of Criminal Identification at Sacramento. They had a computer that would match up the characteristics of a crime under investigation to the known proclivities—MO's—of criminals on file. Upon locating significant similarities, it would suggest suspects and produce their fingerprints.

"Nothing yet."

"That it?"

"I also had a word with Doctor Death."

"Dave . . ."

"Sorry," he said, grinning unrepentantly. "He hasn't finished his protocol yet. Said he might have it by tonight. Tomorrow for sure. Oh, and he said, call him."

"Okay." Kathryn nodded, making a note in her appointment book. "Did he give you any indication of his preliminary findings?"

"He confirms it's pretty much the same MO," Dave told her, reading from his notes. "Asphyxiation this time instead of strangulation, but that's about the only difference. No tissue damage to the throat. Traces of cotton thread in the nasal passages and bronchial tract. Pinpoint hemorrhages in the conjunctivae and the skin of face and neck. Classic symptoms, he says. Everything points to the victim having been smothered with a pillow."

"Any sign of sexual assault?"

"Ligature traces on the wrists and ankles; she'd been tied up at some point. No vaginal or anal trauma. Said he couldn't get anything off the body. She'd been in the water too long."

"You said pretty much the same MO. Does that mean . . . what about the other injuries?"

Dave consulted his notes again. "Same as the other one, Nelson says."

"That it?"

Dave shrugged. "If you want an opinion, I'd say what they're saying is, forget it. Another Jane Doe, probably the same perpetrator, no physical evidence. We've got nothing to work with."

"Tell that to Walt Earheart," she said. "He's relying on us to come up with something."

"Everybody's got problems," Dave grunted.

The door to the left of the judge's bench opened and Alice Hernandez came in. Plump as a Bavarian barmaid, she wore her blond hair combed tightly against her skull with a pigtail in back. A Glock automatic pistol, standard issue for the Sheriff's Department, rode high in its holster on her ample hip. Behind her was the defendant, Eric Burke.

The NAACP lawyer had gone to a lot of trouble to make him look good, Kathryn thought. Twenty-four years of age, dressed in a tweed sport jacket and dark slacks, white button-down shirt and neat tie, Eric Burke looked like an accountant. He swung his arms as he walked across the courtroom. His clean-shaven black face was expressionless as he sat down next to his lawyer, Albert Blakely.

"Jury's coming in," Dave said.

Kathryn kept her head down as the jury took their seats.

"How do they look?" she muttered, hardly moving her lips.

"You ever see *Invasion of the Body Snatchers?*" he said.

Kathryn watched covertly as the jury took their seats. There were fifteen of them in all, five men, seven women, and three female alternates. A couple of the men were swapping jokes with Deputy Hernandez about last night's ball game.

She wondered what color the jury had chosen today. Early along in the trial, Kathryn had noticed that each day they would all wear something the same color: one day purple, the next green, and so on. It was unusual; it could mean they were united in purpose. That would be a big plus: a single-minded jury was much likelier to bring in a conviction than one divided. She gave a little mental shudder at the thought of a hung jury and a retrial.

The buzzer sounded and Deputy Hernandez snapped to attention.

"All rise!" she intoned, sharply. Judge William Stevenson came in and took his place on the bench. He looked briefly around the courtroom, smiled at the jury, bade them be seated.

"Let the record show the defendant and his counsel are present, and that the jury is seated," he said. "Are you ready, Ms. Mackay?"

"I am, Your Honor," Kathryn said, standing up. Stevenson nodded, proceed. He's glad we're coming to the end of this, Kathryn thought. Aren't we all? Albert Blakely regarded her impassively, tapping his chin with a pencil. He was a thickset black man, maybe forty years old, well dressed. He leaned over and whispered something to Burke. The younger man nodded, his eyes on the jury.

Kathryn glanced toward the spectator area. Mac McCaskill and one of the younger assistant DAs, Ben Robson, had come in and were sitting in the rear row. Mac gave her a little nod of encouragement, and Kathryn felt a lift of gratitude. No matter how often you stepped up to bat, it was always good to know someone was out there rooting for you. She smiled at the judge.

"If it please the court," she began, using the time-honored courtesy, turning to face the jury as she spoke. "Ladies and gentlemen. As I explained yesterday, I have the opportunity to speak to you again on behalf of the People in what is called rebuttal. That means I have the opportunity to rebut—to challenge, if you like—what the defendant's attorney told you. That is what I am going to do now."

She walked around the table and stood in front of the jury. They looked at her expectantly.

"Sometimes, ladies and gentlemen, defense lawyers play little tricks on juries, especially in rape cases. One of them is called transferred guilt. The idea is to make the defendant look less guilty by trying to make the victim look less innocent. That was what happened here yesterday. By implying that the victim didn't fight enough, or didn't scream, or didn't seek immediate aid, the defense sought to put Patricia Morales on trial in this court instead of Eric Burke. It's the oldest trick in the book, ladies and gentlemen. And I know you're not going to fall for it."

She turned and walked across the courtroom until she was standing in front of Eric Burke.

"Often, in such cases, juries are asked to use their common sense," she said. "But right now, I want you to use your imagination. I want you to try to imagine you are in a darkened store, at ten o'clock at night, alone. This man, Eric Burke"—she pointed at the sullen Burke, whose hostility was almost tangible—"is coming after you. He tells you he's got a gun and a knife and you'd better do what he wants. What are you going to say, I don't believe you? Let me look in your pockets? Is that what a terrified woman alone in a darkened building would do?"

She pointed at Burke again.

"Look at him! Look at Eric Burke! He's six feet tall. He weighs a hundred and eighty pounds. Patricia Morales is what? Maybe a tad over five feet, and about a hundred and five. Yet the defense wants you to believe that if Patricia Morales didn't want to have sex with Eric Burke, all she had to do was fight him off. Don't you find that ridiculous? Don't you think that's preposterous?"

She went back to her table, ostensibly to look at her notes. She didn't need to, but it would give the jury a moment or two to think about what she had said. She didn't want to hurry them.

"The defense also tried to cast doubt on the victim's testimony by challenging the testimony of Nurse Hennessy, who examined Patricia Morales after she was sexually assaulted," Kathryn went on, turning back to face the jury. She could sense she had them with her now. They were listening intently. No shifting in their seats, no looking at the ceiling or yawning, or making notes.

"Nurse Hennessy is highly trained and very experienced. Her examination established Patricia was raped and sodomized against her will. The defense contends that because Patricia had no bruises or abrasions on her body, she consented. Yet they produce no evidence of any kind to support that allegation. I think you and I know that if they had a witness—any witness—who could controvert Nurse Hennessy's expert opinion, they would have presented such a witness. But ladies and gentlemen, we *know* why there were no bruises, no signs of violence. Patricia Morales didn't, couldn't, fight! Because she was frightened to death by this man here, this man who told her he had a gun and a knife and if she didn't do exactly what he said he would kill her!"

There wasn't a sound in the courtroom. She glanced toward the spectator area; Mac and Ben were still there, watching intently. She walked over to face the jury, looking into their eyes, one after another.

"At the beginning of this trial I told you I am the prosecutor. But that's not all I am, ladies and gentlemen. Don't be misled by the title of the defendant's attorney—'Public Defender.' It is I who defend the public. I am the advocate for the victim: the raped, the maimed, the murdered. In prosecuting Eric Burke I defend not only Patricia Morales but you, and you, each of you and your families, from such criminals. This is the only time, the only place the public's voice and the victim's voice are heard. Remember that."

She turned toward the defense table, looking directly at Eric Burke for a long, silent moment. Burke scowled; his lawyer remained impassive.

"Yesterday, the defense told you he was angry," she said, turning back to face the jury. "You remember how he banged the table? Well, ladies and gentlemen, I'm angry, too. I'm angry because I know what this man has done to Patricia Morales. And I ask you for justice in her name. Find Eric Burke guilty. Thank you."

She went back to her seat and sat down, trembling, suddenly close to tears. Dammit, she thought, I always get so emotional. Now that it was over, she was as limp as a rag. Behind her she heard the door open and close, and knew that McCaskill and Ben Robson had slipped out of the courtroom. She heard the judge instructing the jury that they must now retire and elect a foreperson, and that the court would recess until such time as they had reached a verdict.

"You okay, Kathryn?" Dave whispered.

"Uh-huh." She blew her nose. "How was it?"

"You never did a better rebuttal in your life," he told her. She managed a smile. Even if it wasn't true, it was good to hear.

6

RICHARD SANCHEZ DROVE WELL, AND THE SLEEK SILVER BMW 7 series convertible slipped through the traffic like a shark. He told Kathryn he'd made reservations at a Mexican restaurant called Patrón's over in the Old Town, ten minutes from the County Building.

"You said you liked Mexican food." He smiled. "Is that okay?"

"I have to be back at two-fifteen," Kathryn reminded him.

"Don't worry. I'll get you back in time."

The restaurant was on Dolores Street, right across from the Southern Pacific railroad crossing. It had umbrella-shaded tables on a wooden deck out front. As she came up the wooden steps, Kathryn was aware of the ripple of recognition among the diners sitting at the tables. A short, portly man came out of the restaurant and hurried over to them.

"Mr. Sanchez, good to see you, good to see you," he said. "I put you in your usual corner, yes?"

"That's fine, Isidro," said Sanchez, smiling. "Isidro's the owner," he told Kathryn. The little man smiled and nodded hello, leading the way to a table in a corner of the sun deck against the restaurant wall. Kathryn noticed when they sat down that Sanchez chose the chair facing the wall, his back to everyone.

"I'll order for both of us," he said.

Kathryn smiled; his self-absorption was almost charming. Sanchez turned to the waiting restaurateur and spoke to him rapidly in Spanish.

"What have you ordered?" she asked, as Patrón made notes on a small pad.

"Chips and salsa while we wait," Sanchez said. "Chicken chalupas with guacamole and sour cream toppings. Refried beans. Okay?"

"Sounds wonderful."

"Would you like some wine or a beer?"

Kathryn shook her head. "I'm in trial. Iced tea will be fine."

"And iced coffee for me," Sanchez said. Patrón smiled and nodded again, making more notes on his pad as he bustled self-importantly away.

"He seems anxious to please you."

"You know how it is. TV people coming into a place brings in the crowd. Now: To start with, do I call you Kathryn? Or do you prefer Kath, or Kathy, or what?"

"Kathryn's fine," she replied.

"And formal."

"I used to be Kath, years ago at law school, but when I became a lawyer I thought Kathryn sounded, you know, more serious."

"Where are you from, Kathryn?"

"Kansas City, Missouri."

"And how long have you been here in Santa Rita?"

"Just over five years," Kathryn replied.

"This isn't your first job, then?"

"No. After law school I worked in Kansas City with the public defender's office. Then again in L.A. before I switched sides and joined the DA's office. I was there four years."

"I was born in L.A. My parents still live there. In the *barrio*," he said, a touch defensively, Kathryn thought.

"Is that where you got into television?"

"I started off as a newspaperman. Then I moved over to radio. You know what a twenty-twenty station is?"

"Isn't that where they play wall-to-wall rock all day?"

"Rock around the clock." He nodded. "Only every twenty minutes you break in with news headlines off the AP wire. Ah, here come our chips."

A young waitress put down the dish of salsa and a basket of tortilla chips, and set their drinks beside them. He smiled at her exactly the way he had smiled at Kathryn. It was just an expression, something he did with his features, she decided, as she took a chip and dipped it into the red sauce. It was good and hot.

"Whoo-ee," she said, sipping some tea. Sanchez smiled his automatic smile again. He was a good-looking man, Kathryn thought; not her type, but women would find him handsome. About six feet tall, maybe a little more, with straight black hair cut short and parted on the left, and dark, deep-set eyes over high, prominent cheekbones. His smile was easy and assured, the mouth full and expressive. He was wearing a casually elegant off-white linen jacket with a copper-colored open-neck shirt and dark tan slacks. Apart from an expensive-looking watch on his left wrist, he wore no jewelry.

"What made you leave L.A. and come up here?" he asked, leaning forward and looking directly into her eyes. It would have been disconcerting had it not been so obviously a TV technique, the intense only-you reciprocity of the professional interviewer.

"I wanted to try important criminal cases. I knew I was never going to get the chance as a very junior assistant DA in a thousand-lawyer office."

"And now you're Hal Benton's senior trial attorney. You must have worked very hard. Did you always want to be a lawyer?"

"You know, I feel like I'm being interviewed for *People* magazine," she said.

"Sorry," he said without a hint of apology. "Asking questions is a way of life with me. It's sort of built into my system."

"Mine, too. How do you handle being recognized every place you go?" Kathryn asked. "Doesn't it get tiresome having people coming up to you all the time telling you how much they like your show?"

"Or hate it. You get that as well." He smiled. "Sure, it's a nuisance sometimes. But it's the nature of the business. And I'd probably feel a lot worse if nobody recognized me at all."

Isidro Patrón bustled over, followed by a waitress who brought their food. It smelled delicious, and Kathryn suddenly felt hungry. Sanchez leaned forward again, the way he had before.

"I had a reason for asking you to have lunch with me," he began. "Can I talk to you about these murders?"

"I had an idea you might ask me that," Kathryn said. "So I met with Hal Benton before I came out. And we agreed: As long as our conversation is strictly off the record. Is that understood?"

"Kathryn!" Sanchez said reproachfully, spreading his hands and smiling his artificial smile. "You don't think I'd burn you on our first meeting, do you?"

There ought to be violins, Kathryn thought, like in one of those old movies.

"You tell me," she said.

"Relax," he said. "Whatever you tell me, I promise I'll do my very best to respect your confidentiality."

Kathryn laughed. "Are you serious?"

"Look, either we talk or we don't. I don't go for this off-the-record business. If you tell me something, how do I pretend I don't know it?"

"The same way a jury disregards evidence the judge tells it to disregard."

He shrugged. "We all know how effectively that works."

"Then I'll only talk for the record."

"I'm disappointed," he said. "I'm trying to find a way we can work together here."

"Sue me," she replied tartly. "You made the ground rules."

"They told me you were tough," he said. "Okay, on the record. My sources tell me the two murdered women were mutilated in an identical manner, and that the consensus is we're dealing with a serial killer. Is that correct?"

Kathryn wondered who his sources were. It was widely believed Sanchez had a snitch inside the Sheriff's Department. Walt Earheart had been heard to say if he ever found out who it was, he'd kick the guy's ass out through his ears.

"It's a possibility," she told Sanchez. "It could also mean we're dealing with a copycat, someone who murdered his wife and cut her up so we'd think it was the same killer. You media people gave a lot of coverage to the way the first victim was mutilated."

Sanchez looked surprised. "We got that information from the cops. Are you saying we shouldn't have used it?"

"I'm saying full and frank disclosure of all the known facts isn't always conducive to best law enforcement results. Every time some TV or news reporter hypes up a murder, it makes it that much harder to get an uncontaminated jury."

"Juries are not exactly our responsibility."

"What exactly is?"

"Getting the news. And the facts behind the news. And giving them to the public."

"Whether they're fit to print or not?"

"That's not for me to decide. Or you, if it comes to that."

"Fair enough," Kathryn said. "I just wish there was some way we could get you to hold off once in a while, understand our problems."

"You law enforcement people are really something, you know that?" Sanchez said. "What you mean is, just print what we tell you. Listen, in my experience, police departments walk all over reporters who understand their problems."

"And vice versa," Kathryn snapped back.

Sanchez leaned back in his chair and regarded her levelly. "You're good," he said. "You don't beat about the bush."

"I never found it paid," Kathryn said.

"Moving on," he said. "What can you tell me about the victims?"

She smiled at his unconscious television anchor style. "You mean, what can I tell you no one else knows? Nothing."

"You must have something."

Kathryn shook her head.

"What about the killer? Any leads at all?"

"Just a little while ago you were complaining law enforcement holds out on the media. Here's proof they don't. You know everything we know."

"What are the chances of something breaking soon?"

Kathryn pursed her lips. "There's always a chance. But it's not something you could take to the bank."

"I imagine you watch my program?"

"When I can. I don't get time for a lot of TV."

"You know the format, though?"

Kathryn nodded. " 'The facts behind the facts,' isn't that what you always say?"

"Right. We've built a reputation for dealing with big issues in a small format. And we've done it well. But in television nothing stands still. So I'm putting together a new program, a twice-weekly report pitched somewhere between Donahue and Geraldo. Thirty minutes each show, with guests and a studio audience. Myself as executive producer. The first show will be an in-depth examination of the murders. That was why I was hoping you'd give me something to run with."

"I see," Kathryn said. "Something you could use to make the Sheriff's Department look like the Keystone Kops, maybe?"

"They don't need any assistance from me in that department," he said sharply, eyes narrowing. "But you're wrong. As I told you on the phone, what we're concerned about is the fact that the victims are Hispanic."

"And that's why you're doing the program?"

"I'm Hispanic. Isn't it okay if I feel strongly about Hispanic girls being raped and murdered?"

"As long as you feel just as strongly about it when they're white or black."

"Of course I do."

"Then don't use race as an angle. Victims have no race. They're just victims."

"Maybe you're not as aware as I am of how strongly feelings are running in the Hispanic community, Kathryn," Sanchez said smoothly.

"Ah," Kathryn said. "And that's why you've invited Sheriff Gylam to appear."

"There are a number of questions he needs to address."

"For instance."

"For instance, whether the quality of protection extended to the Hispanic community is a contributory factor in these murders."

"That's a crock and you know it. There are no second-class citizens in Santa Rita."

"I didn't realize you were quite so touchy."

"And now you do."

"Look," he said, smiling, "let's not argue. How about some dessert?" The TV anchor's technique again, she thought, and wondered if he even knew he was doing it.

"I need to be getting back," she said, making it final.

"Of course," Sanchez said, signaling for a check. They got into the car and drove to the County Building in silence. Sanchez pulled to a halt at the foot of the steps leading inside.

"The food was wonderful," Kathryn said. "Thank you." Sanchez gave no indication he had heard her.

"Do you want to be a prosecutor forever?" he asked abruptly.

The question caught her off guard. It was one she asked herself often; she still didn't know the answer.

"Why do you ask?" she hedged.

"You're wasted here," he said abruptly, gesturing toward the County Building. "Small-town prosecutor, small-town cases. You could do a lot better."

"In what way?"

"I ran some tapes. TV interviews you'd done, sound bites. You're good on camera. With proper handling, you could be terrific. Suppose I ... made you a proposition? Would you be interested?"

Was there more to it than the words? She decided it was her imagination.

"What sort of proposition?"

"I've been watching you, over lunch," he continued. "You're a natural. You think fast, you know what you want to say. And you're attractive. Very attractive, if I may say so."

"What is this?" Kathryn said. "An audition?"

"Television could be very good for you," he said, avoiding the question. "Especially if you ever decided to run for office. You could shoot for district attorney, to start with. Or aim even higher."

Kathryn shook her head. "What you see is what I am, a very good prosecutor. I'd be a second-rate anything else."

"Hear me out before you say no," he said. "I think you might find what I have to say worth listening to."

"All right, go ahead," Kathryn said. Something told her to be on guard; Richard Sanchez was a taker, not a giver. What was he after?

"We work together. I get you the media exposure you need. The top shows, the maximum audiences. Donahue, Geraldo Rivera. *Good Morning America. Hard Copy.* I know these people personally. We get you out there confronting the issues. Start building you an image that would carry through to the voter when the time comes."

"I don't think so. Being a TV personality doesn't appeal to me one bit."

"We're talking tomorrow here, Kathryn," he said. "It's not about who you are now. It's about who you're going to be, a year, five years from now."

"And if I say yes? What do you get out of all this?"

He smiled blandly. "Simple. This new unit you're heading up for Benton. You'll be concentrating exclusively on the murders, right?"

"Right."

"All you have to do is see to it whenever anything breaks in the investigation I'm the first to know."

Kathryn stared at him in astonishment.

"That's all?" she said. "I sell out my office, the Sheriff's Department, and myself—and you'll get me into politics?"

"You won't get there any other way. You want to go for the big time, there's a price to pay. Nothing's for nothing."

"You don't even think it's wrong, do you?"

"God decides what's right and wrong," Sanchez said. "I just do the best I can with whatever breaks I get."

"I don't even want to discuss this," Kathryn said. "You can drop me right here."

"Is that your answer?"

"Did you really think it would be anything else?"

"You disappoint me, Kathryn," Sanchez said. "Most people would jump at an opportunity like this."

"Then thank God I'm not most people," she said, opening the car door and getting out.

Sanchez shrugged. "Idealism's an expensive luxury. I hope you can afford it."

He lifted a hand in farewell—or maybe dismissal, she thought—and the silver BMW pulled out of the parking lot. She watched it go, still angry. Damn the man, she thought. Damn him for his gall. It probably never even occurred to him I'd be insulted.

She looked at her watch and made a face. Without regret, she put Richard Sanchez from her mind.

7

THE SANTA RITA COUNTY MORGUE WAS LOCATED IN THE basement of the County Hospital. Kathryn showed her ID to the cop at the door, then went into the lobby and across to the reception desk. She was told that Dr. Nelson would be with her shortly. The receptionist directed her to a simply furnished waiting room, one of a series of more or less identical suites known as the ID rooms. In these, the identification of a body could be effected by showing the face on closed circuit television, sparing grieving and apprehensive relatives the ordeal of having to go down into the refrigerated depths of the subbasement to personally identify the often horribly mangled bodies of their kin.

Through the glass-paneled door she watched the nonstop

movement of personnel in the lobby area—white-coated technicians, secretaries, police officers, doctors, moving from basement to upper floor, office to office—and wondered exactly why she had come.

"Well, well, Katie Mackay."

Morgan Nelson was the only person she knew who called her Katie. A tall man with the round, cherubic face of an Irish priest, he was wearing green surgical garb and rubber boots that squeaked on the tile floor. Bright, inquisitive eyes gleamed behind gold-rimmed granny spectacles. The boyish grin made him look a lot younger than his fifty-four years.

"I thought maybe you'd moved to Boston," he said. "It's so long since I saw you."

"Hi, Doc," she said, smiling. "Do you have a few minutes?"

"For you, always," he said, gesturing her to one of the chairs before subsiding into the other like a collapsing tripod and running a hand through a thatch of close-cropped gingery hair. He took off his glasses, polishing them industriously with a tattered Kleenex. "What can I do for you?"

"That's the trouble," Kathryn confessed. "I don't really know. I'm not even sure why I came up here. I just felt I needed to talk to you."

"About the two Hispanic girls who were killed?"

Kathryn nodded. "How d'you know?"

"Knowing you, it wasn't difficult to figure," he said with a smile.

"I don't like the smell of this one, Doc," Kathryn said. "And I've got a feeling worse things are going to happen before we find this bastard."

Nelson nodded. "You could be right, Katie," he said. "There's something weird about the whole thing. Off the wall, if you know what I mean."

"You look tired," Kathryn said.

Nelson sighed heavily. "I've been down in the Hellhole all day."

The basement—known to everyone who worked in it as the Hellhole—was Nelson's fiefdom. He had designed it, overseen its construction, and written the rules by which it was run. He was tough on his people, but no tougher than he was on himself. It was a rare day he didn't work fifteen hours, and often it was more like eighteen.

Bodies came first to the staging room, where they were put on a gurney and weighed, then meticulously photographed before being taken to one of the three autopsy suites. The largest of these had three stainless steel tables, with the usual weighing scales, sinks, sluices, steel lockers, tools, and sound-proof booth for dictating notes. The second, for cases requiring special study, had only one table. It was known as the VIP room. The third suite was used for autopsies on bodies with known or suspected infectious diseases or which were in an advanced state of decomposition. Here, special air-conditioning systems vacuumed out the noxious gases and directed them to an incinerator. Also on the same level were a complete X-ray and color photoprocessing facility.

"Dave said you might have your protocol on the Sedge-wick Park victim finished," Kathryn said. "That what you've been working on?"

Nelson nodded. "Among other things. Did he give you a rundown?"

"Cause of death asphyxiation. No vaginal or anal trauma. Traces of Valium in the stomach. Genital injuries similar to the Shelter Island victim. Is it the same killer, Doc?"

"I'm pretty sure it is. I remembered something I came across when I examined the Shelter Island victim. I didn't attach much significance to it at the time. But when I examined the Sedgewick Park victim I found a small incision, maybe three-quarters of an inch long, high on the inside of the left thigh. It was more or less exactly the same as one I'd seen on the Shelter Island body."

Kathryn frowned. "And?"

"It wasn't a deep cut, like the others. Barely broke the skin. As if the killer was trying out the weapon."

"Or . . . demonstrating it?"

Morgan nodded, a small smile touching the corners of his mouth. "That's what I like about you, Katie. You never miss a trick."

"Demonstrating it," she repeated. "Reveling in his power over her. The sadistic bastard."

"That's what these things are usually about, Katie."

"So we've got a serial killer on our hands."

"Looks like it," Nelson said. "And he knows a thing or three."

"What do you mean?"

He shrugged. "We got nothing at the crime scene, and the fact that the victims had been dead so long meant there was never much chance of our coming up with anything significant. But there are some . . . oddities."

"Give me a for-instance."

"Okay, take the Sedgewick Park victim. It's not like in the movies, Katie, where they just toss somebody out of a boat and the body obligingly disappears. It doesn't work that way. Even after death the lungs are still full of air. That's why the cops call them 'floaters.' There are only two ways to be sure a body will sink. The first one's the method the old-time gangsters used: you've heard of cement overshoes."

"And the other?"

"The method I'm pretty sure our killer used. It's crude, but it works. You just stick a hose down the victim's throat and fill the lungs and stomach with water. That way when he put her into the lake she went down and stayed down."

"But why? Why would he want to do that?"

"Maybe to confuse us as to the time of death. Maybe to delay discovery of the body. Or maybe something even simpler: he didn't like her."

"You told Dave Granz the genital injuries were unusual. How about this business with the water? Would the guy need medical knowledge?"

Nelson shook his head. "Like I said, it's pretty crude. He could have read up on it in a medical textbook. There are more than enough in the public libraries."

Kathryn was silent for a moment, thinking. "You said oddities. Plural."

Nelson smiled. "Indeed I did. For instance, during my examination I noticed a faint perfume on the body of the Shelter Island victim. I took swabs. The lab confirmed there were faint traces of bath soap on the skin."

"Bath soap? Dave didn't mention that."

"We hadn't finished all the tests then. Still haven't."

"Is it significant?"

"These women weren't willing partners, Katie. There are clear subcutaneous traces of ligatures on the wrists and legs, enough to suggest the killer had to restrain them. That being the case, he'd hardly untie them so they could take a shower or a bath. Which has to mean he washed the body himself, probably after he killed her. If he did that, he had a reason.

One reason for that might be he was making sure he didn't leave any biological traces of himself we could pick up."

"But you don't think it is?"

Nelson shook his head. "He could just as easily hose them down."

"So?"

"So maybe ... just maybe, you understand, this is some sort of caring gesture."

"Are you kidding me, Doc? He cuts them up like this and then ... ?"

"I did say maybe."

"What you didn't say was why."

"Ah," Nelson said with a wry smile. "For that you need a soothsayer, not a pathologist. I don't know, Katie. I truly don't know. It's all maybes and possiblys. But it could mean—and this is pure guesswork, you understand?—he ejaculates on the body and washes it afterwards."

"The body? You mean when they're dead?"

"Maybe. Or maybe in the act of killing them."

"I begin to see what you meant when you said this was off the wall," Kathryn said. "Were there any physical injuries other than the mutilations?"

"Some evidence of bruising of the face and body in both cases. They were slapped, and in the case of the Shelter Island victim, punched. And before you ask, I can't tell you over how long a period the women had been physically abused."

"It all fits the pattern, though, doesn't it?" Kathryn said thoughtfully. "He kidnaps them, keeps them tied up, probably beats any kind of protest out of them. The bastard even gives them a demonstration of the knife or whatever it is he's going to use on them. And then ..."

"And here's something else for your theory file," Nelson said. "We couldn't get much off the Sedgewick Park victim; she'd been in the water too long. But the Shelter Island body was in unusually good condition. She wasn't beautiful, you understand, but the deterioration of the organs was minimal. No tissue damage, no insect depredations."

Kathryn frowned. "Insect depredations?"

Nelson shrugged again. "We have a lot of taboos about the dead. Flies and ants—and if the body is out there long enough, beetles and rats—don't. If they find a dead body lying about, they move right in. And since there was no indication of any damage from insects or small predators, that means the body wasn't just hidden in a shed or a culvert. I won't bore you with all the data on decomposition, but it goes something like this: postmortem hypostasis—lividity to you—is visible within a couple of hours, and complete between six and twelve. Dependent on ambient temperature, decomposition commences anywhere between eight and forty-eight hours. Fastest between seventy and a hundred degrees, most slowly below fifty. Arrested if the body is kept in an environment above freezing, at about forty degrees. You see where I'm going, here? The body had to be kept somewhere with temperature control. Somewhere cool enough to arrest the decomposition process."

"He keeps the bodies somewhere . . . after he kills them?"

Nelson simply nodded yes.

"Why?"

"Two reasons. He might be doing it so we won't be able to determine the time of death."

"But we can?"

Morgan nodded. "There's something called a vitreous potassium test."

"A what?"

"We extract one and a half cc's of the fluid from the white of the eyeball. The lab does a potassium test and gives me a number. Using a formula—it's imprecise, but it works—I can estimate a span of time in which death may have occurred. Or make an educated guess, anyway."

"Which is?"

"My educated guess? The woman in Sedgewick Park was killed first. The Shelter Island victim has been dead a week, ten days. The other woman was killed, oh, maybe two weeks earlier."

"And two?"

"What?"

"You said there were two reasons he might keep the bodies hidden somewhere."

"Right. The second reason—and this is another guess—might be because he prefers them that way. They don't talk back."

"Necrophilia?"

"Possibly. That could explain the washing."

"Let's suppose you're right," Kathryn said. "Where is

there such a place? Where could someone take a victim, hold her till he's ready to kill her, keep the body there—for what, a week?—then load it into a vehicle and drive away without anyone seeing him do it?"

"You're good at what-iffing," Nelson replied, smiling. "You tell me."

"It would have to be someplace very isolated," Kathryn said. "Someplace where people don't poke their noses into other people's business. Out in the country, or way up in the mountains."

"It's not much," Nelson said. "But it's something to keep in mind. Listen, I'm thirsty. How about something to drink. Coffee, tea?"

"I ought to be on my way," Kathryn said, standing up.

"Katie, Katie. Make a little time, for godsakes."

The way he said it reminded Kathryn of her father. She hadn't thought about him for a long time. *Patrick Mackay, twenty years as a traffic controller with the AT&SF railroad, a short, squat leprechaun of a man who never missed a Royals game at the Truman Complex, who smelled of beer and cheap cigars and always forgot her birthday. Katie-me-darlin', come here and listen while I tell you.*

"Sorry, Doc," she said, and meant it. "I've been waiting two days for the Burke jury to come in. I guess I'm a little antsy."

"You, antsy? I thought you were one of those aggressive, hard-nosed, tough, ambitious types."

"What?"

"I read that profile they did about you in that magazine. *California Attorney,* is it?"

"You saw that?"

"They were pretty rough."

"It was a hatchet job. They were trying to make me look . . . I don't know, soulless. As if all I care about is winning."

"Maybe you ought to let people see the nice-guy side of you, once in a while." Morgan smiled again.

"I can't be a Pollyanna while I'm trying a homicide," Kathryn protested. "When I'm in court, it's like . . . like I'm a soldier and it's a war. The only difference is I use words instead of guns."

"You make them just as lethal."

"What am I supposed to do, ask the murderers to stop

murdering, the rapists to stop raping? I'm the senior trial attorney. I worked my tail off to get the job. I can't let down now that I'm there."

"I know, I know, and I'm not saying change. Only ..." He made a vague gesture.

"Only don't be such a tough, aggressive bitch, huh?" She was smiling as she said it, and he grinned back at her.

"What they said was a tough, aggressive, hard-nosed, ambitious bitch," he said. She took a mock swing at him and he held up his hands.

"I know you better than that, Katie. But I'm probably one of the few who do."

"It's the job, Doc," Kathryn said. "You think there aren't times when I'd like to just scream and scream, blow it all out of my head? You think my favorite thing in the whole world is trying to work up a case against a psycho who cuts off women's genitals? That there aren't days when I feel like walking away, and probably would if it wasn't for Emma?"

"I know. And I'm proud of you, Katie. You're one of the best prosecutors in California, and everyone knows it. But I still think you ought to make some room on your schedule for your own life. Take a trip to Florence, fall in love, do something utterly self-indulgent."

"Like you do, you mean?"

"Touché." Nelson smiled wryly. "Okay, I've said my piece. So, are you going to dash off, or do you want to talk some more about the fun and games we've been having down here?"

"Fun and games," Kathryn said. "That's a new name for it."

The work of the pathologist was a lot of things, but fun and games it was not. No matter how many times Kathryn attended autopsies, it was always an ordeal; she could never quite erase from her memory the whining bite of the electrical saws, the constant ambience of formaldehyde. She always wore cologne, and lots of it, to mask the omnipresent visceral stink, but there was nothing you could do to blot out what you saw and heard.

"I've got one more theory I want to run by you," Morgan said, consulting his notes again. "It has to do with the genital injuries."

"What about them?"

"Okay, we're dealing with gross physical mutilation. The

skin of the entire pubis, including the hair, fleshed off the body with a sharp, small-bladed instrument—not unlike the technique leatherworkers call flensing. I wish I could be more specific about the weapon, but it just isn't possible. Think of something between a very sharp pocketknife and a razor, and you'll get the picture."

"I've got it," Kathryn said, suppressing a shudder. "Why would anyone do something like that?"

Nelson looked thoughtful. "It would have to have some special significance for the killer. Some reason that probably only makes sense to him."

"You said you have a theory."

"You really want to hear it?"

"Go ahead."

"I think he's scalping them."

"What?"

"Trophies," Nelson said. "I think he is cutting off their pubic hair like an Indian taking a scalp, a trophy to mark his kill."

"That's disgusting."

Nelson shrugged. "It's a theory."

"Well, keep it to yourself, for God's sake," Kathryn said. "Have you got any idea what would happen if the media got hold of it?"

"They may well do so anyway, Katie. If this man kills again."

"You think he will?"

"I think I'd bet on it."

"One other thing," Kathryn said. "Dave Granz said you concluded that the killer drugged the Shelter Island victim before he killed her. How do you know that?"

Nelson smiled. "A simple enough assumption, if you think about it. How could the victim have gotten Valium any other way?"

"Okay. Next: Why?"

"Maybe just to keep them doped out when he can't be there. So they don't struggle or scream. Or maybe ... to make it easier. For himself, not them. Ten milligrams of Valium would be like a double Scotch on an empty stomach. Twenty-five and the victim would be pretty well out of it in about twenty minutes. Any more and there'd be a danger of OD'ing, but I doubt our boy would care much about that."

"Okay, I'm sold," Kathryn said. "When can I have all this?"

"It's being keypunched right now. I'll give you the file reference and you can call it up whenever you're ready."

She put her hand on his forearm. "I must seem like an ungrateful little bitch sometimes. Thanks for giving me so much of your time."

Nelson smiled. "You're always welcome," he said. "How about lunch one day next week? Or maybe dinner?"

"Give me a call. We'll set up a time. Okay?"

He made a gesture with the clipboard. "Sorry I couldn't give you more."

"That theory of yours is more than enough," she said. "Scalps. Yeccch."

"And then there's the next question," he said.

"Go on."

Nelson's face was deadly serious. "What does he do with them?"

8

WHEN KATHRYN GOT BACK TO HER OFFICE SHE LEFT A MES-sage for Dave Granz to call her when he got in; a quick check with Marcia revealed that no major crisis had occurred during her two-hour absence and that the Burke jury was still out. What were they having a problem with—she wondered.

It was hard to know which was the toughest, the weeks spent trying to convince a jury of a defendant's guilt, or the open-ended waiting to find out whether she had succeeded. At least during the prosecution of a case she was in control. Once the jury was locked away, it was out of her hands. The trick was to get on with something else and try not to think about it; but it was always there, on the edge of her awareness. She kept waiting for the phone to ring, for a voice to say, "Superior Three, jury's coming back."

A frown of concentration creasing her forehead, Kathryn laid a legal pad on the desk and marshaled her thoughts. Three years ago, before Hal Benton had appointed her his senior trial attorney, she had won a place on the Visiting Fellowship Program of the National Institute of Justice, founded in 1971 for researchers, prosecutors, police, and other criminal justice practitioners.

While she was there, Kathryn wrote a paper recommending that although FBI experts were available on request to all law enforcement agencies and investigators, each county ought to have at least one prosecutor on its staff capable of conducting basic criminal profiling. It had been adopted by Santa Rita County, and as a result, she spent six weeks studying the techniques of criminal profiling with the Behavioral Science Unit—the mind hunters, as they called them—at the FBI Academy in Quantico, near Washington.

It had been quite an unusual departure back then. These days, she knew, the State of California had its own mind hunter, a Special Agent Supervisor of the Department of Justice's Criminal Investigation Response Team who had completed a ten-month fellowship at Quantico, one of only twenty-four graduates of the Criminal Investigative Analysis Program nationwide. She picked up the Justice Department's directory of services for the Sacramento Division of Law Enforcement and checked. There he was: Stephen A. Giordano. Maybe if she talked to him? Without letting herself think about it any further she picked up the phone, called the Department of Justice in Sacramento, and asked for Special Agent Giordano.

"Criminal Investigative Analysis Program. Giordano speaking." The voice was well modulated, neutral. She told him who she was and explained why she was calling.

"I know you can't get into specifics over the phone," she said, "but I'd be grateful for any guidance you could give me."

"With certain reservations I'll be happy to help," Giordano said. "It'll be pretty general, though."

"I thought if I could just run the facts by you?"

"Fine," Giordano said. "Why don't you just go ahead and give me a brief rundown of the killings. If I need more you can always fax the details to me."

She tried to visualize the person she was talking to. The name Giordano sounded Italian. Dark hair, dark brown eyes, tall, volatile?

"We've got two victims," she said. "Both young females, both Hispanic. Killed fairly close together, maybe two weeks apart, one strangled, the other smothered. Both bodies mutilated."

"Be specific, please." His tone was businesslike, just short of peremptory. She described the crime scenes, the mutilations, the condition of the bodies, and Morgan's theories regarding both. Giordano listened without speaking until she was finished.

"Okay, that gives me a rough idea of what you're up against," he said. "What's bothering you?"

"I don't know whether I'm wasting your time. I don't even think we have enough facts to put together a victimology."

"Never mind what you don't have," he said. "Concentrate on what you do have. Evaluate the criminal act itself. How did it happen? Where? Did the killer find his victims in some other town, kill them there, and just dump them in Santa Rita?"

"It's a possibility."

"Write it down. If they were local women, why hasn't anyone reported them missing?"

"We checked Missing Persons files on the first victim. There was nothing."

"Check again. While you're at it, see if CAL-ID's computers have come up with any similar cases. Is there any significance in the fact that both victims were Hispanic?"

"Maybe. There's no way we'll ever know unless or until we have an ID of the victims, and so far there's no sign of that happening."

"What about the killer?"

"We don't have a thing."

"You're thinking negatively, Ms. Mackay," Giordano said patiently. "Start at the beginning. Criminal profiling reverses the techniques of the psychiatrist, remember?"

Of course. The purpose of criminal profiling was to formulate a psychological, or even in some cases a physical, profile of a suspect from a variety of types of information: crime scene information, for example, a victim's statement, even a victimology—a summary of facts known about the victim. Instead of studying a person and deducing what his personality and behavior patterns were likely to be, the profiler studied the subject's deeds and tried to deduce what sort of person he was.

"Although we don't yet know what it is, he has a specific reason for doing what he does."

"Good," Giordano said. "But . . . ?"

Her memory flashed back to Quantico, the sun coming in through the classroom window, the dry voice of the FBI instructor.

"Don't try to make sense of it. The killer's behavior isn't logical to us because we don't think the way he does, we don't have his *need* to think that way, which is to maintain and later re-create the excitement of the actual act of killing. Never forget the importance to him of the fantasy that triggered the crime. It's keeping alive the fantasy that's important, it's the fantasy that drives him."

"What he thinks is what he does and what he does is what he is."

"Good," Giordano said again. "So, your killer abducts, physically abuses, and finally kills his victims. Not with a weapon, but with his hands. Then he mutilates their corpses. What does that tell you?"

"It has to be a man," she said. "Quite apart from the fact it's statistically very rare for women to commit this kind of crime, the killings reek of sexual domination."

"You're doing fine," Giordano said. "Think about what he likes doing. And what that might mean."

"He could be what the shrinks call a dominator sadist. We wondered whether he might also be a necrophiliac," Kathryn said. "That might explain why he washes the bodies after he kills."

"It might. If so, on to the next question: Is it a ritual, part of the fantasy, or is it, as your pathologist suggested, a way of removing any physical trace of himself that could be analyzed for genetic fingerprinting?"

"We don't know," Kathryn said glumly. "We just don't know."

"Don't let that stop you," Giordano told her. "Keep chipping away at it. It's like sculpture. It's just a block of stone for a long, long time."

"What about Dr. Nelson's theory? Could he be . . . taking trophies?"

"Nothing's impossible. Some of these guys do things to the sexual organs—well, we needn't get into that. Let's suppose Dr. Nelson is right. We have to ask ourselves, Why?

What *for?* You understand? Try to figure him out. Think like him. The way he thinks directs his behavior. Try to envisage what it is he *wants.*"

"It's hard to visualize a motive."

"There may not be one," Giordano said. "One in five of all the murders analyzed by law enforcement has an unknown motive."

"You think he might be a thrill killer?"

"I don't think anything, Ms. Mackay. I'm just trying to channel your thought processes."

"I know. And I'm grateful. You don't mind my calling?"

"That's why I'm here," he said cheerfully. "Feel free to call again if you think it would help."

"Thanks, I will."

"I'll look forward to meeting you," Giordano said.

"Excuse me?"

"This guy you're trying to profile," he said. "He'll kill again. And go on doing it. I imagine sooner or later I'll get a call from your boss."

"You may be right."

"I often am," Giordano said. "Good luck."

She sat staring at the wall for a long time after they hung up. Giordano was right: it was a bit like sculpture. It took a long time to turn a block of marble into a Michelangelo. Come on, Kathryn, concentrate. Think it through. Think what through? She could sit on her butt for weeks conjecturing and never pin it down. He was an abused child, he was tormented in school, he was a delinquent adolescent, he's repaying society for an imagined wrong, he's . . .

Revenge?

She wrote down the word and stared at it. Revenge for what? For something the victims had done? But the killer probably didn't even know them. Were they paying for someone else's sins? There was a medical symptom called referred pain; the body sometimes camouflaged its weaknesses by sending distress signals from the wrong place. The mind was the same. Give it something it could not handle, something it did not wish to face, and it would refer that pain to something or someone else. So the killer might be exacting revenge for something someone had done to him. Both his victims were Hispanic. Did that mean he, too, was . . .

"Hispanic?" she mused aloud.

"Do I have to be?"

It was Dave Granz. He stood in the doorway smiling, untidily elegant in his tweed sport jacket and tan slacks. "Or will you accept a previously owned WASP?"

"Come in," Kathryn said. "Grab a chair."

"I got the Black Spot," he said.

"What?"

"You remember, *Treasure Island?* Jim asks Captain Flint what the Black Spot is, and Flint says, 'That's a summons, mate.' So here I am. How was Doctor Death?"

"Dave, how many more times . . ."

"Okay, okay, sorry. Did he come up with anything new?"

"Quite a lot," Kathryn said. "Most of it theoretical." She gave him a quick rundown of her conversation with Morgan Nelson.

"He thinks this guy is collecting scalps. Trophies?"

"It's just a theory, Dave."

"But what would he do with them, for Chrissake?" Dave said. "Make ear muffs?"

His macabre humor didn't make her smile. She gestured at the legal pad.

"I was looking for ideas. I talked to the Department of Justice profiler in Sacramento."

"Steve Giordano," he said, leaning over her shoulder to look at what she'd written. She was conscious of his closeness, the familiar remembered mixed smells of cigarettes and peppermint.

"You know him?"

"We've met."

"You weren't impressed." She felt disappointed and wondered why.

"He's one of those collar-and-tie types," Dave said, without enlarging on it. "You really think the killer might be Hispanic?"

"Why not?" she replied. "Most killings are intraracial—whites killing whites, blacks killing blacks, and so on. Statistically, at least, he's likely to be Hispanic."

"The racial divisions blur a little more here," Dave observed. "But let's go with the assumption. Read me what you've come up with."

"Hispanic or white, between twenty-five and forty, a loner

from a disturbed family background," she said, leaning back in her chair, her expression rueful. "Pretty good, huh? That only fits about half the population of California."

"Think positive: you've eliminated half your suspects already. What else do we have?"

"Possibly a dominator sadist. Possibly a necrophiliac. Possibly keeps the victims after he kills them—Morgan said the bodies would have to have been kept in a controlled environment. Temperature between freezing and forty degrees."

"So he has to have someplace he can keep the air-conditioning so high the ambient room temperature is about the same as inside a refrigerator."

"Is that possible?"

"Sure. A well-insulated room with no windows and flush-fitting doors. A couple of industrial air conditioners ... it could be done. The trouble is, it could be in the house next door to you and you'd have no way of knowing."

"It would need to be somewhere he can come and go without too many questions being asked. Somewhere isolated."

"Kathryn, they had a mass murderer in Cleveland about a year ago, killed a dozen people in his apartment. He lived on a city block with about forty other families. Nobody asked him any questions."

"So that's another dead end."

"What made you think revenge?"

"It was just a hunch. But when I thought it, I went cold. Like precognition, you know what I mean?"

"Unfortunately for us, precognition doesn't lend itself to investigation. What about the MO?"

"I made a note to call CAL-ID."

"Worth a shot," Dave said. He didn't sound optimistic, and Kathryn had to admit she shared his doubts.

"You know what time it is?" Dave said, hitching his thigh on to the corner of her desk. She looked at her watch: twenty after five. She sighed.

"Damn it, Dave, I hate to give up."

"In spite of the churlish way it was originally received," he said, "my offer still stands. Let's go pick up Emma and I'll take you both for pizza in Espanola. We can talk it through afterwards. What do you say?"

Kathryn looked at the profiling chart and the notes of her conversation with Steve Giordano. Analysis of the crime scene(s), forget it, the victims were killed someplace else. Analysis of the victims, impossible without an ID. Evaluation of the pathologist's autopsy protocol, still in the pipeline. It looked as if there wasn't a damned thing they could do until the killer struck again. What a cheerful thought to end the day on, she thought. She threw down her pencil in disgust.

"I have to call Walt Earheart," she told Granz. "I promised him I'd try to get something to him tonight."

She put in a call to the Sheriff's Department and talked to the big lieutenant, briefing him on Morgan Nelson's findings and giving him her own thoughts on the killer.

"You don't have to tell Sanchez all this," she reminded him.

"He probably knows already," Earheart replied. "I sometimes think that bastard knows when we change our underwear around here."

Kathryn thought about her own conversation with Sanchez. She didn't flatter herself he hadn't already put a similar proposition to someone else, maybe someone in the Sheriff's Department; in his world, everyone had a price, and sometimes it was surprisingly low.

"Good luck tonight," she said.

"Thanks," Earheart said. "I get the feeling I'm going to need it."

She put the phone down, and Dave looked up expectantly.

"That it?" he said.

"That's it," she replied. "Let's go get that pizza."

9

KATHRYN PICKED UP HER BRIEFCASE AND LED THE WAY DOWN to her little red Mazda in the parking lot in front of the County Building. Dave didn't offer to carry the bulky case: they'd had that one out a long time ago. He stood and watched as she put it and the files she had brought with her into the trunk and slammed the lid down. It was like a ceremony, he thought. The end of that for now, the beginning of this till later. She did it every day at this time, consciously shucking the formal identity of Kathryn Mackay,

Assistant District Attorney, adjusting to being Emma Mac-kay's mommy as she drove to Alameda Heights.

By the time they got onto Alameda Drive, the air conditioner had made the interior of the car bearable. About twenty minutes after leaving the office, they pulled into the parking lot outside Emma's school on Lighthouse Drive. Kathryn had a standing arrangement for her daughter to stay on until five forty-five; a lot of kids with working mothers did. She parked and went through the classrooms and out into the playground in back. She could see Emma on a swing, her dress ballooning, her long black hair flying out behind her.

"Hi, Mommy!" Emma called.

"Hi, there, honeypie!" Kathryn shouted back. "You have fun today?"

"I got a gold star! For being good!"

"Hey, terrific!"

Emma jumped off the swing and ran across the sun-dried lawn and into Kathryn's outstretched arms. Kathryn whirled her around and hugged her, feeling her heart lift the way it always did.

"Look who's come to see you," she said, putting Emma down. Emma cocked her head and squinted up at Granz.

"Hi, Dave," she said. "You coming home with us?"

"You inviting me, princess?" He was looking at Kathryn as he said it.

"We're going to get pizza," Kathryn said. "Would you like that?"

"Yeahyeahyeah," Emma said, grabbing Dave's hand. "And can we go to the beach after, can we, Dave, can we?"

"Anything's possible," he told her. "But you better ask your mommy."

"Come look," Emma said imperiously. They followed her across to the far wall, where there was a board with the names of the children in her class on it. "Lookit, Mommy," she said. "There's my gold star I got today."

"Clever you," Kathryn said. "You think maybe I could get one of those?"

Emma put her hands on her hips and shook her head, giving a theatrically patient sigh. "Mommy, you're being silly. You know they don't give gold stars to grown-ups. Grown-ups get money."

"I guess so," Kathryn said. "But sometimes I sure wish they'd give us gold stars, too."

"Why, were you special good today?"

"I think so," Kathryn said. "I sure tried to be. Didn't I, Dave?"

"Sure did," Dave said.

"Then maybe you'll get one tomorrow," Emma told her, and ran off to get her things from the cloakroom. Kathryn smiled as she watched her go. That's what's wrong with growing up, she thought. Somewhere along the way we forget how to believe in tomorrow.

They got back into the Mazda and Kathryn headed south on Lighthouse Drive. By the time they reached the freeway underpass, Emma was giggling at Dave's silly jokes. He was a natural with kids. He'd once told Kathryn that not having had kids of his own was one of his greatest regrets.

As Kathryn turned right onto Beach Avenue, Dave was asking Emma if she knew how you could tell when an elephant had been in the refrigerator. The sidewalks were crowded with kids in beach gear and tourists. Ahead, a line of cars inched slowly through the packed, narrow streets.

"Elephants can't go in refrigerators," Emma told Dave loftily.

"Can too. Know how you can tell?"

"Nope."

"You can see their footprints in the butter." Emma was still giggling when Kathryn spotted someone backing out of a parking space.

"Hey, how about that for timing, you guys?" she said, signaling left and sliding into it.

"That's what you get instead of a gold star." Dave grinned. He got out of the car and tipped the seat forward so Emma could clamber out. She was gone in a whirl of legs, Dave loping after her toward the pizza place up the street. Kathryn fed the meter and followed at a walk, smiling at Emma's excitement. Sometimes Dave made her laugh so much Kathryn had to act mock-stern, and tell him he just better quit before she got sick. Seeing the two of them together always made Kathryn conscious of the absence of a man in her life. Little girls needed a daddy who was around all the time, not just someone who came to see her on holidays and at vacation time the way Jack did. Kathryn smiled. Someday, my prince will come.

"I'll take a slice of vegetarian," she said.

"Me, too, me, too," Emma said. "And a Coke, Dave, a Coke."

"Kathryn?"

"A Coke's fine."

"Okay," Dave told the girl behind the counter. "Two vegetarian, one pepperoni, two Cokes, and a root beer to go."

"You got it," the girl said automatically.

When the pizza was hot they walked back toward the car and found an empty bench facing the low wall between the sidewalk and the beach. The sun was already dropping behind the cliffs at Lookout Point. Kids were playing in the surf, their voices a single sound mixed with the noise of the waves. A flock of sea gulls wheeled overhead and settled on the beach near a tidal pool. Out at sea pelicans flew low over the water.

"Want some more pizza?"

She shook her head. Dave would go get another, like he always did. Then he would clown about on the beach with Emma for a while, like he always did. Then she'd call time, and Emma would beg to stay a little longer, like she always did. And when they got into the car, he'd come back with them for a glass of wine, like he always did. And when Emma was tucked up in bed and fast asleep, he would say, "Why don't I sleep over?" And she would say no, like she always did now.

There was an inevitable sexual tension in working as closely with someone as she worked with Dave. But getting involved with him again just wasn't on the agenda. They had been through all that a long time ago, not long after she came to Santa Rita. She had just won her first murder case, and Dave, who'd been her inspector, took her out to celebrate. They had an expensive dinner, champagne. Perhaps a glass too many. What happened then had seemed a natural, perhaps even inevitable, consummation: their awareness of each other had grown more intense as the weeks of the trial had gone by.

After a couple of months of seeing each other fairly regularly, Dave moved into her life on a semipermanent basis, sleeping over some nights and most weekends. Something told Kathryn from the start that it was a mistake, but she overruled her instincts: there was a part of her then that needed reassurance, someone caring, someone Emma could love. Dave seemed to have all the right stuff. As time went by, however, his mañana approach to life's problems collided with her do-it-now mentality. With Dave always around, she didn't work as hard, and as a result her performance suffered. She wasn't used to losing, and it was a shock when it happened. In addition, his stormy love-hate relationship with his ex-wife Rita, a bond neither seemed able or inclined to sever, created problems. Kathryn found herself growing less and less sure that she wanted a full-time partner. Maybe she'd grown out of the condition, like a domestic animal that had been too long in the wild.

So she'd bitten the bullet. This way at least, she told herself, there would be no bitterness: she and Dave could remain colleagues and friends. At first, Dave was resentful and hurt; he hadn't understood, maybe still didn't really understand, Kathryn's reasons for wanting to call it a day. She still wasn't altogether sure herself. It had taken her a long time to get all their lives back on an even keel, but she liked to hope she'd managed it not badly. A strong yet fragile bond linked them now, forever.

An hour later they were all back at Kathryn's Seaview Heights condo, and Emma, showered and shampooed, was sitting up in bed in her nightgown while Dave read her the story of the Three Billy Goats Gruff. Kathryn could hear him doing the sound effects of the troll, and Emma's delighted squeals of fright. She poured some apple juice into a glass and sipped it, waited till the goats were on the other side of the hill eating the fresh spring grass, then went down to kiss Emma good night.

"There's wine in the refrigerator," she told Dave as they passed in the hallway. "Or—"

"Wine's fine," he said. "You want a glass?"

"Sure."

Usually between the time Emma went to sleep and she went to bed herself, Kathryn would work on upcoming cases, catch up on legal updates. Tonight she felt oddly restless. She went back into the living room and stood by the window looking out across the bay. Down below and to the right the lights of Espanola glittered brightly in the growing darkness. To the left she could see the long arm of Shelter Island, the intermittent flash of the lighthouse at its western end where the first murder victim had been found.

Dave came over and stood beside her, looking out over the ocean, his left hand on her right shoulder. It was like he knew what she was thinking.

"We'll find him, Kathryn," he said. He squeezed her shoulder encouragingly. "Don't let it get under your skin."

She turned and went back to the kitchen counter where her briefcase and papers were stacked. She opened the case and got out the legal pad on which she had made her notes earlier.

"Maybe we ought to call Sacramento again," she said, "and get that guy Giordano down here."

"You talked to him," Dave said. "Listen, babe, without some hard facts, he wouldn't be able to do any better than you."

"It just seems weird that this man can kill two women and nobody misses them. Nobody calls in and says, my girlfriend, my daughter, didn't come home, maybe one of these women is she."

"Jack Burrows worked that angle real hard," Dave told her. "He ran a make on both victims through the statewide register of missing persons, then tried every contiguous state: Nevada, Oregon, Arizona. He came up empty every time. Both victims were young, probably unmarried. You know the way kids are. They're sharing a place with a friend who figures they just up and left, what the hell, why would she call the cops? Or they rent an apartment someplace, and when they don't turn up after a while the landlord figures they've skipped, sells their possessions for back rent. Think he's going to report it?"

"Come to think of it, the killer could have abducted them someplace else."

"Why would he need to? Hell, half the people in Santa Rita at this time of year are from someplace else," Dave told her. "And that's not counting what Jake Gylam calls the homeless by choice or the runaways or the battered wives and debt-skippers and all the other people who just drop out of the system without telling anyone where they're going."

"What time is it?"

"Nine twenty-five, why?"

"Don't want to miss Sanchez."

"I heard you had lunch. What did you make of him?"

She debated telling him about Sanchez's offer, then decided to confide in him.

"Hard to say, exactly," she fenced. "But . . . there's something about the guy. I don't think I could ever trust him."

"I've got a pal who works for KKPP-TV down in Santa Barbara," Dave said. "Been in the business twenty years. He says Sanchez is the most ruthless, self-centered bastard he ever encountered. Everybody hates his guts. But people hang in there with him because he looks like he's going places and they hope he'll take them with him. Some more wine?"

"Switch on the TV," Kathryn said, shaking her head. "It's time for the program."

The picture swam into view. *Channel Seven News* anchors Steve Brace and Jane Brondini were just doing the wrap.

". . . and that's the news as we saw it, here on KKSU Monterey, this June Thursday," Brace was saying. "From Jane Brondini and myself, Steve Brace, good night. Stay tuned for *Here and Now*—Richard Sanchez examines two bizarre murders in Santa Rita."

The familiar signature music swelled as the titles rolled up. The camera switched to Sanchez, wearing an immaculate cream lightweight two-piece suit with a light blue silk shirt and a midnight-blue silk tie.

"Good evening, ladies and gentlemen. I'm Richard Sanchez, bringing you the issues people want to discuss—*Here and Now.*" His voice was strong, deep, well modulated. It demanded attention. He swung in his chair to face camera two as the logo of the show dwindled to a small rectangle above his left shoulder.

"About a week ago, twenty-two-year-old Steve Jackson took his dog for a walk on Shelter Island Beach. Nothing very unusual about that, he does it regularly, after he gets off the night shift. He said he likes it down there at night, the idea of having one of the most beautiful beaches in the state all to himself . . ."

KKSU had sent a crew to the beach to film. Sanchez's voice continued over an establishing shot taken from the south, down by the marina, up the gentle outward curve of the beach, with the long rollers coming in off the Pacific, and the Shelter Island lighthouse stark and white on its green knoll. The film cut to a shot taken immediately below the lighthouse, the telephoto lens closing in on Sanchez, standing in the place where the body had been found.

"Right where I am standing now, in this idyllic beauty spot, a body was lying. The body of a young Hispanic woman, brutally murdered. Despite a full-scale investigation launched by the Sheriff's Department, no clue to the identity of either the murder victim or the murderer has been found. In fact, our law enforcement agencies had made no progress on the case whatsoever until yesterday, Wednesday afternoon, June nineteenth."

Another establishing shot filled the screen, this time filmed from a helicopter flying over Santa Rita, heading southeast along Montecito, then turning north over the railroad depot toward State.

"Sedgewick Park, Santa Rita," Sanchez said, voice-over. "A place of quiet beauty. A bird sanctuary and nature reserve created from a tule-cattail marsh in the mid-seventies by city benefactor Thomas P. Sedgewick. A tranquil oasis in the bustle of the city. Picnic areas and pathways shaded by live oaks and white alders. And there, fringed by arroyo willow and eucalyptus, the lagoon where over the years thousands of Santa Rita children have come to watch marsh and bird life."

Cut to an interview scene, with two men facing camera. Behind them, the lagoon, near the spot where the second body had been found.

"The day before yesterday, two of Santa Rita's homeless population, Pete Salazar and Johnny Mace, decided to spend the afternoon right here in Sedgewick Park," Sanchez said, off camera. "Pete Salazar, tell us what happened to you."

"Listen, man, it was weird, you know?" Salazar said. The cameraman zoomed in slowly for a close-up. "I mean, I was, you know, I had a few beers, right? I was walking down the side of the lagoon, over here behind where I'm standin', and I sort of slipped and fell into the water."

Cut to Sanchez in a cream jacket and tan slacks. He must have gone straight to the park after we had lunch, Kathryn thought. "Just there, where I'm pointing? By the willow tree?"

"Right, man, I just sort of put down my hands to save myself falling all the way in, you know? And there was somethin' in the water, sort of soft, slimy, you know what I mean? An' then this, it just bobbed up like a cork, this body, this woman's body, this naked woman."

"And Johnny Mace, where were you when this happened?"

"I was back over there a ways, on the bank," Johnny said. "I'm dozin', you know, just takin' it easy. And I hear this splash and I think, hey, poor old Pete's fallen in the pool, man. And I thought maybe I better go see if he's okay, you know, we had a few beers, and then I heard him scream."

"You screamed, Mr. Salazar?"

"You better believe it," Salazar said. "I mean this lady floatin' in the water, she wasn't no Miss America, you know what I'm tellin' you?"

The interview ended and Sanchez came back on screen in the studio.

"Another young woman murdered. Like the first victim, she was Hispanic, and like the first victim, she remains unidentified. Who are these women? Where did they come from? Why were their bodies left to be found in public beauty spots like Shelter Beach and Sedgewick Park? In an attempt to find out more, I talked to Santa Rita County Chief of Detectives Lieutenant Walter Earheart. Join us for that after these messages."

The commercials began; as they blatted away Dave got up and refilled his glass. "I talked to those two," he told Kathryn. "Couple of grab-and-run winos who work the supermarkets over on Mercado. If there ever was anything at the crime scene, they trampled it to death long before our people got near the place."

"Welcome back to *Here and Now*," Richard Sanchez's voice announced over the titles, which whirled away to be replaced by a prefilmed studio interview. Walt Earheart sat facing Sanchez. A caption identified the detective.

"Aw, come on, Kathryn," Dave said impatiently. "Do we need to watch this?"

"Shhh," she said, watching Sanchez slip effortlessly into the role he played so well, that of the probing, merciless interrogator.

"Lieutenant Earheart. Two young Hispanic women brutally murdered, their mutilated bodies dumped in county beauty spots. A serial killer stalking the streets. Yet not only is your department unable to even identify the victims, it doesn't have a single lead to the killer, or any idea when he will strike again. What is your response to that?"

"It's not true we have no leads," Earheart began. "In fact we're following up a great many. I'm confident—"

"Let's hold it right there. Does your department have any idea of the identity of this psychopath, Lieutenant? Yes or no."

"What I'm saying is—"

"Yes or no?" The two men glared at each other.

"No."

"You have no idea who he is, where he comes from, or when he will strike again?"

"It's very early in our investigation. We'll catch him, sooner or later."

"Sooner or later. While thousands of young Hispanic women right here in Santa Rita walk the streets in fear of their lives."

"Getting hysterical isn't going to help, Mr. Sanchez."

"Neither is being complacent, Lieutenant," Sanchez snapped. "I'm expressing the public's disquiet here."

"You mean you're doing a scare story," Earheart flared back.

"Wrong," Sanchez retorted. "People are scared enough already. There's a maniac out there. And your department's inability to apprehend him isn't making anybody feel any more secure."

"I can only repeat, we're doing everything we can," Earheart said doggedly. "You probably know the district attorney has set up a special investigation unit which will concentrate exclusively on these murders. I've assigned every available officer we have to the case. All we need is a break."

"Oh, Jesus, Walt," Granz groaned.

"A break, Lieutenant?" Sanchez pounced, putting just the right amount of disbelief into his voice. "A break? You've got a criminal psychopath on the streets murdering young women and cutting off their sexual organs—and you're hoping for a break?"

"Every lead is being followed up, checked, double-checked," Earheart said, trying to repair the damage. "Every phone call we receive, every piece of forensic evidence. But we can't do miracles."

The filmed interview ended.

"That was Chief of Detectives Walter Earheart, telling us the Santa Rita Sheriff's Department is hoping for a break," Sanchez said. His expression had not changed, but the beautifully weighted shade of contempt in his voice said it all for him. "Meanwhile this brutal killer stalks our streets. If the police can't find him, what can we as citizens do? Join me in an extended examination of this timely question here on KKSU in Monterey, nine-thirty, Sunday night."

The end title music swelled and Kathryn got up and switched off the set.

"Poor Walt," she said. "That was rough."

"I told you we'd get clobbered," Dave said, getting up to fill his glass from the bottle in the refrigerator. "That's the problem with appearing on a show like Sanchez. He can say anything he wants. All the nice, emotive buzz words: serial killer, maniac, psychopath. And you have to just sit there and take it. This is nice wine, by the way. You want some more?"

"You know I get high if I have more than one," Kathryn said. "Besides, I'm still on call."

"Till when?"

"Ben Robson takes over Monday, thank God."

"I guess this means I don't get to stay the night."

"You guess correct." Kathryn smiled. "But to show you my heart's in the right place, I'll drive you down to Espanola. You can catch a bus in from there."

"Don't bother. The walk will do me good." He paused. "You got plans for the weekend?"

"Shopping. Washing. Ironing. All the fun things. Sunday, Jack's coming up to see Emma. They'll go off someplace for the day."

"How about we have brunch together? There's a new Italian place in Catalina—Pasta Forgetting. They do great fettuccine."

"Where do they get these names?"

"Guy in Encino, ex-scriptwriter, turns them out fifty bucks a throw," Dave said, grinning. "How about it?"

"I'm tempted," she said. "But I really have to stay home

and work. I've got jury selection on the Broadwick trial starting Monday."

He shrugged. "Sick of the sight of me, huh?"

Kathryn nodded. "Absolutely," she said. She kissed him lightly on the lips and pushed him toward the door. "Now go on, get out of here."

He stopped in the doorway, turned, looked right into her eyes. "You like Sanchez?" he said. It was unexpected, and for a moment, Kathryn didn't know what to reply.

"A lot of women would say he's attractive. But ... I got the feeling it wasn't really me he was interested in so much as who I am, what I do. Why do you ask?"

He smiled. "Just checking," he said, and let himself out.

10

HIS WIFE KNOCKED SOFTLY ON THE DOOR OF THE STUDY. "I'VE made some coffee," she said.

"I'll be right out," he said. "I'm nearly through."

"What are you doing?"

"Grading homework," he said.

"I thought I heard the TV."

"Talking to myself."

He never allowed her into his den anymore. The holy of holies, he called it. He'd heard her talking to neighbors. "Lee needs somewhere quiet to work," she told them. "He likes to get away from it all."

He had watched the Richard Sanchez program with mounting disbelief. Could they really be that stupid?

Yes, was the answer. Just like Nam.

He would never forget his own sheer terror when he realized how stupid, how careless he had been. Scrubbing himself again and again, burning the clothes he'd worn, throwing the key to the shabby little shanty into the river. Forty-eight hours harrowed by the certainty that any moment the MPs were going to burst in shouting, hustling him out to the Jeep and down to the provost marshal's office.

He couldn't concentrate, he couldn't eat or sleep or think

in a straight line. His brain was like a broken mirror. He broke into a cold sweat every time a door banged, flinched every time he heard raised voices. Three days passed, five, a week. He bought all the papers, desperately searching for some mention of the girl's death. He found one on the ninth day.

Some people living near the shanty had complained of bad smells coming from it, and police broke down the door. Inside, they found the decomposing body of a young girl, murdered and mutilated. She carried no identification. No one knew the names of the owners of the shanty. No one had come forward to claim the girl's body. Murder by a person or persons unknown. The police were pursuing several lines of inquiry, a spokesperson said. The girl could have been killed by a pimp using her as an example to keep his other girls in line, by some freaked-out grunt in from the jungle who'd flipped his lid, or even by the VC, disposing of an informant who was of no further use to them. All avenues would be explored.

His sense of relief was almost sexual. It was quickly replaced by a sense of enormous power, the knowledge that the inside of his life was different from the outside. And knowing no one but he knew it. He had done it. And no one would ever, ever know except himself. There was no way the police could ever link it to him, and there never would be. And anyway, nobody gave a fuck. Just another gook whore dead in a filthy shanty.

Watching the Sanchez show filled him with the same heady feeling of invulnerability. They were all stupid. They didn't even know who the dead women were. They probably never would. The knowledge that he could do it again, whatever he wanted, whenever he wanted, surged through him. The memory of hot frantic lips, pleading eyes, and swallowed sobs of pain started up the familiar odd, uneasy longing inside him.

He unlocked the door and went into the living room. His wife was sitting in front of the TV watching some dumb soap. That was all she ever watched, dumb soaps.

"I thought you said you made coffee?" he said.

"Yes, yes, I'll get you some, you sit down, I'll switch this off . . ."

"Leave it," he said. "Just get the coffee."

He could see the relief in her eyes when she realized he

wasn't angry and he smiled as he watched her go into the kitchen. She had never disobeyed him. And she never would. She smiled hesitantly at him as she poured the coffee.

She'd been quite presentable once, no beauty queen, perhaps, but pleasant enough in a girl-next-door way, good teeth and long glossy blond hair. Not anymore. Drab was the word for Carol now. Drab and boring.

He had married her only because he had to. The principal had called him into his office, a personal matter. Some concern among the parents. An all-girls' school, a single male teacher. Hate to make an issue of it, but he had to appreciate the school's position.

So he played out the game of courting her, and they were married; she turned out to be a homemaker. She sewed curtains and embroidered cushions and at first there was more sex than he wanted, but he broke her of that the same way he broke her of all the rest of it, like a man training a dog, short sharp words for displeasure, fulsome praise for correct behavior. She was a born victim. The harder she tried to please him, the deeper his scorn lacerated her. The more she tried to widen their circle of friends, the more his insults alienated them, just as his treatment of her mortified the colleagues who invited them into their homes.

Stupid cow, he thought.

He opened the paper and turned to the back pages. He liked puzzles. They relaxed him. Crosswords. Anagrams. Scrabble. Best of all he liked codes and ciphers. There was a cipher game in the newspaper every day, a quotation by a famous person. They told you one letter, and you had to work out the rest. Today's was a short one:

IFOH RK YIJYDK RS CNH TFFX FP UHIRHORSB
RS
TRMYLIHK.
—WFNS LFJGHM GFJDK.
Today's clue: U = B.

The commonest letters in the English language, in descending order, were *e, t, a, i, o,* and *r.* Code breakers and cryptanalysts used this rule to help them break whatever code they were presented with. The only unbreakable codes were what were known in espionage circles as one-time pads. The system was simple: sender and recipient had identical copies of "pads," usually around fifty pages, each covered with lines of letters or figures chosen at random. The sender used letters or numbers from one of the pages; the receiver, having been told the page being used that day, used his copy to decode the message. And since no one else knew the contents of the pads, the code was unbreakable.

He looked at the puzzle. *U* equals *B*, but it only appears once; not much help. He wrote down the alphabet on a piece of paper. The letter most frequently appearing was *H*. So *H* was probably *E*. If so, the three-letter word *CNH* was probably *the*. So *C* was *T*, and *N* was *H*. Each time he decoded a letter he crossed it out on his piece of paper. *RS* appeared twice, *RK* once. *R* was probably *I*. *K* would be either *S*, *N*, or *T*. Make a couple of guesses. He wrote down what he had; the puzzle now read:

IFOe is YIJYDs in the TFFX FP beIieOinB in
TiMYLIHs.
                        —WFhn LFJGeM GFJDs.

The eighth word was *believing*, so *I* was *L*, *O* was *V*, and *B* was *G*. That meant *F* must be *O*, and the first word was *love*. Love is *something* in the *something something* believing in *something*. It was going to be fairly easy. There were three *Y*s and two *M*s. Try *A* for *Y* and the third word was probably *always*. So *J* was *W*, and *D* was *Y*. Now try *R* for *M*.

Love is always in the TFFX FP believing in TiraLles.
                        —WFhn LFJGer GFJDs.

The last word of the quotation had to be *miracles*. Of course, he thought, John Cowper Powys. "Love is always in the mood of believing in miracles," he said aloud, and looked at his watch. Twelve minutes. Fairly good. He laid down the newspaper and looked up as Carol came in with the coffee. She smiled uncertainly at him, then went back to watching her stupid soap, her expression as blank as a saucer.

He picked up his pen and wrote out the alphabet again on the yellow ruled legal pad he'd bought in the stationery section at the drugstore. Beneath it, he wrote the alphabet backwards: better not make it too difficult for them. When he was finished it looked like this:

ABCD EFGH IJKL MNOP QRST UVWXYZ
ZYXW VUTS RQPO NMLK JIHG FEDCBA

Next, he worked out his message.

GSV LMV RM HVWTVDRXP KZIP DZH
XZOOVW ZMMZ.
HSV SZW Z HNZOO XFG LM SVI RMMVI GSRTS.
ZMLGSVI LMV HLLM.

He folded the sheet twice and put it in an envelope. The big detective's name was Earheart. Walter Earheart. Lee got up and opened the phone book to the government pages, ran his finger down the listing until he found what he was looking for: Santa Rita County Sheriff-Coroner, Investigation Division, County Building, 701 Pacific Street.

Okay, Walter, he thought, smiling; this one's for you.

11

KATHRYN GOT IN EARLY. SHE COULD GET MORE PAPERWORK done in the quiet forty-five minutes preceding the official start of the working day than in any other part of it. Early as she was, Marcia was already there. Fridays were always hectic. Because trials weren't in session, everyone in the office would be frantically trying to catch up on all the unanswered phone calls, the responses to motions, and all the trial work that had piled up. Friday was also staff meeting day, when Mac assigned cases and kicked around any problems any of them might have.

"Hi, Kathryn," Marcia said. "You see Sanchez last night?"

"I saw it. Is Hal in yet?"

"He's in, and he wants to see you. Premeeting meeting. In the conference room, now."

"Bad as that, huh?"

"They're using real bullets out there."

As if to prove her point, Marcia threw a copy of the morning paper on her desk. A headline in the middle of the page said it all: SHERIFF'S DEPARTMENT SLAMMED: PERFORMANCE "NOT GOOD ENOUGH" SAYS TV'S SANCHEZ.

"Oh boy," Kathryn said, and followed her down the corridor to the conference room. Hal Benton sat at the head of the table. He was a big man, with nice gray-blue eyes and sandy blond hair parted on the left. His face was strong and square, with a good jawline. His nose looked as though it might have been broken once. He looked up as Kathryn came in.

"Sit down, Kathryn." He nodded. "I want to get this TV show crap out of the way before we begin the meeting, okay?"

"Go ahead."

Only four people were present. Mac McCaskill sat on Benton's right; opposite him was Norm Podnoretz, chief of inspectors. Tall, deceptively amiable looking, Norm had worked his way up the ladder from detective sergeant in the Sheriff's Department. He ran his division with a single-minded efficiency that was the envy of every other district attorney's office in California.

"Okay. We all know Walt got fried," Benton said. "If that was all there was to it, we could write it off to experience and get on with more important business."

"But—?" Podnoretz prompted.

"Sanchez called me this morning. He's doing a special on the murders. Jake Gylam has agreed to appear."

"I heard," Kathryn said. "Sanchez must have done the snow job of the century on him."

"Probably reminded him how badly he needs the Hispanic vote," Podnoretz said. "Jake's sensitive to that kind of persuasion."

"Well, it's his funeral," Kathryn said. "And Sanchez'll bury him."

"We can't just sit back and let that happen, Kathryn," Mac said. "Jake being an asshole is one thing. Jake making the rest of us look like assholes is another matter entirely."

"My thoughts exactly," Benton said briskly. "So I told Sanchez I want someone from this office up there with him. I suggested you, Kathryn."

"What did he say?"

"He jumped at the idea. Why wouldn't he?"

"He and I banged heads a couple of days ago. We didn't exactly part the best of friends."

Benton shrugged. "He didn't mention it."

"You surprise me," Kathryn said thoughtfully. "He didn't strike me as the forgetful type."

"So, okay?" McCaskill asked. "Can we call KKSU and tell them you'll do it?"

"What exactly is it I'm supposed to do?"

"Limit the damage," Benton told her. "I don't care how."

"Okay," Kathryn sighed. "When is it?"

"It'll be prerecorded. Two o'clock, Sunday afternoon."

"Sunday?" Kathryn said, dismayed. "Hal, I've got a six-year-old daughter I don't get to spend half enough time with as it is. Now you want to steal my Sunday from me as well."

"Look, Kathryn, I need this from you," Benton said, as if that ended the discussion. Before Kathryn could protest further, there was a tap on the door, and one of the secretaries put her head into the office.

"Kathryn," she said. "The Burke jury has a verdict."

Kathryn leaped to her feet, her heart pounding. "Hal, excuse me, I've got to go."

She ran along the corridor to her office and grabbed a legal pad. Next, she buzzed the inspectors' secretary, Patricia Page, and asked her to try to locate Dave Granz.

"Tell him the Burke jury is coming in, and he should meet me at Superior Three, okay?"

"Ten-four," Patricia said. She was married to a cop, and often used police codes as replies. Ten-four meant message received and understood.

Kathryn left the office by a side door that led into the central corridor and ducked into the rest room to check her makeup. Oh, God, she thought, I look awful. She began shivering and couldn't stop. She wet a towel, pressed it against her temples, and took a deep breath. It didn't help. The face that looked back at her from the mirror was still pale and drawn.

If only it didn't *matter* so damned much, she thought. If only I didn't *care*. Well, there was no use wishing it otherwise: she cared, it mattered. Getting the rapists and killers off the streets and into prison was a duty and a special responsibility she willingly undertook, knowing the cost, knowing its effect on her as an attorney, as a mother, and as a woman.

There were only a few people in the spectator seats. One was the victim, Patricia Morales, who looked up and smiled as Kathryn came in. Kathryn went over to speak to her, but was intercepted by Dave Berry from the *Gazette*.

"Hi, Kathryn," he said. "What do you think?"

"It's hard to tell," she replied honestly. "I hope they'll come back with a guilty verdict, but that doesn't mean they will."

"Here comes Burke," he said.

"I'd better get in there." She went through the gate and put her pad on the table, then turned to face Patricia Morales, sitting in the front row of the spectator area, as Burke and his lawyer walked across the courtroom and took their seats at the defense table. Neither of them looked at Kathryn or the victim.

"How do you feel?" she asked.

Patricia Morales shook her head. She was a dark, pretty young woman, not much over five feet, dressed in an off-white linen suit. "I'm shaking from head to foot," she confessed.

Kathryn squeezed her shoulder. "I don't know if it's any consolation to you, Patricia, but so am I," she said. "Just hang in there, okay?"

"I'll try," Patricia said. The courtroom door opened and Dave Granz hurried in. He came through the barrier and sat next to Kathryn.

"Jesus," he whispered. He was breathing heavily. "I thought I wasn't going to make it."

"Where were you?"

"Up in Mission Heights. They got me through my beeper."

"Mission Heights? How'd you get here so fast?"

Dave smiled his lopsided grin. "Only touched the ground about twice," he said.

Kathryn gripped Dave's hand as the jury filed in and took their places. They looked very solemn. There was a lot of folklore about juries: how if they had found a defendant guilty, they always looked away from him when they came in, and so on. Only the foreperson looked at Burke. His name, Kathryn remembered, was Vincent O'Neill.

Alice Hernandez snapped her command and everyone stood as Judge Stevenson came in.

"Be seated," he said, and turned toward the jury. "Ladies and gentlemen of the jury, have you reached a verdict?"

The foreperson stood. "We have, Your Honor."

Stevenson nodded to the bailiff, who went across and took the slip of paper from the foreperson and handed it up to the judge. Stevenson read it and handed it to the court clerk. His expression did not change.

"The clerk will read the verdict," he said, leaning back in his chair.

The court clerk cleared her throat. "On the charge of rape: guilty. On the charge of sodomy: guilty. On the charge of oral copulation: guilty."

"Mr. Blakely, do you wish to have the jury polled?" Stevenson asked. The defense lawyer shook his head and the judge nodded acknowledgment.

"Ladies and gentlemen of the jury," he said, "this court would like to thank you for your exemplary conduct. This trial is concluded and you are now dismissed. You are free to discuss this case with others, including the attorneys on both sides. You also, however, have the right to refrain from discussing the case with anyone if you so desire. Thank you again."

Kathryn watched as the jury filed back into the jury room. Dave squeezed her hand and then let go.

"The defendant will stand," Stevenson said. Burke got to his feet.

"Eric Thomas Burke, you have been found guilty of rape, sodomy, and forced oral copulation—"

"I'm innocent!" Burke shouted. "You know I am! You know this is just some story they made up against me, her over there, that hotshot from the DA's office!"

"I'll set sentencing for six weeks from now," Stevenson said, as if Burke had never spoken. He glanced at the wall calendar. "August thirtieth."

"Everybody lied!" Burke shouted, ignoring Blakely's urgent signals to be quiet. "They all lied! I didn't do it!"

"Get him out of here," Stevenson snapped, his urbane manner evaporating. "Court's dismissed."

As the judge rose and went into chambers, Albert Blakely put a sympathetic hand on Burke's shoulder. The younger man shrugged it off angrily, his fists clenched, brows knitted. Deputy Hernandez walked over to the defense table and gestured for Burke to precede her out of the courtroom. As he went, he glowered at Kathryn, who was hugging a weeping Patricia Morales. Over Patricia's shoulder she saw Burke's lips move, although his voice was inaudible. *Fucking bitch,* he said, and then he was gone.

Gloria Zanecki, a reporter from *Channel Seven News* whom Kathryn knew quite well, came in and asked if she had time to do a quick interview on the steps of the Courts Building.

"Sure," Kathryn said. "Listen, Gloria, can I ask you a question?"

"What about?" Gloria asked warily.

"Richard Sanchez."

"What about him?"

"You don't like him, obviously."

"He makes my skin crawl. He has a way of looking at women, as if they were meat on a hook and he's wondering whether to cut off a slice. Why do you ask?"

"We had words."

"Don't worry about it," Gloria said. "Everybody does. You have to get on line to hate him."

"That's not my problem. I'm going on his show."

"And you want to know how to play it?"

"Something like that."

"Okay, here's what will happen. He'll be Mr. Charm. 'Put yourself in my hands, my dear.' He'll tell you something like, 'Don't worry about it if I come on adversarial. It's nothing personal, I'm doing it in the interests of good television.' "

"And?"

"He lies. Does that answer your question?"

"Pretty much," Kathryn said. "Thanks, Gloria. Let's go do the interview."

"How about you, Ms. Morales?" Gloria said, turning toward Patricia, who was dabbing at her eyes with a handkerchief. "Can you give us a few seconds also?"

"I don't . . ." Patricia said tentatively.

"All you have to do is tell us how you feel about the verdict," Gloria told her reassuringly. "It won't take a minute."

She led the way outside into bright sunshine yellowed by the TV lights that had been set up to flatten the shadows.

"It's just a quick sound bite, okay?" she said to Kathryn.

She checked her makeup in a mirror, fluffed up her blond hair. "You ready?"

"Ready," Kathryn said. "Do you think it will make the news?"

Gloria shrugged, one of those what-can-I-tell-you gestures. They did the interview in one take; the technicians were checking it on playback when Dave Granz came out.

"Kathryn." His voice was low-pitched and urgent. "Mac wants us upstairs. *Inmediatamente.*"

Kathryn bade Patricia Morales and Gloria a hasty good-bye and followed Granz through the empty courthouse, across the atrium, and along the corridor, hurrying to keep up with his reaching stride.

"Any idea what this is all about?" she asked as they clattered up the stairs. Dave shrugged.

"He just said, 'Get up here fast.' "

The receptionist buzzed them in and they went straight along the narrow white-walled corridor to McCaskill's office. His secretary waved them in. When she opened the door, Kathryn saw Walt Earheart sitting in a leather chair facing McCaskill. Mac looked up.

"Kathryn, Dave, shut the door," he said. "Grab a seat."

"Hi, Walt," Kathryn said. "What brings you down here?"

"We just got a break on our serial killer," Earheart said.

"What kind of a break?" Dave said sharply.

"Take a look," Earheart said, and spread the coded note on the desk in front of them.

12

"IT'S GOBBLEDYGOOK," DAVE SAID.

Earheart shook his head. "It's a simple code. Like the ones they have in the *Gazette* every day. The bastard even made it easy for us. You see where it says $V = E$? That's the key. I've got a deputy does these things for fun. Took him about ten minutes to work it out; the alphabet backwards. Z is A, Y is B, and so on."

Kathryn frowned at the printed lines and the scrawled

translation beneath them, conscious of Dave peering over her shoulder.

THE ONE IN SEDGEWICK PARK WAS CALLED
ANNA.
SHE HAD A SMALL CUT ON HER INNER
THIGH.
ANOTHER ONE SOON.

"Jesus," Dave breathed. "If this guy knows about the thigh cuts ..."

"He has to be the killer," Earheart confirmed.

"What's this little figure, here, the Pillsbury Doughboy?"

"Na. Some kind of signature, maybe?"

"Who the hell knows?" Earheart said impatiently.

"Where did it come from?"

"It arrived about an hour ago," McCaskill said. "Addressed to Walt."

"Handed in at ground-floor reception," Earheart said. He held up a hand. "And before you ask, we checked. A young boy about twelve delivered it."

"Has he been found?"

Earheart shook his head. "We don't even know what he looks like. All the girl at the desk remembers is, it was some kid."

"This is a copy, right? Where's the original?"

"We've rushed it to Sacramento for fingerprinting," Earheart replied. "I didn't want to take any chances on messing it up. If it was on card or plastic, anything with a surface, we could do it ourselves, but to get anything useful off paper you've got to do Ninhydrin and argon-ion laser tests. We don't have that kind of equipment."

"How many people handled it?"

Earheart shrugged. "Three, four. We're trying to eliminate them."

Dave shook his head doubtfully. "Something tells me

we're not going to get anything, Walt," he said. "This guy wouldn't be that dumb."

"I know, but we've got to try."

"What kind of paper is it written on?"

"Standard ruled yellow legal pad," Earheart told him. "Available at any stationery store."

"Was there an envelope?"

"No, it came like this, folded."

"Printed capitals," Kathryn observed. "A ballpoint, by the look of it. Maybe we can do something with the handwriting."

"Maybe," Earheart said. He didn't sound too optimistic.

"Anna," Dave said. "You think it's worth running through the computers?"

"We're already doing that," Earheart said. "National Crime Information Center is checking its missing persons files and foreign fugitive lists, and DOJ in Sacramento is checking out illegal immigrants, escaped prisoners, parole violators, armed forces deserters—"

Dave held his hands up in the surrender sign and smiled. "All right, Walt. Sorry I asked."

"Jack Burrows is coordinating," Earheart said. "You want anything, ask him."

"Anna. It's not much to go on," Kathryn said.

"Maybe that's all he knows," Dave suggested.

"Everybody carries ID," Earheart said.

"Not everybody," Dave persisted. "Suppose he picked her up on the beach? Maybe she was out walking, or jogging. She might have been wearing just shorts and a T-shirt, or a swimsuit. Maybe all he ever knew about her was her first name."

McCaskill held up the note so they could all see it.

"Nobody's mentioned the most important part," he observed. "He says, 'Another one soon.' "

"The bastard is playing games with us," Earheart said, letting his anger show. "He's probably enjoying jerking us around."

"Why did he write a note?" Kathryn asked nobody in particular. "Why not make an anonymous call?"

"You think maybe he has a distinctive voice?" Dave guessed.

"It's a possibility," Kathryn said, making a note. "He

probably knows all incoming calls are taped. He could have a speech impediment, or a strong regional accent, or—"

"I tell you, the bastard's showboating," Earheart said. "He's showing us how goddamn clever he is."

"And by definition," McCaskill said quietly, "how stupid we are. So stupid he can write to us with impunity, give us clues, tell us a victim's name, and we can't lay a finger on him."

"Not yet, maybe," Kathryn said. "But we will."

"Hold the dream," Earheart said.

"I talked to Steve Giordano, the profiler on the Criminal Investigation Response Team in Sacramento," Kathryn said. "He was real helpful. Maybe we should call him in. What do you think?"

McCaskill looked at Earheart. The detective shook his head.

"I'm not being territorial about this, Kathryn, but I don't want to call in outside help at such an early stage. It'll make it look like we don't know how to handle it."

"And do we?"

"As well as anyone. Give us a chance, for Chrissake. We're busting our butts. I don't know what else we can do."

"What about the note? The warning?" Kathryn asked.

"What about it?"

"Do you plan to release it to the media?"

McCaskill frowned. "Walt?"

The big detective shrugged. "Why not?"

"I'll tell you why not," Dave said. "Give the note to the media, they'll splash it all over the front page like he's some kind of goddamn celebrity. He'll feel like Mr. Big. That's his kick, power, right, Kathryn?"

"Look, we're groping about in the dark here," she said, nodding. "But that's what it feels like. I think the more we deny him the glory he's looking for, keep the whole thing low key, the likelier it is he'll react. Or better still, overreact."

"That's one argument," McCaskill said. "But say we release the note. I know it's a chance in a million, but someone out there might recognize the handwriting. This guy isn't the Invisible Man, for Chrissake: he has a job, a home, friends, colleagues. Somebody knows him, feeds him, works with him."

"You decide," Kathryn said.

McCaskill looked at the piece of paper for a few moments.

Then he laid it down on his desk and put his right hand on it, palm down.

"I'll have to check with Hal Benton," he said. "If he okays it, the note is buried. What now?"

"We wait," Earheart said.

"You guys wait," Kathryn told him. "I've got a murder case to get ready for."

The three men nodded. Sensational though the crimes were, there was only so much time any of them could devote to the serial killer. In every one of the twenty-four hours of every day the drug dealing, the auto thefts, the prostitution, rape, robbery, manslaughter, and murder went on, just about anywhere within the four hundred forty square miles that comprised the county.

"You want to grab a sandwich downstairs, Kathryn?" Dave said. "It's nearly one."

"I'm going to skip lunch," Kathryn said. "Check what happened at the staff meeting."

"Nothing exciting, I'll bet," Dave said sourly. "Walt, we through here?"

"Looks like it," Earheart said. "Good luck on Sunday, Kathryn, okay? And watch that tricky bastard."

"Like a hawk, Walt, like a hawk." She grinned.

The first impression a visitor got on entering Kathryn's office was one of brightness and space. Two white wicker armchairs with bright blue cushions gave the room a cheery, welcoming appearance supported by prints and a framed collage of photographs of Emma that camouflaged the flat drabness of the walls. There was nothing anyone could do about the institutional furniture, but the personal touches of fresh flowers and indoor plants, of brass hatstand and wicker étagère, ameliorated the deadening effect of the mat beige walls, the dull striped carpet, the steel-framed windows, and the gray concrete buttresses above eye level.

"Maybe I ought to go see Jake Gylam," Kathryn mused aloud.

"What about?"

"This damned TV show, what do you think?"

Dave shrugged. "You need me anymore today?"

"Why do you do that?" she asked him. "Act like you don't give a damn about anyone else but yourself?"

"Is that what I do?"

"You just did it, and you know you did."

"I guess I learned it the hard way, kiddo," he said. "In the Sheriff's office, when I was on the streets. There was only one person I could count on one hundred percent all the time. And that was me."

"You believe that?"

"I believe in everybody kill his own snakes. You get into a bind, you get out of it. There are exceptions, but I don't allow them to cloud my judgment."

"That's a real sympathetic outlook you have there, Inspector."

He shrugged. "In our line of business, it's better not to get too involved with other people's problems. Leave that to the parole officers."

"Not to say cold-blooded," Kathryn said.

"If that's how it sounds, I'm sorry," Dave said. "But I just can't get worked up about it. You sure you don't want to get a sandwich?"

"I'll just have some tea."

"Change your mind about brunch on Sunday?"

"Get out of here, Granz."

He grinned and went out, closing the door behind him. Kathryn got up and walked over to the window, looking out over the red roofs of the city to the sea beyond. Down in the park she could see joggers on the running path that flanked the river. It would be nice to just put on shorts and join them, run and run and run until she sweated all the uncertainties and doubts out of her body. When she'd first come to Santa Rita, running was Kathryn's never-failing remedy for stress, but these days there just never seemed to be enough time to do it, or to ride the bike she kept in a locker at the side of the building.

The CSI files on the two murder victims were still on her desk, labeled SHELTER and SEDGEWICK in the absence of identification. It still bothered her, not only that the two women had been brutally killed, but that they had been and remained anonymous. It somehow made the butchery seem even more gratuitous. And somewhere out there, on the streets of Santa Rita, the killer walked free.

Where are you? she wondered fiercely. *Where are you?*

13

HE SAT IN THE PICKUP TRUCK IN THE PARKING LOT OF THE Linda Vista Mall, a dark-haired, compactly built man wearing a light tan Windbreaker, dark brown slacks, a pale blue shirt, and leather loafers with soft rubber soles. The clothes were carefully chosen. Nothing memorable, that was the trick. Nothing for anyone to remember. Like the truck: a tan '87 Dodge Adventurer Club Cab 100 with out-of-state plates. Even if anyone remembered it, even if someone took the license number, it wouldn't matter because the plates were false. The genuine ones were under the driver's seat. He could change them in two minutes flat.

The girl had gone into a bookstore that was also a coffee shop. It had one of those cutesy names: American Espresso. Next door was a movie theater showing old horror movies. He had swung the truck over and parked in a space outside, looking around to see if anyone was taking any notice of him. Nobody was. The parking lot was only about a quarter full. The early shoppers had mostly gone home and the late shoppers hadn't yet begun arriving.

He looked out of his window at the people going by. If they knew, he thought. If any of them knew. The hunter's joy, the butcher's ecstasy. That was power, too. He shifted in his seat, feeling the slow pulse of life moving through his body. Sweat at the base of his spine, the center of his chest, beneath his arms. The soft wetness of the inside of his mouth. The steady thump of his heart, beating slightly faster than normal. And the throb of lust in his groin. Thinking about what he was going to do was always exciting. Anticipating the terror that words, touch, and even caresses could instill. The power.

Beside him on the bench seat of the truck was a copy of the Santa Rita *Gazette*. He had smiled when he read the headline. That Richard Sanchez hit it right on the head. The cops were full of what made the grass grow green. They all said the same things. Wide-ranging investigations, all leads being pursued, an early arrest expected. Clichés concocted to conceal the fact that they had no hope of putting it together, any more than the dumbass cops in the other places had. Dumbass: the word made him think of Jack Sarsby. That bastard, he thought.

One day in high school when Miss Paterson was handing out English homework, she wrote the names of three books on the board and told the class to read one and then do a report on it. One was *The Catcher in the Rye,* the second was *Cannery Row,* and the third was *The Three Musketeers.* He chose *The Three Musketeers* because he had seen the movie once on TV. They had to tell her which one they had chosen.

"The one by Alexandre Dumas," he said when it was his turn, pronouncing it "dumb-ass." Everyone laughed.

"That's Dumas, Lee," Miss Paterson said. "Doo-mah."

"Dumbass way to pronounce it," he said to Connie Jovanovich, sitting next to him on his right. Everyone laughed even more. Outside after school he went across to where Connie was standing talking to Jack Sarsby. She was a little over five feet tall, with naturally wavy blond hair and impish blue eyes like one of those girls you see on calendars.

He was crazy about her. He contrived "accidental" meetings just so he could say hello. He stole violets from a flower vendor in the street and put them in her desk. He wrote her poems he never showed anyone. He clipped her photograph from a yearbook and kept it in a little glassine envelope in his wallet.

He wished he could get up the courage to ask her for a date, but he didn't get an allowance like most of the kids at his school and his father wouldn't let him have a paper route. Anyway, she always had four or five guys hanging around, buying her Coke or ice cream or candy. Alan Riddock once spent thirty-eight dollars he'd saved for his summer vacation just to take her to a touring Broadway show.

"Hi, Connie," he said, smiling.

"Well, look who it is," Jack Sarsby said. "It's the dumbass himself. What do you want, dumbass?"

Jack was captain of the school basketball team, tall, muscular, and good looking; all the things Lee was not. Just wearing beaten-up sneakers, a blue sweater, and Levi's, he made Lee feel like a bum. Lee shook his head, shifting his feet uncomfortably. He wished he could think of something really sharp to say, but he was no good at that.

"I uh, just, uh, came over to say hello to Connie," he mumbled.

"Okay, you said it," Sarsby told him harshly. "Now get lost."

"Aw, Jack, don't," Connie said. "He's funny."

"Not funny," Sarsby said. "Weird. He's weird. Aren't you, dumbass?"

Connie giggled, and Lee felt heat rise in him.

"Don't call me that," he said.

"Or what?"

Lee stared at him, hands curled, seething with hate and impotence. He wanted to strike out blindly. But he was afraid, and Jack Sarsby saw it. He smiled contemptuously.

"Fuck off, lizardbreath," Sarsby said, turning away. "Go find some fifth graders to hassle."

Lee felt rage explode inside him. He grabbed Sarsby by the shoulder and threw a punch at him, but Jack turned and blocked it, and as he came round he hit Lee hard in the face. Lee fell down, his jaw and mouth numb. He looked at his hands. There was blood all over them. His blood. He made a strange sound, somewhere between a scream and a shout, surging to his feet and throwing himself at Sarsby, fists flying. Kids came running, shouting "Fight, fight!" Screeching with hatred and rage, Lee threw blow after clumsy blow at the hated face in front of him. He could hear the kids shouting. He caught a glimpse of Connie's face. She was watching Jack Sarsby. They were all rooting for him. That made it worse.

Jack Sarsby set himself, then hit Lee hard in the belly. Lee felt bitter bile rise in his throat. His body felt paralyzed. Then Jack hit him hard on the side of the head and Lee reeled to one side, his head ringing. Vision blurred, he lurched forward. As he did, a fist crashed into his face and he felt the brittle snap of cartilage in his nose. He sank to his knees, snorting blood.

"How's it feel, dumbass?" Sarsby panted. "How d'you like fighting someone your own size for a change?" Lee shook his head. His whole face was swollen and numb. The front of his shirt was spattered with his own blood. His legs and arms were shaking. He could not stand up. He wanted to, but his body wouldn't do it.

"You had enough, dumbass?" Sarsby said. "Or you want some more?"

"Bastard," Lee coughed, spitting blood. "Bastard."

"Ah, look," someone said. "He's cryin'."

"Does him want his mamma, den?" another kid jeered. The ring that had formed around the two fighters broke up, and they all went away in a crowd with Sarsby, laughing. After a while, Lee got painfully to his feet and stumbled off down the street. His mind seethed with fantasies of revenge. Jack Sarsby *killed* by a block of masonry "accidentally" falling from a roof as he walked by, Jack Sarsby *killed* in a downtown alley by an "unknown" assailant, Jack Sarsby *killed* by an "unidentified" hit-and-run driver. And Lee, laughing as he pushed the concrete block over the edge of the roof, laughing as he plunged the knife into the bleeding body, laughing as he accelerated away from the broken thing lying in the street.

He went into a gas station rest room. His face looked like a Halloween mask. Shit. He cleaned off as much of the blood as he could and then headed for home. Home. That was a fucking joke to start with. Home was a street of row houses off Sturges Boulevard. He hated the place. He hated his gutless father and the fat Puerto Rican cow he had married, a waitress in some Mexican joint. He hardly remembered his own mother. She'd died when he was just a kid.

The old man and Paulita, all they lived for was the church. The Church of the Living God. They spent so much time there they might as well fucking live there. And Lynda. She's your sister now, the old man told him. She's family. Yeah, the fuckin' Addams Family.

Lynda was two years older than him. Someone had once told her she looked like Rita Moreno. What she really looked like was a spic whore. The way she walked around the house when their parents were out, practically nothing on, looking over her shoulder to make sure he was watching her swing her ass, to see if it was having any effect on him. Sometimes she would sit on the sofa opposite him, her legs apart so he could see the faint white gleam of the tight triangle of her panties. And the blood would pound in his head and she *knew,* the prick-teasing bitch, she knew what she was doing. She'd look at him *there* and she'd smile a smile as old as Eve's. She was asking for it.

She was in the kitchen when he got home. He tried to go upstairs without her seeing him, but she heard him and came out. She was barefoot, wearing only a short cotton slip. She was not tall, but sturdy, with a ripe figure, wide hips, and high, firm breasts. He could see her nipples through the cotton. She leaned against the door frame, one rounded hip stuck out.

"Hey, *cholo,* why you sneakin' aroun' like that for?" she said. She took hold of his arm and pulled him back. When she saw his face she put on a comical expression of surprise. *"Que mamarracho,* wha's hoppen to you?"

"I fell," Lee mumbled.

"You fell?" she said, her voice rising. "You fell? You spec anyone to b'lieve that?"

She always put on this big act when her mother was around, how she didn't like him. Like she pretended she didn't like boys. They're all the same, she'd tell her mother, they're only after one thing. And Mama would nod like some fat old Buddha. Mama didn't know shit from Shinola. Lynda had probably been fucked more times than Cleopatra.

"I fell, I tell you," he shouted.

"¡Mentiroso! Malvado! I tell you wha' hoppen. You got in a fight an' somebody beat the sheet out of you."

"Let me alone," Lee mumbled. "I want to go upstairs."

Her mother waddled out, fat and blowsy. She looked at Lee with eyes like black olives and shook her head.

"You wait till you fother seess you," she said. She raised her voice. "You gonna be in trobble."

"Yeah, deep sheet," Lynda said. "Hey, Pops! *Venga!* Come on out here, take a look wha hoppen to your lil baby!"

"I'm reading." Donald Russell's voice was thin and querulous. Lynda gave a contemptuous laugh.

"You're alwayss readin'," she shouted. "Books, books, books. You're a bigger wimp than he is!"

Donald Russell made no reply, and Lee felt the shame and hatred well up inside him the way it always did when Lynda badmouthed his father. She wasn't even his daughter, for Chrissake. What kind of man let another woman's kid walk all over him like that? Why didn't he come out and slap her down?

"I got to go and clean up," he said. His mouth felt like a block of wood. One of his teeth was loose. He thought about having to go back to school tomorrow. Everyone would know. They would all be laughing at him. That bastard Sarsby. He'd pay him back one day. He'd show them. All of them.

"You make sure an' put tha shirt in some col' water ri' now, you hear me?" Paulita shouted as he went slowly up the stairs.

"Yeah, deekhead," Lynda echoed. "Get you act together."

Twenty years ago, Lee thought, and every one of them I see reminds me of how much I hated her, still hate her.

All this time, his eyes had never left the entrance of the bookstore. As he watched, the girl came out. He sat up, his hand moving to the door handle. Eighteen, nineteen, maybe. Medium height, enough pounds overweight to give her a slightly plump appearance, she had long black hair and dark eyes. She was wearing a pale gray sweat suit and Adidas running shoes. The pants of the sweat suit had a dark blue double stripe down the side. As she drew level with the pickup he opened the door and got out, his back to the setting sun.

"I wonder if you could help me?" he said. "I'm sort of lost. I want to get to Espanola?"

"Sure," she said. She was quite pretty, he thought. The olive-dark eyes and smooth brown skin reminded him of Kim *No don't God don't no more God no* and he felt the growing swell of excitement in his groin. "Where exactly do you want to go?"

"I'm supposed to meet some friends in a pizza place down there, uh ..."

"Little Pizza Italy?"

"That's the one," he said, smiling. "How'd you know?"

"Everybody goes there," she said. "It's neat."

"Right," Lee said. "Is it far from here?"

"Naa," the girl said. "Look, here's what you do: See the exit over there? Just make a right, keep going. You'll come to East Bayshore, that's the coast road. Turn left and it'll take you straight into the center of Espanola."

"I'm a real klutz when it comes to directions," Lee told her. "Look, I've got a map here. Could you maybe show me?"

He went over to the pickup and spread the map on the

hood, standing half aside so she could get to it. He took a quick look around. Nobody. As she passed between him and the vehicle, he half-turned and jammed the stun gun hard against her chest. There was a crackling buzz and her eyes rolled upward. As her legs folded, he caught her with his right arm, opening the door with his left and lifting her up into the cab. He looked around again. Nobody was taking the remotest interest in him.

He went around to the driver's door and got in. The girl lay limply on the seat, her face smooth and calm. He had the needle ready in the glove compartment. All he had to do was slide it into her thigh and wait. The drug was midazolam; he'd bought it from an orderly at the County Hospital who stole it from the dispensary. It would keep her out of it for maybe an hour.

When he reached his destination, he lifted the girl out of the truck and took her inside. He laid her on her back on the bed in the little room in the cellar and using strips of cloth, carefully tied her hands and feet to the bedposts so that they made an *X*. That done, he went methodically through her purse, taking out her driver's license, tissues, two tampons, a bottle of clear nail polish, and some loose change, carefully placing everything on a window ledge in the corridor outside. A place for everything, and everything in its place. Then he closed the door and waited beside the bed in the darkness. He was in no hurry. This was one of the best parts, when they realized what had happened to them. When they realized what was going to happen. When he saw that realization in their eyes.

He sensed rather than saw the girl's eyes flicker open. He heard her draw in her breath sharply and let it out in a quivering sigh. Lust pounded through his body like a steam hammer.

"Hello, Barbara," he said.

At first Barbara thought she was dreaming.

Then she heard herself moan, and opened her eyes. It was pitch black; she could see nothing. She tried to move and found she could not. Her brain was sluggish; something was wrong, but what? Then it all came back to her in a rush of memory. Coming out of the bookshop. The parking lot. The man coming across toward her, his back to the setting sun.

Then an immense pain, as if her entire body had been squeezed in some gigantic hand. She had tried to shout, but the strength had run out of her like water down a sluice.

Oh, God, no.

Don't panic, she told herself. You mustn't panic. She opened her eyes again. The blackness was not quite so intense this time; she could discern a faint light, although not enough to see by.

"Hello, Barbara."

The man's voice beside her made her cry out with fright.

"Just relax," he said. "Relax."

She recognized the voice. *Him.* She tried to move again and realized she was tied up. She was lying on her back on a bare mattress. She tested the rope holding her wrists.

"Don't bother, Barbara," the man said. "It won't come undone."

How does he know my name? Her mind was alert now. He went through my purse, found my driver's license. What does he want? she wondered. Stupid, stupid, you know what he wants. She felt a sudden drowning wave of despair engulf her. Tears welled up in her eyes.

"Please," she croaked. Her lips were parched and cracked. Her voice scratched in her throat. "Let me go. I'll do anything you want. Just let me go."

He did not answer. She could hear him breathing; she spoke again into the silent darkness.

"Please. If you want money—"

She sensed movement, and saw him stand up, a blacker shape against the blackness. He looked much bigger than he had in the parking lot.

"How . . . what did you . . . ?"

"It's called a stun gun, Barbara," he said. His voice sounded as if he was smiling as he spoke. "Quite harmless. Some police forces use them to pacify arrestees."

"What do you want?" she shouted. "What are you going to do to me?"

Colored lights exploded in her head and she realized he had hit her. Her head spun. She was shocked, sickened. No one had ever struck her in her life. She drew in deep, ragged breaths, only half-conscious. She could feel the warm salt taste of blood in her mouth.

"Don't raise your voice, Barbara," he said, quietly. "It's not ladylike."

"Let me go!" she screamed. "Let me go, let me go, let me go!" She was still screaming when he hit her again. This time she passed out.

Barbara came to. She felt the groan of pain form in her throat and quelled it. The side of her face was throbbing and sore. She tried to work her mouth and felt the swollen lips chafing. She was still tied to the bed in the same position. Her arms and legs were stiff. She opened her eyes cautiously, afraid of what she might see.

Nothing. And yet ... he was nearby. She could sense his presence.

As her eyes became accustomed to the darkness, she could see that she was in a room. Directly above her hung an unshaded unlit light bulb. She turned her head all the way to the right and saw a faint gleam of diffused light emanating from another room beyond the door, which was about three inches ajar. It was cold, as if someone had just come in from outside on a winter day.

She turned her head to the left. A blank wall, the darker bulk of a piece of furniture: a chest of drawers, perhaps, or a table. It was cool. She realized he had taken off her sweat suit; she had on just the T-shirt and shorts she'd worn to play tennis.

When was that? How long have I been here? she wondered. Is it night or day? She took a deep, deep breath, and in spite of herself, it came out a soft sob. She shook her head to stem the tears, but they came anyway. She let them come, her body twisting with despair. She knew he was there, watching, listening. He made no sound. Finally, she stopped crying.

"No more of that," he said. "Do you understand me, Barbara?"

There was no emotion in his voice. He came nearer, looming darkly over her. She flinched reflexively.

"Please," she sniffled, realizing how futile, how pointless the word was in this context, but knowing no other to say.

"I asked you a question," he hissed.

A slap rocked her head to one side.

"Answer me!"

He hit her again, backhand now.

"Answer me!"

She saw his hand move for the third time and screamed, "Yesyesyes."

"Yes what?"

"Yes, I understand."

"Good," he said. She thought he might be smiling. "I don't like women who keep me waiting."

"I ... I'm s-sorry ..."

"Very well. Keep still."

He sat down on the bed next to her. He smelled fresh and clean, like someone who has just had a shower. It made her conscious of her own grubbiness. His hand moved and she felt cold metal against her skin. Her mind blanked and the breath rushed out of her body. But it was not a knife. Scissors, she thought. He cut up the left-hand side of her shorts from thigh to waist. Then he went around the bed and repeated the exercise on her right side. He put his hand under her, lifting her up to jerk the separated halves away and toss them aside. Then he cut off her panties.

That.

In the uttermost depths of herself she had known ultimately it would be that. She squeezed her eyes shut, trying to blot out the drowning sense of nakedness and shame that assailed her. No, she thought. This can't happen. My name is Barbara Gates. I am nineteen years old. I live at 1812 Coronado Drive, Alameda Heights. She tensed herself against the expected touch of his hands on her skin, the weight of his body, the hurting thrust of his entering her.

Nothing happened.

She opened her eyes very slowly. He was sitting on the bed next to her in the darkness. He was very still. She tried to see his eyes but they were hidden in pools of shadow.

"How old are you, Barbara?" he asked.

"N-n-nineteen."

"Are you a virgin?"

What did he want her to be? Suppose he was some sort of religious freak, ready to punish anyone who wasn't ... pure? Her fears scurried around in her mind like rats in a maze. What did he want? *What did he want?*

This time she didn't even see his hand move. Galaxies exploded behind her eyes. She blacked out, hovering on the edge of consciousness. No, no, she thought, no, hanging on to awareness, opening her eyes as his hand went back to hit her again.

"I'm, no, I'm not, I'm not a virgin, I'm not!" Her voice was a tight, controlled shriek. The side of her face was numb; pain was a long, slow, dull throb throughout her body. All she could think of now was stopping him from hitting her anymore. All the other things that could happen were of no importance as long as he didn't hit her again.

"I knew when I first saw you that you were an intelligent girl, Barbara," he said. He stroked her long dark hair away from her face. The gesture was almost tender. "What are you thinking?"

She shook her head.

"Tell me."

"You . . . know," she gulped.

"No," he said. "Tell me."

"I . . . is . . . are you . . . going to rape me?"

"Would you like me to?"

He put his hand between her legs; it was as cold as ice. She felt his finger touch her vagina and her skin crawled.

"Uuuh." She choked on speech, her throat closed in terror. "I don't know, no, yes, whatever you want. Only don't hit me. Don't hit me anymore."

"That will depend on you," he said.

He reached across her body and picked up the scissors again. This time he cut off her T-shirt. He tossed it into the same corner he'd thrown the pants. She had no bra. She shivered in the half-light. The room was cold, slightly dank; like a cellar, she thought. Was it a cellar? The man stood up and went across the room, then came back with something in his hand. He held it up so she could see it. Something small and metallic that caught a faint flicker of light.

"Do you know what this is, Barbara?" he said. There was a strange, crooning lilt in his voice.

"I . . . can't see."

"It's a scalpel," he said. "You buy them through surgical supply catalogs."

A scalpel?

"You wouldn't believe anything so cheap could be so . . . perfect," he said, his voice retaining its odd crooning sound. "So . . . sharp. If I were to cut your throat, you wouldn't even know it had happened. Until you were drowning in your own blood."

She felt her naked skin go clammy with terror. He laid the delicately shaped blade against the inside of her thigh, high up, near the crotch.

"Can you feel that, Barbara?"

"Uh . . ." Her whole body was rigid with fear.

"This?"

His hand moved. She felt a tiny thread of pain, like iced fire, then the soft trickle of blood that told her he had cut her.

"Please," she said. Her voice was clotted with fear; the word came out of her throat like a ball of tar.

"You understand that I can do anything I like to you?"

"Please . . ." She saw the gleam of his eyes, remembered. "Yes, yes, I understand."

"Will you do whatever I tell you to do? Without question?"

She didn't know what to do. The silence seemed to last an eon.

"I . . . don't know what to s-say."

"Don't worry," he said. "I'll teach you how to please me. You do want to please me, don't you?"

"What . . . what are you going to do to me?" she faltered.

"Don't be in a hurry, Barbara. You'll find out. Soon."

"Oh, God, please don't hurt me," she wailed. "I'll do anything. Whatever you want."

"I know you will," he said.

14

JACK ARRIVED LATE, AS USUAL. DID HE DO IT ON PURPOSE? she wondered. Jack knew how she was about punctuality; to her, being where you were supposed to be, on time, was almost a religion. She decided it wasn't deliberate; it was just that Jack hadn't given her needs a thought. Nearly ten years, she thought, and he doesn't know much more about me now than he did right at the beginning. A perfect example of Peter Pan man: a few more wrinkles around the eyes, a few more creases down the face, otherwise the same gangling, diffident preppie she'd met all those years ago on campus. Who was it who said, Everything changes? Whoever it was, he obviously never met Jack.

Today her ex-husband was wearing a light gray cotton denim long-sleeve shirt with the cuffs rolled back halfway up the arm, blue jeans, and Reeboks with pale blue trim. It was his off-duty uniform. At work he almost always wore charcoal gray suits.

"You're looking good, Kath," he said. "How is everything going?"

"Busy-busy," she said. "Hectic but happy. What about you?"

"Same," he replied with a small shrug. "We seem to spend half our time these days prosecuting street gangs."

"Where are you thinking of going today?" she asked. He was standing over by the bookcase; a stranger, looking at her books. The odd feeling she always had when Jack was around assailed her: a sort of unease about not caring more for someone who had once meant so much. He gave a noncommittal shrug.

"You mean you didn't make any plans?" Kathryn said.

"How am I supposed to know what's going on in this part of the world?" he said. "Anything you specially want to do, Em?"

"We could go to the beach," she said hopefully. Emma would go to the beach in a hurricane.

"You got any ideas, Kath?"

"Not really," Kathryn said. "You're too late for Father's Day and a little early for the Fourth of July parade."

In spite of herself, it came out snappy.

"Oh, terrific," he said. "Put-down time already, right?"

"You were always the put-down expert, remember?" Kathryn retorted. Jack shrugged again and put on his wounded look. She had once been charmed by that boyish vulnerability; now it irritated her.

"Maybe we could go up to San Francisco, spend the day," he said. "How about that, Em?"

"Sure," Emma said. She had been excited all weekend about her outing with Jack. She asked specifically if she could wear her white dress with the blue polka dots and brushed her hair a hundred times so she would be pretty for her daddy. Now that he was here, she was acting nonchalant. Kids were funny.

"I have to go to Monterey," Kathryn told Jack. "A TV show."

"It's about the *murders*," Emma said, making it dramatic.

"Oh, yeah, Sanchez, I forgot. You mentioned it on the phone."

"I'm running late, Jack," Kathryn reminded him. "It's a forty-minute drive down to Monterey."

"Hey!" he said, "here's an idea. How about we come with you? Em and I can go to the aquarium. You want to go to the aquarium, Em, see the sharks?"

"Do they eat people?"

"Only in the movies," Jack said. "We can go to the aquarium, then later we'll find a McDonald's and have cheeseburgers and fries. What do you say?"

"Can I have a chocolate shake?"

"Sure you can," Jack said. His enthusiasm sounded forced to Kathryn's ears. She wondered if it did to Emma's, too. She didn't miss much. "Shall we go in my car? It's got more room than that dinky little thing you zip round in."

"Okay. But can we go, please?"

"Nag, nag, nag," he said, and went out.

She locked up and followed Jack and Emma downstairs to the parking lot. Seaview Heights faced the bay on a bluff above Beach Avenue, about halfway between Espanola Drive and Lighthouse. Each of the blocks was named after a European city. Kathryn's second-floor one-and-a-half-bath condo was in London House. It wasn't perfect, but she loved the view from her balcony out over the wide bay, with the slim white finger of the Shelter Island lighthouse off to the left and the pier at Espanola poking out into the dark blue water on the right. The morning mist had burned off and flights of pelicans were winging their way toward Monterey, a purple smudge on the horizon.

Jack opened up the car, a Pontiac Grand Am, '89 model. Spick and span, as always, she thought; he even had one of those pine-tree-shaped air fresheners hanging from the rearview mirror. She couldn't help but compare it ruefully with her own car, the interior of which usually looked like a closet a wildcat had been locked up in.

"You're not seeing anyone, then?" she said to Jack as he

made a right on Beach Avenue and headed up Bay toward the interchange.

He looked at her sharply. "How d'you know that?"

"The car." Kathryn smiled. "No kid mess, no used Kleenex. You always were finicky, Jack."

He shrugged. "How about you?"

"Like I said, too busy," Kathryn told him.

"What about that inspector?"

"That's over."

"I read a piece about you. In *California Attorney*."

"That," Kathryn said, making a face.

"It took me back. All that stuff about how ambitious you are ..." He didn't finish the sentence.

"How are your parents?"

"Good. My father retired. They're buying a place down in Laguna."

Tom Hallam, Jack's father, was a building contractor, a heavily built man completely devoid of any sense of humor, who said trivial things in a ponderous tone and referred to his mousy, spiteful-eyed wife Elaine as "herself." They had disapproved of Kathryn from the start and never made any attempt to conceal their dislike. There had been Sunday afternoons in their spotless, depersonalized house in Whittier Heights when she had wanted to hang out of the window and scream, like Dorothy Parker in Hollywood, "Somebody get me out of here, I'm as sane as you are."

She made a rueful face. It had probably been just as hard for the Hallams to get along with her as it had been for her to get along with them. Jack was an only child. A spoiled only child. In their eyes, their boy could do no wrong. Kathryn had made the error of trying to make them see otherwise. They in turn made it very clear they didn't want to know.

"You've gone quiet," Jack remarked.

"Just watching the people," Kathryn lied. "I don't often get the chance to be a passenger and look out the window."

Once they were on the Alvarado Highway they made good time. The scenery between the two places was pretty uninteresting, mostly wide flat fields of the brussels sprouts, broccoli, and artichokes for which the area was famous. Jack took the Del Monte Avenue exit and they got lucky and found a parking place near the aquarium that stood on the

site of the old cannery. Kathryn hadn't been to Monterey
for a long time; it hadn't changed much. Other than its pre-
served adobes, it was just another little coastal town, making
its living from tourism and the ghost of John Steinbeck.

"Okay, you guys, have a great time," Kathryn said. She
gave Emma a hug and watched the two of them go off down
the street toward the aquarium. Again the feeling of guilt
swept over her. I ought to care about him more, she thought.
It was no use; it was as if Jack was just some guy she'd
known a long time ago, at law school or back home in Kansas City. In every other respect he was a stranger. Only
Emma kept the bond between them alive.

The KKSU-TV building was just a couple of blocks over
from the old Pacific Biological Laboratories building—The
Lab, as they called it today—once the domain of "Doc" Ed
Ricketts, but now used mostly for social functions. She
pushed through glass doors into a brightly lit foyer. Behind
a desk to the right a blond receptionist sat using a word
processor. She looked up and smiled dazzlingly as Kathryn
came in.

"Welcome to KKSU-TV," she sparkled. "How may I assist you?"

"Kathryn Mackay for Richard Sanchez," Kathryn said.

"Oh, yes, Ms. Mackay," the girl said, "you're expected.
Please take a seat momentarily."

She was about twenty-two or -three, with a good figure,
and a pouty-pretty face with too much makeup on it. A sign
on the desk said her name was Polly Zimmerman. Gonna
have to change that when you break into the movies, kid,
Kathryn thought, hiding a smile. The foyer was lined with
wooden paneling not unlike that used in the Santa Rita
courtrooms. Big framed portraits of KKSU personalities
looked down on visitors: Jane Brondini, Steve Klarsfeld,
Richard Sanchez, Steve Brace, Emilio Johnson. Comfortable
vinyl armchairs were grouped around a low table with a
centered vase full of fresh flowers, the latest news magazines
fanned in a half circle around it.

A door in the far wall opened and a dark-haired young
woman wearing a pair of horn-rimmed glasses and a slightly
distracted look came out and looked around. She put on a
professional smile and came across toward Kathryn.

"You must be Kathryn Mackay," she said, extending a

slim, cool hand. "I'm Karen Bolsover, executive assistant to the producer. I hope you haven't been waiting long?"

She was dressed in a crisp white silk blouse and a close-fitting black skirt; she looked neat and efficient. Kathryn told her she had just arrived and refused an offer of something to drink.

" 'Kay, here's what will happen," Karen Bolsover told her. "I'm going to take you down to the hospitality suite, where you'll meet Richard—you've met, haven't you? Yes, I thought so—and the other guests. Later, someone will take you down to makeup. Then we'll go on set to do voice level tests and camera setups. Are there any questions you'd like to ask me?"

Yes, Kathryn thought: How do I get out of this? She smiled and shook her head.

" 'Kay," Karen Bolsover said. "Shall we go in, then?"

They walked along a corridor lined with offices, and down some stairs to an open space with composition floors. Double doors to the right bore a big sign: STUDIO A: DO NOT ENTER WHEN RED LIGHT IS ON. Karen Bolsover led the way through a door opposite into a brightly lit room furnished like an airport lounge, with a bar off to the left-hand side. As they entered, Richard Sanchez came across the room.

"Kathryn, good to see you again," he said as they shook hands. "Look, I'm sorry about our little argument the other day."

"It wasn't a little argument," Kathryn said.

Sanchez favored her with a long, thoughtful look. "I really don't want us to be enemies," he said. "We can be very useful to each other, you know."

"I don't see how," she said coolly.

"Give it time," he told her. "Come over and meet Alexander Feinstein."

"The criminologist?"

Alexander Feinstein was a professor of criminology at the University of California, Berkeley. He appeared frequently on TV as a sort of all-purpose expert on matters criminal. He was a short man with heavy eyebrows and thick curly hair cut in what was almost an Afro style.

"I've heard of you," he said, when Sanchez introduced them. He had a deep, mellifluous voice with a trace of a

German accent. He sounded like Henry Kissinger. "You look very young to be a senior prosecutor."

"I started early," Kathryn said, smiling to take the sting out of the words. "Hello, Sheriff."

"Kathryn," Jake Gylam said. "Always nice to see you."

He was a big, tall, slow-moving man with a thatch of black hair, a lined face, grave manner, deep hoarse voice. The gravity and the thoughtful way of speaking were a pose that concealed Gylam's inability to think quickly. All the same, he was a master of what Dave Granz called "the Texas two-step," the art of being someplace else when the manure hit the air-conditioning. He was drinking whiskey.

"I have to circulate," Sanchez said. "Excuse me, please. Someone will take you down to makeup in a few minutes. As soon as everyone's ready, we'll get started."

"Slippery bastard," Gylam said, loud enough for Sanchez to hear. He took another slug of whiskey.

"Tell me, Sheriff, what made you change your mind about appearing tonight?" Kathryn asked.

"It seemed to me a gesture of reassurance to the public would not be amiss at this time," Gylam said ponderously.

"Do you want to take a minute to discuss what we're going to say?"

Gylam stared at her. "I have done this before, you know," he said.

"Just a thought," she said. Gylam was one of those men who always expected a helping hand to be holding a concealed weapon. Nothing you could do about it, but there were times it was a pain.

Kathryn felt someone move closer to her and turned to find herself facing the producer of the show, Jayne with a *y* Kellerman, a willowy woman of about forty with a thin, high-cheekboned face and long dark hair. She had a large glass of red wine in her hand, and her cheeks were slightly flushed. She inspected Kathryn with frank curiosity.

"I half-expected Jane Fonda," she said. "But you're more the Debra Winger type."

"What do I do, apologize?" Kathryn said, taken by surprise. Jayne Kellerman smiled enigmatically.

"I just wondered what you'd be like. It isn't everyone who can rattle Wonder Man."

"Is that what you call him?"

"He told me about your lunch. He said you were tough. A tough cookie, those were his words."

"We seem to have disagreed on pretty much everything except the food."

"One way or the other, you seem to have made quite an impression."

Kathryn smiled. "Perhaps he's one of those men who only remember the women who say no."

"A little sweeping, perhaps. But you may be right. He likes to get his own way."

"And you try to see he does?"

Jayne Kellerman lifted her eyebrows a fraction. "If you're asking, Am I on his side, the answer is yes. If you're asking, Do I worship the ground he walks on, that's another matter. Richard is a major talent. He's going places."

"And you want to go with him."

"We all want success, don't we? This show is important to me. I want it to succeed as much as he does."

"No matter what?"

"Oh, let's not be melodramatic, please. Richard offered you an . . . arrangement. You turned it down. End of story. Nobody got hurt, unless you count the dent in Richard's ego."

"You can dent it?" Kathryn asked sweetly.

"My, my," Jayne murmured. "It bites. Well, I suppose it all makes for good television. Look, I have to go. We'll be ready to start as soon as you've been down to makeup. How do you feel? No butterflies?"

"I'm fine."

"Good. Look, there's something I want you to know before we begin," Jayne Kellerman continued. "We want to make *Here and Now* timely and relevant and gutsy. It's important to him, to me, to the station. So if Richard seems . . . adversarial when you get out there, please don't think there's anything personal about it. It's all in the interest of giving the people a good show. You understand?"

"I understand the words," Kathryn said.

A few minutes later the young production assistant told her it was her turn to go to makeup. With a shrug, she followed her to the mirrored, brightly lit suite. As the makeup artists wielded their brushes and tissues—a dab of Max Factor Number Five to take away a dark shadow beneath the eyes, a brush of powder to remove the highlights from forehead and nose, a checkup as professional and dispassionate as that of a plastic surgeon—Kathryn stared at her reflection in the mirror, Jayne Kellerman's words echoing in her head. Nothing personal. All in the interest of giving the people a good show.

That's what the Romans said to the Christians, she thought. Just before they threw them to the lions.

15

THE SET WAS A BRIGHTLY LIT ISLAND IN THE DARK CAVERN OF the studio. It was an informal layout: a sofa, a low table, two armchairs. Your typical suburban living room, Kathryn thought, as Sheriff Gylam and Alexander Feinstein were shepherded to two seats on Sanchez's right, Kathryn to his left. The camera operators swung the cameras around to check angles; lighting men laid light meters on their chests to set exposures, sound assistants clipped lapel mikes to their clothing and asked them to speak a few words for sound levels.

It was pleasantly warm sitting beneath the hot studio lights. Kathryn watched the technicians talking desultorily among themselves as the audience filtered in, staring with frank curiosity at the people. She could see the set as they saw it on a monitor positioned behind and to her left. An assistant brought in carafes of water and glasses and placed them on the table in front of each guest.

"Five minutes, studio," a disembodied voice boomed. Kathryn watched Sanchez checking his appearance on the monitor. He signaled for a makeup girl to come over and dab away a shine of perspiration on his forehead, checking his notes as she worked.

"One minute! Quiet please!"

Here we go, Kathryn thought, as the music of the opening title sequence came through the overhead speakers. She glanced at Gylam. He was sweating. The floor manager crouched in front of the camera signaled the countdown with splayed fingers. Three, two, one . . . He pointed at Sanchez.

"Good evening and welcome to this special edition of *Here and Now*," Sanchez said. "I'm Richard Sanchez. Tonight, an in-depth report on the savage murders which have shocked the seaside community of Santa Rita. Two murders committed, as the police have now confirmed, by the same person. A cold-blooded killer who strikes without warning and disappears without a trace. I'm joined tonight by Dr. Alexander Feinstein, eminent authority on criminal behavior, Santa Rita County's Sheriff Jacob Gylam, and Assistant District Attorney Kathryn Mackay, heading up the special investigation unit investigating the killings." He swiveled his chair. "Dr. Alexander Feinstein. Perhaps you could outline the present state of thinking on sexual murderers."

Feinstein drew himself up self-importantly as the camera swung around to focus on him.

"The most comprehensive work in this field is the FBI's Criminal Personality Research Project," he said. "It's an ongoing study of sexual murders. Briefly what happens is this: Each murderer who consents is extensively interviewed by FBI agents regarding his background, his behavior at the crime scene, and his postoffense behavior. In addition, his criminal records are reviewed. Data is also collected on the victims of these murderers."

"And what does that tell us?"

"Statistics show sexual murderers are predominantly white, usually elder sons, first or second born. In nearly half the cases studied the father had left the home before the subject was twelve. Forty percent of the subjects lived outside the family home before age eighteen. Nearly all of them had experienced some form of abuse as children: physical, psychological, or sexual."

"And what kind of men are we talking about here, Doctor—average IQ, bright, or what?"

"The majority were of average or above-average intelligence. One or two were exceptionally bright. And there were other significant common denominators. Despite their intelligence, these men had similar life patterns. They were low achievers at school, they wound up in unskilled employment, they had poor work or military service records. Nearly all reported feeling a sense of failure, of low social attachment, at an early age. So they retreated into a fantasy which became more real than reality."

"How do you mean, more real than reality?"

"I'll give you an example. One murderer's fantasy involved an exceptionally good sexual experience. When his victim's behavior did not match the fantasy, he became enraged and killed her."

"What does that tell us?"

"I touched on some of this in my book, *The Wilder Shores of Self*," Feinstein replied. "Male sexual fantasy is common. Universal, even. But a normal male does not respond to disappointment in real sexual encounters with antisocial behavior. It is the abnormal male who cannot control his reactions, and responds with sexual homicide, an act of control, dominance, and performance representative of an underlying fantasy embedded with violence, sexuality, and death."

"Let's just hold it there a moment, Doctor. Can you simplify that a little for us? Control, dominance, and performance ..."

"The killer needs to control the situation, make the victim fit into his fantasy for his own sexual satisfaction. The violence is part of that, the sex is part of it, and of course, the victim's death is its culmination."

"And do we have any way of classifying such murderers?"

"Yes, we do. The FBI's special profiling agents type them and the crime scene in terms of an organized or disorganized dichotomy. The premise for this dichotomy—"

"Let's try not to get too technical here, Doctor," Sanchez interrupted. "Are you saying sexual murderers come in one of two varieties—organized and disorganized?"

"No, of course not. That's how the FBI classifies them."

"They're either organized or disorganized killers?"

"That's correct."

"Can you explain what that means?"

"An organized killer is very much in control throughout. Knows what he's doing. He's socially adept. Passes for normal, if you like. Plans his murders and carries them out calmly and dispassionately. His victims are usually strangers, and there is often an element of sadism in the killing. If he uses a weapon, he takes it away afterwards, and is careful to avoid leaving evidence at the crime scene. He will often move the body from the crime scene to another location."

"And the disorganized killer?"

"Usually a man of below-average intelligence, socially inadequate, probably sexually incompetent. He tends to kill spontaneously, or at random, and with no set plan for eluding detection. No attempt is made to hide the body or get rid of the murder weapon."

"And to which of these groups would you suggest the Santa Rita murderer belongs?" Sanchez asked.

"No question in my mind," Feinstein said. "This is the work of an organized offender."

"All right, Doctor," Sanchez said, leading. "Tell us, now. Is there one word to describe such a killer?"

"There is," Feinstein said. "Psychopath."

There was a solid hum of audience reaction; Sanchez let it build for a moment before asking his next question.

"Would you say such a man was insane, Doctor?"

"*Insane* is a legal term. The medical term would be *mentally disordered*. You say *insane* and most people think of someone foaming at the mouth, mad the way a rabid dog is mad. This man is not like that. He would appear to be as normal as you or I. But he is mad, just the same. And dangerous."

"And you think he may kill again?"

"I'd say it was extremely likely."

Once again there was an audible audience reaction. Once again Sanchez let it build to its peak, then he stood up. His timing was impeccable, Kathryn thought. She watched as he took a large card and pinned it to the back wall behind his chair.

"You heard what Dr. Feinstein said. This man may kill again. Tonight, *Here and Now,* I can exclusively reveal that the killer has announced his intention of doing just that. Last Friday afternoon, this note was delivered to the Sheriff's Department in downtown Santa Rita."

The cameras zoomed in on the printed card till it filled the screens of the monitors. "The one in Sedgewick Park was called Anna," Sanchez intoned voice-over. "She had a small cut on her inner thigh. Another one soon."

Kathryn heard the swift collective intake of breath in the audience as Sanchez spoke the last three words.

"Yes, it's genuine," Sanchez said, building the moment.

"There's no question of that. To learn more, stay tuned. We'll be back right after these messages."

The monitors went blank; a disembodied voice filled the silence. "Three minutes, studio."

"Okay, everyone, relax," the floor manager announced. Jake Gylam got to his feet and glowered at Richard Sanchez.

"God damn it, Sanchez," he snapped. "How the hell did you get ahold of that note?"

"You know I can't tell you that, Sheriff," Sanchez said with a disarming smile.

"That's classified documentation relating to an ongoing investigation," Gylam fumed. "God damn it, I'm tempted to hit you with a charge of obstructing the course of justice!"

"It would be great publicity for the show," Sanchez said, still smiling. "Go right ahead, Sheriff."

"You know what a copycat killing is, Sanchez?" Gylam said. "Do you have any idea what I'm talking about?"

"Why do I think you're about to tell me?" Sanchez drawled. Gylam flushed with anger.

"A copycat killer," he scowled, "is someone who gets a sick thrill from the grisly details of a murder. So much of a kick he goes out and tries to duplicate it. That's why in nearly every homicide, we in law enforcement try to keep certain details confidential; that way, we're able to identify when a copycat killing takes place. There'll always be something the killer doesn't know, some detail that doesn't tally with the others."

"I take it there is a point to all this, Sheriff?" Sanchez said impatiently. "We'll be back on the air in ninety seconds."

"Yes, there is, dammit!" Gylam snapped angrily. "By revealing the contents of that note, Mr. Sanchez, you have just made it possible for someone to become a copycat killer. You've told him the one thing about this murderer no one else knew, and I'm going on the record here as saying that what you did is irresponsible in the extreme."

"Not only that," Kathryn said. "You conveniently neglected to mention the means by which you got the note. We'll have every newspaper and TV station in the state on our backs ten minutes after this show is broadcast, demanding to know how and why you got an exclusive. What are we supposed to tell them?"

Sanchez shrugged. "You could tell them Richard Sanchez said, tough." He smiled.

"Good God, doesn't it even bother you?" Gylam said.

Sanchez shrugged. "You do your job, Sheriff. I do mine."

"Thirty seconds, studio," the disembodied voice announced.

"Quiet, please," the floor manager snapped, turning to face Richard Sanchez. He splayed the fingers of both hands and held them up. After a few more moments he gave an exaggerated nod and then started counting down, closing his fingers to mark the seconds passing, four, three, two, one, pointing at Sanchez as he said the last word.

"You're back with us, *Here and Now,* talking about a brutal killer. A man who has killed twice and plans to kill again. Soon." He let the word hang for a long moment.

"Turning now to you, Sheriff Gylam," he said. "Would you agree with Dr. Feinstein's assessment of this killer?"

Gylam's face was still set in anger. "It's an assessment. I'm not qualified to comment on its accuracy."

"You mean you won't."

"I mean exactly what I said, Mr. Sanchez," Gylam snapped. "I'm not qualified to comment."

"Kathryn Mackay, you're head of the special investigations unit set up to probe these killings. Do you have any thoughts on what Dr. Feinstein has to say?"

The empty eye of the camera swung round to fix her with its gaze and Kathryn tried to remember all the things she'd been told about appearing on TV. Sit still. Don't blink. Talk slowly. Don't use your hands. Talk to the camera, not the interviewer. Smile.

"Dr. Feinstein laid out the general parameters of offender profiling," Kathryn said, taking her time. "While his comments may be fine in the most general sense, we in law enforcement are trying to put together a more ... realistic picture of this particular offender."

"Realistic?"

"People are inclined to think if we use the word *organized* about a killer, it means he's some sort of master criminal. It doesn't. In actual fact, this man is stupid. So stupid he thinks he can kill and kill again and never get caught."

"Stupid," Sanchez said thoughtfully. "But didn't Dr.

Feinstein say most of these serial killers have average or above average intelligence?"

"You're talking about IQ, Mr. Sanchez," Kathryn said. "I'm talking about an asocial attitude. We're dealing with someone who kills young women and mutilates their bodies. And believes he will not have to pay for his crimes. That makes him stupid."

"But not unintelligent, surely. After all, the note the killer sent was originally in code, was it not?"

"Plenty of intelligent people do stupid things," Kathryn said. Gotcha, buster. "The killer's sending a note to the Sheriff's Department supports my proposition that he is stupid. And while we're on the subject of the note, perhaps we ought to mention that you didn't get it from either the Sheriff's or the District Attorney's office."

Sanchez smiled the smile of someone who appreciates a good adversary. "I don't think I ever indicated otherwise, Ms. Mackay. A good journalist never reveals his sources, you know that. But let's get back to the killer . . ."

"Let's do that," Kathryn said. "And let's try to avoid the cheap sensationalism while we're at it. Stop suggesting there's some sort of horror movie monster stalking the streets."

Sanchez's eyes glinted with malice. "Are you contending there isn't?"

"I'm contending that words like savage, violent, and dangerous paint exactly the sort of picture the killer wants us to have of him, rather than what he is really like."

"Which is?"

"He's a wimp. A gutless coward, a pathetic imitation of a human being. Intelligent, maybe. But cunning rather than clever. And vain. And treacherous. A pathological liar. In other words, a drab little social misfit who only feels like a man when he's brutalizing defenseless women."

"Strong words," Sanchez said, swiveling around. "Would you agree, Dr. Feinstein? The killer is—what was it Ms. Mackay said?—pathetic? A drab little social misfit?"

Feinstein blinked rapidly, pursing his lips.

"I'm afraid I really can't go along with that. I mean, while there is certainly . . . uh, what Ms. Mackay says does to some extent reinforce my earlier comments, that the fantasies of such men are often generated to conceal a colorless, obsessive personality, to compensate for the anomie—the social detachment we spoke about. But that doesn't make him any less dangerous. Don't let us forget he's killed two defenseless Hispanic women."

"I don't think any of us is likely to," Sanchez said, turning around to face Jake Gylam. "Any more than we're likely to forget he's promised to kill another. Unless your department can come up with something more substantial than promises, Sheriff."

"Let me say this about that," Gylam blustered. "One of the reasons I agreed to appear here tonight was to place on record the fact that we are not in a negative outcome situation here. Every member of personnel in my department, every law enforcement officer in Santa Rita County, is dedicated to the pursuit and apprehension of this perpetrator. Every aspect of these killings will be examined and reexamined, every grain of evidence checked and rescrutinized. The facilities of the Department of Justice and the National Crime Information Center have been placed at our disposal. I feel quite sure—no, I'm confident—that this momentum will enable us to move toward a resolution. It's only a matter of time."

"Time may be the one thing you don't have, Sheriff," Sanchez said, turning away haughtily, like a matador turning his back on the bull he has dominated. "And the same, alas, is true of us. I'm Richard Sanchez, as always, *Here and Now* with the topics that matter most. Thanks to my distinguished guests for their valuable insights. Most of all, thank *you*. Good night, and—be vigilant."

It was a great wrap and he knew it. The audience didn't need prompting to applaud. From the corner of her eye, Kathryn could see Jake Gylam staring stonily at them like an Easter Island monolith. Well, they'd come through. If it hadn't been a triumph of law enforcement public relations, neither had it been the eight-on-the-Richter-scale disaster she had feared it might turn into either. Thank God for small mercies, she thought.

16

"THAT WAS QUITE SOME SHOW."

As Kathryn switched off the VCR, Laura Foster got up, stretched, and walked across to the window to look out at the ocean. She wasn't a frequent visitor, but she came over to Seaview Heights whenever she needed to talk through a case, or get some advice on the best way of handling some tricky legal problem. Right now she was here because at Kathryn's request, Mac had assigned her to assist on the Broadwick trial.

"Even if it begged a few questions," Kathryn said, referring to the Sanchez show.

"Like what?"

"Well, for one, the brutal statistical fact that out of the twenty-five thousand–plus murders committed every year in the United States, one in four is never solved."

"Why is that relevant?"

"Because anyone who knows anything about law enforcement knows that probably up to half of those unsolved murders—more than six thousand of them, Laura, seventeen every day of the week—were probably committed by someone who just popped up like a malignant mushroom, killed once, twice, then moved on. That's why they're almost impossible to solve."

Look at some of the more sensational cases of the last couple of decades, she went on: the Seattle sex killer Ted Bundy, who had killed twenty girls over a two-year period; Dean Corll, the Houston homosexual mass murderer; or nearer home, Ed Kemper, the necrophiliac Santa Cruz "Co-ed Killer." Because their killings were so random and unplanned, luck played as large a part in their capture as investigative techniques.

"I'll tell you one thing," Laura said. "You saved the Sheriff's bacon."

"Twice," Kathryn said, grinning at the recollection. "The producer invited us to stay and watch the show in the studio, then join them for dinner afterwards, but I couldn't stay, I'd already arranged to meet Emma and Jack."

"How about you, Sheriff?" Sanchez then said to Jake Gylam.

"I'd rather eat untreated sewage," Gylam snarled. Sanchez smiled his shark smile.

"I guess you know what you like, Sheriff," he said smoothly.

"I got Jake out of there before it got any worse," Kathryn told Laura. "He was mad enough to bite a chunk out of a redwood."

After the show, Jack had driven her and Emma back up to Espanola and she made him a sandwich before he left. It was typical of Jack that he didn't stay to see the Sanchez show with her. She supposed it was his way of showing he wasn't interested anymore. She wondered why he thought she cared one way or the other. After Jack left, Emma related her day's adventures: the sharks and turtles and "huge big fish with starey eyes" she'd seen at the aquarium, the cheeseburger and fries and chocolate shake at McDonald's, the walk along the beach looking for starfish.

"You always have a good time with your daddy, don't you?" Kathryn said as they headed for the bedroom. "I'm glad you're such good friends."

"He's nice," Emma said. "I sometimes wish we lived with him."

"You do? Why?"

Emma grinned mischievously. "Because then I'd have someone to fix my skates."

Kathryn took her daughter by the shoulders and pointed her toward her bedroom. "Go brush your teeth, young lady," she said mock sternly, "and stop teasing me."

Emma giggled. "I was, wasn't I?"

"You're bad clear through," Kathryn said, and hugged her. "Okay, go!"

"Mommy, come in and say good night," Emma called from her bedroom a few minutes later.

"I'll be right there, sweetheart," Kathryn replied. "I just have one call to make."

"Don't be lo-ong," Emma caroled. "I'm getting slee-py!"

"Did you brush your teeth yet?"

"Sure. I used my yellow toothbrush you bought me."

"Very good. I'll just be a little while. Why don't you read a story?"

"Because," Emma said.

"Because what?"

"Because I want you to read it to me."

Kathryn smiled. "Okay, just let me make my call."

Hal Benton answered the phone himself. "I hate to bother you this late," she said. "Did you watch Sanchez?"

"I watched," he said. "How are you feeling?"

"Like a used Kleenex," she said. "Will we get a lot of flak from the media about the note?"

"None we haven't had before. You covered just fine. I talked to Mac. He saw it too, and he agrees. Don't worry so much."

"I don't know if that makes me feel any better," Kathryn said with a smile. "But at least it doesn't make me feel any worse."

"That would seem to be about the right philosophical attitude," Hal said.

"Nothing more from Sacramento, I suppose?"

"Only what I told you on the phone. No identifiable prints on the note. Our killer probably wears latex gloves. Why wouldn't he? It's in all the true-crime books and the TV cop shows."

"I suppose we should have expected it," Kathryn sighed. "I was just hoping against hope—"

"Mommy!" Emma called.

"Be right there, sweetie," Kathryn said.

"Aha!" Hal chuckled at the other end. "Got a strapping young surfer up there, have you?"

"No such luck," Kathryn said, thinking, Maybe a strapping young surfer wouldn't be such a bad idea right now.

"Anything else you want to talk about?"

"No. I just needed a friendly ear."

"You did just fine, Kathryn," he said again. "Sleep tight."

Kathryn put down the phone. Just talking to Hal always made her feel better. He had a way of taking all the strain off. She cradled the phone and went through to Emma's room. Her daughter was curled up under the blankets. When Kathryn came in she leaped up, tossing the blankets aside, and threw her arms around her.

"You were a *long* time, Mommy!" she scolded.

"I know, honeybun," Kathryn said. "I'm sorry. I was talking to my boss."

"Mm," Emma said, unimpressed. "C'n we read the story now?"

Kathryn opened the book. "Once upon a time," she began, "there were three billy goats whose name was . . ."

"Gruff," Emma said gruffly.

"The three billy goats Gruff lived on the side of a hill. At the bottom of the hill was a river, and over the river there was a wooden bridge."

"Oh-oh," Emma said. "That's where the troll lives."

"That's right."

"Oh, Mommy, is the tro-o-o-oll coming?"

"Pretty soon," Kathryn said. "You better get right down tnere where he can't see you."

"Okay, I'm down," Emma said, her voice partly muffled by the blankets pulled up under her nose. "Go on, go on."

When the story was finished Kathryn hugged Emma tight, kissed her, and held her close before tucking her in.

"Love you, Mommy," Emma said, her voice already sleepy.

"Love you, too, sweetheart." Kathryn stood for a few moments, looking down at her daughter. So precious, so unique. *I wonder if she knows how much I love her? Do children ever know? When you're a child, you take your parents' love for granted. When you become an adult, you remember other things.* She tiptoed out of the room. Emma would fall asleep in minutes; she always did. Laura had arrived a little over half an hour later, just as she was putting the Sanchez tape into the VCR.

"Would you like anything?" she asked now. "Tea, coffee, a glass of wine?"

"Maybe later," Laura said, glancing at her watch. "Let's get started on the case book first, okay?"

Kathryn opened up her briefcase, and they settled down to work. Preparing properly for trial was in many ways as important as trying the case itself. Prepare carelessly and a good defense attorney would shoot you down in flames. Organize badly and you would suffer the torments of hell as you tried to find a vital piece of paper while a judge and twelve jurors stared silently at you for what seemed like hours.

"Okay, we start with a case book," she said. "I've got one ready for you. Here, take it."

She handed Laura a big three-ring binder with several sections filled with blank paper. In the first section, she told her, she must log every action she took in connection with the case, however small, however trivial, which she might later have to substantiate or verify.

The second section would be a list of things that had to be done—witnesses to be subpoenaed, priors to be obtained, instructions to be pulled, cases to be looked up and read. Another section would contain copies of all relevant police reports and notes made by the law enforcement agencies, and still another the statements of all the witnesses.

"I've already got you copies of the *Gazette* covering the day before, the day of, and the day after the crime. Here, put them in the file."

"What do I do with them?"

"Maybe nothing. But if the defendant or any witness uses a TV show or a movie he claims to have seen as an alibi, you can check him out in the appropriate issue of the paper."

Yet another section of the case book, she told Laura, should list exhibits, and another reports of any other crimes in which the defendant had been involved.

"Now comes the important part," she told her. "I want you to read every single piece of paper not just once or twice, but over and over again until you begin to get a clear picture of how we'll present the case. We'll visit the scene of the crime so that if the defense produces photographs we think distort the scenes they're supposed to depict, we can challenge them or insist the jury be taken there."

"When do I get the time to do all this reading?" Laura said, crestfallen.

"Make time," Kathryn told her uncompromisingly. "And update the case book every day. Before you get through, you'll probably have six as thick as this one. Now, how about that glass of wine?"

"I think I need one." Laura grinned. "Do you do this with every single case you prosecute?"

"Every single one," Kathryn replied, taking the wine from

the refrigerator and pouring them each a glass. "No exceptions."

Laura raised her glass in a silent toast.

"You know something, Kathryn?" she said, mischief in her eyes. "We're nuts."

"Nuts?"

"Look at us, for godsakes. We're both over the age of consent. It's Sunday night. Neither of us is exactly a frump. So why are we sitting here compiling a case book instead of out having a good time with a couple of good-looking hunks?"

"I don't know," Kathryn said. "Maybe it's because all the good-looking hunks are either married or spoken for."

"You heard about Bill Calhoun?"

"No, what?"

"The governor blocked his appointment to the Appellate Court. Apparently he got the whisper about him and Janie Welsh."

"How's he taking it?"

"Pretty badly, I heard. The funny thing is, he and Janie split up. Before it happened. He went back to the wife and kids."

Poor Bill, she thought. And poor Janie. Everyone a loser.

"Dangerous business, love," she observed.

"Ain't it the truth," Laura said.

Kathryn was still thinking about their conversation as she got ready for bed. Face it, kiddo, frump or not, there weren't that many good-looking hunks around. At thirty-nine you were out of the first-love stakes and into the second-time-around handicap. Kick the idea of an affair with someone else's husband or being some older guy's mistress, and what were you left with? Most of the men she met in her line of work were already married; the ones who weren't, like Dave, were often badly bruised. The rest were lowlifes you wouldn't want to be on the same side of the street with.

She yawned and rubbed her eyes. It was nearly eleven. She took off her clothes and slid into bed. Tomorrow would be a demanding day. They only seemed to come in the one variety. She switched off the light, and fell asleep almost instantly.

* * *

Having the secret place meant he could do it whenever he wanted. There was no need to hurry. Yet he wanted to do it. He couldn't wait another week. He wanted to do it now. He took off all his clothes and laid them in a neat pile at the top of the stairs. Then he opened the door and went down to the cellar. The cold air on his skin felt clean and pure. She was sitting on the bed the way she had been when he left her, wearing the white T-shirt and white cotton shorts he had bought at the drugstore in the Laguna del Mar Mall. He didn't need to keep her bound anymore. It was like having a slave. Better. She looked up as he came in. Her eyes widened when she saw him naked. He could see the fear in back of her eyes. He liked that.

"Hello, Barbara," he said.

"I didn't hear you coming." She was looking at him. *There.* She couldn't take her eyes off it. He liked that, too.

"Were you looking forward to seeing me?" he said, his voice soft, almost caressing.

She swallowed noisily. "Yes. I am. I was." She looked at him uncertainly, anxious not to make a mistake. "I ... uh ... do you want me to ..."

He lifted his chin, as if considering options. "Yes," he said. "You know what I like, Barbara."

She came toward him, trembling with fear, holding his eyes with her own, ready to flinch at any threat. She knelt down in front of him and began. Her tongue was rough and dry. He looked down at her, felt the power, felt the slow uncoiling of lust in his belly. Knowing made it so much more intense. Knowing what was going to happen.

"You love doing that, don't you, Barbara?"

"Mmmm," she said, looking up at him. "Yes. Yes, I do."

"Say it the way I told you!" he snapped. "Say *cholo!* I love it, *cholo!*"

"I love it ... *cholo.*"

"That's better. Now lie down," he told her. "On your back."

She did as she was told and he squatted over her. "There," he said. "I'll make it easier for you."

"Yes," she said. She was crying softly. That made it even better.

"You do love it, don't you?" he said. "Tell me how much, Barbara."

"It's ... it's—" Her voice broke and she began sobbing. He stood up and looked down at her, straddling her body with his legs. He shook his head sadly.

"Don't lie to me."

"I'm not. I like it, I told you I do."

"Cholo!" he shouted and hit her with his open hand. She hunched herself up in a ball, her hands in front of her face, knees pulled up to protect herself.

"Oh, God, no, please, I'm sorry!" she sobbed. He hit her again, blindly.

"Haven't you learned anything?" he hissed.

"Yes, I have, I have," she wailed piteously. "Please, give me another chance." She got up on her knees, throwing her arms around his naked thighs, frantically kissing his crotch. He took hold of her hair and yanked back her head, slapping her again and then again, dragging her across the floor.

"I told you!" he shouted. "I thought you'd learn. Why do none of you ever learn?"

Still holding her hair bunched in his fist, he yanked her upright and hurled her onto the bed. She cried out with pain as her head hit the wooden bedpost with a flat smack. Her face was contorted, her eyes glazed. She knew now, he thought. She knew what was coming now. She beat at him ineffectually as he ripped the T-shirt off her, grabbed the waistband of the shorts and yanked them off. He felt engorged, hot, eager. It was coming, it was here again.

He took hold of her throat with both hands, pushing her down on the bed, and half fell on top of her, forcing a guttural animal sound from her. She thrashed her head from side to side and arched her body to try to dislodge him, and he felt part of himself going up and away from there, and as he went he tightened his grip, tighter, tighter. He heard her begin to wheeze. Her fists beat an ineffectual tattoo on his forearms. He felt himself going farther away from there, a roaring inside his head like the crowd at a Super Bowl as he increased the pressure, pinning her body down with the weight of his own.

He felt the life go out of her in the same moment he reached orgasm.

17

AT THIRTY-SEVEN YEARS OF AGE, DEPUTY PUBLIC DEFENDER
Marty Belker was about medium height, narrow shouldered
and thin, with a high forehead and receding sandy hair. His
vanity was expensive shoes: he claimed to have over a hundred pairs. Being in a stuffy courtroom with him was a trial
in more ways than one: Belker was less than careful about
personal hygiene. It wasn't the first time Kathryn had faced
him in a courtroom; she didn't think she was going to enjoy
it this time any more than she had the others.

Jury selection had taken four days, with both prosecution
and defense vying to find jurors who would understand the
strengths and perhaps forgive the weaknesses of their case.
Jurors were either *for* or *against;* it was each attorney's job
to try to choose properly. Kathryn's approach was based on
a formula she'd worked out over the years: she looked for
jurors she would be happy to have a conversation with, people she sensed were something like her. The ones she didn't
like, she bumped.

Although he was charming and likable throughout the selection, smiling at the ladies, firm and direct with the men,
going to a lot of extra trouble to try to find jurors who might
be sympathetic to the defendant, Belker didn't fool Kathryn.
He was theatrical, tricky, and unprincipled. His attitude
would change completely once the trial began.

By four o'clock Thursday, the jury had been accepted by
both sides and sworn; *voir dire* was complete. She'd got as
good a jury as she could hope for under the circumstances,
Kathryn thought. No lawyers, no shrinks, no writers, no
poets. Just the usual mix of American citizens. A man of
sixty who liked to watch football on TV, a car salesman of
thirty-five who read *Playboy,* a pleasant-faced middle-aged
woman who was knitting a sweater for her grandchild, a
black woman who worked at a supermarket checkout, an
Oriental man who owned a shoe store in Mountain View.

Kathryn watched as the last of the jurors-to-be filed out

of the courtroom. Marty Belker came across and sat on the corner of her table.

"Why are you asking to see the judge in chambers, Kathryn?" he asked. "What are you up to?"

"We haven't talked dispo, Marty."

He put on a pantomime look of astonishment. "What? Attila the Hen wants to make an offer?"

"Oh, can that, will you?"

"What kind of an offer are we talking about?" Belker asked. Today he was wearing lizard skin loafers with gold chains across the instep. Mr. Bojangles, Kathryn thought. A real fancy dancer.

"Patience, Marty, patience," she said. "That's why we're going to see Calhoun."

"He didn't look too delighted when you asked him."

"He never does," Kathryn said.

The door to judge's chambers opened and Pete Zabriskie, the tubby, blond deputy from the Sheriff's Department who was court bailiff on this case, stuck out his head.

"Judge'll see you now," he announced. Kathryn looked over at Belker. He smiled and made a gesture: after you. She shook her head in amusement at his spurious gentlemanliness. Marty was one of the biggest chauvinists she knew. They went around the bench and into chambers, a comfortable book-lined room that felt more like a study than the adjunct of a courtroom.

"Take a seat, people," Calhoun said. He looked as if he was in a good mood. So far everything was going smoothly. That was how he liked it; a friendly courtroom, nobody rocking his boat. "I think we've got a good jury out there, don't you?"

"They'll do," Belker said. "Can we get to it, Your Honor? I've got an appointment."

"Me, too," Calhoun said urbanely. "Ms. Mackay?"

"I want to open up an area we haven't really explored, Your Honor," Kathryn began. "Mr. Belker and I haven't had any meaningful discussions about this case in terms of a plea."

"You're making an offer?" Calhoun said, raising his eyebrows in exaggerated surprise.

"We might be able to cut this thing short," Kathryn said,

ignoring Calhoun's humor, which was as leaden as Belker's. "What about it, Marty?"

"I'm listening," Belker said.

"Okay, here's what I have in mind: If Broadwick's convicted of first, he's not eligible for parole until he's done eighteen years," she said. "If he pleads to second, he'll be eligible in eight to ten. He'd be out before he's forty. I'm prepared to let him plead guilty to a second-degree murder charge if the defense can put something in my file supporting dim cap. I imagine you can?"

"I might," Belker said. "But I don't like the offer. I think we can do better."

"Are you kidding me?" Kathryn said. "How?"

"Our position is that not only was his capacity diminished, but he killed his girlfriend in the heat of passion. Voluntary manslaughter. That's max eleven years."

"Your Honor!" Kathryn said impatiently, turning to Calhoun. "Talk to this guy!"

"You don't really think you can get a jury to buy heat of passion, Mr. Belker?" Calhoun asked.

"We can try."

"Marty, we've got a witness who testified at the prelim that your client left her house telling her he was going to kill the woman," Kathryn reminded him.

"Maybe she misunderstood him."

Calhoun looked dismayed, and Kathryn knew why; he could see his nice friendly trial turning into a knock-down drag-out fight.

"Look, why go through all that?" Calhoun said. "We can settle it right here. Save ourselves a lot of time and the taxpayer a lot of money."

Belker hunched his shoulders and stared at the floor. Body language: I don't care what you say. He shook his head. "No deal."

"You haven't talked to your client yet," Kathryn reminded him.

"I know what he'll say."

He did, too, Kathryn thought. Danny Broadwick was a very confused human being, and Belker had a great deal of control over him. He would have no trouble persuading Danny to go to trial, which was what Marty wanted. He knew copping a plea wouldn't get him any headlines. He had never defended a murder case before. It would be good for his image and his career.

"You're still obligated to convey the offer to your client, Mr. Belker," Calhoun said gravely. "I suggest you do so. And let me say something else: I don't often see Ms. Mackay offer a deal. Damned rarely, in fact. You should think very carefully before you turn it down."

Belker's expression didn't change. He shrugged and got up, going out through the rear door that led into the corridor and down the stairs to the basement where Danny Broadwick was being held. When he was gone, Calhoun looked at Kathryn and shook his head.

"Imagine," he said, smiling. "The Iron Maiden, making an offer."

Kathryn didn't reply: there was no point. She'd learned the rules long ago. It was all part of being a woman in what was still perceived as a man's world. The funny names were little jibes thrown at you to point out you weren't being feminine enough. Come on strong, you were a pushy bitch. Fail to do so and they'd patronize you or, worse, ignore you.

"It's a good deal," she said. "Belker knows that."

"I agree," Calhoun said. "You think he'll go for it?"

When Kathryn shook her head Calhoun looked disappointed. "I hope you're wrong," he said. "But at least you put it on the table. I want you to know I appreciate your doing that."

The door opened and they looked up expectantly as Belker came back in.

"No dice," he said, sitting down in the bentwood chair facing the judge. "My client doesn't want any part of any deal."

"Surprise, surprise," Kathryn murmured.

Calhoun's face showed his disappointment. "Pity," he said. "Still, if that's the way the ball bounces. Anything else, Ms. Mackay?"

Kathryn shook her head no. Calhoun stood up, taking off his robe and hanging it on a bentwood coat tree behind the desk. It was as if he hung up his judicial *persona* with it. In his gray lightweight suit, pale blue shirt, and plain dark blue tie, he looked more like an ad executive or a commodities broker. It was hard to imagine what Janie Welsh had ever seen in him.

"That's it, then," he said. "See you both Monday."

Kathryn picked up her papers and led the way back into the courtroom. It was just a few minutes after five; she would have time to check her office before she left to pick up Emma. She shoveled the papers into her briefcase and headed for the door, followed by Deputy Zabriskie, who'd lock up the courtroom after their departure. Marty Belker fell into step alongside her as she hurried through the atrium and into the main building.

"So," he said as they came to the stairway. "You ready to do battle Monday?"

"How can you do a thing like that to your client, Marty?" Kathryn asked him.

"Do what?" Belker said.

"Don't be disingenuous. You told him not to accept my offer, didn't you?"

Belker shrugged; it was an admission, and Kathryn had to control her anger. How could a responsible attorney put his own interests before those of his client?

"I'm going for first-degree murder, Marty. All the way. Twenty-five to life."

"Straight for the balls, as always," Belker said. "No wonder you're so popular."

"Just don't forget I made you an offer," Kathryn said. "You want to chance it. But it's your client who'll do the extra years."

"It ain't over till the fat lady sings. You don't have your first yet."

"I'll get it, Marty. He's guilty and he'll go down."

"God," he said, turning sarcastic, "you really get off on the idea of sending someone away for life, don't you?"

"Dammit, Marty, he beat a woman to death with a tire iron! What do you want me to do, give him a medal?"

"It was heat of passion, for godsakes, can't you at least admit the possibility? The woman was a bitch. He'd had a few drinks. She called him an asshole, and he lashed out. The poor shlub didn't know what he was doing. When I get to his diminished capacity at the time of the killing—"

"Don't waste it on me, Marty," Kathryn said. All at once she felt enormously tired. "Save it for the jury."

Belker made one of those what-can-you-do-with-someone-like-that gestures he was always making and went down to the stairway to the cafeteria. Kathryn walked upstairs to her office. She couldn't believe the day had gone so fast; she felt out of kilter, as if she had jet lag. She made herself a cup of tea and walked down the corridor to the conference room. Animated voices: some of the younger prosecutors were sitting around bullshitting.

One or two of them greeted Kathryn as she came into the room. Sitting with his back to her was David Agostino, as dark and Italian-looking as his name. To his right sat Martin Lucero, who specialized in narcotics cases. Next to Martin was blond, stocky Vic Carpenter, his face sun-reddened as usual; take him out of his neat, gray, three-piece suit and put him into a pair of shorts and he'd look more like a surfer than a prosecutor. At the far end of the table was Laura Foster; she wiggled her fingers hello. Kathryn regarded them all with affection.

"How's that embezzlement case of yours coming along, Martin?" she asked.

"No sweat," he said. "A dead bang case." The others laughed and Martin frowned, surprised by their reaction.

"We've got everything except video of the guy with his hand in the cash register," he said. "What can go wrong?"

"Don't ask," Kathryn told him, smiling. "Just remember, no one's dead bang guilty until the verdict's in."

It was something she tried to impress on all of them: no trial ever went entirely according to plan. Call it what you like: glitches, gremlins, Murphy's Law, something always went awry. The ground rules—the Evidence Code, the Penal Code—were there, and the formalities of the courtroom never changed. All the rest, the credibility of witnesses, the reactions of the jurors, the decisions of the judge, remained completely unpredictable. And God help the prosecutor who wasn't ready for that.

"Hey, I saw you on TV," Martin Lucero said to Kathryn. "I thought you handled Sanchez pretty well."

"Well, thanks." Kathryn grinned.

"I saw that," David Agostino said. "He did a real number on the Sheriff, didn't he?"

Vic Carpenter grinned. "Jake's still stamping about upstairs like an elephant with hemorrhoids. How the hell did Sanchez get ahold of that note, anyway, Kathryn?"

"I wish I knew."

"Any other developments?" Laura asked.

Kathryn stood up, shaking her head. "Nothing. And Dave Granz says it isn't going anywhere unless we get some kind of real lead. Look, I'm sorry to break this up, but I've got to go pick up Emma."

She went out to the parking lot, got into her car, and wound down the windows to let in some air till the air-conditioning bit. She pulled out into Pacific and zipped over to the lane that would take her left at the lights onto Bonita. Apart from the usual bottleneck where Bonita joined Alameda, the traffic was light, and she made good time up to Alameda Heights. Near the college the road made a long, climbing curve that gave a magnificent view of Santa Rita, spread around the bay below.

He was down there, somewhere, she thought. But where? He had to have a job, which meant he had colleagues. He had to have someplace to live, which meant he had neighbors and acquaintances. He had to eat, so they knew him in some coffee shop or supermarket. He drove a car, so someone somewhere sold him gas. A lot of people knew this man. But who was he, what was he like? Tall, short, fat, thin, blond, dark, ugly, ordinary?

What was he *like?*

Lee watched Kathryn Mackay as she put her briefcase into the trunk and then got into her little red car. She was wearing a royal blue linen suit and a white blouse, white earrings with blue centers, blue pumps. Pretty lady, he thought. She had long dark hair. That was good. He liked them with long dark hair. She looked smaller than she had on TV. Her words burned inside his brain. He had been very angry with her when she said those things, but now it was controlled.

He slid the car out of the visitors' parking space he had been occupying for the last hour and followed her down Pacific and then left on Bonita. She would be heading for Espanola. She had a condo on Seaview Heights. He'd checked her out in the deed transfer books in the County Recorder's office. That was the great thing about government offices. You could just walk in and ask them anything you wanted to know, and they had to tell you.

She was a good driver, taking no risks, always signaling

well in advance. He followed her up onto Alameda Drive, down the long curving slope into Alameda, and then up the hill on the far side of the valley, heading east past the college, where she made a right on Lighthouse. About two hundred yards down she made a left turn. He coasted to a stop by the curbside opposite a sign that read MARTHA JANEWAY SCHOOL. He turned off the engine and waited.

Ten or twelve minutes later he saw the red Mazda nose out of the school entrance and turn left on Lighthouse. Heading for home, he thought, putting his Honda into gear and moving into the traffic about three cars behind Kathryn's car. On the far side of the underpass beneath the Alvarado Highway, it turned in to a small mall on the right-hand side of the road. Lee followed, coasting past as Kathryn got out of the car and a little girl clambered out on the other side. She was wearing a print dress and leather strap shoes. She was dark and pretty, with a pug nose powdered with freckles, brown eyes beneath dark brows, long dark hair, slender tanned arms and legs. So Kathryn Mackay had a daughter. He wondered who the father was.

He parked and watched them go into a frozen yogurt shop. The little girl said something. Kathryn Mackay laughed and hugged her. They looked happy, close. When they came out with their cones they got back into the car and drove out of the parking lot. The woman was driving one-handed, the little girl in front eating her yogurt. He followed the car down Lighthouse to Beach Avenue, the boulevard that ran along the ocean front. He could see the stark white finger of the Shelter Island lighthouse on its bluff across the shining strip of water that formed the inlet. A flight of pelicans was dive-bombing a school of fish off the beach.

The last time he had been down here it had been just before dawn. He had driven across the bridge and coasted along the sandswept road above the bluffs with his lights out. Gulls wheeled above him, shrieking their lost-soul cries, as he made a three-point turn so that the rear of the pickup was right at the edge of the road where the sand hills shelved steeply down to the beach. He pulled the dead girl out of the vehicle.

Andrea. He had never known her last name. She was now known as the Shelter Island victim. Little Andrea with the small breasts and the wide brown eyes. A nobody, and he had made her famous. He had picked her up on the highway near Carmel, hitchhiking. She wouldn't do any of the things he wanted and he had been so angry he killed her sooner than he had planned; because she had been so disappointing he didn't keep her long. Holding the body by the shoulders he tipped her over the edge. She rolled down, arms and legs flapping. Then he took off the latex gloves, folded up the plastic sheeting, and stuffed it into a trash can liner that he later left in a dumpster on the other side of Santa Rita.

He followed Kathryn's car up to Seaview Heights, coasting on past as the red Mazda turned into the driveway of the condo and dropped out of sight on its way to the underground parking lot. He looked up at the lighted windows and tried to picture them in there together. Home.

It was just a word, a concept, like *mother*. Sometimes he thought that somewhere in the farthest reaches of his memory, he could remember a smiling woman. Or maybe it was just wishful thinking that made the fading photograph of his mother come alive in his memory. He never had a mother, or a home. Just fat Paulita, who wanted him gone. Especially after what happened with Lynda.

I wan you out of here. I don wan you hangin' aroun my daughter, you hear me?

She's lying to you. She always has.

You don call Lynda a liar. You jus a disgustin', you know it? I don wan you aroun my place.

Your place? Hey, Pa, come on, tell her the facts of life, here. Tell her whose place this really is.

Now, Lee. I don't want you talking to Paulita that way.

How about the way she's talking to me?

Is the same every time he's comin' back here. Thinkin' he's mister big-important. Don like this, won eat that. I don wan him here. I won have him around.

You won't have? You don't want? What about me? This is my home too, you know.

You don live here no more. You don belong here.

Listen, son, maybe . . . Look, you're in college now. Maybe if you found a place of your own?

You telling me you don't want me here? My own father?

Go on, tell him. Tell him to leave us in peace.

Is that what you want? Is it, Pa?

What do you want from me? It's ... Paulita's right. Every time you come back, there's trouble. Arguments, fights.

Why don you go back to San Francisco an stay there? This isn your home no more. You hear? This isn your home no more.

He looked up at the lighted windows of the condominiums and smiled, remembering. Nor yours, either, you fat bitch.

An hour later he was back at the secret place. He looked at Barbara Gates lying stretched out on the bed, his eyes feasting on her naked body. Her white skin shone in the faint light coming in from the open door at the top of the stairway. She was beautiful. He had washed her carefully and combed her hair. He was glad now he hadn't cut it. It was a small enough reward. She had tried hard, much harder than any of the others. He sat down beside her and took her hand in his.

"Nearly time for you to be going, Barbara," he said.

He already had the place picked out. That would shake them up some. He smiled at the thought. But there was work to be done first. He slid his arm under her shoulders and lifted her up; her head lolled on his shoulder, the long dark hair falling over her face. He brushed it back gently. She was silent and still and beautiful, like a statue. He carried her to the big stainless steel caterer's draining board he'd installed next to the stone sink and laid her down. One arm lolled over the edge; he put it gently by her side. It was a pity that it had to end, he thought. Barbara had tried very hard. But it was never really the way he wanted it to be.

He padded naked across the cellar floor and took a scalpel from the stone jar he kept them in. He set the chemicals out, then opened the book he had got from the mail-order company in Washington State. When everything was ready, he set to work. He'd messed up at first but he had the hang of it now.

Barbara lay unmoving, her eyes wide as if in surprise. As he worked, he hummed his favorite lullaby to her.

> Hush little baby, don't say a word.
> Daddy's gonna buy you a mockingbird ...

18

THE BROADWICK TRIAL WAS IN ITS FOURTH DAY. MARTY BELker was examining a witness when the court telephone gave its muted ring. Harry Greenbaum, the bailiff, picked up the phone and listened, cupping his hand over the mouthpiece when he spoke. He scribbled something on a notepad, nodded, put down the receiver, and came across on silent feet to the prosecution table, putting a folded note in front of Kathryn. She opened it; Harry's writing was ornate and looped, with circles for full stops.

"Dave Granz called," she read. "Another note in code just turned up. It was addressed to you. It says there's a body at Cabrillo Park High School. He's going up there with Jack Burrows. If a hoax he'll call again. If not, wants to know can you get away lunchtime?"

Kathryn looked at the quartz clock above the courtroom doorway. Eleven-fifteen. It was a possibility, but not much more than that. She scribbled a note on her own pad, and signaled Greenbaum to come get it.

"Please call Granz. Tell him I'll get there if I can, but it won't be for an hour or so."

She watched Greenbaum go back and make the call, then redirected all her attention to picking up the thread of Belker's questions to the witness while a separate part of her brain puzzled over Dave Granz's call. What did the note mean? Why had the killer sent it to her this time? She forced herself to concentrate on what was going on in court. In here, they were arguing about a man's life. Whatever happened outside while she was in trial would just have to wait.

Half an hour later, she got an unexpected break. As Belker finished with his witness, and prior to Kathryn's cross, Judge Calhoun called a recess. He probably had a lunch date, Kathryn thought as she stacked up her files. She hurried out into the parking lot and got into the Mazda.

Cabrillo Park High School stood in a wooded ravine that lay between the southern perimeter of Cabrillo Park and the northern edge of Outlook Heights, a nice middle-class residential area on the northeast edge of town with well-kept houses, neat lawns, shaded gardens, shuttered windows. Kathryn pulled her car to a stop in front of the main building next to Granz's battered old Ford sedan. There were no green-and-whites, no uniforms in sight, but parked further along was a white KKSU panel truck with a satellite dish on its roof. So much for keeping things low key, she thought. She went inside and identified herself to the receptionist at the counter in the main hall.

"Oh, yes, Ms. Mackay, your colleagues are in the principal's office. Straight down the corridor, fourth on your right. I'll call and say you're on your way."

"Thank you," Kathryn said, and hurried along the hall. A cluster of male students were standing together, shooting the breeze. As she passed, one of them turned to his friends and said something inaudible. They laughed, looking at her. Some things never changed.

The principal's office was a high-ceilinged study with dark wood paneling and fitted bookshelves; tall windows that let in a lot of sun looked out across the quadrangle at the rear of the building. Grouped around a leather-topped antique desk were Dave Granz, Jack Burrows, and the principal, a tall, slim man in his mid-fifties. A large-scale map of the school grounds was spread out in front of them.

"You made good time," Granz said as she came in. "We only just got started here."

"Calhoun called an early recess," Kathryn said. "I have to be back by two."

"Kathryn, this is the principal, Dr. Ethan Jameson," Burrows said. He was a thickset man of about fifty who looked as if he worked out with weights. "Dr. Jameson, this is Kathryn Mackay, district attorney's office. She is in charge of the special investigation unit I told you about."

"I think I saw you on TV," Jameson said as they shook hands. "About a week ago?"

"Take a look," Granz said, sliding a sheet of paper across the desk toward her. She picked it up. The message printed on it read:

WMSJJ DGLB YLMRFCP YR
AYZPGJJM FGEF
FCP LYKC GQ
ZYPZYPY.
P=R

It was signed with the same little figure. Beneath that was the decoded version.

YOULL FIND ANOTHER AT
CABRILLO HIGH.
HER NAME IS
BARBARA.

"When did this arrive?" she asked Burrows.

"Don't know. It had been left in the mail slot at the downstairs reception desk in the County Building. It could have been put there anytime."

"You're sure it's our man?"

Dave Granz answered. "Looks like the same printing as before. This time the code was a little more difficult. But only a little."

"Original gone to Sacramento?"

"Sheriff's office sent it up by car with a deputy who'll hand-deliver to Jack Clayburgh." Clayburgh was head of latent fingerprinting at the Department of Justice there.

"You asked for priority." It wasn't a question.

"Yup. They'll get back to us as soon as they can. Oh, and it looks like someone tipped off Sanchez. There's a camera crew waiting outside in a van."

"I saw it," Kathryn said. "I'm sorry, Dr. Jameson. We wanted to do this quietly. I'm afraid there's not much chance of that now."

"Not your fault," Jameson said with a diffident shrug. "Nobody's fault." He glanced at his watch.

"The question is, where do we start?" Burrows said, glaring at the map as if he could scare it into telling him where to start looking. The campus covered something over ten acres altogether.

"I must say I still find it difficult to believe anyone would do a thing like this," Jameson said primly. "I mean, a body? In my school?"

"Shock value," Granz said. "The real question is, if he did, how did he do it without being seen?"

"Exactly," Jameson said. "There are"—he waved a hand in a vague gesture—"so many people about."

"How about at night?" Granz asked.

"All the school buildings are locked up at eight. There are alarms. No one could get in without the janitor knowing."

"Janitor?"

"I've sent for him. His name is Buchholz. The students . . . we call him, ah, Mr. Buck." There was a knock at the door. "I expect this is he now."

He went across and opened the door. A short, powerfully built man came into the room. He had a broad, flat-planed face with a bulging jawline, a flattened nose, and thick iron-gray hair. With his powerful forearms and big knuckles, he looked like a saloon bar brawler. He wore blue coveralls.

"You send for me?" he said to Jameson. His voice was guttural, accented. "What you want?"

"These . . . these gentlemen wish to talk to you, Mr. Buck," Jameson said. "They are from the police." Looks like I became invisible again, Kathryn thought resignedly. It was not a new experience.

"Mr. Buchholz, I'm Detective Jack Burrows, Sheriff's Department. This is Kathryn Mackay and Inspector Dave Granz from the district attorney's office."

"Police?" Buchholz said belligerently. He looked at Jameson. "Is some problem?"

"Mr. Buck's English is . . ." Jameson waved a hand. "If you'll allow me?"

Burrows nodded, go ahead.

"The, ah, detective believes . . . a body . . . that a body may have been concealed somewhere in the school," Jameson said. "He wants to ask you . . ." He let it trail off with another of his vague hand gestures. Buchholz's expression changed to one of astonishment.

"Body? You mean *dead* body?"

"We're investigating a possible homicide," Burrows said

patiently. "And we have reason to believe someone may have hidden the body somewhere in this school . . ."

Buchholz shook his head. "No. Is not possible."

"Why not?"

"I lock up every night, mister. Nobody can't get in after I lock up."

"You live on the premises?"

Buchholz nodded, jerked a thumb at the window.

"Mr. Buck has a small apartment in the basement of the main building," Jameson interpreted.

"So what you're saying is, no one could get in without you knowing?"

"Night time, no. Nobody."

"You said each building has a burglar alarm, sir?"

"We were experiencing a problem with vagrants," Jameson told them. "We had alarms fitted. Each one is linked to a central control panel in the main administration building."

"Are there any buildings which don't have alarms?" Kathryn asked the janitor. He looked surprised, as if he hadn't expected her to speak.

"Maintenance shed don't got no alarm," he said. "Pumping unit don't neither."

"Maintenance shed? Pumping unit? Are they on this map?" Burrows wanted to know.

"Back here," the janitor said, tapping the map with a stubby finger. "Here is north parking lot. Next to it, swimming pool. Behind, pumping unit. You know, mister. Makes the water hot. Keeps it clean."

"Filtration machinery?"

"Yah, yah." Buchholz nodded enthusiastically. "Keeps hot, filters water."

"Could anyone get into either of them without your knowledge?"

Buchholz shrugged. "It's possible."

"What do you keep in the maintenance shed?"

Buchholz clearly considered the question stupid. "Mowers," he said. "Brooms. Rakes. Shovels. Garden stuff."

"What about the filtration unit?" Kathryn asked. "How often do you go in there?"

Buchholz looked at Jameson and then at Burrows. "Is it okay she can ask questions?"

Burrows didn't say anything, just waited. The old man

shrugged, making no effort to hide his surprise at them letting a woman question him.

"How often I go in there? Once, maybe twice in the week. Lately not so much."

"Why not?"

Buchholz looked at Kathryn and shook his head, as one might do with someone being deliberately tiresome. "You remember we had an earthquake?" he said patiently. "You remember that, lady?"

"Sure," Kathryn said, refusing to let his attitude bother her any more than Jameson's had. "What about it?"

"After the earthquake there was a sub . . . subside?" He paused, looking at Jameson.

"A subsidence," the principal supplied.

"Yah, yah, subsidence. County Planning Department say is not safe."

"But that was well over two years ago."

He shrugged his heavy shoulders. "They still didn't fix. I told Dr. Jameson, yah?"

"He's quite right," Jameson confirmed. "We've complained to the County Planning Department half a dozen times. But with the budget cuts . . ." He moved a hand and sighed.

"They don't fix. So I don't go in no more than I got to," Buchholz said.

Kathryn looked at Granz. He knew what she was thinking.

"And when was the last time you were in there, Mr. Buchholz?" she asked.

Buchholz frowned. "Last week. Maybe ten days."

"I think maybe we better go take a look," Burrows said. Jameson sensed their tension.

"You think . . . ?" he said.

The detective shrugged. "Let's go find out."

"I'll come with you. In case . . ." Another movement of the hand.

"No," Granz said, firmly. "Mr. Buchholz here can show us the way. If there's anything to report, we'll get right back to you."

They hurried through the main school building, its hallways thronged with students changing classes. As they crossed the quad she heard her name called and saw Richard

Sanchez coming toward her. Behind him was a tall, bearded cameraman with a video camera on his shoulder.

"What's happening, you found something?" Sanchez demanded.

"Nothing yet," Kathryn told him.

"Where's everyone going?"

"We're on our way to check some outbuildings. Just stay clear till we tell you otherwise, please."

"The hell we will," Sanchez said. "Come on, Tom."

He and his cameraman followed Kathryn as she hurried after Granz, Burrows, and the janitor along a path that ran parallel to the front of the classrooms. A narrower, unpaved path ran around behind the low, flat building that housed the swimming-pool complex and led to a rundown area with knee-high clumps of weeds backed by cyclone fencing topped with barbed wire.

Standing adjacent to each other in the center of this area were two squat cinderblock buildings with heavy steel shutter doors. One had a sign that said PUMP AND FILTRATION UNIT. KEEP OUT. Buchholz unhooked a bunch of keys from his belt. They jangled noisily as he turned the lock.

"Get this, Tom," Sanchez said urgently, and Kathryn heard the whir of the videocamera as the heavy door swung back, making a hollow metallic sound as it hit the wall. Jack Burrows turned and saw Sanchez and the cameraman for the first time.

"What the . . . ?" He caught himself before he said anything else and looked at Kathryn. She shrugged.

"I did tell him, Jack," she said.

Burrows nodded. "Sorry, Mr. Sanchez," he said. "You'll have to stay back. This may be a crime scene. I can't allow you any closer."

"Sure, Detective," Sanchez said, holding up his hands palm out. "No problem."

The janitor reached for a switch; fluorescent lights flickered on overhead but did little to illuminate the interior. A short corridor opened into a rectangular, concrete-floored area. Beneath metal arches supporting a low roof, a maze of piping funneled down to huge pumps housed within metal cages. The filtration machinery throbbed and hummed. The air was stale and damp and smelled of chlorine. Buchholz went into a little office and came out carrying a flashlight.

"What's in back?" Granz asked him.

"Maintenance pit, workshop," Buchholz replied, leading the way. "It's dark back there."

They went about ten paces, then the janitor stopped, wrinkling his nose.

"Ach Gott!" he said. "What's stink like that?"

They could all smell it now: a sweet cloying pungency. Burrows grabbed the janitor's shoulder and pulled him back.

"Okay, Mr. Buchholz," he said tightly. "Here's what you do. Go back to the principal's office. Have him call the number on this card. Tell whoever answers we want a crime scene investigation unit up here, Code Three. Got that?"

"Crime scene investigation unit, Code Three," Buchholz said with a nod, breathing shallowly. He made a gesture toward the shadows. "Is it . . . ?"

"Just do what I asked you," Burrows told him. "And let me have that flashlight."

Buchholz handed over the flashlight and went out. Burrows looked grimly at Dave Granz and the two of them went forward together toward the unlit area at the rear of the building with Kathryn a few feet behind them. The big detective shone the light down into the inspection pit.

"Shit," Kathryn heard Granz say.

"Dave?" she asked.

"It's another one," he told her, biting off the words. "Young woman, nude."

Kathryn stepped forward. To one side stood a workbench with tools scattered on it. In the floor was an inspection pit, maybe six feet deep. At the bottom, lying on her back with arms and legs extended in an *X,* was the shining white body of a young woman.

"Looks like she's been carved up the same as the others," Granz observed. "Not much blood. Probably just dumped here."

"Look at that," Burrows said, aiming the flashlight beam down on the victim. The skin of the stomach showed the greenish-red patches that signaled the onset of decomposition. "What do you think, Dave?"

"Couple of days," Granz said.

As he spoke the words the area was suddenly bathed in bright light and they turned, startled, to see Richard Sanchez coming across the open area behind them, holding up a floodlight, the KKSU cameraman beside him filming. For a second they were immobile, like figures in a frieze, then Burrows erupted into action. He ran at Sanchez and the cameraman, batting the camera aside, pushing them back away from the inspection pit.

"Hey, watch out for the camera, Mac!" the cameraman said, retreating. "This is valuable equipment."

"Then get it out of here before I bend it over your fucking head!" Burrows stormed. "You hear me? You, too, Sanchez. Get the hell out of here, you goddamn creep!"

"Jack," Kathryn said, stepping to his side quickly and putting her hand on his forearm. Burrows clamped his mouth shut, but she could feel the angry tension in his body. Kathryn turned toward Sanchez, who was glaring defiantly at the detective.

"This is an official police crime scene, Mr. Sanchez," she told him crisply. "You'll have to leave immediately. And I'll want your shoes and both of you printed as soon as CSI gets here."

Sanchez shrugged and tapped the cameraman on the shoulder. "Let's take it outside, Tom," he said, and left without another word.

"Can you believe that guy?" Burrows said. He had control of himself again, but his voice was still rough with anger. "Can you believe it?"

"Forget that," Kathryn said, taking control without thinking about it. "Close this place down, Jack. Tape it off right here. Another perimeter outside. You know the routine. Nobody else in until CSI gets here. Make a note of what time we came in, where we stood, where everyone else stood. Send for Dr. Nelson or the deputy coroner. Dave, you notify Podnoretz. Let's get Walt Earheart up here, too."

Burrows moved back toward the inspection pit. He looked down at the naked body. His face was cold and angry.

"Bastard," he said softly. "You bastard."

Who did he mean? Kathryn wondered. The killer? Or Richard Sanchez?

19

THE CORRIDOR OUTSIDE HIS CLASSROOM WAS CROWDED, knots of students clustered together, talking heads down.

"What's all the fuss?" he asked one of them.

"It's another one, sir," someone said. "Another girl murdered."

They found her, then. That was fast.

"Do they know who it is?"

"Don't know, sir."

The classrooms were housed in a long, four-story brick building with casement windows and wide stairs leading up to multiple glass door banks. He went along the corridor and out into the quadrangle at the rear of the main school building. It was bordered on its other three sides by the assembly hall, the theater, and the main administration building facing west on Cabrillo Parkway. He could see the flashing strobe lights of the police cars over by the swimming pool building.

By the time he walked over there, the coroner's deputies and the white crime scene truck had arrived. A big, bulky man in a dark gray lightweight suit who he recognized as Lieutenant Walt Earheart was watching four deputies ringing off the area with yellow police crime scene tape and keeping the milling crowd of curious students at bay.

And there was Kathryn Mackay, standing by the entrance to the maintenance facility building. Hello, Kathryn, he thought. Some men were donning zippered white paper coveralls, protective masks, overshoes, and latex gloves prior to entering the filtration unit. Crime scene investigation team, he thought, maintaining the integrity of the crime scene. Protective clothing to make sure they don't contaminate the area with their own hairs or fibers from their clothes, a deputy at the door logging the names of everyone who enters the scene in case their fingerprints or shoe tracks are needed later to exclude a suspect print near the body. It won't get you anywhere, boys.

He saw Richard Sanchez going over to talk to Kathryn Mackay and edged closer, trying to hear what they were saying. One of the deputies put a hand on his chest.

"Stay back, please. There's nothing to see. Just stay back, please."

Whatever Sanchez was saying, it was making Kathryn Mackay mad. He saw Sanchez stretch out his arms wide.

"Shoot me, shoot me," Sanchez said. "I did what I get paid to do."

As he spoke, another car came to a rocking stop at the taped perimeter. Three men got out. One of them lifted a hand in greeting to Kathryn Mackay, and went inside. Two other men followed him; one of them carried a video camera. They looked expectantly at Earheart, who had just emerged from the building.

"What we got, Lieutenant?" the one with the camera asked.

"Young woman," Earheart told him. "Get yourselves some face masks, it's not pleasant in there."

"When was it ever?" the man said. The second one picked up his bag and followed him into the building. Earheart looked around, saw Sanchez for the first time.

"Mr. Sanchez," he said. "You mind keeping your people on the other side of the tape?"

"I just need thirty seconds for this shot, Lieutenant," Sanchez said, ignoring the injunction. "We ready, Pete?"

"On five," the unit manager said. "Okay, nine, eight, seven, six . . ."

"Good afternoon," Sanchez said into the camera as the lights came on. "This is Richard Sanchez, at Cabrillo Park High School, Santa Rita. *Here and Now,* a dramatic new development in the macabre murders that have brought anger and outrage into every home in the county. More on that story after this."

How bizarre, Lee thought, as Sanchez turned away from the camera, to watch a man smiling and talking to an electronic box with such sincerity and conviction, as though it were another human being.

"Steve?" Sanchez asked.

A man hunched over a monitor listened, eyes lifted heavenward, then took off his cans and nodded, giving a thumbs-up signal to indicate the take was okay. Sanchez turned toward Earheart.

"Lieutenant?" he said. "How about giving us a sound bite on this?"

You had to admire him, if only for the balls, Lee thought.

"Sorry, Mr. Sanchez," the detective said, clearly trying to be polite. "There'll be an official statement later. I can't give you anything now."

Sanchez was about to reply when someone yelled his name. The body trolley was being brought out by the coroner's deputies. It looked like some strange form of beetle on wheels. Lee was surprised to see how the crowd had grown; it looked like the press was arriving in force.

Sanchez hurried away. The cameraman hoisted his camera to his shoulder and the sound engineer moved off after him, poking his mike forward to pick up anything that might be useful later. Someone up on the TV truck swiveled the lights to cover the scene as the body trolley was loaded into the coroner's van. Lee could hear the mechanical chatter of camera power drives and see the bright stars of flashbulbs as the van took off. After a few minutes, he saw Sanchez coming back. The other reporters were still milling around near the doorway of the filtration unit. They were all like Sanchez, he thought. All waiting for an angle, something, anything. Great story over here, boys, he thought. If only you knew.

The crowd was beginning to disperse. He wanted to stay, but he didn't want to draw attention to himself. A group of students was clustered around the TV crew. He eased over toward them.

"Hello, Mr. Russell," one of the girls said. He recognized her. Diana? Dana. Dana Kinsley. "Isn't this awful?"

"I still don't know for sure what's going on," he said. "Some girl murdered, or something."

The girl ignored him, turning to watch as the unit manager, Peterson, shouted orders at the crew, and the lights were swung into place. Kathryn Mackay followed Sanchez into the bright pool of artificial sunshine, standing where the unit manager indicated she should. Lee watched Sanchez position himself in front of the camera. His whole demeanor was different. He looked relaxed, almost uninvolved. Only his eyes betrayed the inner tension.

"I'm Richard Sanchez. We're back at Cabrillo Park High School here in Santa Rita," he said. "Let's move right away to the sensational new development in the series of murders that have rocked this small central California county. About half an hour ago, the body of a young woman was found here, in the maintenance facility you can see behind me. All that we know about her is her name was Barbara. It was her body you just saw being speeded away for forensic examination."

He turned to face Kathryn Mackay. She looked tense, Lee thought. He tried to get closer so he would hear her better.

"With me now is Assistant District Attorney Kathryn Mackay. Ms. Mackay, what can you tell us about the victim?"

"I can't add much to what you've already said. The victim is a young woman aged between eighteen and twenty-one with long dark brown hair and brown eyes. She is five feet seven inches tall—"

"Hispanic?"

"Yes."

"And how was she killed?"

"Preliminary findings indicate manual strangulation. Without a full autopsy we can't be sure."

"Was the body found here today mutilated?"

"Yes."

"In the same way as the others?"

"We can't know that for sure until an autopsy has been conducted."

"Gross physical mutilation of the genital area, I believe the phrase was, Ms. Mackay. Isn't that what happened here?"

"I can't comment on that."

"But you don't deny it?"

"I neither deny it nor confirm it," Kathryn Mackay said. She's angry, Lee thought, and trying not to show it. "And until the pathologist has completed his examination, neither will anyone else."

Sanchez turned away from her toward the camera.

"That was Santa Rita Deputy DA Kathryn Mackay. From other sources we understand the young woman found here today was indeed mutilated in exactly the same way as the earlier victims found on Shelter Island and in Sedgewick

Park. She is undoubtedly the latest victim of the vicious serial killer who is stalking the streets of Santa Rita. Richard Sanchez, *Here and Now*, Cabrillo Park High School."

He stared at the camera, holding the frank, caring expression until the cameraman stopped filming. Then he took a deep breath and let it out in a long exhalation. He seemed surprised to find Kathryn still there. Completely engrossed in watching, Lee did not even notice that the students had dispersed until the bulky figure of a deputy sheriff materialized at his shoulder.

"All right, buddy, move along, there's nothing more to see here," the deputy told him. "On your way."

"It's all right, Deputy, I work here at the school," he said.

"Sorry, sir," the deputy said, plainly unapologetic. "You still have to leave. This area is off limits."

"Of course," Lee said. He could see Earheart and Sanchez glowering at each other and wished he could hear what they were saying. As he walked away, the technicians doused the lights and Sanchez waved the KKSU station wagon over. It overtook Lee as he crossed the quadrangle toward the main administration building. He could see Sanchez in the passenger seat, his face tense. Lee smiled.

All in good time, *cholo*, he thought. All in good time.

Dave Granz let Jack Burrows take his car and bummed a ride back to town with Kathryn. He sat preoccupied as she threaded the Mazda through the busy lunchtime traffic, and didn't speak until they got into the parking lot outside the County Building.

"You want something to eat?" he asked. Kathryn shook her head. "Listen, walk down to the cafeteria with me anyway."

They went down into the basement. Obsolete computer terminals waiting for pickup were stacked along the walls. Outside the parking citation window, six or seven people were already in line waiting for it to open at two. Granz got some black coffee and a chocolate chip cookie. They sat at a table under the pop art mural of Santa Rita.

"I've been thinking," Dave said. "About you and Sanchez."

"There is no me and Sanchez, Dave. That guy is . . . I

don't know the right word. It's like he has no moral conscience."

"They have to have it removed, like a lobotomy," Dave said. "Or they can't work in TV. No, what I meant was, there's a kind of respect thing going on there. You have an identity with him."

"You didn't see the interview," she said.

"Hear me out," Dave said. "I got talking to that unit manager, Peterson, up at the school. I told him I'd fix it so when CSI gets through he can get some shots of the crime scene. He got real friendly, told me a lot of stuff about how Sanchez claims he's going to ride this case all the way to a network show."

"So what? We can't stop him."

"I don't want to stop him. I want him to think we're on his side."

"Are you out of your mind?"

"Oh, come on, Kathryn, you know I'm not really suggesting you sell out to the bastard. But he wouldn't know that. If he thought he had you in his pocket, we could feed him all sorts of disinformation. Maybe get this psycho out there to make some kind of mistake."

"Sanchez is greedy but he's not a fool. He'd know in a flash if we were blowing smoke. Don't forget, he's probably got other sources in the Sheriff's Department. Maybe even in the DA's office for all I know."

"There has to be some way to get a line on this damn killer. Make him do something, anything, that would give us a lead on him."

"I wish there was, too, Dave. But we're not going to get to him by using Sanchez. Even if we could, I don't want to go down that road."

"I guess you're right. I just wish we could give the bastard some of his own medicine."

"Our day will come," Kathryn said.

"I'll hang on to that thought." Dave grinned. "You doing anything later?"

"Early night."

"How about if I came by? We could talk."

"What about?"

Dave hesitated for a moment, then shrugged. "Things," he said. "In general."

"Why not?"

"Your enthusiasm is overwhelming," Dave said, touching the end of her nose. "Eight o'clock suit you?"

"Make it eight-thirty," she said.

She ran up the stairs and through the length of the building, and got into Superior Two just as Harry Greenbaum came in with the jury.

Tiger stripes of late evening sunlight coming through the dusty venetian blinds slatted the worn carpet. He sat in the darkening den thinking about Barbara. He visualized her lying on the bed, her body a white *X* in the semidarkness, the terror always in her eyes. He tilted his recliner back and closed his eyes. *He untied her hands and feet and she wound her arms around his neck, her mouth close to his. Her body was hot.*

"Tell me what you want," she whispered.

Lust pulsed in his groin as he got up, went over to the desk, and unlocked the center drawer. He took out the panties he had cut off her body. They still smelled of her. He buried his face in them.

"Hurry," she whispered.

Clumsily, urgently, he unfastened his pants and with his face still buried in the remnants of the panties, he masturbated. He reached orgasm quickly. When it was over he wiped himself with the crumpled scraps of underwear and tossed them back into the desk drawer, his mind spinning back over the years, all the years ...

And he was in his room, just back from the beach. He'd gotten a tan and he wanted to see how he looked. He was standing in front of the mirror in his shorts when Lynda came in. Lynda.

Hola, hermano, she said. Wha you doin'?

Nothing, he said. Nothing. His voice stuck in his throat. She was wearing a short slip. Nothing else. His ears felt hot.

"Anyone ever tell you you got a nice body?" She put her hand on his back. "You hot, *cholo?*"

"Uh ... I ..." He couldn't speak. All he was conscious of was a pounding in his head that seemed to stifle all other sound. She slid her hand around in front, caressing, stroking his hard belly. He felt her fingers edge inside the elastic of his shorts.

"You like thees, donyou?"

She pressed herself against him, and he could feel the hot dampness of her body down the back of his own, the soft roundness of her belly against his buttocks. Her fingers moved lower, circling, stroking, twining into the hair in his groin. When she took hold of him, he groaned, unable to move, his entire body shivering. She moved her hand up, down, very very slowly.

"Nice, eh, *cholo?*" she whispered. "Listen, you wanna do it with me?"

"Oh, Jesus yes, yes!" he said, turning as she peeled the shorts down around his hips. He tried clumsily to kiss her but she avoided his mouth, stepping back. He stood, foolishly erect, in front of her.

And then she laughed. Pointing at him. *There.*

"Look at you! You know how estupid you lookin'?" She laughed. "You really t'ink I wanna do it with *you,* hey, you really t'ink I let you anywhere *near* me? You t'ink I'm innerest in that thing? I seen ababies with bigger dicks. I seen ashrimps bigger than that! You *pathetic,* you know that? Pathetic!"

Don't think of her. Think of Barbara. She had been the best one yet. Somewhere a police siren wailed, and he tensed. Then he smiled. No way, he thought. That knownothing sheriff who'd been on the Sanchez show? IQ of a boiled potato. Those dumbass pseudo-experts? Forget it. He knew more about psychology than they would if they lived to be ninety, and they'd already demonstrated that they couldn't find their asses at high noon using a concave mirror. Kathryn Mackay had called him stupid. Wimp. All those other names. She didn't know how dangerous it was to make him angry. She better not be so smart-mouthed. She better just not.

He looked at his watch. Time for the news. He switched on the TV. The screen flickered in the semidarkness. He watched without interest as Steve Brace and Jane Brondini went through their nightly routine, waiting for them to get to the local items.

"Today in Santa Rita, a shocking development in the serial murder case baffling law enforcement there," Jane Brondini said. "Taking us through it, Richard Sanchez."

Her words were swallowed by the spuriously urgent title

music that introduced Sanchez. This was it, this was what he had been waiting for. He put the can of beer down on the floor and leaned forward with his arms resting on his thighs. They were at Cabrillo Park High. Sending Sanchez the note had been an inspiration. He had reacted exactly as expected. Very good, *cholo,* he thought.

". . . dramatic new development in the macabre murder mystery that has brought anger and outrage into every home in the city," Sanchez was saying. "More on that story after this."

A fat man in a polyester suit filled the screen yammering about great cars, easy terms, generous trade-ins. Come see me, he said, sweating like a pig in a sauna, Dan, Dan, the Nissan man.

"Fucking station breaks," Lee hissed at the TV. "Get off, you fat faggot!"

The intro music swelled and faded again and Sanchez filled the screen, OB lights putting a yellow tinge on his skin. "I'm Richard Sanchez," he said. "We're back at Cabrillo Park High School here in Santa Rita. Let's move right away to the sensational new development in the series of murders that have rocked this small central California county . . ."

In the darkened room he watched the hand-held camera pictures of the coroner's team trundling the body trolley to the van as Sanchez's voice-over told the story of its discovery. The watcher smiled. Good-bye, Barbara. He wondered if they'd notice the hair. They were all such dumbasses, probably not. Next time he would have a little more fun, make it a little more difficult for them.

"With me now is Assistant District Attorney Kathryn Mackay," Sanchez said. "Ms. Mackay, what can you tell us about the victim?"

Hello, bitch. Lee watched closely as she answered Sanchez's questions. She looked slightly defensive. On guard, he thought. She doesn't trust Sanchez. Smart cookie.

"Was the body found here today mutilated?"

"Yes."

"In the same way as the others?"

"We won't know until an autopsy has been conducted."

"Gross physical mutilation of the genital area, I believe the phrase was, Ms. Mackay. Isn't that what happened here?" Sanchez's voice was harsh, hectoring. Lee smiled again. *Make the bitch sweat, cholo.*

"I can't comment on that." She was angry now. *Got you on the run, too, Kathryn,* Lee thought. After a couple more questions, Sanchez shut down the interview and turned to the camera.

". . . she is undoubtedly the latest victim of the vicious serial killer who is stalking the streets of Santa Rita. Stay tuned for more, after this."

Bravo, cholo, Lee thought, *that's exactly right. Stay tuned for more.* He picked up the can of beer and drank what was left in it.

20

"ALL RIGHT, MAC," HAL BENTON SAID BRISKLY. "LET'S GET started."

The hum of conversation faded away as everyone present took their places. Following the third murder, Benton had inaugurated daily meetings so that he was kept constantly in touch with developments. Held during lunch hour in whichever room was vacant, today's was in the conference room. Benton was in his usual place at the head of the table, with Mac on his right and Norm Podnoretz opposite.

"We're going to be pushed for time," McCaskill said. "Walt, you want to bring us up to speed on the Cabrillo Park murder?"

"We got a positive ID within a couple of hours of releasing the artist's sketch," Earheart said. "The victim's name was Barbara Gates. She was nineteen. Studying at UCSR."

The University of California at Santa Rita was a beautiful tree-sheltered enclave northwest of town in University Heights, a name locals shortened to The Heights.

"How come she hadn't been reported missing?" McCaskill wanted to know.

"Damnedest thing," Dave Granz interposed. "She lived at home in Alameda Heights with her parents. They were on a two-week cruise to Antigua, didn't get back till last night. Barbara wasn't home, her bed hadn't been slept in. The dog had shit all over the house. They were about to call the Sheriff's Department to report her missing when her father saw the sketch in the paper."

"They been interviewed?"

Dave nodded. "I went up there with Jack Burrows. The father's a marketing executive with Olympus Foods in Catalina, mother's Hispanic, works part time as a nurse at County Hospital. They cooperated all the way down the line, gave us anything we wanted. We've got the kid's diaries, letters, yearbooks, photo albums, everything. Jack's working on them right now, that's why he's not here."

"What about boyfriends?" McCaskill asked.

"Just one. Guy named Ted Baker, student at The Heights, lives in the same neighborhood. We talked to him. He said they'd been going together nearly six months, but they broke up about three weeks ago."

"Anything there?"

"Naa, no big deal, they're just kids."

"So were Leopold and Loeb," Benton grunted.

Granz grinned. "Baker hadn't seen Barbara since the breakup. Said he'd tried calling her a few times in the last two weeks and left messages, but when he got no reply, he figured she just didn't want to talk to him."

"Why'd they split?"

"Her idea. He wanted to get engaged, but she didn't want to be tied down till she was out of college."

"It could still be a motive. Did we check him out, Walt?"

"Of course," Earheart replied, a shade impatiently. "He couldn't do enough to help. Volunteered to take a poly, agreed to be printed and to give a blood sample. We'll set up the poly anyway, but ..." He stopped, shrugged dismissively. Clearly, Baker was no suspect in his book.

"What about family, friends, teachers, neighbors?" McCaskill asked.

"Jesus, Mac, we're doing our best. You know what our caseload is like. I'm stretched to the limit at the moment."

"Give me an update on what you've got, anyway," Benton said.

"Okay, you know the scenario. It looks as if the girl was killed someplace else and dumped at the school. The rest is pretty much the same as before. Nothing at the crime scene.

Almost certainly the same killer—there are a lot of similarities. Coded note, small incision in the thigh, mutilation of the genital area. Doc Nelson says it's practically impossible to estimate time of death."

"What, again?" Benton said angrily.

"Yes, again," Kathryn said. "He said he'll guess if you want him to, but it wouldn't mean much. All we know for sure is Buchholz, the janitor, hadn't been inside the building since Monday, June twenty-fourth."

"So suppose the killer snatched the girl sometime in the first week her parents were away, say about ten days ago," Granz hypothesized. "He could have killed her anytime in the intervening period, kept her body someplace until he was ready to dump it."

"Kept her someplace?" McCaskill leaned forward, frowning. "In what, a freezer?"

"Not a freezer," Kathryn interjected. "I asked Doc about that. He says freezing creates tissue changes a pathologist would spot in a second."

"That's not something everyone knows. Maybe this guy's some kind of refrigeration technician?"

"Not necessarily," Podnoretz said patiently. "He could go down to the library and find out all this stuff in five minutes. You can keep a dead body in almost perfect condition for quite some time, providing the temperature remains constant somewhere between thirty-two and forty degrees. Decomposition only begins when the corpse is exposed to ambient temperatures."

"And that's what the killer's doing?" Benton asked. "He's keeping the body in a cool facility somewhere?"

"We don't know, Hal," Granz said wearily. "It's possible. If he had a well-insulated room, if he kept the air-conditioning really high . . . it's possible. Maybe he dumped her up at the school over the Fourth of July holiday. Then again, maybe he just killed the girl Friday night, took her up there right away. On the physical evidence alone, that's possible, too. No way Nelson can tell which."

"I still like the idea of him being a technician of some sort. Isn't there some way we can check this cool facility thing out? What about meat-packing plants, vegetable storage depots?"

"Give us a break, Hal," Earheart said. "There must be a

couple of hundred places like that down in Catalina alone. Not to mention the rest of the county. We just don't have the people."

"You said Catalina, that puts a thought in my mind," Podnoretz said. "Most of the people who work in those produce storage places are Hispanic. We've got Hispanic victims. Are we looking at a Hispanic killer here?"

"It's a distinct possibility."

"Okay, let's pursue that. Male Hispanic, working in the Catalina area, may be some kind of technician, unlimited access to some kind of storage facility—"

"It would have to be one that isn't used much," Kathryn said. "This guy needs privacy. He can't have anyone walking in on him."

"Okay, okay, it's just a thought," Benton said impatiently. "Anything else?"

"We got latent prints and shoe tracks," Dave told him. "It'll take time to get elimination prints. Frankly, I seriously doubt this killer was dumb enough to leave any. The body was naked, so we haven't got any clothing to examine. No blood, no semen, no drag marks. Nelson says the body was washed, same bath soap as before." Granz glanced at his notes. "Exterior of crime scene: no tire tracks or shoe tracks; the service roads are all hardtop. We got some tracks in soft ground in front of the filtration unit. They might be from bicycle tires, or they might just have been made by a wheelchair."

"He rolled her body in there in a wheelchair?"

"It's a possibility we're examining. Might explain how he got her in without being noticed."

"And without leaving drag marks," Podnoretz said.

"Dave, what else?"

"I want to talk to the girl's parents again," Dave said. "I'll interview school friends, teachers, relatives, as soon as I can get around to it. Maybe Kathryn can work up a victim profile."

Benton looked directly at Kathryn. "How about that, Kathryn? You want to try, or do you think we ought to call in your profiler friend from Sacramento, see if he can help us with this?"

"What can he give us that Kathryn can't?" Granz asked.

"Oh, come on, Dave, this guy's a specialist."

"So was the guy who designed the *Titanic*," Dave said stubbornly. "All you get from specialists is theories. What we need here are some answers. And in this case the answers are on the street, out there where it happened."

"Kathryn?"

She went for the diplomatic reply. "Without more information, I don't know what else Giordano could do. But if you think it might be worth trying, let's give it a shot."

"I'll discuss it with you later," Benton said. "Before we move on, I want to spend a few minutes on Richard Sanchez. I imagine most of you saw the interview he did with Jake Gylam and Kathryn. Last night he did a number on us from the crime scene. The guy is making us look bad. I don't like that. Someone is feeding him information, and I want to know who. I want to know as a matter of priority."

"Hell, there are a couple of hundred people working for law enforcement," Pete Avery, one of the inspectors, said. "It could be any of them. Or maybe even more than one."

"Look, I don't care if it turns out to be the Mormon Tabernacle Choir. We've got a leak and I want it plugged," Benton said.

"Listen, Hal, there is something," Mac said. He looked at Kathryn as he spoke. "I don't know whether to bring it up or not."

"What, what?" Benton said irritably.

"Greta Brotherton came to me before the meeting. She said she knew who was leaking information to Sanchez."

Greta Brotherton was a member of the misdemeanor trials team. A tall blonde in her mid-thirties, separated from her husband, she wasn't so much beautiful as striking, with high cheekbones and pale blue eyes that seemed to say, Come on, baby, light my fire. At one time or another most of the single guys upstairs in the SO had tried to date her, and even one or two of the married ones. She never quite said yes and she never quite said no. The boys called her the Ice Maiden. And one or two other names.

Benton sat up. "Who?"

"Kathryn."

Kathryn felt her face stiffen at the unexpected accusation. "What did you say?" she snapped.

"I know, I know," Mac said, holding up his hands palm out. "But that's what she said."

"Get her in here," Kathryn said angrily. "I want her to say this to my face."

"No need for that, Kathryn," Mac said. "Just tell us it isn't true and that'll be the end of it."

"First tell me exactly what she said."

"She said Sanchez offered you a sweetheart deal. You give him inside information, he gets you on all the talk shows. So you'll look good when you run for DA."

Kathryn looked at Hal Benton. He was watching her.

"Who told her that?" she asked Mac.

"You're not going to deny it?"

"No, I'm not," Kathryn said, keeping a tight rein on her temper. "Sanchez invited me to lunch. Hal, you knew about it. And he tried to talk me into doing a deal, giving him information. I turned him down flat."

"According to Greta, you told him you'd think it over."

"You know, I never thought I'd say this about another woman," Kathryn replied flatly. "But Greta Brotherton is one dumb blonde."

Benton cut in. "I don't think we need waste any more time on this, Mac. Kathryn's told us she turned Sanchez down, that's it as far as I'm concerned. Greta's way off base. Whoever Sanchez's informant is, it isn't Kathryn."

"She said she heard it, she thought we ought to know," Mac said.

"And no hard feelings, right?" Kathryn said.

"I want you to drop this, Kathryn," Benton said. "I'll talk to Greta. Understand?"

She drew in a deep breath and let it slowly out.

"Whatever you say, Hal," she said, although she was still mad clear through. Why would someone you'd worked with for years suddenly come out with something like that? Why was Greta Brotherton trying to make trouble for her? What on earth had gotten into the woman? She looked at Granz. He smiled uncomfortably and lifted a shoulder: search me.

"Are we through here, Mac?" Benton said.

"That's it, I think. Unless anyone's got anything else?"

On that sour note they returned to their respective duties. Back at her desk, Kathryn attacked her paperwork, trying to keep herself from thinking about what had happened. But no matter how hard she tried, she couldn't put Greta's spiteful accusation out of her mind. Outside it began to rain. You couldn't rely on anything anymore.

The Gates house was a newly remodeled three-bedroom, two-and-a-half-bath contemporary. It stood on a large lot in a quiet street in Alameda Heights, a middle-income residential area scattered along both sides of a broad valley down which, perhaps a hundred years earlier, the Rio Espanola had run.

"I hate to bother you again, Mr. Gates," Dave Granz said.

"It's no bother," Gates said. "We want to help. Anything. Come in, come in."

He was a burly man of about forty-five, who looked like he might have been a football player at college.

"My partner is going through the papers you gave us, Mr. Gates," Dave said. "I wondered if . . . would it be possible for me to see Barbara's room?"

"It's still just the way she left it," Gates said. "Through here."

The house was tastefully furnished. Granz knew Josefita Gates was originally from Cuba, but there was nothing about the place that said Hispanic except maybe the *ristra* of chiles hanging on the wall.

Charles Gates led the way upstairs to a bedroom door, opened it. A neat, square, airy room, predominantly pink. The window looked out on a neat, sloping yard with shrubs and flowers; between the roofs of the houses below Granz caught a glimpse of the ocean.

"You have a nice garden," he said.

"Jo does most of the work," Gates said. "Barbara used to . . . help her." He made an apologetic gesture. Behind the rimless eyeglasses his pale blue eyes looked close to tears. Granz looked around the room. The furniture, wallpaper, even the bedspread, were in complementary shades of pink. A full-size drawing board stood by the window, half a dozen glass jars jammed full of brushes, pencils, marker pens on the window ledge. On the wall above the headboard of the bed was a small crucifix. There were paperbacks on a bedside shelf: Gabriel García Marquez, Carrie Fisher, a thesaurus, *The Secret Diary of Laura Palmer*. A Toshiba portable TV and a Panasonic CD player and a row of discs: Madonna,

Julio Iglesias, George Michael, Gloria Estefan. A poster behind the door: Bogart and Bergman in *Casablanca*.

"Shall I stay?" Gates asked.

Granz shook his head. "I'll call you if I need anything," he replied. Gates nodded and went out, closing the door behind him. Tucked into the frame of the dressing-table mirror were half a dozen curling Polaroids, the colors of some of them starting to fade. Barbara in a red swimsuit on a beach someplace, laughing. A group of girls at a party. Barbara shaking hands with Donald Duck at Disneyland. A young man in T-shirt and blue jeans: Ted Baker, the boyfriend. If I'd had a daughter, he thought, this is how she would have been.

One by one, he opened her bottles and boxes, checking each. Barbara's clothes were still in the drawers of the dresser; a faint trace of her perfume came off them, startling him. Working methodically he checked every item of clothing in each of the drawers, then the pockets and seams of every blouse, jacket, dress, and pair of jeans in the closet. One by one he opened shoe boxes, taking out the shoes and feeling inside each. He riffled through the pages of each of the paperbacks on her shelf, holding them by the spine and shaking them to dislodge anything that might be filed inside. He opened and looked inside each of the CD boxes. He unpinned the poster and looked behind it. He lifted the mattress of the bed and checked beneath it, then the edges of the carpet. Nothing. He hadn't really expected anything else. Barbara Gates had no dark secrets.

He sat on the bed and looked at the poster. You must remember this, a kiss is still a kiss. Unexpectedly, his eyes misted with tears. He shook his head angrily. *No*, he thought. *No damned tears.* He had done this a thousand times; it had never got inside him before. You steeled yourself so it wouldn't. You couldn't function objectively. And yet in spite of himself, anger coursed through him like electricity. He opened the door and went back to the living room. Charles Gates was standing by the patio door, looking out at nothing in particular. He turned as he heard Granz come in.

"Finished?" he said.

"Thank you," Granz said. "Is Mrs. Gates out?"

"She's making some coffee."

"There are some photographs. I brought them down. I wondered if you could identify the people in them."

"She wanted to be a teacher, you know," Gates said. "She was studying art. Graphic design."

"I saw the drawing board. She enjoyed school?"

"She's . . . she had lots of friends. Lots. Didn't she, Jo?"

Josefita Gates came in carrying a tray. She looked like an older version of the girl in the photographs. She was not tall—few Hispanic women were—but she was slender and carried herself well. She had on a linen-and-cotton-blend dress with random diagonal stripes. Her hair was long and black and looked as if it was naturally wavy. Her eyes were dark and sad.

"They were round all the time. Such a happy crowd. Boys, girls. Havin' fun. Ay, the noise they made."

She glanced around the silent room, as if comparing it now with when it had been full of her daughter's friends.

"You have other children," Granz said, watching her pour the coffee.

"Two," Charles Gates said. "Paul's married, lives in Bakersfield. Anita is away at college, Berkeley. She's studying anthropology." He said it as if he still could not altogether believe it.

"They wanted to come home, but we tol' them no, wait," his wife said. "Please, sit down, Mr. Granz. You like cream, sugar?"

"Black is fine, thank you," Granz said. Wait, she had said. Wait until they let us have your sister, our daughter back, wait until we can give her love's last sad gift of all, her funeral.

"The photographs?" he prompted.

Charles Gates took them from him. His wife sat on the arm of the chair and looked over his shoulder.

"This one was taken on her birthday," he said. "Right here in the house. Let's see. That's Mary-Beth Forgan, she lives right across the street. Next to her is . . . what's her name, Jo? The nice little girl from Laguna del Mar, father works for the city?"

"Margarita Lopez," his wife supplied. "Jaime's in the controller's office."

"Right, right." Gates nodded. "The one on Barbara's left is Susanna Portola."

"You have addresses on all these girls, sir?" Granz asked, writing the names down.

"They'll all be in Barbara's address book," Gates said. "I already gave it to you. Susanna lives in Alameda. And the one on the far left, that's, oh, the funny kid who plays tennis, what's her name, something-mann?"

"Waldemann," his wife said. "Irene Waldemann."

"Thank you, ma'am," Granz said. "I'm sorry to have to ask you to do this."

"No, don't be sorry," she said. "We will do anything to help you find whoever . . . whoever did . . ."

Charles Gates got up and put his arm around her. She didn't look at him.

"Anything," she said again. "Anything."

Granz sat and talked with them for perhaps half an hour, encouraging them to tell him about their daughter and her friends; there was always a chance one of his questions would trigger a recollection that might be helpful.

"Even now, I hear a car door slam, I look up, I think, she's home," Josefita Gates said. "And then I remember. It's . . . I still can't really believe she's . . . gone."

"Have you any idea where she went to meet her friends?"

"Their homes, usually," Gates said. "Or they came here."

"What about public places? Did she go to the beach? Over to the park?" Cabrillo Park was just a quarter mile away.

"Sure, I guess so, but pretty nearly always with the other kids," Gates said. "She played tennis a lot."

"She might have gone to the mall," the woman said. "She liked to look around in Robinson's. An' the bookstore."

"Would that be the Linda Vista Mall?" Granz asked.

"She goes . . . she used to go to that espresso place. So she could look at the books."

"You mean alone?"

Gates frowned. "Is that important?"

"She would have had to be alone, sir."

"She knew not to talk to strangers," Gates said. "She knew that."

"We think this guy probably looks pretty harmless," Granz said. "They're good at that."

There was a little silence. When she spoke into it, Josefita Gates's voice was a haunted monotone. "Why . . . how could anyone do somethin' like that? She never hurt anyone in her whole . . ."

Tears ran suddenly down her face. She turned blindly and laid her head against Granz's chest, making no sound. He put his arms awkwardly around her shoulders and held her. He looked over her head at Charles Gates and he saw the pain and loss in the man's eyes.

"I'm sorry," Josefita Gates said, stepping back and knuckling away her tears. "I just . . ."

She turned her face away and looked out at her garden, and Granz felt anger surge through him again. This time he made no attempt to control it. He knew it wasn't smart to get personally involved, but the sight of Charles Gates's stricken eyes, the woman weeping silently by the window, and the photograph of Barbara shaking hands with Donald Duck conspired to make it impossible to remain uncommitted. Maybe I want it to be personal this time, he thought. Maybe I need it to be personal.

"I'd better be on my way," he said. "Is there anything you need?"

Charles Gates looked at his wife, then shook his head. "You must have a lot to do," he said dully. "We'll be all right."

"Thank you for the coffee, Mrs. Gates."

"De nada," she said automatically.

Normalcy was their refuge from the agony. Go to work, mow the lawn, pay the bills; vacuum the carpets, cook supper. Just get through the day, then the next, then another. Most of all, don't think. Don't think about what was. Don't ever think of what might have been. You bastard, he thought. You have no right to cause such pain.

"We'll get him, Mrs. Gates," he said. "That's a promise."

She stayed at the front door; Charles Gates walked out to Granz's car with him.

"Listen," he said, his voice low-pitched. "Do something for me: when you catch this bastard, shoot him in the balls. And don't call an ambulance. Let him fucking bleed to death."

Granz glanced at the woman standing in the doorway, a hand shading her tear-filled eyes, and then back at Charles Gates's bitter face.

"I work with a lot of innocent victims, Mr. Gates," he

said, "and it's nearly always the same. They want whoever hurt them to be hurt the same way. But it's got to be done according to the law. That's how you know us from the bad guys: we have rules and they don't."

"Fuck the rules," Gates said harshly. "You find him, kill him. That way the goddamned shrinks won't be able to hand the judge a sob story and get the bastard off."

Granz put the car in gear; as he drove away, he could see Gates standing on the sidewalk staring after him.

"You know what, Charlie?" he said to the mirror. "That's not such a bad idea."

21

"THIS IS JAYNE KELLERMAN," THE VOICE ON THE PHONE ANnounced. "Is that you, Kathryn?"

"Jayne," Kathryn said, surprised. "What can I do for you?"

"The other way around," Jayne said. "Richard asked me to call you. To offer our apologies."

"Apologies? What for?"

"Greta Brotherton."

"How on earth do you know about that?"

"It doesn't take long for that kind of news to travel," Jayne said smoothly. "However, we were concerned you might think she got her information from us. She did not."

"Then where the hell did she get it?"

"That's what I'm calling about," Jayne said. "Do you have someone on your staff called Granz? David Granz?"

"What about him?"

"Did you tell him about your conversation with Richard?"

"I don't know. I may have. Why?"

"I just wondered if you knew he was seeing this Brotherton woman on a fairly regular basis. Hello? Kathryn?"

"I'm still here," Kathryn said. "How do you know all this, Jayne?"

"It just . . . came to my attention. Is it helpful?"

"I don't know if that's the word I'd have chosen," Kathryn said. "But thank you for telling me."

She put down the telephone as if it were Ming china and stared at the wall. She was still thinking through what Jayne Kellerman had told her when a voice broke into her reverie.

"Hello in there." Kathryn looked up. Mac was standing in her doorway, a file under his arm. "Got a moment?"

"Hi, Mac," she said. "I was just getting ready to leave. Come on in, grab a chair."

McCaskill, who had a certain gravity of manner that discouraged small talk, sat silently for a moment as if he was trying to decide how to begin. He looked formal in his dark three-piece suit; Kathryn had never seen him without a tie. He was a first-class chief deputy DA; everyone respected him because he never forgot what it was like in the trenches. Behind his back, defense attorneys called him No-Deal Neal because of his uncompromising attitude: plead to the sheet or go to trial.

"Never asked you this before," he began, "but I've often wondered why you have all this stuff on the walls. Newspaper clippings of cases you've won."

"I've got an oversized ego."

"Come on, Kathryn."

"You really want to know?"

"Sure I really want to know."

"Okay," Kathryn said. "Look at me."

He raised his eyebrows. "And?"

"Come on, Mac, what do you see? How would you describe me?"

McCaskill shrugged. "Thirty-something, petite build, long dark brown hair, brown eyes, green two-piece suit with a pale yellow blouse—"

"You forgot one thing," Kathryn said. "Female."

He frowned. "Is that an issue?"

"Sometimes," Kathryn said. "And that's why I have all the news clippings on the walls. I'm concerned that someone coming in here—a victim, a cop, a witness—won't take me seriously."

"You worry about that? With your record?"

"Makes me sound pretty insecure, huh? Well, maybe. But record or no record, when it comes to the really serious crimes, the rapes and the homicides, the first thing people see is a woman. Relatively young, small, and not ugly. A lot of them aren't ready for that."

"Never really thought about it," McCaskill said with a shrug. "Everybody here knows you more than pull your weight."

"You remember the Rodriguez case?"

"Sure. Long time ago. He was that old man got murdered up in Mountain View. Couple of drunken construction workers picked a fight with him. Johanssen and . . . who was the other guy?"

"Barkley."

"Johanssen and Barkley, right. They beat Rodriguez to death with an ax handle."

"It happened right after I was made senior trial attorney. When the family found out Hal had assigned the case to me, they told him they didn't think I'd be tough enough to handle guys like Johanssen and Barkley. They said he ought to put a man on to it. They were afraid they'd intimidate me."

McCaskill gave a short, explosive laugh. "That would be something to see. You don't let much intimidate you."

"I know that, you know that. Victims coming in here don't."

"Talking about victims," McCaskill said. "You remember at the meeting we discussed calling in the profiler on the Barbara Gates killing? Hal and I decided it's worth giving it a try. What do you say?"

"I agree," Kathryn said. "In spite of what Dave says, my feeling is we can use all the help we can get. Thanks to Sanchez, right now the DA's office is about as popular as toxic waste."

"My feelings prezackually."

Kathryn frowned. "What?"

"It's what Carey says," he said, grinning. "Prezackually. I think it means something more emphatic than exactly."

Mac had a son, Carey, and three daughters. They were a big, noisy, happy family.

"He must be what, now, ten?"

"Eleven, going on thirty-four," McCaskill said. "The things that kid does with the English language."

"I guess I've got some of that to look forward to," Kathryn said. "Although I can't imagine Emma being eleven, somehow."

McCaskill smiled. "It sneaks up on you. How is Emma, by the way?"

"She's fine. She's spending the evening with a friend. I've got a dinner date."

"Glad to hear it," he said. "Candlelight and wine? A little table in the corner?"

"With Doc Nelson?" she said. "You must be joking. We'll probably spend the entire evening talking about autopsies."

He looked at her for a moment before speaking. "Why do you do it, Kathryn?"

"Do what?" She frowned.

McCaskill waved an arm to encompass the room, the building, the world.

"This. You're always on call. You have a dinner date, it's work. You beat your brains out, sixteen hours a day, seven days a week. And for what?"

"Truth and justice, Mac." Kathryn smiled. "Truth and justice."

"Come on. You're young. There are so many other things you could do . . ."

"You mean like specialize in collections? Or bankruptcy?"

McCaskill shook his head doggedly. "You know what I mean. You need to make some time for your own life. You don't get a second go-round. I was talking to Margie last night. I said to her, Dammit, I don't get to see half as much of the kids as I'd like to. And she said, Don't come crying to me, you're the one who never leaves the office until eight every night."

"What is this, Mac? You trying to break my heart?"

"Hell, no," McCaskill said hastily. "Just . . . you must wish you had more quality time with Emma?"

That hit a tender spot. Only this morning Kathryn had overslept slightly and they had barely enough time to get breakfast; in fact, Emma hadn't finished hers when Kathryn dropped her off at school; she was crying because they never had time to hug anymore. Kathryn had reached for the phone half a dozen times to call her daughter at school and then later at Parks and Rec's after-school program, but she had known it would embarrass her.

"Never a day goes by I don't," Kathryn said. "And I keep on wondering whether in about ten years she isn't going to give me a very hard time over it. But in the meantime, this is what I do and this is who I am. I like my job, Mac. I know I'm doing something useful."

She didn't add that she knew, and he knew too, that if she were to let up even a little, she'd lose her position at the office in an instant.

"Well," he said defensively. "It was just a thought."

"But it's not what you came in here to talk about, is it?"

He shifted uncomfortably in the wicker chair. All at once she caught on.

"Greta Brotherton," she breathed. "Right?"

"You don't think I—you don't think any of us took what she said seriously?"

"I don't know," Kathryn said. "I did."

Mac made a frustrated gesture, like a man bothered by a bug he can't swat. "I hate gossip," he said.

"If you're going to tell me about her and Granz, don't bother," she said. "I already know."

"You do? How . . . ?"

"Does it matter?"

Mac sighed. "Probably not. Except it might explain . . . it seems he broke it off, quit cold on her. I guess she thinks you're responsible."

"She thinks I'm sleeping with Granz?"

McCaskill hesitated. "You see a lot of him."

"I see a lot of Hal Benton."

"You know what I mean."

Flashes of memory popped up in her head like menus on a computer screen.

Who would you like?

Dave Granz.

Why did I ask?

Of course. "Then you think so, too," she said.

"It doesn't make any difference to me one way or the other. It's none of my business."

"Mac, it's not true."

"You two were . . . you know. Not so long ago."

"God, was the whole office talking about that, too?"

"You know the rule. Three can keep a secret as long as two of them are dead."

"It's been over between Dave and me a long time, Mac," she told him. "A long time."

"Okay, okay. But Greta obviously thinks otherwise. Maybe Granz is using you to keep her out of his hair."

You doing anything later?

Early night.

How about if I call round?

"And that's why she said what she did?"

McCaskill shrugged. "I don't know. Maybe. Probably. Listen, Kathryn . . . I'm sorry this happened."

"Don't worry. I'll handle it."

"Okay. About the profiler: I'll call Sacramento. With any luck at all we can get him down here sometime next week. I gather you already talked to him."

"Just the once," Kathryn said. "He sounds like a nice enough guy."

"Can you make time to show him around, introduce him to everyone?"

"I'm still in trial, Mac. But okay, I'll try. By the way, does Dave Granz know you're bringing him in?"

McCaskill nodded. "We discussed it. It's his case."

"And?"

"You want the truth, he was pissed, pardon the expression."

"Let me see if I can guess what he said when you told him," Kathryn offered. "He said, 'We want facts, not theories. And where we'll find them is out on the street, not in some goddamned library.' "

McCaskill smiled. "Hey, pretty good," he said. "He also said, 'Mac, what can this guy do we haven't already done ourselves?' Not quite as politely as that. You know what? He's got a point."

"Maybe," Kathryn said. "But it's a pretty outdated one."

"Look, I know how he feels. He's like a lot of cops, it's his case, he doesn't want some whiz kid telling him how to run it or, worse still, taking all the credit for solving it."

"He's still going to have to learn to work with Giordano."

"He knows that. He said he has a few ideas of his own he wants to check out first."

"What sort of ideas?"

"He wasn't too specific. You know Dave."

I thought I did. She said, "Did you get a chance to read the transcripts of his interviews with the Gates family?"

Mac nodded. "They told him a lot about Barbara. Smart

kid, by all accounts. One thing the father said stuck in my mind: She knew not to talk to strangers."

"Yet she must have. Tells us something about the killer, doesn't it? He must come on as pretty harmless."

"Goddamned psychos," McCaskill said. "It's like each one comes along is freakier than the last."

"I know," Kathryn said. "That's why I think it's probably a good idea to bring Giordano in. A little fresh thinking won't hurt. Maybe he'll spot things we've missed."

"Let us pray. I just hope he fits in around here, that's all. I don't need any more hassles."

Kathryn grinned. "You sound like Granz," she said. "I've been to Quantico, Mac. They're not all buttoned-down college boys."

"I know, I know. You about through for the day?"

Before she could answer, the phone rang. Kathryn grimaced.

"I was," she said wearily and picked up the receiver. The caller was a sheriff's deputy named Fred Waite who was at a homicide scene. A fifty-year-old woman had been shot and killed by her son-in-law, who wanted to confess. Kathryn told him to wait and she'd come out with an inspector.

"Looks like you're going to miss dinner," Mac said, and left her to it. It turned out he was right; it was after seven by the time she left the crime scene, got into her car, and drove along the coast toward Espanola. On the way she used the car phone to call Morgan.

"I got hung up on a homicide," she explained. "I haven't even changed yet. I'm sorry, Morgan, but it looks as if dinner tonight is out."

"You don't know it, Katie, but you're doing me a favor," he said. "I'm still in the autopsy suite and only about half done. I was just thinking of calling you."

"Just as a matter of interest, where were we going to eat?"

"Oh, someplace really ritzy. Burger King, or maybe even a Taco Bell."

"Boy, what am I missing!"

"If you're going to be sarcastic, I'll eat with my, uh, client, here," he said. "He's not as choosy as you. Talk to you tomorrow, okay?"

She turned onto Lighthouse and left again into Seaview Heights. It would have been nice to dress up, go to a nice restaurant, but it would have meant a real late night. She wondered if Ruth and Emma had eaten yet. It still wasn't too late to go down to Espanola and get pizza, she thought.

The thought reminded her of Dave Granz. She still didn't know how she felt about what she had learned. Jealous? No, not jealous. Disappointed, maybe. Something had changed, but she couldn't pin down exactly what. Instinct told her not to make any decisions about it right now. She parked in the driveway and went through to the gardens. Skip the pizza, she decided, we'll have quesadillas instead.

"Mommy! You're early, you're early!"

Emma had seen her getting out of the car. She ran toward her across the garden, arms outstretched, and Kathryn whirled her around in her arms, laughing. Ruth came over and stood watching them.

"Well!" she said, when Kathryn put Emma down. "What happened to your dinner date?"

"Don't ask," Kathryn said. "Hey, did you guys eat yet?"

"We were just about to go in and start supper," Ruth told her. "No problem, I got enough for three."

"Let's go out," Kathryn said. "My treat. What do you say?"

"You know how I hate not to have to cook," Ruth said dryly. "Let me get a sweater. I'll be right with you."

As her friend turned and went inside, Kathryn squatted down on her haunches. Emma regarded her gravely.

"I thought you were going out," she said. "I thought you had a date."

"I canceled it," Kathryn told her. "So I could be with you."

"Is that a really-truly, Mommy?"

Kathryn smiled. "No, it's more of a sort-of-a-kind-of-a," she said. "Will that do? Now, how was school today?"

"It was okay," Emma said philosophically. "I was glad when it was lunchtime, though."

"Gee, I'm sorry about breakfast, sweetheart," Kathryn said. "I just ran out of time, that's all. You forgive me?"

"Oh, Mommy," Emma said patiently, her dark eyes wide and serious, "I don't mind really. I mean, everyone knows life's not fair."

Kathryn put her hands on her hips and regarded her daughter in amazement. "Now where in the world did that come from?"

Emma gave an offhand shrug. "Julie Corcoran says it all the time."

Julie was one of Emma's classmates, a precocious only child whose parents were both highly paid professional people. Out of the mouths of babes and sucklings, Kathryn thought. She put her arms around Emma and gave her another big tight hug.

"My daughter, the philosopher," she said.

22

MARTY BELKER STARTED HIS CLOSING AT TEN. TODAY HE WAS wearing black Gucci loafers, a dark brown three-piece suit, a cream cotton shirt, and a striped tie. The courtroom lights caught the sheen of perspiration on his face as he paced up and down in front of the jury. At the defense table, Danny Broadwick sat, as he had sat throughout the trial, a blank stare on his face, apparently indifferent to what was happening around him.

"It may come as a surprise to you, ladies and gentlemen," Belker was saying, "but I do not expect to persuade you my client did not commit the crime with which he is charged. Quite the contrary. Danny Broadwick killed Pamella Cowan. But not with premeditation, not with malice aforethought. He walked into the apartment. They quarreled. In the heat of that quarrel he picked up a tire iron leaning against the wall and struck her down. It was an act of passion, of uncontrollable rage."

He stopped, and went over to the podium to check his notes. Kathryn scanned the faces of the jury. Every one of them was watching Belker intently. Their perception of him was so much different from the reality; but that was how the system worked. Belker was a *defender,* a good man, fighting to save the life of another, innocent until proven guilty beyond a reasonable doubt, just like in the movies or on TV. What they didn't know was how many of the rules Belker had violated during the two-and-a-half-week course of this trial.

Every evening, after court recessed, Kathryn spent an

hour going over the day with Laura, pointing out just such violations. Not so Laura would know how smart she, Kathryn, was for spotting them; but so that when she found herself in a courtroom with Belker or someone like him, she'd know what she was up against and maybe how to handle it.

"Juries often perceive defense counsel as the good guy," she told Laura. "And you've got to sit there and let them believe it, even though you can see him flouting the rules of professional conduct, intentionally misleading the judge, and persistently violating his duty of candor with the court. Every fiber of you will be screaming to tell them he's a smooth-talking bastard who doesn't give a damn about justice, only winning. But you can't."

"How about if we gave him some of his own medicine?"

Kathryn shook her head. "Even though we know his investigator misrepresented himself to a witness in order to get her to talk to him, even though we can show Belker subpoenaed records about the victim for the trial although the law requires they be delivered first to the judge, we're not allowed to tell the jury."

A DA had to turn over information favorable to the defense even though defense might not even know of its existence, and disclose to the defense anything that might exonerate or mitigate. A DA could not conceal or suppress evidence. A DA was required always to be fair to the opposing party and counsel. A DA must never intentionally mislead a judge. In fact, a DA could not do a whole lot of things that fancy dancers like Marty Belker got away with every day of the week.

"Surely Judge Calhoun knows what Belker is up to?" Laura said.

"There are judges and judges, kiddo," Kathryn replied. "A lot of them get their jobs because of political connections, not because they were great lawyers. They're insecure up there, so they develop little ways of showing the jury who's in charge. One will insist you always use the microphone, another that you always address him standing up. Some of them deliberately set out to demean an attorney in front of the jury so that he or she will lose stature—and eventually the case. And then there are the ones who, no matter how often he breaks the rules, won't slap down a defense attorney who oversteps the mark. Calhoun is one of those. You remember last week, Belker *ex-parte*'d us?"

"You mean when he talked to the judge without you being there?"

"That's the name of the game. He bends the judge's ear any way he wants to without us there to raise objections, makes points he knows he'd never be able to make in court. Slick, huh? You'd think the judge would know better, wouldn't you? After all, it's forbidden by the Rules of Professional Conduct."

"Then how does Belker get away with it?"

"He knows Calhoun has such a big ego, he feels he couldn't possibly be influenced by an *ex parte* conversation, although in fact that's probably exactly what happened. So instead of coming to it with an open mind, the judge has a preconceived notion of the case or the issue and we have to break it down. You think that serves justice? More importantly, do you think Marty Belker could care less?"

Well, Laura would learn the hard way, the way they all did. You could tell someone they were in a minefield, but you couldn't always stop them from blundering straight onto a mine. Concentrate, Kathryn, concentrate. She forced herself back into the present. She wasn't expecting any surprises from Belker—she could probably have written his closing for him— but that didn't mean she could take a single thing for granted. The fact that they were approaching the end of the trial didn't mean Marty wouldn't try to pull any more stunts.

He stopped in front of the jury box, slapped both hands onto the rail in front of the jurors, his face no more than a couple of feet from theirs. She recognized the movement; it meant Belker was coming to his big finish.

"Consider the evidence that Pamella Cowan was a sharp-tongued, vindictive, overbearing woman," Belker continued. "Consider the evidence of her heavy drug use. Consider the evidence of her flirtatious behavior with other men. Consider the evidence that on the very day she was killed she told her boyfriend, Danny Broadwick, that she had slept with another man. Ask yourself, how did that make Danny feel? Ask yourself, what must have gone on in his head when she told him that? Pamella Cowan goaded Danny Broadwick to his limits. Beyond them. Until . . ."

Belker took a pencil between the thumb and forefinger

of both hands, held it up where the jury could see it, and snapped it. The sound was sharp and loud in the quiet courtroom. Hokey, Kathryn thought. But effective.

"It was a tragedy that ended in an explosion of violence," Belker said. "No one is going to ask you to forget that another human being died. But you have to try to understand how it happened, and why. If you do that, if you have listened carefully to all the evidence, you must find that what took place was a voluntary manslaughter committed in the heat of passion. Thank you."

He went back to his table and sat down, staring at nothing. Kathryn looked at the clock and then at Calhoun. The judge caught her glance and nodded.

"Ms. Mackay, are you ready?"

"Yes, Your Honor," she replied.

"You think we'll get through this by noon or thereabouts?"

"I do."

"Good," Calhoun said smoothly. "Please proceed."

"If it please the court," Kathryn said, turning to the jury. "Ladies and gentlemen of the jury, you have been very patient and attentive throughout this long and difficult trial, and I thank you. I will do my best to make my closing remarks to you as brief as possible. To begin with, let me go back to my first argument and remind you again of what I said about heat of passion and provocation. The classic example of heat of passion killing is when a husband finds his wife *in flagrante delicto* with another man, takes a gun, and kills him. That provocation, that uncontrollable passion, mitigates an intentional killing from murder to manslaughter. But remember, the defendant must have been provoked. He must have acted upon that provocation and that alone. There can have been no prior settled intention to kill.

"In other words, ladies and gentlemen, we are looking for provocation which, by the objective standards of any reasonable person, would be sufficient to make a man—or a woman—lose control and kill. Is that what we had here? Defense has suggested to you that Pamella Cowan was a slut, a user, a nagging shrew who brought her death upon herself. And that she brought death upon herself because she goaded the defendant until he snapped. And killed her.

"But that flies in the face of the evidence. According to

the evidence, he told his sister just thirty minutes before the killing, 'That bitch keeps screwing me up. I'm going to shut her mouth once and for all.' Then he went into the apartment and beat Pamella Cowan to death with a tire iron.

"This was not uncontrolled heat of passion, ladies and gentlemen. This was the cold, deliberate action of a man who had found out about his girlfriend's infidelity and had decided, rationally and impassionately, to kill her."

Kathryn walked across to the evidence table and picked up the murder weapon, an inch-thick bar of steel, eighteen inches long. She took it across and leaned it against the table at an angle. From a box, she took out a slightly deflated soccer ball, which she put on the table in front of her. There wasn't a sound in the courtroom.

"And then," she said, turning so that the jury could clearly see everything she did, "he went into the apartment. He walked over to where the tire iron was leaning against the wall."

She walked around the table.

"He picked it up and raised it over his head. And then . . ."

She picked up the tire iron and raised it over her head in both hands and brought it down on the soccer ball. The metal bar thudded heavily into the soft leather. The jurors flinched.

"Pamella Cowan fell to the ground, trying to protect herself with her hands."

Kathryn swung the tire iron up and brought it down again.

"Then he hit her again! And again! And again! And again!"

The flattened ball fell off the table onto the floor. She was panting with exertion, her whole body shaking. She put the tire iron down, staring at her trembling hands. She turned to face the jury.

"Her skull was crushed, all the bones in her hands and forearms were smashed. The ceiling and walls were spattered with her blood. And after that awful crime, do you know what Danny Broadwick told the deputy who arrested him? He said, 'I had to do it, man. She'd been asking for it for a long time. This was just the last straw.' "

She drew in a deep breath and looked at the jury. Their faces were set and somber.

"The defendant knew exactly what he was doing, ladies and gentlemen," she said quietly. "He went into that house determined to kill Pamella Cowan. He made his intention perfectly clear. He wanted to end their relationship and he did just that, not in the heat of passion, but with premeditation and deliberation. This was murder in the first degree, and I ask you to find accordingly. Thank you."

She went back to her chair and sipped from the glass of water Laura slid over to her.

"Jesus, Kathryn," she muttered.

Kathryn hardly heard the words. She felt sweaty, shaky, depleted, and as always, uncertain how effective her presentation had been. It seemed as if she had been out there for hours, but a look at the clock told her she had only been on her feet thirty-eight minutes. There was a school of thought that held if you could not hit pay dirt in thirty minutes you ought to sit down anyway. Like all courtroom rules, it was susceptible to infinite variation.

She half-listened as Calhoun instructed the jury, already feeling the onset of the letdown that always accompanied the end of a trial. The bailiff snapped, "All rise!" and she got to her feet as the judge left the courtroom. As she watched the jury file out behind Yablonski, the telephone on the bailiff's desk gave its muted shirr. She picked it up.

"Superior Three," she said. "Kathryn Mackay."

"Kathryn, it's Mac. What's happening down there?"

"Jury is out," she told him. "What can I do for you?"

"The profiler has arrived. Giordano. Can you make a meeting in my office, two o'clock?"

"I'll be there. Mac, have you seen Dave Granz?"

"He finally came in from the cold," McCaskill said. He sounded as if he might be smiling. "You want to talk to him?"

"Not on the phone," Kathryn said. "Ask him if he'd mind coming over to my office. In ten minutes, say?"

"My pleasure," McCaskill said, and rang off.

"You need a hand with this stuff, Kathryn?" Harry Di-Stefano, who'd been her inspector on the case, gestured at the files on the table.

"Thanks, Harry," Kathryn said. "We can manage."

"Anyway, you don't want to be drummed out of the division for being chivalrous to an ADA, do you?" Laura said. "I'll schlepp them up later."

Harry grinned and ambled out toward the atrium, where he could grab a smoke. Kathryn looked across the courtroom. Marty Belker, head down, shoulders hunched as if to ward off eavesdroppers, was deep in conversation with Dave Berry of the *Gazette*. She could probably have dictated word for word what he was telling the newspaperman. Dave glanced over Belker's shoulder at Kathryn and raised his pencil and his eyebrows. She nodded.

When he was finished with Belker, Dave came over. He carried a dog-eared shorthand reporter's notebook in his left hand.

"Any comment on today's proceedings, Kathryn?" he asked her.

"What did Marty tell you, he's confident they'll bring in a manslaughter verdict?"

"Right. And you?"

"I never try to predict what a jury will do, you know that. But I think we made our point."

"That routine with the tire iron," he said. "That was something else. I never saw anything like it. You could practically see the blood flying."

"I was afraid it might be a bit too melodramatic," she confessed.

"Maybe it was. But it worked," he assured her. "Believe me. Marty's burning. He thinks you completely upstaged him."

"Poor baby," she said. They went out into the sunlit hallway together and walked over to the main building.

"I'll get someone to call you as soon as the jury comes in," Kathryn promised. Dave touched two fingers to his forehead and went out down the steps into the sunlight. She climbed up to the second floor and checked in past the empty reception desk, wondering what she was going to say to Dave Granz.

He was waiting for her when she got to her office, leafing through a booklet on forensic voice identification put out by the Michigan State Police. He looked up as she came in and dumped her files on the desk.

"Hi," he said lazily. "What's up?"

She sat down in her swivel chair and looked at him. Same old Dave. Same tweed jacket, light gray slacks, same boyish good looks, same disarming manner. Nothing showed. It was probably just as well it never did, she thought. Or how could we bear one another?

"I haven't seen you for a while."

"Been out there," he said, making a gesture toward the window. "Everyone's running round trying to get something on this Linda Vista Mall killing."

An elderly man, Elliot Tavares, had been mugged in a parking structure near Robinson's, a newly opened department store in the Espanola mall. When the deputies got there, they found him dying of massive head injuries. A blood-stained piece of two-by-four about two feet long was lying nearby. Witnesses said they had seen a young man apparently trying to help the seventy-seven-year-old man into the passenger side of a small pickup. When they approached and saw the blood, he ran away. White, blond, about twenty; that was as much as the witnesses who saw it were able to give the cops.

"I read about it in the paper," Kathryn said. "You're having trouble with it, right?"

"Ted Krell is having trouble with it," Dave said. Krell was chief of the Espanola police department. "He had the dogs out right away and the witnesses were real good. Nobody expected it to die on the vine. But after a week, he hollered help."

"And?"

"As of this moment, we've got a list of about two hundred leads. The biggest problem is this perp looks like Joe Regular. The description fits about twenty thousand guys you can find on the beach anyplace between here and San Diego."

"You on it full time?"

Granz grinned. "That'll be the day. Na, I got the usual caseload. And on top of that, I've been playing a sort of hunch I've got. Trying to get a line on the Gates killing."

"Have you come up with anything?"

"Nothing yet. Nothing I'd call concrete, anyway. I'm just poking around, an idea. But it might lead someplace. Was that why you wanted to see me?"

"Greta Brotherton," Kathryn said, blurting it out.

"What about her?" he asked, frowning.

"She tried to put a knife in me. You want to tell me why?"

"How the hell should I know?" he said, but as he said it

he got up and went past her over to the window. She swiveled around in her chair; he stared fixedly out at the street.

"That's it? You don't know?" Kathryn asked.

"What am I supposed to say?"

"How about the truth?"

"Listen, Kathryn, I—" he began. The protest died on his lips as he turned and looked at her. He stared at the floor, shrugged. "Who told you?"

"Woman's intuition. Telepathy. A message from the occupant of an interplanetary craft. What difference does it make who told me?"

"I . . . it just happened, Kathryn. One of those things. It was over as soon as it began. Except she—" He sighed and spread his hands helplessly.

"So you used me."

He looked uncomfortable. "I didn't . . . I just let her think whatever she wanted to think."

"You told her you were seeing me. And that was why you couldn't see her anymore?"

"It was true in a way, I was coming to see you. I just didn't explain it was . . . business. So she . . ." He shrugged and came back across the room to sit in the wicker chair in front of her. "Are you angry?"

"I thought I was. But no, I'm not. Just sad."

"I never—I couldn't tell you. That would have made it worse."

"Worse than this?"

"You would have disapproved."

"What am I, Mary Poppins?" she said. "Look, go sleep with the Radio City Rockettes if you want to. What you do with your private life is your own business. But don't drag me into the middle of it."

"Hell, Kathryn, I didn't mean to cause you grief," he said. "It never occurred to me she'd go to Mac with that story."

"You sat there and said nothing."

"I didn't want to make it any worse. And I felt . . ."

"What did you feel, Dave? Like you'd betrayed me?"

"Look," he said, "you and Emma, you're important to me. Greta Brotherton is not. So do me a favor and act like this never happened, okay? I screwed up, but it's history."

"Okay. Now one of us has to put Greta straight on it. Right?"

He stared at the wall, making no reply. Kathryn had a struggle to conceal the smile that kept threatening to spread across her face. He was like a damned school kid.

"Would you like me to repeat the question?" she said.

"Okay, I got the message," he said. He stood up, patted his pockets. "I need a cigarette."

"Those things'll kill you."

"Yeah," he said ruefully. "Me and my death wish."

"You know about the meeting with Giordano? Two o'clock?"

"I saw Mac." He went to the door, opened it, stopped. "You know what's funny?" he said.

"Tell me."

"She said she prefers younger men."

23

"KATIE!"

She hadn't seen Morgan Nelson since their dinner date had gone down the tubes. He got to his feet, beaming, as she came into her office.

"I've been waiting for you. Thought we could have a few minutes before the meeting."

"Hi, Doc," she said. "It's good to see you."

She meant it, too. She would never forget how he befriended her in those chilly early days when she first came to Santa Rita and didn't know a solitary soul. The gap in their ages didn't seem to mean much. He listened well, he had a good sense of humor, he loved Emma. In spite of the sometimes not-very-subtle innuendos of her colleagues, sex was never involved. Talking to him was the closest thing to going to a shrink that she knew.

"How did the Broadwick trial go?"

"We'll get a conviction. How about you? You busy?"

The green eyes twinkled mischievously. "What's that proverb—death keeps no calendar? There are no recessions in my line of business, Katie. Yours either, come to that."

"Don't remind me," she groaned.

"Tell me something about this profiler Hal has called in."

"I don't know much more than you do. He's with the Department of Justice in Sacramento and his name is Steve Giordano. I've talked to him on the phone, he seems like a regular guy. Hal thinks he may be able to come up with some ideas on these serial killings."

"Can't you do that?"

"Not as well as he can. Now that I'm out of trials I'll be able to concentrate on the investigation. We'll work together."

"Richard Sanchez is giving your office a hard time."

"That's his specialty."

"I take it the investigation hasn't gone anywhere?"

Kathryn made a face. "Nope. We thought getting an ID on the last victim might give us something we could get our teeth into, but it fizzled out."

"Barbara Gates," Nelson said reflectively. "A pretty girl."

It was hard to imagine him thinking of any girl as pretty or plain or anything else. They rarely looked pretty on the autopsy table and what he did to them certainly didn't make them any prettier.

"You by any chance free tonight?" Kathryn said, surprising herself. The remark was totally spontaneous; she'd had no idea at all she was going to make it.

"I can be," Nelson said.

"I owe you dinner. How about coming over to my place?"

"I'll pick up a bottle of wine. Eight o'clock?"

"It's a date."

They went together into the conference room. Jack Burrows and Dave Granz were over by the window, talking quietly. Neal McCaskill was bent over a spread of crime scene photographs with a broad-shouldered younger man whose dark brown, almost black hair had flecks of silver in it.

"Ah, hello, Doc," McCaskill said, straightening up. "Steve Giordano, this is Dr. Morgan Nelson, our pathologist. And Kathryn Mackay, Assistant DA in charge of the special investigation unit."

"I've already talked with Ms. Mackay," Giordano said as they shook hands. "Good to meet you, Dr. Nelson."

His grip was firm and dry. Kathryn recalled her mental picture of him when they had first talked: tall, slim, volatile.

Giordano was none of those things. Of medium height, athletically built, he had watchful brown eyes and eyelashes as long as a girl's. About forty, Kathryn judged.

"Steve's attached to the Criminal Investigation Response Team of the Department of Justice," McCaskill told Nelson. "He'll be with us for a while."

"You come direct from Sacramento?" Nelson asked him.

"I've been working out of San Francisco," Giordano said. "I drove down this morning."

"Everyone here? Okay, let's get to it," Mac said, waving them to their seats. Giordano sat next to him at the top of the T-shaped conference table. Granz and Burrows sat opposite each other, Kathryn and Morgan Nelson taking the lower end.

"I've had Dave and Jack give Steve a brief rundown on the three killings, and we've had a preliminary look at the crime scene photographs," he continued. "Steve has given us a list of his requirements. Jack, you'll coordinate. Kathryn, I want you on this with Steve full-time as of now."

"I've got a jury out, Mac," Kathryn reminded him.

"I know that. But Hal's pushing hard for some kind of break on this thing. Any kind. Now Broadwick's finished, he wants you on it full-time."

"Do I get Dave and Jack full-time, too?"

"Dream on, dear heart," Jack Burrows told her.

"Dave will give you as much of his time as he can. As for Jack, I'll talk to Walt Earheart, see what I can do," Mac promised. He looked at Giordano. "Steve?"

Giordano nodded. "I want you all to know I'm very glad to have this chance to work with you," he said. He had a well-modulated speaking voice with a faint New York accent. "The first thing I'd like to do is deformalize our relationship. So please call me Steve, and if I may, I'll call you by your first names also."

He looked around for their affirmation, got it, and continued.

"Fine, good. Let me start by saying I haven't come here to try and razzle-dazzle you. Most of you've probably got more years in the bag than I've had breakfasts, and it may well be that one or two of you think, Who the hell does this hotshot think he is, coming down here to show us how to do our jobs? Well, I want it understood, I'm not a hotshot, I'm not trying to show you how to do your jobs, and I'm not in the miracle business. What I'm here to do is try, if I can, to come up with some ideas that will help you— you, not me—to pin down this serial killer." He looked around. "Any questions so far?"

Nobody spoke.

"Okay, we'll begin with a little general information. The profiling process—by the way, the FBI Behavioral Science Unit no longer refers to it as profiling, but as criminal investigation analysis that may result in a profile. CIA for short."

"Aren't you afraid the spooks at Langley will object?" Dave Granz asked. Was it her imagination, Kathryn wondered, or was there a hint of hostility in the question?

Giordano smiled but didn't respond. "Let me just run through what I'll need to get started. First, a really detailed map of the area with the crime scene locales designated. Second, a victimology, a summary of everything known about the victims: age, race, educational level, employment—"

"We got pretty much nothing on the first two victims," Jack Burrows interrupted. "Way we see it, they could easily have been abducted someplace else, maybe Santa Clara or San Jose, and brought over here."

"Understood," Giordano said. "Just let me have whatever you've got."

"You'll want to visit the crime scenes, I imagine?" Mac said. "Kathryn, can you take care of that?"

"No problem," Kathryn said. "Any idea when you might want to do that, Steve?"

Giordano shrugged. "As soon as possible. I'd like to get a clear mental picture of the physical layout of each scene. I can get a lot of what I need from the CSI photographs, of course, but nothing beats actually seeing the location. Let me ask you something, was that you I read about in *California Attorney?*"

"Oops," Morgan Nelson said. Giordano looked up, surprised, and Kathryn smiled.

"Not my favorite press clipping, Steve," she said.

"Glug glug," Giordano said, reacting very fast. "Sound of a man trying to talk with his foot in his mouth. Sorry."

"Forget it."

"Thanks. You told me you had some profiling experience."

"I spent six weeks at Quantico with the Behavioral Science Unit. I imagine it's all become a lot more sophisticated since I was there."

"Some," Giordano said. "But it's like I told you when we talked on the phone, the basic principles haven't changed. We're still trying to identify the major personality and behavioral characteristics of the offender based on an analysis of his crimes. You remember the seven points?"

"Sure," Kathryn said. "Evaluation of the criminal act, evaluation of the specifics of the crime scenes, analysis of the victim, evaluation of preliminary law enforcement reports, evaluation of the autopsy protocol, development of a profile, and investigative suggestions predicated on it."

"We went through all that," Dave Granz said impatiently. "It got us precisely noplace."

"Happens sometimes," Giordano said imperturbably. "Weren't you able to draw any conclusions at all after we talked?"

"I'd hardly call them conclusions," Kathryn said. "Generalizations, maybe."

"Tell me."

"To begin with, we're almost certainly dealing with a sexual dominator: Morgan found indications of restraints and physical abuse. We judged the one victim we know anything about to have been a moderate-risk subject."

"We can explore that more fully in due course," Giordano said, leaning forward with his hands clasped together. "Go on, please."

"This was a nice middle-class college kid. She didn't hitchhike, she didn't hang around street corners. She wasn't the type who'd go off with just anyone. So he had to abduct her from someplace fairly public."

"You're postulating abduction by force?"

"We can go on *postulating* till our teeth drop out," Granz snapped. "It won't get us anyplace."

"Dave's right, Steve," Jack Burrows added. "It's like this guy knows all the angles. He hasn't given us a damned thing to work with."

"That in itself may tell us quite a lot about him," Giordano replied, apparently oblivious to the hostility in Dave Granz's voice. "In fact, it's surprising how much we know already."

"Yeah?" Granz said, ignoring McCaskill's warning frown. "You want to run that by me?"

"Kathryn's already done some groundwork. She thought he might be a dominator sadist. Possibly a necrophiliac. Possibly Hispanic, but just as likely to be white. Statistically likely to be between twenty-five and forty years old. Possibly keeps the victims in some kind of cold storage facility. He may not be a rocket scientist, but we know he's intelligent—the coded messages, the lack of a crime scene, tell us that. We know he wants us to recognize his work: he puts his signature on it."

"Something else," Kathryn said. "He probably knows quite a lot about police procedure."

"And where does he get this information?"

"Hell, that's easy," Burrows said disgustedly. "He watches TV. He could go in a 7-Eleven any day of the week, pick up half a dozen paperbacks that would tell him anything he needs to know."

"Books, magazines, movies, videos," Granz said, more to himself than anyone else. "There must be half a dozen mail-order houses that specialize in that kind of stuff."

"Let's talk about the mutilations," Giordano said. "Why does he chop the bodies up the way he does?"

"Doc thinks he's taking trophies," McCaskill said, "scalps."

Giordano looked at Nelson, raising his eyebrows. "Dr. Nelson?"

"Most people just call me Doc, Steve. Or Morgan, if you prefer."

"Doc's just fine." Giordano smiled. "Go on, please."

"We know serial killers like to relive their crimes," Morgan said. "We know they frequently take something from the victim, an item of clothing, something of no tangible value except insofar as it helps the killer to relive the murder. I wondered if . . . ?" He ended with a shrug.

"For the purposes of this argument, let's assume you're right," Giordano said. "We then have to ask ourselves what does he do with the . . . scalps."

Morgan shrugged. "You mean, does he keep them?"

Giordano said nothing. He was good at getting other people to talk, Kathryn thought.

"If he does," Morgan mused, "how, where? In a refrigerator, or a specimen jar like they have in labs? Or does he dispose of them . . . some other way?"

"Jesus, Doc!" Burrows said, his face twisted with disgust. "You're not suggesting . . . ?"

Morgan shook his head. "I don't think our killer is a cannibal, Jack. I just wonder if he mightn't be preserving these . . . trophies in some way."

"Can that be done?"

"The Indians did it."

"But . . . why the hell would he?" Burrows wondered. Giordano looked at the pathologist.

"A guess? The same reason hunters put the heads of the animals they have killed on the walls of their studies and dens," Nelson said.

"You already said it, Doc," Giordano said softly. "Trophies."

Dave Granz, who had been scribbling furiously on the pad in front of him, looked up.

"So you're saying what we're looking for here is a guy with female pubises hanging on his walls, is that it?" he asked Giordano.

"Hey, Dave, take it easy," McCaskill said quietly.

"It's okay, Mac," Giordano said softly. "Yes, Dave, that's exactly what I am saying."

"You sound pretty sure of yourself," Granz said. "For someone who only arrived here an hour ago."

Giordano shook his head, refusing to let Dave get under his skin.

"No, I'm anything but sure of myself," he confessed. "One thing I do know, with this kind of killer, nothing is certain. We can conjecture all our lives and never pin it down. Was he abused by his father, was he molested as a child, is he paying back society, is he showing his contempt? The longer I do this, the more I believe what the shrinks don't want to hear. A lot of these guys kill because they like it."

"Okay," McCaskill said into the silence that ensued. "What next, Steve?"

"A ride to the morgue," Giordano said. "I want to take a look at Barbara Gates. Then I want to see the school facility where the body was dumped." He looked at his watch, then at Kathryn. "I was thinking of doing that tomorrow, but it's only three-thirty. Do we have time to do it today?"

"Sure," she said. "We'll take my car."

"I'll call my office," Morgan said, going to a phone. "They'll get a pass ready for you."

"While you're at it, ask them to make me copies of your autopsy protocols, tox results, and all the photographs."

"Got it," Morgan said, pushing buttons.

"No sweat on the crime scene," McCaskill said. "I'll just need to clear it with the SO. You also want aerial photos and color eight-by-tens of the crime scenes, right?"

"Yeah. As soon as you can get them."

"What about the Broadwick jury, Kathryn?" Mac asked. "How long you think they'll be out?"

Kathryn raised her eyebrows and held out her hands palms up, like someone checking for rain.

"How long is a piece of string? Yablonski or DiStefano will contact me on the car phone if we have a verdict. I can be back here in twenty minutes. In a pinch, Laura can take the verdict for me."

"That's it?" Granz asked. "We all through here?"

He sounded impatient, as if he wanted to be somewhere else fast.

"For now," Giordano told him levelly. "I'll check with you and Jack tomorrow morning and we'll get down to some serious work."

"You be careful out there," Granz said, and left.

24

"TELL ME ABOUT GRANZ," GIORDANO SAID.

They were on their way to the County Morgue, Kathryn driving. She glanced at him. His face was expressionless. It was like he showed anyone only what he'd decided he wanted them to see. Good-humored and pleasant meeting everyone at the DA's office, serious but uninvolved when he was dealing with Granz. For some reason it vaguely irritated her. Which of these faces was the real man? Any of them? None of them?

"Not much to tell," she said. "He's a local boy, born and

bred right here in Santa Rita. Career cop. Ten years with the Sheriff's Department before he joined the DA's office. Three commendations. He's one of the best inspectors we've got."

"He doesn't like me much, does he?"

"It's not you personally," Kathryn said. "It's what you do."

"I got some of that," he said softly. "Back there. So he doesn't think much of profiling. Or the people who do it. Look, if he sees me as competition, I can't do anything about it. And I won't lose a lot of sleep over it, either."

"He doesn't see you that way, Steve." Kathryn smiled. "He's too much of a pro for that. He knows we're all on the same side, and he'll adjust to the situation. But these murders . . . it's become personal with him. Especially the Barbara Gates killing."

"A good cop shouldn't let that happen."

"If you knew Dave better, you'd know he'd never ordinarily let it."

"Did he tell you this?"

Kathryn shook her head. "I know him pretty well, but I doubt . . . it's not something he'd talk to me about. Norm Podnoretz told me. What happened was, Dave got the job of interviewing her family and friends, going through all her effects. I don't have to tell you, usually that kind of thing is routine. But this time . . . it seems like it got to him. He just couldn't keep it at a distance."

Giordano nodded, his face as impassive as before. "I can relate to that," he said. "It's something a lot of cops experience. You never know what will trigger it. I had the same thing happen to me once, back in 1986. The department had just activated Criminal Investigation Response Teams throughout the state. We were called in to assist investigating a series of child killings up in Mendocino County. There'd been five murders. And I was doing my job and they were just . . . victims. Then . . . we found this pair of cowboy boots. You know, like miniatures. I guess it made me think about the vulnerability of my own kids; it really broke me up."

He shook his head as if to rid himself of the memory. It was an unexpected admission; cops usually kept a tight rein on their emotions. Kathryn made a left past the Alvarado Highway interchange and took Mission Heights Boulevard.

Three minutes later they rolled into the parking lot outside the County Hospital.

"Let me get this straight before we go in," Giordano said. "Nelson works for the county as a forensic pathologist, right?"

"The coroner's office is part of the Sheriff's Department," Kathryn said, nodding. "But more often than not coroners are politicians. A lot of them have about as much appreciation of forensic pathology as a truck driver. We contract it out; Doc Nelson is our main man."

"Okay," he said. He absorbed information without any visible alteration in his expression. Like a computer, she thought. You put it in and you know it's there. They got out of the car and went inside, showing their IDs to the cop at the door before checking in at reception.

"Dr. Nelson left these for you," the dark-haired young woman behind the counter said, and handed them VISITOR tags. "Will you be going down right away?"

Giordano looked at Kathryn. "I can't think of any reason to wait," he said. "Can you?"

"Let's do it," she said.

They took the elevator down to the subbasement. To their surprise, Morgan Nelson was waiting for them as the doors opened. He was wearing his uniform, green surgical garb and rubber boots, powerful forearms protruding from the short sleeves. There were traces of talc on the backs of his hands.

"Hi, Doc," Kathryn said. "Back at work already?"

"Got a ride in a police car," Morgan said.

"Looks pretty busy down here," Steve observed.

"Death never sleeps," Morgan said with a tired smile, and waved a hand at the assignment board on the wall. "We're flat out most of the time."

You forgot, while you were getting on with the business of living, that down here the nonstop procession of the dead never ended. Unless they were from natural causes, the circumstances, manner, and cause of all deaths in the county were investigated and determined. In addition to murders—and these days even sleepy little Santa Rita had its share—the pathologist's office investigated all suicides, accidents, nursing home deaths, and any death by illness where the decedent had not seen a doctor for twenty days prior. Call it one death in every three; that was about two hundred and fifty autopsies a year, an average of five a week. Twenty to thirty of those would be murders. That made every day a busy day, and Mondays busiest of all. Outside the autopsy suite there would be a line of plastic-sheeted gurneys, preternaturally still amid the bustling hubbub, corpses awaiting their cue: lights, camera, action.

"Busy weekend, huh?" Giordano said.

"Only kind we get." Morgan glanced at his clipboard. "And if you think it's bad down here, you should take a look in the emergency rooms some Saturday night. Katie, I'll have to take a rain check on dinner again. I've got an evening of cutting ahead of me."

"Sure, Doc. We'll do it some other time."

"I was looking forward to it," Morgan said, his tone aggrieved. "But"—he waved a hand at his domain—"I can't stop the carnival. By the way, Steve, those autopsy protocols you wanted? You can pick them up when you leave."

"I appreciate it," Giordano said. "Especially when you're under such pressure."

"Just as easy to do it right away as later," Nelson said, and led the way diagonally across the hall to the massive stainless steel door of the refrigerator. As he swung it open they were enveloped by a wave of cold, foul air; if she'd been brought in blindfolded, Kathryn would have known immediately where she was. She'd attended her first autopsy down in L.A. She had never been inside a morgue before then. It was like something out of science fiction. Bright harsh lighting, the sullen gleam of the stainless steel autopsy tables, the sounds of water drumming in a sink, the metallic clatter of surgical instruments. She could still remember the rough banter of the cops as they waited until the pathologist came in.

The body was that of a middle-aged woman, victim of a vehicular homicide. There were massive head injuries; the face was practically unrecognizable. The pathologist was a tall, thin man in his middle fifties, with the tapering hands and long fingers of a pianist. Kathryn steeled herself as he made the first incision, starting at the left shoulder, slicing through the pectoral muscles in an arc that ended up at the same point on the opposite shoulder, completing the Y with a deep vertical cut all the way down to the pubis. He used a pair of rib cutters to nip out the sternum, removed the breastplate of ribs, and lifted the organs out of the chest cavity, recording his actions into a microphone above his head. A flat, lambent, unavoidable odor filled the air.

The pathologist made a special effort to involve Kathryn, inviting her to ask questions, explaining what he was doing and why he was doing it. The words poured out of him like a foreign language: epithelial tissue, stenosis, infarcts. She could feel the cops watching her as he peeled back the scalp and showed her the fracture lines in the skull.

After it was over, it was time for lunch. The cops invited her to join them. They waited to see how hungry she was and what she would order, making jokes about chopped liver. What she wanted more than anything else in the world was a long, hot shower, but she toughed it out, ordered a cheeseburger, just like they did. Somehow it had been important to disappoint them, to show she could do it. Nowadays she went to autopsies voluntarily. Seeing the victim made the crime somehow more real, more painful. A sense of reality and pain were crucial to good prosecution.

Morgan Nelson located the correct gurney, checked the toe tag, made an old-fashioned gesture of the after-you variety, and stepped aside.

"Need me for anything else?" he said to Kathryn.

"We can manage, Doc," Giordano replied. "You carry on with whatever you were doing."

"Next one's a floater," Morgan said, with a grimace. Nobody liked floaters, the decomposed bodies of murder victims or suicides found in the ocean or on the shore. He'd want to get it over and done with, Kathryn thought. She felt the same way about the task ahead of her now.

Giordano peeled back the sheet. Kathryn forced herself to go closer, as close as she could without making contact. The girl's face was still grotesque, swollen, dark bluish in color. Dull brown eyes like marbles showed behind slitted lids. The hair was tucked neatly into an elasticized skullcap that concealed the incisions made by the Stryker saw. Kathryn steeled herself to take in the entire body, trying to memorize the details and at the same time trying to imagine what Barbara Gates had been like in real life.

A pretty girl. She remembered Morgan saying it, and how odd it had sounded. Barbara Gates had long eyelashes. Her finger- and toenails were manicured, and she'd had a wax job on her legs. She was slim, her figure almost boyish. The hip bones projected upward sharply, the stitched autopsy incision stark against the marble white skin. Below the belly, the wounds at the apex of the legs looked like pulped fruit. She looked at the girl's face again. Its expression was blank, as if what had happened to her body had nothing to do with her.

Kathryn shivered, remembering another conversation with Morgan Nelson, right after he did the autopsy.

"The physical findings lead me to believe her death was quick, Katie," Morgan had said. He meant it kindly, to alleviate any distress he thought she might be feeling.

"That doesn't bother me anything like knowing how long she had to realize she was going to die."

Death by asphyxiation took only a few minutes. But when every fiber of your being was screaming *please God somebody help me,* minutes were eons. Eons of knowing.

They stayed in the holding facility for maybe a quarter hour while Giordano made notes about the victim's injuries. These, and whatever information he excerpted from Morgan's autopsy protocol, would become part of his analysis of the killer's MO, and would also be used for the victimology, a summary of everything known about Barbara Gates.

"Okay, that's it," he said, putting the gold Cross pen into his inside jacket pocket. "Let's get back to the real world."

They went back upstairs and picked up the autopsy protocols at the reception desk. Giordano put them into his briefcase and they went out into the warm, welcome sunshine.

"Where now?" Kathryn said. "The crime scene?"

"It's four-thirty," Giordano said. "Let me buy you a cup of coffee."

"I could use something," Kathryn said.

They got into the car and she headed east on the freeway.

"There's an open-air café near the entrance to Cabrillo Park," she told Giordano. "It's on our way."

"The Café on the Park," Giordano said, reading the sign as she came off the freeway exit and swung in. There was a circular central building of glass and redwood with white slat tables and chairs ranged outside beneath blue and white striped umbrellas.

"The high school is about half a mile away," Kathryn told

him. "It backs right onto the park. Pretty much the biggest recreational area in Santa Rita. Scenic walks, archery, golf, and baseball. It's even got a covered bridge. No river, just the bridge."

Giordano let a smile touch his lips briefly. "California," he said. They walked over to a table and a young waitress came out to take their order.

"You don't drink coffee?" he said when she asked for tea. "That's practically un-American."

"But espresso is?"

"Hey, I'm Italian," he said. "Make allowances."

"You're from New York, right?"

"I was born on the Lower East Side. Little Italy."

"How long have you been in California?"

"Since 1984. You?"

"Ten years."

"Where you from originally?"

"Kansas City, Missouri."

"He called you Katie," Giordano said. He didn't push; she could respond if she wanted or let it go past her if she preferred.

"We go back a long way," she said. "Back to when I first came up here from L.A."

"He's what, fifty-five?"

It always surprised her that men her own age thought that mattered. Like, How could you be interested in that old man?

"Maybe you have to be a woman to understand."

"Try me."

"Morgan was there for me when nobody else was," she said. "I don't think I could have made it up here without his help—when I was seen as another pushy broad *intruding* into an all-male preserve."

"That bad, huh?"

"I didn't catch on for a long time. It was like when I was at law school, too naive to realize the excuses they were giving me when I wanted to borrow someone's notes were all part of the male freeze-out. For a little while, I felt like, oh, I don't know, like a lamb in a cage full of tigers."

"And Morgan kept them from eating you up?"

She smiled. You're just feeling sorry for yourself, Morgan had told her. Go on doing that, and they'll put you down as an easy mark. The boys have got to find out you can bite. You've got good teeth, Katie. Go bite someone.

"He listened, Steve. Whenever I needed a shoulder to cry on, whenever I needed someone to hold my hand. I don't need that so much anymore, but it's good to know he's still there. He's the nearest thing to a real father I've got."

She saw the flicker of his eyes that told her he had made a mental note of that last remark. The computer again.

"You have a daughter," he said. Just another simple, declarative sentence. He was good at those. She could simply talk about Emma in general if she wanted to. Or tell him the whole story.

"I was divorced just before I came up here," she said.

"A lawyer?"

"How did you know that?"

"It's a joke," he said. "Lawyers marry lawyers. Who else would have them?"

"Ouch."

He smiled his slow smile; it softened his whole expression. "Tell me about Emma," he said.

"She's nearly seven. She has long black hair and brown eyes and freckles. She likes dressing up pretty, going to the beach, oh, and quesadillas." She dug into her purse and came up with a snapshot Jack had taken a couple of months ago.

"Going to be a beautiful lady," Giordano said. Why did I think he was going to say, Like her mother? Kathryn wondered.

"I have to pick her up by six," Kathryn said. "We'd better move if you want to see the crime scene."

He paid the check and they got back into the car and drove down through the quiet streets of Outlook Heights to Cabrillo Park High. Kathryn used the car phone to advise the school administrator that they were coming in, and drove straight past the school building and around back, parking in front of the squat cinder block buildings. She clipped the crime scene seals and opened up the filtration facility. It smelled the same as before, of damp and stale air and chlorine. Kathryn flicked on the lights.

"You'll need a flashlight," she said. "There's probably one in the office."

She went into the cubicle, looked around. A cheap desk,

a hot plate, a rusty gooseneck lamp, some papers bunched together with a spring clip shaped like a giant clothespin, a battered old office chair. The flashlight was hung on a nail beside the door. She handed it to Giordano and followed him into the unlit area at the rear of the building. The beam of the flashlight picked out the workbench and the inspection pit in the floor.

"Down there," Kathryn said, gesturing.

"I saw the photographs."

He squatted down on his haunches, staring into the dark depths of the inspection pit as if its oil-streaked walls could somehow tell him something. His face was solemn, thoughtful.

"He must have taken quite a lot of care with the body," he said. "You'd think he would have just . . . let her fall. But he didn't. He lowered her in gently. So she'd look . . . just right."

"Why would he do that?"

Giordano shook his head, stood up. "The earlier victims were left out in the open, in public places, right? He just dumped them and ran?"

"That's right."

"You think maybe there could have been something . . . special about this one?"

"How, special?"

He shook his head again. "It's too soon to say. I don't go in for gut feelings, but if I did I'd say my gut feeling is, it's some kind of a game he's playing with us."

"Game?"

"He's saying, I can do whatever I like. Anytime I please. And there's nothing you can do about it. That's what the notes are about. With the little gingerbread man."

"I meant to ask you about that. You think that's what the little figure is?"

"It would fit," he said. "Run, run, as fast as you can, you can't catch me, I'm the gingerbread man."

"But would he be that dumb, putting himself deliberately at risk?"

"We're not dealing with someone stupid, Kathryn," Giordano said impatiently. "I suspect this man knows exactly what he's doing, and why he's doing it."

He put the flashlight back on its hook and they went

outside. Kathryn locked the door and put on fresh seals. Giordano stood staring at the unlovely building from which they had just emerged.

"Who'd know about a place like this?" he said, as if to himself. "Who'd know?"

He didn't seem to expect an answer. She looked at her watch—5:28.

"What now?" she asked.

He let out his breath in a long, frustrated sigh. "I burn some midnight oil over Doc Nelson's autopsy protocols."

"Where are you staying?"

"A friend who lives in Laguna del Mar loaned me his place. It's just a studio."

"I have to pick up Emma. If we could do that first, I can run you over to Shelter Island, then give you a ride home."

"Fine with me," he said, and got into the car. Kathryn drove down Outlook Heights Avenue to Alameda and swung east. The home-going commuter traffic was heavy; it took her nearly twenty minutes to get through the valley and up the hill to the college. When they reached the crest of the hill she pulled over so Giordano could see the view.

"That's Monterey?"

"Santa Rita to our right, Espanola right below us, Catalina to the left. And yes, Monterey way across the bay."

"All those lives going on down there," he said, almost as if to himself.

"Funny you should say that. When Barbara Gates was killed, I stopped here one evening," Kathryn said. "I sat here, and I thought pretty much the same thing: He's down there someplace. Maybe I can actually see the house he lives in. He has a job, he has friends, just like the rest of us. And we can't even begin to imagine what he looks like."

"So," he said slowly, "it's getting under your skin, too?"

She nodded. "I think about the life I'm living, the future ahead of me. And it being all over for them. Never having a chance. Young women like me, Steve. Like I was, once. It . . . haunts me."

"It's the same for all of us," he said. "Cops on the beat, detectives, you, me. We have to cope with things that are beyond coping with. Other people are lucky, all they have is nightmares."

She put the car into gear and headed down toward Lighthouse.

"Hey," she said on impulse, as they turned into the parking lot of Emma's school. "Do you like pesto?"

Giordano looked surprised. "Are you serious? I'm from Little Italy, remember?"

"I was going to cook some for Morgan. I've got all the fixings. Why don't you eat with us? I'll drive you down to Laguna later."

"I think I'd like that," Giordano said.

It wasn't a success.

When she saw Giordano, Emma's face changed; it was obvious she had been looking forward to having Kathryn all to herself. She knew by now that if there was a stranger in the car, it meant Kathryn was going to have to go out again, or intended to work at home. Either way, that was not what Emma wanted.

"Is he coming home with us?" she asked pointedly as Kathryn turned out of the school driveway onto Lighthouse.

"Emma!" Kathryn remonstrated. "This is Mr. Giordano. Not 'he.' "

"Well, is he?" her daughter insisted.

"Yes he is. I'm going to cook pesto. We can all have supper together. Would you like that?"

"What's pesto?"

"It's a way of cooking spaghetti," Steve told her, turning in the front seat so he could look at her.

"Yech!" Emma said. "I hate spaghetti."

"What do you like?"

Emma ignored the question. "Is he going to stay late, too?" she said to Kathryn.

"I think I've had enough of that face, Emma," Kathryn said, putting a warning into her voice. "And I think you'd better watch your manners, too, young lady."

Emma shrugged and fell sulky-silent; nobody said anything during the rest of the journey up to the condo. When Kathryn opened the door, Emma ran straight into her room. Kathryn pretended not to notice.

"She wants you all to herself," Giordano said. "Listen, we can forget this if you want to. I can grab a bite at the beach."

"She'll get over it," Kathryn said. "Can I get you something? I have orange or apple juice, Perrier, wine."

"Apple juice would be fine," Steve said. "This is a nice place you have."

They were standing at the kitchen bar, an L-shaped counter behind which were the stove, refrigerator, microwave, sinks, and cabinets. A cordless phone stood on a stand on the counter. The main living room opened out to the right of the entry. Straight ahead was the big window that led onto the balcony. To the right were floor-to-ceiling bookshelves, which also housed the CD player and a Sony portable TV. Two cream-colored armchairs flanked the window, and a sectional sofa with a glass-topped coffee table stood at about the center of the room. In one corner was a circular cherry table with four upright chairs. Steve walked over to look through the window.

"That's a great view."

"It's the main reason I bought the place," Kathryn said from the kitchen. "You sure you don't mind eating early?"

"No, it's fine," he said absently. She saw him looking at the CDs and the books, not casually but one by one. He moved about the room, noting the pale golden striped wallpaper and matching curtains, the complementary green of the patterned rug, the framed numbered print of the primitive painting depicting Espanola, the white painted wicker chairs and the copper planters on the balcony.

"Are you profiling me?" she asked, handing him his juice. The lines at the corners of his eyes crinkled, but it wasn't a real smile.

"Force of habit," he said. "I can't not do it anymore. Every time I go into a strange home, I find myself looking at things . . . getting a sense of the person."

"And?"

He raised an eyebrow. "If I had to use only one word, I'd say self-sufficient."

"What does that mean?"

"Living alone . . . women do it better than men."

It might have been an invitation to ask him about himself, but she let it go. She didn't want to have him feel uncomfortable, although another part of her brain assured her that Steve Giordano wasn't going to answer any question he didn't want to answer; later she'd feel that perhaps she should have taken the moment. Almost as soon as they were through eating, he thanked her, made his excuses, and left. It was only a couple of miles to Shelter Island; the walk would do him good, he said. As he left, he turned to face her.

"Listen, I appreciate your inviting me to your home. I enjoyed it."

She thought about that after he'd gone, and wondered what it was that he had enjoyed. The food had been adequate, and they had drunk a couple of glasses of zinfandel, talked about shows and movies and people they both knew. Emma had sulked a little at first, but he asked her without condescension to tell him about her school and what books she read, and after a while she'd responded to his unforced courtesy.

"So, did you like Mr. Giordano?" Kathryn asked her daughter as she tucked her into bed. Emma cocked her head to one side and considered the question with grave seriousness.

"Is he sad, Mommy?" she asked.

"I don't think especially. Why?"

"He has a sad look on his face when he doesn't know you're looking." She did one of those who-knows? shrugs. "Maybe he's lonely."

Kathryn laughed out loud. "You're a pretty smart kid," she said, "you know that?"

25

HE ALWAYS THOUGHT OF IT AS HUNTING. FINDING A PLACE where the innocents went their innocent way. Watching. Waiting. Until he found the right one. Then take her. Never the same place twice. Never the same way. And always, for the thrill of it, always a little more danger.

He decided on Marina Village, a high-income resort area a few miles down the coast where it was extremely unlikely he would be seen by anyone who knew him. The Village overlooked the inlet lying behind the long thin arm of Shelter Beach. The main streets ran east–west. Pedestrianized

Central had the stores and larger restaurants; Shoreside had the concessions and burger joints and open-air cafés facing the serried rows of berthed sailboats.

He wandered along Shoreside, mingling with the crowd. Christ, the *freedom* kids had today. Most of them dressed like they were going to a come-as-you-are party in Venice Beach. Girls everywhere: in tank tops and shorts, in minimal halter and short sets, in bikinis with cotton T-shirts over them, or cutoff denims that hugged their buttocks and crotches. Couples rolled past on bikes; ponytailed skaters in short-shorts whisked by, earphones tishing metallically. Nobody took any notice of him; he looked like any other visitor. A girl climbing over the rail of a medium-sized powerboat caught his eye. She was maybe five-three or -four, with long dark hair tied back with a hank of yellow ribbon. Dark eyes, long slender legs, smooth brown skin. The name of the boat was *Suzie Q*. He watched her for a while, the movements of her body as she bent and turned triggering the first pulse of desire. There were people everywhere; far too many people. When did it quieten down? Wait, wait. No hurry, yet. Let it build. That was part of the excitement.

He sat down at a table outside a café opposite the yacht harbor and watched the women come and go, blondes, brunettes, plain girls, pretty girls, thin girls, fat girls. Amazing how many fat girls there were. Lardy buttocks, dimpled thighs, blowsy breasts, ugly, ugly, ugly.

The girl he had seen on the boat appeared out of nowhere. She was wearing an unbuttoned white cotton blouse over a one-piece swimsuit cut low at the top and high at the thighs. Her figure was trim and neat, her legs firm and brown. Legs were important. You couldn't be beautiful if you had ugly legs. He followed her along the waterfront, mingling with the crowd so she wouldn't notice him. She turned left on Third. By the time he got there she had disappeared.

He went back to the yacht harbor and walked along to where the *Suzie Q* was docked. A young blond guy of maybe twenty-four was hosing down the deck of a sailboat in the adjoining berth. Lee stopped and pretended to take an interest.

"Nice boat," he said. "Yours?"

The kid looked at him with lazy insolence. "Ahuh," he said.

"This one here, the *Suzie Q.* Would you happen to know the name of the guy who owns it?"

"Sure. Kenny Brayfield."

"Does he live down here?"

"Na. Catalina, I think."

"I was talking to his girlfriend the other day," Lee said. "Long hair tied back with a yellow ribbon?"

"Oh, Linda," the kid said.

Linda!

"Linda, right. I've seen her around."

"Ahuh," the kid said. "She works over at Feltrini's."

That explained her disappearance. She'd gone into the staff entrance of the pizza joint she worked in.

"Going to take a sail?"

The kid squinted at the sky. "Na," he said. "Too late."

"See you around," Lee said.

"You have a safe one," the kid replied.

By about eight, Marina Village was much quieter, and after sundown, the streets were almost empty, the yacht harbor silent. Only in the brightly lit cafés and fast food places was there activity and laughter. By eleven, those too were closed and the kids moved up to a place called Everly's on the corner of Fourth and Central.

Perfect.

He walked back to where he had left his car and drove home. He would not go back to Marina Village again that week. Give the kid on the sailboat time to forget him. He sat in the dimly lit den and thought about Linda bending over the side of the boat until the wanting built inside him like steam in a pressure cooker. He checked that the door was locked and unzipped his pants.

Her name was Linda Diaz, and she was twenty. She lived with two other girls in a second-floor apartment on Second between Shoreside and Central, and worked at a pizza joint called Feltrini's on Shoreside between Third and Fourth, open seven days a week from eight in the morning till eleven at night. Staff worked two shifts; eight till four and three till eleven. Linda had an almost unvarying routine. If she was on the early shift she would go down to the yacht harbor after she got through and hang around until her boyfriend turned up, usually around six.

If she was working the late shift, she would meet him and the rest of the boating crowd at Everly's after she got through. They'd stay maybe an hour, drinking beer, then Kenny and Linda would walk down the hill to her place. If it was a Saturday he might sleep over. Otherwise, he'd head home for Catalina.

Tuesday night was warm, with a cooling breeze coming in off the ocean. At ten-thirty Lee slid the pickup into a vacant parking place near the corner of Fourth, about fifty yards from Feltrini's; there were only a few cars parked there at night. He got out and waited. The yacht harbor was silent except for the soft slap of water on boat hulls, the occasional creak of a mooring line; reflected lights danced on the water. A woman's laughter came from somewhere, but there were few people about. The pizza place was pretty much empty, too, just one or two late owls in there, the waitresses tidying up their stations, the kitchen staff cleaning and scouring.

She came out at eight minutes past eleven. She was wearing tennis shoes, white slacks, and a blue sweatshirt. He waited till she got nearer then started walking toward her. As they drew level with each other he stopped.

"Linda?" he said.

She stopped, frowning, wary. "Excuse me?"

"I'm a friend of Kenny Brayfield's," he said. "You're his girlfriend, aren't you?"

"Yes, I am," she said. She was alert, but not frightened. Good, good.

"I've got a package for him." He showed her the parcel he had made. "Something he ordered for the *Suzie Q*. He said it was urgent so I brought it down but he's not there."

"He's up at Everly's," she said. "You want me to show you where it is? I'm going up there now."

"Hey, fine," Lee said. "Lead the way."

He had his hand on the stun gun as they rounded the corner onto Fourth, out of the brighter lights and into the darker shadows. He grabbed her, slamming her against the wall of a building, clamping his left hand over her mouth as he tugged the stun gun out of his pocket. In the same moment, she brought up her knee into his crotch, flailing away at his face with clawed hands. He sensed the knee coming up, and managed to twist his body to deflect the worst of it, but it winded him and he involuntarily loosened his grip. One of her flailing hands hit him clumsily across the face, bringing tears to his eyes, and then she bit his clamping hand, screaming.

"Bastard, bastard, get away from me, you fucking bastard!"

He grabbed her again, trying to get the stun gun against her body, but she was strong, writhing, screaming, flailing at him, kicking, spitting.

"Help me!" she screeched, "somebody help me!"

"Shut up, you bitch!" he snarled, and hit her with his fist. She bounced back against the wall and off it, collapsing askew, her mouth a bloody rose, her eyes wide with fear. Her sweatshirt was torn at the neck and there was a black streak on the thigh of her slacks.

He stooped to grab her again, shut her up, anything, but she scrabbled away from him, screaming like a factory whistle, a loud, piercing sound. *Jesus Christ. She'll have the harbor patrol down here in a minute!* He turned and ran blindly back to the harbor pursued by the unbroken sound of her screams *helpmehelpmehelpme.* He scrambled into the cab of the pickup and sat slumped over the steering wheel, trembling from head to foot, soaked with sweat, his heart pounding. *Jesus, Jesus, Jesus!* He could still hear her screaming and he thought he saw some men running toward the sound. Had anyone seen him running around the corner? Getting into the pickup?

Don't panic, he told himself. *Act natural.* He made himself move with slow and normal deliberation. Drawing in deep, ragged breaths, perspiration streaming down his face, he started the engine, backed out of the parking space, and drove slowly along Shoreside, every nerve tensed for someone's yell behind him. Nothing happened. As he turned up East Laguna Drive, a good half mile from the yacht harbor, a police car sped by in the opposite direction, siren blaring.

Ten minutes later, just after he passed beneath the freeway and turned west on Alameda, he pulled over to the side of the road and pounded the steering wheel with his fist, exorcising his anger. *Bitch, bitch, she'd ruined everything.*

"Slowly," he said, over and over again, like a mantra, slowly, slowly, slowly, slowly, until his breathing and pulse rate were normal. Then he went back over every single second of what had happened, rolling the film of it in his mind like a video engineer running a tape, again and again and again, so that he knew every frame, every movement. Think it through. It had been a mess, but he had got out of it clean. Maybe the bitch had seen his face, maybe she'd give the cops some kind of a description. He could live with that: there were a thousand men in Santa Rita who would fit his general description.

He checked his watch; it was a little after eleven. It probably wasn't necessary, but he would take all the usual precautions. That was another rule: never take chances. He got back on the road, swinging north off the freeway onto University Drive and heading for the mountains. It was after twelve-thirty when he finally got back home; the lights in his wife's bedroom were out. So much the better. She knew better than to ever again ask him questions, but at least there would be no stupid conversation: Did you have a nice day? No clucking about whether he had eaten, whether he would like something warm to drink, as if he were some kind of fucking moron. He was wearing his usual street clothes now; everything he had worn earlier was burned. That way, even if he had lost a button or left a shoe track at the scene, it wouldn't matter. He was just going to sleep when he thought *Jesus fucking Christ, the stun gun.*

There was nothing in the paper the next morning. He was tempted to get into his car and go back down to the Village, look around; but that would have been stupid. Someone would have found the stun gun, either a passerby or one of the cops he'd seen going to the scene. It didn't matter; no one could trace it to him. Years ago he'd read in a gun magazine and filed away the information about which states had the fewest restrictions on buying weapons: Kentucky, Delaware, Tennessee, North Carolina, and Virginia. Visiting Richmond for a convention, he'd paid cash for the stun gun in a store around the corner from the John Marshall Hotel. There would be no prints on it; he always wore surgical gloves when he was hunting. The clothes he had worn had been burned; the ashes sifted out of the window of the car as he drove back to Santa Rita. His hand was bruised where she'd bitten it, but the latex gloves had prevented her teeth from breaking the skin.

He walked through his day like a zombie. At four he

bought the earliest edition of the evening paper and scanned it eagerly. There it was:

GIRL FIGHTS OFF ATTACKER

Linda Diaz, 20, of Marina Village, was hospitalized last night at County Hospital suffering from shock following a vicious midnight attack. Her assailant is described as a man of medium height with dark hair, between forty and fifty years of age, wearing a tan jacket and slacks. Laguna del Mar police spokesperson Sgt. Mary-Jo Kupfer said a number of leads were being followed up.

Nothing much there. It was hardly likely that the police would mention the stun gun, assuming they had found it. It was still possible some kid had picked it up and walked away with it.

At five he drove home, put his car in the garage, and went into the den with the pot of tea Carol always had ready for him. He switched on the TV, flicking from channel to channel, hoping to catch a local newscast, but everything was sitcoms or talk shows. He was drinking his second cup of tea when the doorbell rang. He frowned; who would be calling at this time of day? He waited; after a few moments Carol tapped on the study door.

"Dear, can you spare a moment?" she said. There was a tremor in her voice. He opened the door and she stared at him.

"What is it?" he said impatiently. She turned and he saw the man standing in the hallway, a good-looking guy with blond hair and a crooked grin.

"Mr. Russell?" he said. "My name is David Granz. I'm an inspector with the district attorney's office." He held up a wallet and flipped it open. Lee stared in disbelief at the shining shield. *Jesus,* he thought, *they know, they know.* Panic paralyzed him, damping down his hearing, blurring his sight. He felt sweat break out all over his body. *Jesus,* he thought, *they've found me, they know.* The words pounded in his head like a heartbeat: *theyknow, theyknow, theyknow.*

"What . . . what do you want?" he managed.

"Just a few questions," Granz said. "It won't take long."

26

FOR KATHRYN MORNINGS HAD ALWAYS BEEN A STRUGGLE; even though she was usually out of bed at five-thirty, most days it still wasn't early enough. Get dressed, pile into the car with Emma's backpack filled with lunch, snacks, sweater, jacket, a swimsuit for the days they went straight to swim lessons. Breakfast from Donaldson's, usually eaten in the car, sometimes checking homework at the same time. A few kisses in front of the school, and then total immersion in work. That was when everything went well; there were also bad days when they were late and she sent a tearful Emma off, her half-eaten breakfast still on the front seat, no time even for a farewell hug.

Lunch hours were the same, always on the run. Shopping, trips to the cleaner or the bank, doctor and dentist appointments, all had to be crammed into that brief hour. At the end of the day, making the switch from prosecutor to mother on the way up to Lighthouse to pick up her daughter. Emma's evening routine was pretty much set: dinner, shower, clothes out for the next day, a game or a story, bedtime. And so was Kathryn's. Hop on the StairMaster—no time these days to jog—and catch up on case summaries and legal updates before collapsing into bed. Next day, start all over again. *The Waltons* it was not.

Working with Steve Giordano had changed all that. For the first time in as long as she could remember she had fat on her schedule. She could get up later, linger over breakfast while Emma prattled on about school, or swim class, or her friend Julie Corcoran, and still have plenty of time to drive downtown. Being off trials meant not having to stay up until the wee small hours reading transcripts, highlighting police reports, outlining the testimony of her next day's witnesses. It meant not having to spend her weekends researching the law and prepping closing arguments. She could relax, shop, spend time with Emma, watch TV.

Instead of the adrenaline rush that came with going to

trial, there was the steadily building excitement of investigation, the construction of the jigsaw puzzle of fact and clue and supposition that went into creating an offender profile. It was slow work, involving meticulous examination of existing evidence and careful reexamination of all the witness statements and investigative reports filed by the SO deputies who had been first to arrive at the crime scenes, CSI, SO detectives, and DA's inspectors.

Among the first things Giordano did was to allocate to Jack Burrows the virtually full-time task of compiling a register of all assaults on females between the ages of fourteen and thirty made between the time of the discovery of the first body on Shelter Island and the present, cross-referencing descriptions of attackers, types of locations, and victim profiles, computer-scanning thousands and thousands of documents for common denominators.

"That's going to be a mother of a document," Burrows commented sourly. "You mind telling me what we get out of it at the end of the day?"

"This guy isn't batting a thousand, Jack," Kathryn explained. "For every time he's succeeded, he must have tried and failed once, a couple of times. You know what he's looking for: concentrate on young Hispanic women between the ages of, say, sixteen and twenty-five, check their statements, see if there are any common denominators in their descriptions of the assailant, the MO, anything."

While Burrows called in all the documentation he would need, Giordano went through the police reports and the autopsy protocols on each murder line by line, asking Kathryn questions about the locations. Time and again he went through the numbered photographs, always in the order they had been taken, from crime scene to autopsy table, studying the body wounds from every photographic aspect and in lighting that varied from natural daylight to lab high-intensity. He spent hours with Morgan Nelson, asking questions, listening carefully.

"I'm beginning to see what you meant about him," Giordano told Kathryn after one of these meetings. "He's ... *offbeat* isn't quite the word. *Idiosyncratic* might be nearer. He has his own way of looking at things. Not to mention saying them. What's that thing about wild herrings?"

"It's a saying he made up. People who never chase after wild herrings or red geese rarely stand the world on its ear."

The small smile that seemed to be all he allowed himself touched the corners of his mouth. "Wild herrings and red geese," he said. "Is that what your friend Granz is chasing?"

"I don't understand."

"Jack Burrows tells me he's collecting mailing lists."

"Mailing lists? What kind of mailing lists?"

"Burrows didn't know. He says Granz made it pretty clear he didn't want to talk about it, said it was just an angle he's working on."

"And it has to do with this case?"

Giordano lifted a shoulder. "He didn't say."

Kathryn frowned thoughtfully. "Dave isn't much on wild herrings or red geese," she said. "He's more the just-gimme-the-facts-ma'am type. Do you want me to ask him?"

"It can wait. We've got plenty to work on."

Amen to that, she thought. The task of compiling a profile involved five distinct phases. First, a minute reexamination of the crimes. Then, a comprehensive evaluation of the specifics of the crime scenes. Third was a victimology, an analysis of everything known about each of the victims; fourth and fifth were evaluations—complete reevaluations really, like everything else Giordano did—of the police reports and Morgan Nelson's autopsy protocols. From these five would develop a profile with critical offender characteristics, as well as investigative suggestions predicated on the profile constructed.

"You know something about the process already," Giordano had told Kathryn soon after they began working together. "It's not dissimilar to the way a clinician makes a diagnosis and treatment plan. We start with the actual crimes: what the man is actually doing and what significance those acts may have for him."

"I took a run at that, right at the beginning when they found the body in Sedgewick Park," Kathryn said. "I had some half-formed ideas. We discussed it, remember?"

Giordano nodded. "I remember," he said.

"I had the thought—hunch, if you like—the motive might be revenge. What do you think? Could he be doing this to women as a sort of ... repayment for something some woman did to him?"

"A specific kind of woman, perhaps? Hispanic, late teens or early twenties?"

"That's what it begins to look like, doesn't it? Which in turn might mean he's Hispanic, too. But that's just statistical. He could as easily be white."

"Who came up with the idea he might be taking trophies?"

"That was Doc Nelson. Why, was another matter. That was about as far along as we got. There were too many holes. No victim ID on the first two cases, no primary crime scene, so we couldn't evaluate that."

"Look, don't let the fact that all we have are secondary crime scenes throw you," he said, "there are still some things there that are useful to us."

"Such as?"

"First, the fact that he changed his MO slightly each time."

"You mean the way he dumped the bodies?"

"How significant do you think that is?"

I'm not the profiler, she thought. This is your bag, not mine.

"Maybe it doesn't matter anymore by the time he comes to get rid of the body," she suggested. "Maybe whatever his . . . fantasy is, it's completed by then."

She thought she saw surprise, but only for a moment.

"Good, yes," he said. "But there's something else. The Shelter Island victim was just dumped on the dunes. After seeing the area, I'd guess he probably brought her there in a car or a pickup, lifted her out, and just let her go, down the slope. You can see"—he pointed with a pencil at the photograph of the sprawled corpse—"she just rolled down there any which way. The second victim, too; he just rolled her into the lagoon. But Barbara Gates . . ."

He fell silent, swiveling the chair in an arc, staring without seeing out of the window, his expression the same thoughtful frown she had seen when they had visited the crime scene at Cabrillo Park High and he had squatted over the dark hole of the inspection pit, visualizing the body of Barbara Gates spread-eagled down below.

As the days went by, she became accustomed to seeing him there like that; swinging in the chair, turning ideas over in his mind, examining some item of information the way an archaeologist would turn an artifact over and over, this way and that, looking at it from every conceivable angle.

Less easy to get used to was the feeling that when he looked into her eyes Giordano was actually reading her mind. It was the same feeling she got when men looked at her a certain, sexual way, mentally undressing her. Only in Giordano's case, his eyes never left hers. It wasn't her body that interested him. Was that flattering? Or not?

"Let me ask you something," she said. "You remember they found a tire track at the Gates crime scene? It made me wonder . . . how does this guy move the victims around without anyone seeing him? There are always people around Shelter Island, even late at night. The same is true of Sedgewick Park; the body had to be taken across open space, or to a boardwalk, then lifted over a rail and dumped into the lagoon. Yet nobody saw anything."

Giordano shook his head. "People tend only to notice the unusual, the out-of-the-ordinary. I had a case where a guy trundled a naked body through a railroad depot in a plastic trash bag loaded on a two-wheel luggage trolley. Dozens of people saw him do it, but nobody really *saw* the guy. You know, they look at him doing it right out there in full view, and they think he must be legit, right? There was a case in Wilmington where one of these creeps killed a woman in his apartment, put her body in a sleeping bag, took a cab to the docks, and dumped it there. The cab driver who gave him a hand loading it into the back of the cab never noticed a thing."

"Someone suggested he might be using a folding wheelchair."

"That's as good a guess as any."

"But the risks the guy would be taking, pushing a dead body around in public . . ."

"May be part of the enjoyment," he said. "Or maybe it isn't . . . real."

"Not real?"

"Like you said. Maybe that part of it isn't in the fantasy. Maybe it's just a chore he has to do when it's all over."

As time passed, the formality that had been there between them at the start of their working relationship dissolved. She got used to being around him, accustomed to the way he moved his body, the half-gestures with which he accompanied certain statements, the way by five o'clock he needed a shave. Every once in a while he would disappear, and she'd learn later he'd been visiting with Benton or had meandered over to see what was happening in Earheart's bailiwick, touching base with everyone he needed to touch base with. He didn't overdo it; that would have been as big a mistake as to try to insinuate himself into the closely knit camaraderie of the homicide detectives, who would have given him short shrift. He was serious but not grave; if he said he would do something, he delivered. He showed them he respected them; after a while they began to do the same.

And day by day, they worked their way through the mountains of paperwork that are generated by any murder investigation, reports, diagrams, photographs, tips from the public. Day by day, they fed it all into the database, which now contained every known fact about the victims, the crime scenes, the killer. Day by day they ran the program, cross-referencing, querying, adducing, canceling as they went. And day by day they grew closer to each other, knowing and yet not realizing it was so.

"How are we doing?" Kathryn asked. They were into the second week of their partnership.

"We're getting there. Why do you ask?"

"I had a call from Richard Sanchez. He wanted to know if we had anything he could use."

Giordano made an impatient sound. "Tell him to go take a . . ." He caught Kathryn's expression and paused, and the small smile moved the corners of his mouth. "You already told him, right?"

"Give the man a kewpie doll." Kathryn smiled. "Want some coffee?"

"Sure. Black—"

"One sugar, I know." Kathryn plugged in the hot pot and spooned instant coffee into the stoneware mug Giordano had acquired from somewhere. When the water boiled, she'd make some tea for herself.

"Tell me something, what are you doing weekend after next?"

The question was so totally unexpected she was taken

aback. "Nothing special I can think of. That is, Sunday my ex-husband is coming to visit Emma."

"So you'd be free the Saturday night?"

She nodded, covering her slight confusion by making the coffee and pouring hot water over a teabag in her own cup.

"The Alameda College Players are doing *Carousel*," he said. "Have you ever seen it?"

"That's Rodgers and Hammerstein, isn't it?"

Once again she detected faint surprise. "Most people say *Hammer-steen*," he said. He made an untypically hesitant gesture. "I thought we might go. If you'd like to."

"Saturdays are iffy," Kathryn said. "I can't always get a sitter . . ."

"No, no," he told her. "I got tickets for us all, you, me, Emma. I want her to see it."

"Isn't she a bit young . . . ?"

"She'll love it. It's sort of a fairy tale."

"I think I saw the movie."

"It's not in the same class as the stage show."

"You sound like an expert."

He made the same diffident gesture again. It was like he was reluctant to let her—or was it anyone?—see any side of him except the formal one.

"I love those old musicals. Kern, Cole Porter, the Gershwins. *Carousel* is probably the best of the Rodgers and Hammerstein shows."

"What time does it begin?"

He took an envelope out of his pocket and looked inside.

"Seven-thirty. If I picked you up at what, six? We could grab something to eat in Espanola, go straight to the college."

"You already bought the tickets?"

"Had to. It's a sellout."

"You were so sure I'd go?"

"There'll be no problem if I have to return them," he told her. "I checked. They've already got a waiting list."

"Answer the question."

"Pretty sure," he replied. His eyes met hers, held her gaze. Something more than the words was being said. Kathryn stood very still, wondering if he could hear her heartbeat in the silence the way she could. It felt like a door opening, as if there were a connection running between the two of them, conducting sexual energy.

"What's happening here, Steve?" she said very quietly.

"It's like in the song. Getting to know you."

"We haven't had much time for that."

He moved his head slightly but said nothing. The brown eyes gazed steadily into her own. "We've earned a break. You already cooked for me. How about if I take you to dinner tonight?"

The telephone rang and they jumped, like guilty conspirators. She laughed and picked up the receiver.

"It's for you," she said. He took the phone with his left hand, touching her fingers with his right.

"So? What about dinner?"

She smiled. "It took you long enough," she said.

Kathryn wore her black dress and her Saks Fifth Avenue shoes. She thought about taking a wrap and decided against it.

"Well, well, look at you," Ruth said. "This Giordano fellow must be something special."

"You look pretty, Mommy," Emma said, and hugged her. "And you smell nice."

"You know, I can't recall how long it's been since I wore a dress," Kathryn said. "I'm so used to wearing suits, I feel . . . I don't know, flighty."

"Have a good time," Ruth said. "Don't be in a hurry. *King Kong* is on *The Late Show*."

"It's just a date, Ruth," Kathryn said.

"Sure," Ruth replied. "Dinner at Paolo's."

Paolo's was probably the most exclusive restaurant in Santa Rita, standing on Lookout Point in Cliffside Park. In a foyer decorated with green silk drapes and oil paintings a maître d' in tails greeted them and asked them if they would care for cocktails.

"We'll go straight in, I think," Steve said. "And take a look at the wine list."

The restaurant was on two levels, and was already nearly full. They followed the maître d' upstairs and were ushered to their table in a corner; it was like dining in space. Menus the size of drawing boards were brought to them. Kathryn smiled.

"Who was it said, The bigger the menu, the lousier the food?"

"Marcel Proust."

"Did he eat out a lot?"

"In his younger days," Steve said. "Would you like me to order, or would you consider that inappropriate?"

"Go ahead," Kathryn said with a smile. "I'm not that militant."

While Steve and the waiter discussed the menu, she studied him surreptitiously. He was a good-looking man, she thought. A slight bump on the bridge of his nose hinted at a break, skillfully mended. The thoughtful eyes, strong jaw, and firm mouth projected an impression of calm reliability. He had large hands and big-boned wrists, a dark shadow of hair poking from under the shirt cuff. He wore a simple gold watch with a black leather strap.

"Well," he said, as the waiter went away. "That takes care of that. Now we can talk."

"Good," she said. "There's something I want to ask you."

She saw the slightly guarded look appear in his eyes. Was he always on guard? And if so, against what?

"What did that mean, about Marcel Proust, in his younger days?"

"He took to his bed when he was thirty-five. Never went out again."

"You know about Proust?"

He cocked his head to one side and stuck out his lip. "Was that really what you wanted to ask me?"

"I had a couple of other things," she said.

"Go ahead."

"You don't wear a wedding ring. But I gather there was a Mrs. Giordano?"

He made a rueful face. "Ah, the interdepartmental grapevine. I forgot how efficient it is. What did you hear?"

"Just that you'd been married. And you mentioned kids."

He looked out at the ocean, across to where the lights of Santa Rita were beginning to glimmer in the deepening blue of the evening.

"Her name is Susan."

"Go on."

"We were married right after I moved out here," he said. "That was what, eight, no, nine years ago. Tony was born the following year. Lisa came along two years later. I was in at the beginning of CIRT, working fifteen hours a day, seven days a week. I loved what I was doing so much it never occurred to me Suze might want things any other way. Then one day she gave me an ultimatum: if I didn't take some notice of my family, start being a husband and a father, she was going to file for divorce and custody of the kids."

"A lot of cops' wives feel that way. I've heard them say they wished it was another woman, they could handle that."

"I didn't want to lose her, lose everything. I told her I'd quit the department, get some other kind of job if that was what it took. I even started looking around. Hopeless. I had no skills anyone wanted. Except law enforcement."

That, too, was a common experience: prosecutors, cops, all of them, were trained to do only one thing. If it became impossible to continue, what else could you do?

"She went ahead with the divorce?"

He looked out at the ocean, the way he had before. "I didn't fight her for custody. It was like I had some strange disease, like I was paralyzed with apathy. I couldn't . . ." He turned his head back to face her, looking into her eyes. "It worked out pretty well for her. She remarried, some guy who's a camera operator with a news agency, had a couple more kids. Lives up in Sacramento, fat and happy."

"And the children?"

"I see them when I can. This kind of work, it's difficult to do it on a regular basis."

A waiter brought the wine in an ice bucket and showed it to Steve, who looked at the label and nodded. The waiter removed the cork and poured a half inch into a glass. Steve wasn't embarrassed by the ritual the way some men are. He picked up the glass, sniffed, took a sip, nodded again. When their glasses were filled, he touched her rim with his, his eyes on her face. The wine was pale and cool, with a tart edge. Kathryn made an appreciative sound.

"It's just a summer wine," he said. "Frascati."

"Frascati. Where is that?"

"Right outside of Rome."

"You've been there?"

"Sure. My people are from Naples."

The waiters served their first course, hot flaky pastries filled with asparagus spears in a chervil sauce.

"Mmmmm-mmmm," Kathryn said. "What's in this sauce?"

"Just cream, butter, lemon juice. And chervil, of course."

"Is this an Italian dish?" she asked.

" 'Sta sera, tutt' il mondo è Italiano," he said. "Tonight the whole world's Italian. Why are you smiling?"

"I just remembered, we were eating Italian when Jack and I had our final breakup."

"In a restaurant?"

"Not like this. It was one of those hokey little trattorias, you know, spaghetti with clams, cheap red wine in a carafe, checkered tablecloths and candles in those wine bottles with basketwork. We were with friends, Dick Martin, a public defender I knew, and his wife Terry. And suddenly, right there in the restaurant, Jack started trashing me. Workaholic, power hungry, hyperambitious, lousy wife, lousy mother."

"People store things up," Steve said, as if recalling a personal experience. "Then the dam breaks. Was it rough?"

"I just . . . sat there and took it because I couldn't believe he was doing this in front of our friends. I could see Dick and Terry were embarrassed, they didn't know what to do. I was too tired to fight: I'd been in trial all day. And then Jack said, Dick, you were in court, tell the truth, didn't you think that closing argument of Kathryn's was the worst damned mess you ever heard in your whole life?"

"Really gave it to you, huh?"

"It wasn't new. He'd been doing me for a long time. That night was just . . . what's the cliché?"

"The straw that broke the camel's back?"

"I got up and walked out of the restaurant. And a little while later, out of his life."

"You met him in law school." There it goes again, she thought, that deceptively simple sentence that invites you to open up your entire life. If you want to. Well, tonight, for some reason, she wanted to.

"If I'd been smarter I'd have known we were a bad match right from the start. Jack went to law school because his parents thought lawyering was a good way to make money."

"Not you, though."

"No." She smiled. "With me it was a crusade. I was going to make the world a better place."

"How come?"

"You sure you want to know all this? It goes back a long way. To when I was a kid."

"I really want to know," he said gravely. "Ah, here's our food."

He had ordered a hot shrimp salad garnished with morels. The sauce tasted of green peppercorns.

"Good?" he asked.

"Heaven," she said, and meant it. Although she loved good food, she was usually dashing about so much she sometimes literally forgot to eat, or grabbed the first thing she saw, some kind of sandwich, a Snickers bar, anything. They ate for a while in companionable silence, enjoying the food and the wine. Then Steve asked a question.

"Did you have freckles, too, like Emma?"

She shook her head. "I was small, skinny, gawky. I never had her kind of self-assurance. She knows more at six than I knew at twice her age."

"They all do."

"My father shielded me from everything. Not my sister, just me. I was his little girl, you know, polka dots and pigtails. He wanted me to stay like that forever. Then when I was fourteen he died. My mother married an old friend of my father's, a widower named Paul Kravitz. He had two sons of his own. He just didn't know how to handle a teenage girl. He'd been brought up in one of those spare-the-rod-and-spoil-the-child families, so he was very big on punctuality at mealtimes, good school grades, doing your homework. My sister Teresa had married and my brother went to work in Oregon. So I got it all. It was like living with Simon Legree."

"Hard for a teenager to take," he said. "Especially with all that life out there waiting to be lived."

"This one didn't wait. You remember that saying, I sold my soul to rock and roll? That was me. I just went right off the rails. The kids I mixed with were, you know, less advantaged than me. So I could feel superior, I guess. I was skipping classes, hanging out with the gang. God, that long, hot summer, I remember it so well. Bobby Kennedy killed, and

Martin Luther King. The race riots in Detroit, remember all that?"

"Nineteen sixty-eight," he said. "My folks took me to see *Hair*."

"There was this boy, Peter Devaney." She smiled as she spoke the name. "I haven't even thought of him in years. I was wild about him. We went to see *Bonnie and Clyde* five times. Of course, Paul disapproved. And of course, the heavier he came down on me, the more I rebelled. I was seventeen and I knew it all. Then one night, I was with Pete and some other kids in a bar for over-21's, using phony ID. The police arrived, and next thing I knew I was on my way to juvenile hall."

"And your stepfather said, I told you so."

"Close. What he actually said was, You made your bed, now lie in it. He didn't come down to the hall and he wouldn't let my mother go either. So there I was, very scared and all alone. Then this woman from the public defender's office came to see me. Her name was Melinda Gray; she'd been assigned to my case. She got me released and placed on informal probation. She gave me the support my parents wouldn't. I can't tell you how important that was to me then."

"Is that where you got the idea of becoming a lawyer?"

"I guess . . . I wanted to be like her. After college, I enrolled in law school. I was pretty naive. No one in our family had ever even been to college, never mind law school. I didn't have the slightest idea what I was letting myself in for."

"And then you met Jack."

"We got married right after we graduated. I became a public defender, Jack went straight into the DA's office. I guess he needed that security, being part of an organization. He wasn't really interested in the criminals he prosecuted or the cases he was handling. He just did the job."

"But you . . . ?"

"I did everything but ride a white horse. You know how you are at that age, you think you can whip the world. I lasted eighteen months. It just ground me down to nothing. When Jack told me there was an opening in the DA's office, I quit. He was great at first, so supportive, so understanding. Maybe he thought he'd won. I don't know. Then . . . I started wanting to move on, move up. He saw that as a threat. We did nothing but squabble about it. After a year, we were at each other's throats morning, noon, and night. I'd yell at him, he'd yell at me. We disagreed on practically everything."

"So you split."

"Melinda Gray told me something I've never forgotten," Kathryn said. "She said there was nothing shameful in the pursuit of excellence. Jack kept trying to make me settle for less and I wouldn't. I'd identified my aims. I wanted to try important criminal cases. I knew if I didn't work twice as hard as everyone else I'd spend the rest of my life trying misdemeanors in municipal court. I wasn't about to settle for that."

"Twice as hard. Because you're a woman, you mean?"

"Twice as hard because I don't have anyone to hold the fort for me. You think about it. I'm on a knife edge all the time. I can't be sick. I can't take time off. If it even looks like Emma might be coming down with something, a cold, a fever, I panic. Then the guilt sets in. Because instead of worrying about my daughter, I'm more concerned about whether I'll be in trial, whether I'll be able to find someone to look after her, hoping she'll be okay till the weekend so I can look after her."

"Does it make you angry?"

"No, I chose the life. It's just . . . just sometimes I get jealous at how easy it is for other people. Especially the men. They have a wife for backup. To do the washing, the ironing, the cooking, the shopping."

"Maybe you should get married again."

He just said it. No emphasis, no meaningful glance. She looked at him for a long moment, not speaking. His eyes didn't waver.

"I don't know. I don't think I'm cut out to be a wife. But I'd make a great husband."

They laughed, and the moment passed. When they had finished, he signaled the waiter and paid the check. Afterwards they drove over to East Bayshore Park and strolled along the path above the ocean. It felt relaxed and comfortable and good. There seemed to be no need for further conversation.

After a while, he stopped and turned to face her, taking both her hands in his. His expression was unreadable in the phosphorescent half-light coming up off the ocean.

"I'm pretty much of an old-fashioned type, Kathryn," he

said softly. "Everything by the book. You know, dinner, the theater, take you home to meet my folks."

"I'd noticed that," she replied, feeling the door swing open again, the same electric energy flow between them.

"It's just that we seem to have reached what they call a certain point in the relationship sooner than I expected," he said.

"I'd noticed that, too."

"So . . . the thing is, I don't want to make any wrong moves with you," he said. "We can keep it at this level if you want to."

She thought about that for a little while. Down below they could hear the ocean surging against the cliffs.

"No," she said. "I don't want that."

He said nothing more. They walked back to the car and drove over to his studio apartment in Laguna del Mar. It was on the second floor, with a big picture window looking out across the lagoon. It seemed to her it took forever to climb the stairs, and then they were in the darkened apartment and his lips were on hers and he was fumbling with the back of her dress and they fell over backwards onto the bed.

"The zipper," he panted. "Where's the goddamn zipper?"

"Here," she answered, breathlessly. "Wait, let me . . ."

His body was broad and strong, and in the faint light coming through the window she could see his eyes were closed. He put his arms around her and held her close, gently at first, until she whispered that she wouldn't break. She ran her hands up the length of his body, feeling the strong swell of his back muscles. She felt his lips on her breasts, the nipples springing erect to meet them. She lifted her buttocks and he slid off the panties. His body hair brushed her skin as his hands caressed her and it was like warm water running through her, and then all she wanted was the hardness and weight of him deep inside her.

He spoke her name softly as he entered her, almost like a question. Afterwards she had no recollection of anything other than the mounting urgency of her own emotions, the answering surge of his, long sweet waves of pleasure followed by sudden, endless aching release. And then when it was over, and they lay there laughing and sweaty and breathless, his arms around her like a shield, he kissed her gently at the nape of her neck.

"That takes care of the lust," he said. "Now let's make love."

Around midnight he drove her home. As they turned into her street, she saw the police car outside the condo, radio squawking. Her mind went blank. All she could think was *Emma.* Her heart pounding, Kathryn got out of the car and ran across to it, fumbling in her purse for her ID. Steve was right behind her.

"I'm Kathryn Mackay, DA's office." She held up the ID so the deputy in the car could see it. She was afraid to put her fears into words. "What's happened here?"

"County Comm has been trying to reach you for two hours, Ms. Mackay," the man said. "Told us to wait till you got back. It's one of your inspectors, Dave Granz. Somebody messed him up real bad. They've got him in the County Hospital, hanging by a thread."

27

"How is he?"

Kathryn sat down, staring out of the window but seeing nothing. Returning to the informal, noisy bustle of the County Building was almost comforting after the controlled tension of the hospital.

"He's still unconscious," she told Steve. "They've done everything they can. All we can do now is wait."

"They've had three days. Have they figured out what happened yet?"

"From his injuries, it looks as if he was attacked from behind. Whoever jumped him never gave him a chance, just stepped up and whacked him over the back of the head with something, they don't know what yet. Whatever it was, it fractured his skull. Granz must have tried to get up and grab his assailant, and the guy pulled some kind of knife and just hacked him to bits. You saw the Polaroids. His hands . . ."

She suppressed a shudder. Crime scene photographs usually didn't bother her; but this was different. She had leafed through the pictures of the splattered blood, steeling herself against a sense of mounting, inescapable horror. When she came to the close-ups of Dave's ravaged face and hands, she thought her heart would tear like paper. The memory of them was burned into her mind as if by acid.

"Did CSI get anything at the scene?"

"They sent his clothes over to the lab. They'll check to see if there's more than one blood type. Fingernail scrapings. You know how it goes. They'll hold their findings till we get a suspect."

"That's it?"

"Until they come up with anything more specific, it's officially classified as an attempted homicide. God knows what actually went down."

The room in the intensive care unit had been cool and clinical, as though it had no connection with the outside world. A nurse stood watchfully at her shoulder like a sentinel throughout her visit. Granz lay as still as death, nothing but his closed eyes visible through the cocoon of bandages. It seemed to Kathryn that she stood there for a long time, with only the electronic bleep of the monitors and an occasional paging call breaking the sterile silence. The nurse's discreet cough was faintly impatient. Don't be long, please, I have work to do.

"Who's on it?"

"Walt Earheart has taken personal charge. He's got every available deputy he can spare out on the streets asking questions."

"Dave's tough, Kathryn. He'll pull through."

She didn't reply. Granz, who was in deep trauma when they got him to the hospital, had needed three pints of blood before the surgeons could begin the four-hour task of repairing the multiple wounds to his head, hands, and face. He had twin depressed fractures of the skull caused by multiple blows from a blunt instrument with a striking face between three and four inches wide. These alone would have necessitated immediate emergency surgery even without the series of incised linear wounds—varying in length between three and six inches—on his face, and the even more serious injuries—defense wounds—to the palms of his hands and lower forearms. The damage to his right hand, in particular, was giving the doctors cause for grave concern.

"I hope you're right," Kathryn said. "They didn't sound exactly what you'd call optimistic up there."

While none of the wounds to his head and face would have been fatal in itself, one downward slash had bisected Granz's cheek from left ear to chin, and another had sliced deep into his throat, damaging the sternocleidomastoid muscle and narrowly missing the carotid artery; they were uncertain yet whether the injury to the larynx would affect his power of speech.

Giordano listened to her catalog of Granz's injuries in silence. When she was finished he shook his head.

"I can't get a handle on it," he said. "There's a . . . ferocity here out of all proportion to the event. First, the guy hits him twice with something . . . what would be that big, a wrench, a tire iron? Then he goes after him with a knife . . . You say his gun was still in the holster?"

"Yes."

"And he wasn't robbed."

Kathryn shook her head. "His wallet and credit cards weren't touched."

Giordano frowned. "Could it have been someone he knows?"

"Why would he meet someone he knows in a parking lot?"

"Why not?"

"I know the way his mind works. If it was a friend he'd meet him in a bar."

"A snitch?"

"Anything is possible. All we know for sure is there was a nine-one-one call from a woman up at Laguna del Mar. Not far from your place."

"Is that what they call the Village? By that sort of Edwardian hotel?"

"The Seacliff, right. Just a little farther over there's a convenience store, some other buildings—a copy shop, an antique dealer, a dry cleaning place."

"I've been up there. There's a big parking lot in back."

"That's where it happened. The woman was dropping something off at the copy shop for next morning. She said as she was turning out of the parking lot, she got a glimpse of a man in her headlights, crawling around on the ground. He looked like he might have been hit by a car, or beaten up, he had blood all over him. It was late, she was afraid to go look, but she called the cops. They went up there, cruised around, couldn't see anything. There's construction work going on at the hotel and there are a couple of big dumpsters behind it. One of the deputies spotted a hand sticking out from behind one of them. It was Granz. God knows how, but he'd crawled about twenty yards from where he was attacked."

"Dammit, what else could he have been doing in a Laguna del Mar parking lot at ten-thirty at night, except meeting someone?" Steve said exasperatedly.

"There's nothing in his appointment calendar or on his message tapes."

"What about earlier in the day? Where was he? Who did he see?"

"I don't know, Steve. You'll have to talk to the detectives."

Giordano made a gesture that betrayed his frustration. "I'm sorry. It's just ... senseless."

"It always is. Always seems to be, anyway. Look, I'm going to call the hospital, see how he is."

"Again?"

She thought she detected impatience in his voice and it surprised her. "What do you expect me to do, just put him out of my mind?"

Steve looked around the room, as though the piled-up files and chart-decorated walls could answer the question.

"Okay, go ahead and call," he said. "If there's any change we'll go up there."

She dialed the number and was put through to the ICU. The voice of the nurse who answered was crisp and business-like. There was no change; the patient's condition was stable.

"No change," she sighed. Giordano nodded and opened the door without a word.

"Come on," he said.

"Where are we going?"

"Just get in the car."

He drove west through the streets of what had once, in the days when Santa Rita had been a fishing village, been the town's own Little Italy; a little while later they picked up Highway One north. She wondered where they were going. Not that it mattered.

"I feel as if somehow it's my fault," Kathryn said.

"I don't understand."

"As if, you know, if we hadn't been together that night, maybe it wouldn't have happened. Isn't that ridiculous?"

He put his hand on hers. "It's ridiculous, all right. Don't think that way."

How nice if you could just tell your brain, Don't think that way. Don't think at all. Brains didn't work like that. She looked out at the ocean. Way out, a sailboat leaned away from the wind. The silence was pleasant. They hadn't run out of things to say, she thought; just the need to say them.

Just before they reached Half Moon Bay, Steve turned off the highway and coasted down a tree-lined lane that led them to a busy little harbor, white-painted clapboard buildings, a restaurant with a belfry topped by a weather vane in the shape of a sailboat. It was like someone had lifted up a piece of Cape Cod and dropped it into this little bay.

"Let's get a cup of coffee," Steve said.

They went into a restaurant that looked as if it had been converted from a film set; it had a white picket fence, hanging baskets, bay windows, wooden floors, fake oil lamps. Steve ordered coffee for himself, decaf for Kathryn.

"I'm glad we did this," she said. "It takes the pressure off a little."

"He's still important to you." Yet another of those simple declarative sentences he was so good at, she thought.

"Yes." The reply was simple, too. And enough; it was as though he knew the rest by telepathy. He reached over and touched the back of her hand with his fingers.

"He's in good hands, Kathryn," he said. "He won't die."

"I'm not afraid of him dying," Kathryn replied. "It's if he lives and he's . . . he can't function. He's a cop, Steve. One of the best. But he'd be no damned use at all as anything else."

"Let's take a walk."

They wandered along the waterfront holding hands. Gulls wheeled over the harbor making their lost-soul cries. There was a secondhand bookstore in a mini-mall at the far end; Steve bought a well-thumbed paperback called *Blues for the Prince.*

"Who's Bart Spicer?" Kathryn said, looking at the cover. "I never heard of him."

"He wrote some of the best private eye stories ever," Steve said. "This is one of them."

She wasn't really listening. They passed a bank of telephones and he saw her looking at them, her thoughts written on her face as clearly as if on paper.

"When was it, Kathryn?" he asked softly. "How long ago?"

He didn't need to amplify the question, she knew what he was talking about.

"Ages," she said. "About a year after I first came up here from L.A. He was all mixed up. I was, too. I think I knew from the start it wasn't going to work, but I needed something. Someone. And he was there."

"What went wrong?"

Kathryn sighed. "I wasn't ready for a full-time partner. Dave wasn't either. Probably never will be."

"So you stopped, like that, cold turkey?"

" 'The coward does it with a kiss.' "

"Is that a quotation from something?"

"You can look it up. When we get back to the office."

Steve grimaced. "You're right. We'd better move."

"In other circumstances it would be nice if we could just . . . stay up here, you know, like ordinary people."

"We're not ordinary people," Giordano said, his voice harsher than usual. They got back into the car and drove up to the highway. Traffic was light. There were sunbathers and surfers on the state beaches; ordinary people. She felt a little surge of envy, but only for a moment.

They pulled into the County Building parking lot and went up to the Special Investigation Unit office. Everything looked just the same. There were no messages. She rang the hospital; no change. The nurse's crisp voice sounded a shade impatient. Kathryn sighed.

"Come on, damn you," she said softly to no one in particular. She walked around the room, touching the charts, the piled-up files, the boxes of photographs and slides. Steve Giordano watched her without speaking or interrupting her reverie.

"How much longer before we do the briefing?" she asked finally.

Giordano stuck out his lower lip, considered the question. "There's a lot more we could do."

"There always is. But would it get us any further? Honest answer, Steve."

He was silent for what seemed a long time.

"Not unless we get further input, no. I think we've gone about as far as we can go."

"Then why are you waiting? Sooner or later you've got to give the Sheriff's Department what we've got, let them run with it."

Giordano shook his head. "I'm not stalling, Kathryn," he said. "We've got a profile, but it's based on so many maybes I'm reluctant to release it without having the experts at Quantico go over it. I'm pretty sure they'd say it needs more work."

"I disagree. I think what you've got is good enough to go with."

"Why this sudden urgency?"

"There's nothing sudden about it. From the first moment Walt Earheart showed me the crime scene photographs, I have wanted to get this guy in a courtroom. I want to put him away for good."

"We all do. First we have to catch him."

"We will. We know what he's like, how he acts, the way he thinks." She stopped all at once, her lips apart, eyes wide. *I know the way his mind works.* "Oh, my God," she whispered.

"What?" he said. "What is it?"

"There was a thought in the back of my mind someplace," she said, her voice so soft he had to strain to hear it. "It's been there all day, it wouldn't come out, I don't know why. Maybe I was scared to put it into words in case it sounded stupid or ridiculous. It was in there all the time we were taking that ride and I was thinking about Dave and what had happened to him, and all of a sudden I thought, Steve, listen: what if it was the same guy who attacked him?"

Steve stared at her disbelievingly. "What same guy? You mean ... the killer? The killer attacked him?"

"It's possible, isn't it?" Her lips were dry, her heart pounding in her chest; the implications of her speculation were so immense she could not contain them. Steve shook his head.

"I can't see it. It's just not likely. In fact, it's off the wall."

"Doc Nelson said that," Kathryn said softly. "About the killer. Something off the wall about this guy, he said."

"Tell me why. Why would he do it? What motive could he possibly have for trying to kill Granz?"

"You remember . . . Dave said if we ever caught this guy it would be because of street work, not theory. You remember that?"

"Yes. And?"

"And you remember when I asked Jack Burrows what Granz was doing, he said Dave was working on something. In his spare time."

"I remember, I remember," Steve said impatiently. "Lists. He was checking out lists. Jack Burrows said he was hardly ever in the office. So?"

"So suppose he found the killer?"

Steve shook his head again, impatiently now. "That's too much suppose for me. And even if we go down that road, I can't believe he'd have gotten that close to someone he suspected of being the killer without telling anyone. Would he?"

"Maybe," Kathryn said. *I know the way his mind works.* "More than maybe. Quite probably."

"Okay, say you're right—and I don't—say he had some private little investigation going, you have to go on from there. You have to have Granz set up a meet with a guy he suspects of being a serial murderer in a darkened parking lot. It doesn't play, Kathryn. He may be a maverick, but he's not crazy."

Her brain was racing, possibilities suddenly coming at her from every angle. "I know. But what if . . . if he didn't know that the person he was meeting was the killer? But the killer thought he did?"

"What is all this, woman's intuition?"

"Dammit, Steve, don't do that to me."

He made an impatient gesture. "Sorry. Look, I told you at the start I don't believe in hocus-pocus, or divine intervention, or flashes of inspiration. That's not the way this business works."

"You also said what you do is as much from the heart as it is from the brain. Why can that work for you but not for me?"

"All right, you win. He set up a meeting with the killer,

only he didn't know he was the killer. So why did he set up the meeting?"

"Maybe the killer set it up."

"Why?" Steve's voice betrayed his exasperation. "Give me a motive. Why does he want to kill Granz?"

"I don't know," Kathryn said doggedly. "It's there looking at us, Steve. We just can't see it. Come on, don't fight me, help me."

"You don't give an inch, do you? Okay, start over. How did Granz find him in the first place?"

"The lists."

"And what was on them?"

"We can find out. They'll be in his desk. Or his apartment."

"Okay. Let's talk ourselves through your scenario. Without telling anyone, not you, not Podnoretz, not even Jack Burrows, Granz is working on these lists. We assume he's getting names and addresses from them. He is then interviewing people at those addresses, all this without official sanction. Why? Where the hell does he expect it to take him?"

I know the way his mind works.

"He'd only be looking for a lead," Kathryn said. "Somewhere to start, something, anything."

"Okay, okay. Let's go the rest of the way," Steve said, not troubling to conceal his impatience. "In one of these unrecorded interviews at one of these unknown addresses he talks to the killer. Except, of course, he doesn't know it's the killer. But the killer thinks he does. And for reasons yet to be explained by you or anyone else, he falls apart. In spite of the fact that everything we know about him says we are dealing with an organized planner who only preys upon young Hispanic women, you now want to alter the profile to accommodate a killer who carefully sets up the murder of a cop and then botches it. Have I got it right? Is that your theory?"

His voice was harsh, challenging, almost contemptuous. Put that way, it did sound ridiculous. For a long moment Kathryn wavered, then anger fired through her. *I know the way his mind works.*

"Yes, dammit," she snapped, "it is!"

"Okay," Giordano said with a shrug. "Take it to Earheart. I can't stop you."

Damned right you can't, Kathryn thought.

28

"NOTHING," WALT EARHEART SAID DISGUSTEDLY. "FOUR days, and we haven't even come up with a lead."

"Take it easy, Walt," Jake Gylam said, his lizard eyes expressionless. "We all knew it might be a dead end."

They were in the cramped conference room adjoining Gylam's office. Hal Benton, who had requested the update, sat on Gylam's right, Norm Podnoretz on his left. Mac Mc-Caskill was not present; in Benton's absence he was, as always, running the DA's office.

"I can't believe it," Kathryn said.

"Look, Kathryn, I put every goddamn detective I could spare on to this," Earheart replied, nettled. "If there'd been anything for them to find, they'd have found it."

"I know that, Walt," Kathryn said. "We all do. It wasn't a criticism. It's just, I felt sure we'd come up with something."

"We did," Earheart said. "This pile of crap!"

He gestured disgustedly at the stack of papers in front of him, the rap sheets and DMV printouts of the long list of names and addresses they had found at Dave Granz's West Bayshore Drive apartment.

Once they had them, it was immediately apparent Kathryn had been right. Telling no one, Granz had embarked on a one-man campaign to turn up a lead on the killer of Barbara Gates. Now everyone realized why he hadn't been seen around any of his usual barroom haunts, why he hadn't been sitting in on the all-night poker games in the squad room as he so often did. All at once, the things he'd been saying around the office made sense. *I've been playing a sort of hunch. Trying to get a line on the Gates killing.* Someone recalled him furiously scribbling notes on his pad when porno distributors had been mentioned at their first meeting with Steve. *I'm just poking around. But it might lead someplace.*

At his apartment they found copies of every girlie magazine, every "adult" paperback, sleazy skin flick, and porno video Granz had been able to find in Santa Rita and some that looked as if they'd come from farther afield, San Francisco or L.A. Cheap paper-covered catalogs for books on S/M equipment were thrown carelessly together with Spanish-language pinup mags and brochures for sex aids and peeka-boo underwear. The cops who went up there were still talking about some of the stuff they'd found.

From ads in these Granz had apparently obtained addresses for video movie distributors, magazine publishers, and direct-mail book dealers who supplied the kind of sleaze he was looking for. From these suppliers he had somehow— his method in such cases, according to Podnoretz, was a judicious mix of charm and veiled threats—obtained copies of their mailing lists, extracting from them names and addresses of subscribers living in or near Santa Rita. Armed with this list, it appeared he had combed Department of Motor Vehicle records for information on the age, race, and occupation of everyone on his lists, discarding anyone who didn't fit by reason of age or disability.

"Then he hit the streets, started knocking on doors," Earheart said. "We still haven't been able to figure out exactly how he was playing it. If he made any notes or taped any of his interviews, we haven't been able to find them. That left us only one way to go: I put people on to telephoning everyone on the list and asking if Granz had visited them. We came up with nearly sixty he'd talked to. Can you imagine that guy, nearly sixty interviews without so much as a single written note on any of them?"

"From what I've heard about him?" Gylam said. "Sure I can imagine it."

"Were you able to get anything out of the people Granz had talked to?" Benton asked.

"They all said pretty much the same thing: that Granz asked some very odd questions."

"You can see why they'd think that," Earheart added. "A cop turns up on your doorstep unannounced, wants to know things like, Does anyone in the family have Hispanic relatives, or own a vacation home or a time-share or spend weekends or periods of days away from home? Is anyone in the family a hunter, or a survivalist, or interested in police procedure, or code making and code breaking, or working with leather? These people he talked to probably just figured, you know, is this guy crazy, or what?"

"Hold it there a moment," Steve Giordano said, speaking for the first time. "This is interesting. Kathryn, you said you know the way Dave's mind works. Think like him now. He knew what he was doing. Why was he asking these questions?"

"It's not so hard to figure out," she replied. "Take the questions about Hispanic relatives. Our guy is killing Hispanic women. For revenge or hate or because he likes them better than any other kind—we don't know yet. So the odds are, somewhere back in his past there has to be an experience—possibly sexual, not necessarily a good one, whatever it was—with someone Hispanic. It might have been abuse. And abusers are often relatives. Dave would know all that."

Giordano nodded, something not unlike excitement in his eyes. "Vacation home?"

"Our killer has to be keeping these women somewhere," she ventured. "Way on back we wondered if he has a cabin someplace, or maybe a trailer, or an outbuilding on a farm maybe, where he'd be close to some kind of cold facility. That's why we've never had a primary crime scene. So Dave figured maybe he might own property someplace, and asked about time-shares or vacation homes."

"Let me ask you guys something," Jake Gylam said. He didn't bother with the tortured English he affected for public consumption when he was dealing with his own people. "Is all this theory going anyplace?"

Earheart held up a hand. "Hold it, Jake," he said pleasantly. "Steve's right, this is damned interesting. Go on, Steve."

"The questions about someone in the family being a hunter link up with the ones about working with leather, right, Kathryn? If the guy is taking scalps, and it looks pretty certain he is, he might be making trophies out of them. A hunter or a survivalist or someone who works with leather might know how to do that."

"The rest is pretty straightforward," Kathryn said. "This guy seems to know a lot about police procedure; and you all know about the coded notes."

"Did Sacramento ever come up with anything on those?"

"Yeah," Podnoretz said. "Same paper, same type of cheap ballpoint. Which gives us zilch, like before."

"So we're nowhere," Gylam said.

"He must have found something," Kathryn insisted. "He must have."

"Maybe he did, who the fuck knows?" Gylam growled. Giordano got up and went across to the coffee machine, pouring himself a cup. His face was expressionless; he came back, sat down, waited.

"How many names are there altogether, Walt?" Kathryn asked.

"Total? A hundred and twenty-four."

"You called a hundred and twenty-four people, but only sixty of them said Granz came to see them."

"Fifty-eight."

"Then maybe our boy is one of the remaining sixty-six."

"Maybe doesn't mean shit," Gylam rumbled. "There's no guarantee the guy we're looking for is even on the list."

"I'd agree," Giordano said, "if it wasn't for the fact Granz was attacked."

"That still doesn't do it," Gylam persisted. "Hell, that could just as easily be because of something happened years ago, some dickhead Dave put in the slammer who got out and decided to pay him back, some guy whose lady he shacked up with, who the hell knows?"

"I thought we checked his cases for a similar MO?" Kathryn said sharply.

"We did, we did," Earheart assured her. "There was no match." He banged the desk with his fist. "God damn him, why couldn't he do it by the book like everyone else?"

"If he'd done that we wouldn't have anything at all, Walt," Podnoretz reminded him quietly.

"I know, I know," Earheart said testily. "It's just so damned frustrating. If I could only talk to him for thirty seconds . . ."

"I called at the hospital on my way in this morning," Kathryn told him. "He's still in intensive care. They say it'll be a while yet before he's strong enough to talk. Always supposing he can talk at all."

"I saw Doc Nelson," Podnoretz said. "From what he says, Dave's in pretty bad shape."

"He's lucky to be alive," Kathryn said. "One of the cuts just missed an artery."

"Well, if that's your idea of lucky," Jack Burrows said quietly, "I'd rather jump in a bucket of shit."

A little silence followed his words. Jake Gylam got up out of his chair and walked across to the window, looking down at the traffic moving along Pacific Street.

"So where do we go from here?" he asked. "You want us to go out and interview the people Granz didn't get around to? Is that all you've got to offer us, all these maybes and probablys?"

"If you can come up with a better scenario, we'll go with that," Kathryn said. "Otherwise, that's the route we take. Start over from the top. Everybody, even the ones Granz already talked to."

"Okay, we'll give it a whirl," Gylam said. "What about your people?"

"They'll be at your disposal. Right, Norm?"

Podnoretz looked at Benton, who nodded. "Anything you say."

"And what exactly are we supposed to ask these people?" Earheart wanted to know.

"The same questions Granz was asking," Kathryn said. "But with a difference this time."

Earheart frowned. "What difference?"

"We've completed the preliminary analysis," Steve said.

"Aha," Gylam said. "The long-awaited profile. And when do we get to see this masterwork?"

"I have copies here," Steve said, ignoring Gylam's lumbering sarcasm. He stood up and took a bundle of stapled pages out of his briefcase. "It's only twelve pages. What I suggest you do is give a copy to each of your detectives and have them read it. Then we'll get them in here tomorrow and I'll answer any questions they might have."

"Okay," Gylam said, making it clear he wasn't overwhelmed by the offer. "I suppose at the worst it might narrow the field down."

"Is that it?" Podnoretz said, standing up.

"One last question before you go, Hal," Gylam said. "You know how long all this is going to take? You know how many people it's going to tie up?"

"No, let me ask you something instead, Jake," Benton replied. "What else have we got?"

It was one of those questions; nobody answered.

"Okay," Giordano said. "Here we go."

Today he was wearing a dark gray lightweight suit with a white shirt and pale gray tie. He sat at the far end of the conference room, which had been set up with rows of chairs so the detectives and the DA's inspectors could all sit facing him.

"I appreciate your all coming in today," he began. "And for taking time to read my preliminary analysis. I know you've all got pretty horrendous caseloads, and I'll try not to keep you any longer than I have to. There are just a few things I want to tell you about what I do and how I arrived at my conclusions before we get to the questions."

The first thing they had to understand, he told them, was that the primary reason for criminal investigative analysis was to narrow the field of investigation. It would not provide the identity of a criminal. Rather, it would indicate the kind of person most likely to have committed a crime by focusing on personal and behavioral patterns.

"Criminal Investigative Analysis has proven particularly useful in serial sexual homicides, where the crimes are apparently motiveless, the victims selected at random. But there is always a motive, even if it's one only the killer can understand, and the selection of victims is never random, but based on his perception of certain characteristics which are of symbolic significance to him. So you'll see we've analyzed the similarities and differences among the victims to hypothesize a motive."

The thing he wanted to stress, he continued, was that CIA was a technique, no more, no less. Like forensics, like DNA, it was not intended as a substitute for beating the pavement, but as a tool to assist good, solid investigative work.

"What we know for sure is that this guy has killed three women in Santa Rita, and could possibly be the guy who put Dave Granz into ICU. On my record, I'd be willing to bet he's killed before, someplace else. More importantly, if we don't catch him soon, he's going to do it again."

He took a sip of coffee, giving them time to think about that. Kathryn looked at the familiar faces in the rows of seats, some attentive, some apathetic, some visibly bored. She'd worked cases with a lot of these guys: Pete Avery, Martin Silvero, Harry DiStefano, Jack Burrows, Pete Bishop, Mike Eastwood. They were good cops. No matter how they felt about the profiling, they'd do the job.

"The thing about this case that interests me most," Giordano continued, "is that the guy has given us nothing. It's like he knows exactly what we'd be looking for, and deprives us of it. No crime scene, no time of death, no prints, no bloodstains, nothing we can identify him with. Until the attack on Granz. The crime scene investigators got two blood types off Dave's clothes, and enough from under his fingernails to indicate he hit the guy, or scratched him, something. If we can find him, we can use DNA to type and match him. This is our first real break, and that's why what happens over the next week or so, while you're checking these names, is so important. We don't want to blow this. If our guy thinks we are on his case, he may freak, destroy all the evidence, leave us nothing. Okay, that's the end of the speech. Now I'll take questions. Since I don't know all of you, it would help if you'd identify yourself as you ask your question, okay?"

There was a pause; none of the detectives wanted to be first. Then an arm was raised aloft in the center of the room; a faint smile moved Giordano's lips at the small rebuff.

"George Tannenbaum, Sheriff's Department."

Tannenbaum was a short, fat guy in a well-tailored dark blue suit, his tie slackened so the knot was in the middle of his chest, his collar open. He wore a lot of expensive gold: neck chain, chunky bracelet, watch. Kathryn often wondered how he could afford it on a cop's pay. Tannenbaum waved his copy of the analysis.

"You want to tell us how much of this thing is guesswork?"

"I prefer to think of it as deduction," Giordano said, "based on solid facts."

"You call him the Gingerbread Man."

"It's just . . . to give him some kind of identity," Giordano replied. "That little figure he uses as a signature. I think that's what it means. He's taunting us. You can't catch me, I'm the gingerbread man."

"You don't know that."

"I don't know anything, George. Like I said, it's deduction."

"Okay, then how do you get it that he's . . . lemme see, he's probably well educated, possibly a single man living with a relative or a sister?"

"You saw in my analysis I classified this man as an organized killer. Everything we know about him suggests planning and premeditation. If you take another look at the charts I included, you'll see that such men usually have average to above-average intelligence. Organization, intelligence, these suggest education. Everything else we know about this man supports that conclusion. As to the relative or sister, experience comes into it again. Most organized killers are sexually competent, and live with a partner. But this man has a secret life: the times he is away from home finding his victims, abducting them, keeping them someplace. You guys are married: let me ask you, if you stayed out nights, disappeared for a couple of days without explanation, would your wife ask awkward questions?"

It got a laugh; Kathryn mentally saluted Giordano for pitching his answers so the detectives could relax and not feel they were being lectured or talked down to.

"That's why I think it may be a relative, someone who wouldn't ask those awkward questions. That answer your question, George?"

"You say he has a soft voice and an ingratiating manner," another voice chimed in. The speaker was big Pete Avery. "How can you know that?"

"He's abducted three young women," Giordano said. "If he was threatening in any way, they'd never have let him get close enough. Which suggests he's soft spoken and mild mannered in appearance. Look, before we go any further, Jack, do you want to give everyone a quick rundown on your survey of the assault reports?"

Jack Burrows stood up. "I checked all the assaults and attempts on women in the county between a date one month before the first victim was found and the present. The theory was that any one of these might have been an attempt by the killer to abduct a victim. I was looking for cases where the victim was a female Hispanic, between the ages of sixteen and twenty-five, and the assailant had to be male, between twenty-five and forty years old. Out of thirty-nine cases examined, there were seven where the victim was Hispanic and the right age. In five of these cases, the descriptions of the assailant were similar: Caucasian, medium height, dark hair, average build, no physical defects, no scars or distinguishing marks."

The detectives were sitting up in their chairs now, all signs of boredom or lack of interest vanished. You could almost feel the electricity, Kathryn thought.

"Using national-average statistics, that makes our man between five-six and five-ten in height, and between a hundred and forty and a hundred and eighty pounds," Giordano interposed. "Go on, please, Jack."

"In two of the cases, the assailant was wearing a tan or ivory windbreaker and dark-colored pants; in three of them, the attack commenced with the assailant grabbing the victim's hair, then clamping a hand over her mouth. In three cases, the most recent three nights ago in Marina Village, a brown or gold pickup was seen parked at or near the scene. No license number, though."

"Now you know where the physical details in the profile come from," Giordano said. "Oh, and by the way, this was found at the scene of the last attack."

He held up the stun gun. About the same size as an electric razor, it worked by shooting an electrical discharge that interrupted messages from the brain to the muscular system, causing severe disorientation for between ten and fifteen seconds.

"This may be what our killer used or is using to subdue his victims without a struggle. We're running checks on it, but we're not too hopeful: they're not classified as firearms so it won't be registered. Just keep it in mind that he may have another. Anything else?"

"You said something about his reaction to interrogation?" Mike Eastwood called out over the surge of conversation that followed Giordano's words. "Could you enlarge on that?"

"I'm glad you brought that up," Giordano said. "Okay, men, listen to this, it's important. If we're right, and the same guy who killed these women also tried to kill Dave Granz, he's a mad dog. He may not look like one, but don't take any chances. If he smells remotely like our guy, back off, call it in, let us take a more careful look at him."

There was a pregnant silence. Walt Earheart spoke into it. "Okay, you guys," he said. "Let's get out there and find this bastard."

Lee called in sick. The registrar, a dried-up old spinster named Muriel Applebaum, said all the appropriate things: keep warm, plenty of hot drinks, soon be as right as rain. She didn't give a damn whether he lived or died, the old bitch. Nobody at the school liked him; not that it mattered to him in the slightest. He had long ago decided the faculty were insignificant mediocrities, every one of them; as for the students, they were a bunch of irresponsible, ungrateful rich kids who evinced no desire to learn anything except how to get a gold AmEx card. Teaching was a thankless job at best; the idea of even having to be inside the school, let alone standing in front of a classroom of unresponsive teenagers discussing the characters of Hamlet or Hotspur while every nerve in his body was singing like a violin string, was unbearable. He told Carol he had a lot of class work to catch up on and locked himself in his study, staring at nothing.

He had been stupid. There was no excuse. Stupid. When he was hunting, finding victims, taking them out of their own lives like an angler taking a fish from the water, he was in control. Going after Granz had been a major error. On the video screen of his imagination, a film loop kept running the events in the parking lot at Laguna del Mar over and over and over until his mind screamed for release. Things had started to go wrong and he could not control them. First the bitch whore in Marina Village, then the boyish-looking detective with the deceptively nonchalant manner that did not fool Lee for one single moment.

"Mr. Russell?" the man had said. "My name is David Granz. I'm an inspector with the district attorney's office." He held up a wallet and flipped it open. *Jesus,* Lee thought, *they know, they know.* For what seemed minutes but was in fact only a moment, panic paralyzed him; he could neither see nor hear. Pounding in his head like a heartbeat he heard the words *theyknow, theyknow, theyknow.*

He took a deep breath. "What . . . what do you want?" His voice felt rough, strange: a croak. Granz didn't seem to notice.

"Just a few questions," the inspector said. "It won't

take long. If it's inconvenient, I can come back some other time . . . ?"

"No," Lee managed, recovering his self-possession. "No. It's fine. Just . . . didn't expect, uh, visitors. I'll . . . We can go in my study."

"Would you like some coffee?" Carol asked. Granz smiled and shook his head.

"This won't take long," he told her. "Thanks anyway."

"Shall I stay?" she asked.

"If you like," he said.

"No," Lee snapped simultaneously. Lee could see that Granz was surprised at Carol's reaction: she had literally quailed. "You'll only get upset. Dear," he added quickly to soften it.

"I'll . . . if you . . . need me I'll . . ." She made a vague gesture and backed into her kitchen, closing the door behind her.

"She suffers from nerves a lot," Lee said vaguely. "Migraines, that sort of thing."

Lee led the way into his study, waved Granz to the armchair, and sat down in the chair by the desk; his legs felt shaky. Instead of sitting in the armchair, Granz took an upright chair from its place against the wall and sat facing him.

"Would you mind telling me what this is about, Mr. Granz?" he asked.

"I'm conducting an investigation, Mr. Russell," Granz told him. "I'd be grateful for your cooperation."

"What kind of an investigation?"

"It's what we call a neighborhood survey," Granz said. "A process of eliminating certain people from our inquiries by means of a system we call comparative referencing."

Lee frowned. He knew a lot about police procedure. They might do a neighborhood survey in Outlook Heights because Barbara Gates's body had been found nearby, but he had never heard of comparative referencing. It might be something new. Or it might just be a bunch of bullshit, he thought. Cops were big on that. Yes, that was what it was. He felt self-confidence flooding back into him, like a swordsman might feel as he made himself ready to fight a duel. It was a pleasing analogy. He put a concerned look on his face.

"Is this about the girl who was killed? Barbara Gates?"

Granz's eyes narrowed. "What makes you think that?" he said, sharply.

"I just assumed . . ."

"Why?" Granz snapped.

"I'm a teacher at Cabrillo Park High."

"Ah. I see." Granz relaxed visibly. "I'm sorry, I didn't know that. Aren't you at school today?"

"Class work," Lee said, gesturing at the papers on his desk. "Is that what this is about?"

"Did you know the dead girl?"

Lee shook his head. "She wasn't one of our students."

"Of course, I forgot. Were you at the school when her body was found?"

"I can't remember. Probably. I remember someone told me about it, one of the other teachers, I think. It sounded pretty gruesome."

"You didn't go take a look?"

"I saw her body being taken away, yes."

"Did you notice anything unusual?"

"What sort of thing?"

"Anything that caught your attention, anything out of the ordinary."

"Nothing I can think of."

"Have you ever been inside either of those outbuildings?"

"I don't think I even realized they were there until . . . Why do you ask? What has this to do with your . . . what did you call it, neighborhood survey?"

Lee allowed himself a secret smile. He could ask questions, too. After all, he was innocent until proven guilty, right? He didn't fail to notice that Granz ducked answering.

"You never know what someone may have noticed, without even knowing they noticed it," Granz said. "I don't suppose you saw anyone hanging around the school grounds who shouldn't have been there at any time prior to the discovery of the body, did you?"

"There are people coming and going all day. You tend not to take much notice unless it concerns you personally."

"You don't mind my asking you questions about it?"

"No, I don't mind. Although I don't think I can help you much."

Lee's initial panic had dissolved; he was totally in control of himself now. He could dance rings around this dumbass.

Any of them. All of them. They were all dumbasses. The thought almost made him smile.

"Can you remember what you were doing the night before Barbara Gates's body was found?"

"I can't even remember when it was."

"July eighteenth."

"Am I under suspicion or something?"

Granz smiled. "There's no question of that, Mr. Russell," he said. "I'm just checking one or two things. You don't even have to talk to me if you don't want to."

That's the second time he hasn't answered the question, Lee thought. He shook his head. "Go ahead, I . . . we've got nothing to hide."

"I'm sure you haven't," Granz said. "So, where were you?"

"I'm pretty sure I was home. The eighteenth was a Thursday, right? Let me check my calendar."

He took out a calendar and flicked through the pages.

"No, nothing there. So I was home."

"How long have you been at Cabrillo Park?"

"A little over three years."

"Which subjects do you teach?"

"Just English. Language and literature."

"You must do a lot of reading." Granz looked around at the bookshelves lining the wall.

"I used to. Not so much now."

"This is a real nice den you've got."

"I need somewhere quiet; I do most of my school work in here. Grading papers, preparing lessons and homework. People think a teacher goes home, that's the end of his day. In fact, it's the start of the next one."

"I suppose you're too busy to have time for any hobbies?"

"As a matter of fact, no. I collect fishing flies."

"Trout?"

"That's right. I have over four hundred . . . Would you like to see them?"

"Some other time, maybe," Granz said. "You do any leatherwork? Tanning, curing, that sort of thing?"

The question caught him unawares. "No. Nothing like that."

"The reason I asked, you've got a book on the subject here." Granz got up and took the paperback down off the shelf. *"Tan Your Hide: Home Tanning Leathers and Furs. With a Special Section on Working with Leather,"* he read from the cover and looked at Lee quizzically. Off balance, Lee managed to put a hint of displeasure into his voice.

"Look, I know you have to do your job, but what's all this got to do with . . . ?"

Granz's face was bland. "I just wondered why you'd need a book on curing leather if it's not your hobby. Looks like it's been on your shelf awhile," he observed, showing Lee the trace of dust he had picked up on his finger.

"Oh, that," he said, making it nonchalant. "It's not mine. I think you'll find it belongs to one of my students. Look inside, you'll see his name. Rother? Rether?"

"Ritter," Granz said, putting the book back. "How about crossword puzzles, Mr. Russell. You do them?"

"No."

"Other kinds of puzzles? Codes, word games?"

"Once in a while, like everyone else, I suppose. I like word games. But things like jigsaw puzzles bore me."

Does he know something? If so, how? Is he just bluffing? Yes, of course he is. How can I be sure? The questions scuttled about in Lee's mind like rats in a sewer.

"You mind telling me your age, sir?"

"Not at all. I'm forty-three."

"Local man?"

"No. I was born in Chicago."

"How long have you lived in Santa Rita?"

"Since 'eighty-eight. We came down here in the spring."

"And before that?"

"Redwood City. I taught at a school up there. Canyon Heights High."

"You have no children?"

"None of my own. Hundreds of other people's."

It was a golden oldie, but Granz gave it a dutiful smile.

"Is this your only home, Mr. Russell?"

"Uh . . . how do you mean?" The change of tack surprised him for a moment.

"I mean, you don't own a time-share, or a vacation home?"

"No." He smiled, although his face felt stiff, as if it was coated in cement. He couldn't know about the cabin. It wasn't possible. "If you knew anything about schoolteachers, you'd know we don't make that kind of money."

"So you don't get away much?"

"A few days fishing here and there."

"Is that with your wife, sir? With friends? Or alone?"

Careful, Lee told himself. He could have already checked with the school or the neighbors or both. You know how cops work.

"Alone, usually."

"And how often would that be?"

"Four or five times a year. It varies. A couple of days at a time."

"And where do you go, sir?"

"Sierra de Salinas, mostly. Sometimes up around Sequoia, Mount Whitney."

"When was the last time you went away?"

"Over the July Fourth weekend, I think. Is it important?"

"Do you have it in your calendar?"

Lee riffled through the pages. "Yes. I went up to Lake Isabella."

"Any luck?"

"I never keep my catch."

"You mind me asking what kind of car you drive, Mr. Russell?"

"A Honda Civic two-door sedan."

"That's it? You don't own a pickup or a four-wheel drive?"

Good, Detective, but not very subtle. You couldn't possibly know about the pickup, either.

"No."

"Must be hard work driving up in the mountains with a small car like that." Granz was looking past Lee at something on the desk. But what, what? Lee wanted to turn his head and look but knew it would be a dead giveaway.

"I don't fish much in the winter."

"Okay, just let me run through this with you again. Your full name is James Leland Russell. You're forty-three years old, your wife's name is Carol. You have no children. You teach English at Cabrillo Park High School. Have I got that right?"

"Correct."

"Your hobbies are fishing and fly-tying."

"Yes," Lee said. "I do a little gardening also."

"I noticed how neat your front yard was," Granz said. "You own no other property except this house, right? You drive a Honda Civic; that's the only vehicle you own. You take short fishing vacations four or five times a year, up in the Sierras, a couple of days at a time. Oh, do you ever get away midweek, sir?"

"It varies," Lee said, leaving it at that.

Granz stood up. "Well, I think that covers everything," he said. "Thank you for your time, Mr. Russell."

"Sure," Lee said. "Look, can't you tell me why you're asking all these questions?"

As he spoke, he glanced offhandedly at the desk. Saw it. How could he have been so *fucking* stupid? Had Granz seen it too? If so, did he know what it was? Was he aware of its significance? The decision came into his mind fully formed. *I'll have to kill him.*

". . . part of a criminal investigation," Granz was saying. "I'm afraid I'm not at liberty to say more at this time."

"I'll show you out," Lee said. He led the way to the door, opened it. Granz stopped on the doorstep, turned.

"Oh, by the way, Mr. Russell," he said. "Are you related either by birth or marriage to anyone Hispanic?"

Did he know about that, too? It was possible. Tell the truth, just in case.

"My stepmother and stepsister," he said. "My father remarried late in life."

"Do they live here in Santa Rita?"

"They're both dead."

"Oh, I'm sorry," Granz said. "Excuse me. When did they die, sir?"

"They died in an apartment-house fire in Chicago when I was about eighteen," Lee said. "Is that all, Mr. Granz?"

"For now," Granz said. "Although I may need to talk to you again. Look, I'll give you my card. If you remember anything, anything at all that might help us with the Barbara Gates case, call me, okay?"

"Of course," Lee said. He smiled at Granz as the inspector tipped him a finger-to-the-forehead salute and crossed the sidewalk to his car. He looked at the card. It had a cellular number. He smiled again. They couldn't monitor cellular phones.

29

HE REHEARSED IT ON HIS TAPE RECORDER MAYBE SIX OR eight times. Granz was streetwise, he wouldn't fall for anything too obvious. At the same time, Lee couldn't risk him calling in backup or trying to set up a stakeout. The next night, when he had the script the way he wanted it, he called Granz's mobile number. It rang for a long time. Then he heard Granz answer. He sounded slightly out of breath, as if he'd had to run to the car.

"Is that Inspector Granz?" he asked, talking the way kids he'd known in Chicago used to talk, what his father had called a "dis-and-dat" accent: *Dis da way ya wanna do dat?*

"Who's this?" The voice sounded tinny, echoing. Car phones always did that.

"My name is Carter? Albert Carter?"

"Yeah. What can I do for you, Mr. Carter?"

"You the one looking into this Barbara Gates murder?"

"What about it?"

"I got some information on the guy who killed her."

"What kind of information?" Granz's voice had changed. Lee smiled.

"Listen, I'm in this phone booth in Laguna del Mar. I see this guy in a pickup, tan, local plates. The heap looks familiar, so I go over and take a look. It's the same pickup I seen driving into the Cabrillo High School grounds the night before they found that girl's body. Barbara Gates?"

"Let me get this straight, you saw a pickup driving into the school? What time was this?" In spite of the poor acoustics, the urgency in Granz's voice was almost tangible.

"Jeez, I don't remember exactly. Eight-thirty, round there."

"You get a good look at the driver?"

"Yeah. Guy about thirty, thirty-five, dark hair, mustache, maybe five-ten, sort of gangling. Wore a tan color jacket."

"And?"

"What caught my eye was he was getting this wheelchair

outa the truck. You know, like they use in hospitals, folded up? I seen him opening it up."

"And then?"

"That's all, really. I was just passing, happened to see him. Then I read it in the paper there was tracks they thought might be from a wheelchair outside the building where they found the body."

"Why haven't you come forward before, Mr. Carter?"

"I didn't place no significance on it right then. I'm a trucker, see, I hauled a reefer of berries up to Seattle, just got back. I'm going for a drink and I see this pickup. And then I remember the guy at the school."

"And you know where he is now?"

"I just told you, up here in this parking lot right here in Laguna del Mar. No question it's the same one. There's a sort of D-shaped dent in the front fender. I'm looking right at it."

"Where in Laguna del Mar?"

"You know the hotel? The Seacliff? Right in back of that."

"I know it. Okay, Mr. Carter, stay put, I'll be there in fifteen minutes." Granz's voice was controlled, but Lee could sense his excitement. "How will I know you?"

"I've got on a red and white checked flannel shirt and blue jeans. Five-ten, brown hair."

He went out to the parking lot and waited. There was no one around; everyone had gone home hours ago. He felt shivery and tense as the minutes ticked away. He could hear the cars on the freeway nearby. The evening was still and silent.

A battered old Ford sedan turned into the parking lot. He saw Granz roll down his window, coasting to a stop. After a while he got out, looking around. It was nearly full dark now. Lee could practically hear what he was thinking. *Where the hell is this guy?* Granz made an impatient sound and walked toward the dumpster behind which Lee was hiding, went past him to the boardwalk in front of the hotel, checking to see if anyone was there. Lee heard him curse under his breath, then he turned to go back to his car.

Now.

As Granz went past his hiding place, Lee stepped out behind him swinging a fourteen-inch stainless steel crescent wrench and hit him on the back of the head with all his strength. The force of the impact jarred his arm. Granz made a sound somewhere between a shout and a groan and fell to his knees, shaking his head. Lee stepped closer and hit him again, this time above the ear on the right-hand side of the head. The inspector fell forward, face down, pulling his knees into his belly, hands clenching and unclenching spasmodically.

Dropping the heavy wrench into one of the big outside patch pockets of his rubberized foul-weather jacket, Lee reached into his shirt pocket and took the scalpel out of its little leather carrying case. He had put a new blade on it before he came out. He grabbed Granz's hair, pulling his head back so he could slide the blade across his throat; in that same moment Granz made an animal sound and came up off the ground, bloody and blind-eyed, reaching for him with both hands.

Lee felt the inspector's fingernails rake across his face. A stifled screech of pain burst from his mouth, and he slashed at Granz with the scalpel, *there!* felt the blade's slicing slide through flesh, temple to chin, another, lower, going for the throat, a third, again, again, *there, you bastard!* hearing his victim's hard, urgent grunts of pain as he tried to fend off the whipping blade with his bare hands.

Granz collapsed to his knees coughing, blood pattering onto the ground like rain, then rolled over on his side, a ghastly gargling sound emerging from his throat. He tried to push himself up on his hand, but it would not take his weight. Then slowly, almost in slow motion, he stretched out, still and silent.

Lee waited, taking no chances; but Granz was as still as death. He inched forward; just as he was bending over to make sure Granz was dead he heard a car engine start up close by and saw headlights cut across the parking lot. Stifling a curse, Lee turned and ran, not looking back as the car moved toward where Granz was lying. The inspector lifted his head, trying to see his attacker, his ruined face streaked with ribbons of blood that looked black in the faint light. The headlights of the car swept across and past him.

It was just like all the other times.

He could not believe it at first, and then he began to

wonder why he had ever thought it would be otherwise. The cops in Santa Rita were just as dumb as all the others had been, all sirens and attitude, useless unless someone gave them the answers on a plate. Every hour that passed increased his contempt: they were pathetic. Sure, let some drunk blow off his wife's head with a Mossberg, they'd have him in custody before the smoke had cleared. Let some dealer set up a crack house in Harbor Park, undercover cops would bust his ass before he could strike a match. Cops were great at rousting the bums in the park, citing some poor jerk who had a beer too many on his way home, but put them up against someone with a brain in his head and they didn't know where to start.

If anything, the media were even more predictable than the cops. On the first day there were front-page headlines in the *Gazette,* BRUTAL MURDER ATTEMPT AT LAGUNA DEL MAR, with an additional page inside. Crime scene newscasts from KKSU-TV, a serious-faced female in a gray suit, Gloria something-Polish, reporting from the Laguna del Mar parking lot, and over to Jane for an interview with one Cara Mae Marable, a middle-aged woman who had called 911. She must have been the one who had started the car up, he thought. What was the stupid bitch doing up there at that time of night?

The next day, the follow-up, just as predictable: DETECTIVES PROBE LEADS IN LAGUNA DEL MAR CASE. Feature writers outlining where the investigation was going, carefully scripted quotes from the SO. On TV, someone called McCaskill from the DA's office said it was just a matter of time before the painstaking investigation being conducted by the task force turned up a concrete lead.

Lee laughed out loud at that: if they had anything concrete there'd have been a green and white patrol car sliding up to his front door a long time ago. It was almost a rule in law enforcement that most crimes were won or lost in the first twenty-four hours. Did the cops think they were the only ones who knew it?

By the third day, the story had been relegated to the inside back page under a headline that said NO BREAK IN LAGUNA ATTACK CASE. Nothing on the TV news at all. Instead, editorializing on *Here and Now* from Richard Sanchez: graphic and glorified portrayals of violence on TV and in the movies, he said, were desensitizing a whole generation to the horror of violent crime. A panel of experts discussed the proposition. Blah, blah, yawn, yawn.

On the fourth day, he came across a small item in the *Gazette* that reported that a citizens' committee had complained to the district attorney's office that Inspector Dave Granz, recently the victim of an attempted murder, had harassed scores of Santa Rita citizens while conducting an unauthorized murder investigation, and that the DA's office had pledged a full inquiry when Inspector Granz was released from the hospital. Lee sat in the den and let the dark laughter inside him bubble up. Chopped up like chicken liver and ending up reprimanded for it: who'd be a hero?

On the fifth day, there was nothing in the paper at all. Dave Berry, who'd written the earlier stories, turned in a splashy piece on a murder/suicide the preceding night. Newspaper readers and TV audiences had the attention span of a two-year-old in Disneyland, and the people who wrote for them knew it. Which was why they monitored the police channels looking for tomorrow's headlines, a flashy SWAT siege, a juicy rape trial, or a gory child murder, something that would attract viewers or bump up readership figures. All it took was a hot one, and they'd be out there giving it their best shot, the on-the-spot report on the six o'clock news, the front-page splash in the next morning's paper. But a story about an investigation that was getting no place, like the attack on Granz, no leads, no suspects, nothing? Give me a break.

It was the same with the cops. The Sheriff's Department, which worked an A-Team/B-Team system, each team four days on and four days off, had pulled shifts twice since the night of the attack, which meant by now they probably had a couple dozen more cases to follow up on. The Granz case would have been pushed out of the way by others more urgent—and more amenable to being solved.

On top of that, if what the papers had said was true, and the whole inquiry Granz had been conducting had been unauthorized, the DA's office would probably sweep it under the carpet before the citizens' committee sank their teeth any deeper into it or, worse, brought up again the hot issue of a police review board.

After a week, Lee felt safe.

True, Granz was still alive, but the papers said he was suffering from some kind of post-traumatic amnesia. If and when he got his memory back, what would he be able to tell the investigators? Nothing. The name of a nonexistent man who set up a meeting in a parking lot and attacked him. Nothing but the most general physical description. He should have known better. The cops were at best only average bright. This one was way out of their league.

He sat in his den with his feet on the desk thinking about Linda Diaz in Marina Village, remembering her long slim brown legs with the golden peach fuzz of hair on her inner thighs, and the swimsuit tight over the darker patch where they met. The need was beginning again. Tomorrow, he thought, I'll go down to Espanola. Can I help you, sir? No, thanks, I'm just looking.

Inside him, the dark laughter bubbled up again.

30

"KATHRYN, IT'S RICHARD SANCHEZ."

The instantly recognizable voice at the other end of the line surprised her. She had been so deeply immersed in the investigation there had been no time to give Sanchez much thought, although she had read or heard somewhere that he had become executive producer of his own show, and knew he had won the twice-weekly half-hour spot, linked to the network news, he had so desperately coveted.

"What can I do for you?" she asked briskly.

"Did you see the show Wednesday?"

"I was working."

"Pity. We did a special on random violence, using the attack on that inspector of yours as the jump-off. Rape, assaults, drive-by shootings. It got great ratings and a lot of positive comment. The station received over a hundred and twenty calls next day."

Was he really so thick-skinned? Kathryn wondered. No, it was a lack of empathy, of any sense of feeling for anyone but himself. Some people just didn't have it. Richard Sanchez didn't have it in spades.

"The inspector's name is Granz," she reminded him.

"Right, right," he said impatiently. "That's not why I called. My sources tell me that Department of Justice hotshot you're working with—what's his name, Giordano?—has finished his profile of our serial killer. Can you confirm that?"

"Off the record?"

"There you go again. Okay, off the record."

"Off the record, yes. And I'd like to know how come you're so well informed."

"I make it my business to be," Sanchez said. "When is he going to release it to the media?"

"Not his decision to make," Kathryn said, surprised at the question. "You could try the Department of Justice in Sacramento, but I wouldn't give you much for your chances. CIAs are confidential."

"Is that a fact? Suppose I take the position that the public has a right to information about its criminal justice system—"

"Oh, spare me the attitudinizing. You know as well as I do that if we released CIAs to the media, we'd be buried by people calling in because some guy kicked their cat, or the next-door neighbor they don't get along with too well is a dead ringer for the guy in the profile."

"I don't agree, but I can see I'd be wasting my time arguing. How's Granz, by the way?"

"He's on the mend," Kathryn said. "But he's still got a long way to go."

"Has he been able to tell you anything about the attack?"

"He doesn't remember it. That whole day is a blank in his memory. The doctors say he's suffering from some form of posttraumatic amnesia."

"Can he talk?"

"Not until his wounds are fully healed. There was some damage to the trachea, and they were afraid at first his vocal cords might be affected, but it healed up fine. It looks like he's going to be okay."

"I don't suppose you'd like to call me and let me know when he gets his memory back, would you?"

"You're the reporter. You call me."

"There you go again. You want to watch that, you might offend me. By the way, how did you like the food at Paolo's?"

"How did you—?"

"Don't miss the show Sunday," he said. "You'll love it."

He hung up before she could speak again. She stared at the phone, frowning. How had he known about Paolo's? And what else did he know?

Carousel was marvelous, the college cast giving it their very best and showing few signs of their amateur status. Emma—wearing a flowered dress that reached almost to her ankles, her hair piled up and kept in place with a band of imitation pearls—loved every moment of it from the colorful opening fairground sequence to the soaring finale. She hid her face in her hands when Billy died, and she cried when the Snow children were mean to Louise. She was so grown up it made Kathryn's heart ache.

Sunday was glorious, the morning mist burning off early to give a bright, hot sunny day that would bring visitors by the thousands to the beaches, creating the usual chaos as radiators overheated in the bumper-to-bumper traffic making the long, slow climb over the Santa Rita Mountains. Kathryn got up early and made breakfast. Still wearing her nightgown, she filled the washing machine and did some ironing, sorting out Emma's clothes for school next day, the standard Sunday routine. Then she went in to wake her daughter.

"Hi, there," she said, drawing back the curtains. "Rise and shine."

Emma opened her eyes, squinting in the bright light coming through the window. "Snuggle," she said, holding out her arms.

Kathryn slid under covers and held her daughter in her arms.

"Hey, remember where we're going today?" she whispered. Jack had called to say he couldn't make it, pressure of work. To counter any disappointment Emma might be feeling, Steve had suggested they have a day out in San Francisco.

Emma nodded. "Is Steve still here?"

Kathryn caught the intonation. "I thought you liked him."

"He's not like Dave."

That one caught Kathryn off guard. "He's a different sort of nice," she said. "So I like being with him for different reasons. Don't you?"

"I guess. Only I wish we could be just the two of us sometimes."

"We're the two of us right now."

"No, Mommy. I mean a whole long day."

"Maybe next weekend. We already made our plans. We don't want to change them now, do we?"

"Why not?" Emma wanted to know with the unassailable logic of the very young.

"What would you like for breakfast?" Kathryn asked, ducking the question.

"Can I have a blueberry muffin?"

"Anything else?"

"I'd like . . ." Emma considered carefully, frowning. "Grapefruit juice. Peach yogurt. And a blueberry muffin."

"I'll get it ready while you take your shower," Kathryn told her. "Wear a shower cap. And don't forget to brush your teeth."

She went into the kitchen. After a while Emma came in, wearing her white terry cloth robe. She said hello to Steve, who was reading the paper out on the balcony, then came in and sat in the breakfast nook and started to eat her breakfast.

"Mommy," she said after a while, "there's a field trip next week. We're going to San Wamperdista."

"San Juan Bautista," Kathryn said. "There's an old mission there. It'll be fun."

"Miss Cordova asked if anyone's mommy would drive."

"I'm sorry, sweetie, I know they need volunteers, but I really can't get away from work."

"Oh," Emma said with a sigh, "I already told her that. I keep on hoping you will one day, but I know really the judges won't let you."

She believed it was the judges who were responsible for Kathryn's being unable to participate in school activities, for her sometimes being called out in the middle of the night, for Emma's always being the last child to be picked up from day care in the evenings.

"Does it make you sad I can't do things with you like other mommies, sweetheart?"

"Sometimes," Emma said. "I don't mean to cry but somehow the tears just run out on their own."

"Hurry up and finish your juice," Kathryn said, turning away so Emma couldn't see her expression. "We'll be leaving soon."

A little after ten they piled into Steve's little red Escort and left for their trip to San Francisco.

"Steve, you've got to get a different car," Kathryn said. "This heap is bad for your image. You need something with a bit more pizzazz."

"You tell my boss that," he said. "He's not very big on pizzazz. Neither am I, if it comes to that. All I want it to do is get me from *A* to *B*."

"Mommy, what are we going to do in San Francisco?" Emma asked.

"We're going to be real tourists," Steve said. "I've got it all mapped out. We'll ride to the top of Telegraph Hill on a cable car, have lunch in Tarantino's, then go for a cruise on the Bay."

"Naaaaaa!" Kathryn and Emma shouted in unison. "Corrrrrny!"

Steve looked nonplussed. "What do you mean, corny?"

"Cable cars are corny. I want to go to Chinatown," Emma said.

"Okay," Steve said. "Okay."

"And I want to go to the Japanese Tea Garden," Kathryn added.

"What is this, a conspiracy?"

"It's our way of telling you us Mackay women are used to making our own decisions," Kathryn told him. "You'll get used to it."

What they ended up doing was walking through the arboretum in Golden Gate Park and finding wild strawberries in the flower beds; Emma fed salted peanuts to the squirrels while old ladies smiled. They sat on the grass in Washington Square and listened to some kids playing guitars, then strolled over to Chinatown and bought Emma a paper parasol in one of the emporia.

"See?" Kathryn grinned as they headed down the hill.

"Aren't you glad you let us women decide how to spend the day?"

"It's been fine," he said.

"Are you sulking, Steve?"

"Why would I be sulking?"

"I don't know. Did we dent your male pride?"

"Not beyond repair," he said. But he didn't smile as he said it and he didn't talk much on the way back home either. It was almost dark by the time they got back to Santa Rita. Emma had fallen asleep on the way down; Steve bundled her up in a woolen blanket and carried her upstairs.

" 'night, Steve," Emma said sleepily, half-waking as he laid her on the bed. "Thank you for my parasol."

"Good night, Em," he said. He went to the door and pointed at the kitchen. "I'll open some wine," he said to Kathryn. "While you say good night."

He took a bottle of Devlin chardonnay from the refrigerator and two glasses from the wall cupboard. Kathryn came in as he poured. They clinked glasses and she took a sip of wine before going over to the answering machine to check for messages. Nothing. She couldn't entirely dismiss a slight feeling of letdown; it was a rare day as a DA when her tape wasn't packed with calls from cops, her inspectors, other prosecutors.

"That didn't take long," Steve said, tipping his head toward Emma's room.

"She was beat." Kathryn smiled. She stood on tiptoe and kissed him. "Thank you. It was a lovely day, wasn't it?"

He didn't answer. She walked across to the window, opened the catch, and slid it back. A cool breeze sighed in as she went out onto the balcony. Down below, the lighthouse blinked against the darkening ocean.

"You seem restless," he said.

"Yes. I am."

"Any particular reason?"

"I think so." Kathryn sipped her wine, choosing her words carefully. "I realized something just now, when I checked the answering machine and there weren't any messages. I miss being in control of my life. Everyone else is out there doing things while we just sit and wait."

"That's the nature of the discipline we're working in. It will change once we start seeing some real results."

"I know that. And I know that what we're doing is important ... but it's not what I do. It's not what I'm best at."

"I think you underestimate yourself. You've shown a remarkable aptitude for this kind of work. Maybe if you gave it more time ... What I'm trying to say is, we're a good team. Don't break it up now just to ..."

"What were you going to say, Just to satisfy a whim? You think that's what it is?"

Steve leaned on the sill of the balcony, looking out at the ocean. "I wasn't going to say that at all. I just don't think your going back to being a prosecutor is so important that you can't stay away from it a little longer."

"Important comes in two varieties, Steve," she said. "Yours and mine."

Her voice must have been sharper than she intended. He blinked, and turned around to look at her.

"Something's wrong, isn't it? It's been there all day."

"I'm sorry. It's not your fault, although what's happened to us is part of it. It's just ... everything is happening too fast. I keep on feeling I ought to be making decisions, and I'm too strung out emotionally to make them, even if I knew what they were."

"Give me a for-instance," he said. "Maybe I can help."

"I don't know, Steve. I think maybe I've got to work all this out for myself. These last few weeks, spending so much more time with Emma, I've realized just how much I don't know about her, about my own daughter. She's growing up, and I'm missing all that. For instance, the other day I was picking up some pizza and sent her into the grocery to buy some muffins and milk. When I came in she was standing at the checkout with her basket and her money all ready and she was upset when she saw me because she wanted everyone to think she could handle it on her own. And I thought, If I was being a real mother, I'd have known that already—before her babysitter, anyway."

He nodded, sipping his wine. "And that's a problem for you?"

"That's just it. One minute, I'm cutting myself to shreds for being such a lousy parent, and then the next, the other side of me takes over, the one who wants to send the rapists to the joint, the one who gets the adrenaline kick out of going to trial, the one who puts the job before everything else. I keep swinging wildly between the two, thinking I ought to give it up, and knowing in my heart that I probably never will."

"Is that what you think? That you'll never give it up?"

"I suppose . . . I can't imagine being a fifty-year-old prosecutor. But I can't imagine being on the bench either. I guess I'll just have to wait and see."

"The wisdom of the ages in three words," Steve said. There was a shade of sadness in his voice and she wondered why. "What time is it?"

"Nine-thirty. Oh, I forgot, Sanchez, right?"

Steve switched on the TV, ran through the channels to seven, and hunkered down in front of the set; a man was saying that if cats could choose, they'd all choose Purina. Then the station logo appeared, the music swelled, and the graphics spelled out the familiar title. Sanchez was wearing a dark blue blazer with a pale blue shirt and striped tie.

"Good evening, I'm Richard Sanchez, bringing you—*Here and Now*—the matters of moment in our state, in our society. Tonight, we return to the subject of serial murder. Tonight, *Here and Now*, we launch a new campaign to apprehend and bring to justice the killer of three young Hispanic women in Santa Rita."

"How does he get away with this crap?" Steve said angrily. "Is he trying to put vigilantes on the street?"

"I don't know, but I'm going to record it," Kathryn said. She shoved a videotape into the recorder and set it in motion as the camera pulled away from Sanchez to reveal a large screen on which was drawn the outline of a man, not unlike those used for police shooting practice but without the target rings.

"Imagine this is he," Sanchez said. "The faceless, featureless, unknown killer of three innocent women. Some weeks ago, we explored the personality of this man. Tonight, we will tell you exactly what kind of man he is. To begin, then, let me tell you about the new criminology, as practiced, if not yet perfected, by the FBI. They call it criminal investigative analysis, CIA for short. You may have heard it referred to as mind hunting, or offender profiling . . ."

"What is this?" Steve said tightly, getting to his feet as Sanchez began to outline the way an offender profile was compiled. "What the hell is this?"

He went across to the telephone and dialed, his stance tense, his fingers drumming on the receiver. Sanchez was now talking about profilers, what their qualifications were, how they were trained. Behind her, Kathryn could hear Steve talking tersely into the phone.

"Jake? Steve Giordano. I think I've got a major problem. Is Chuck there? Do you have his home number? Yes, I know what day it is and I know what time it is."

"A summary of the findings of the Department of Justice specialist who has been working on this case has come into my possession," Sanchez was saying. "As I go through it, our artist, Cliff Nagel, is going to add the information to this blank outline. When we are through, we will have the fullest picture yet of the man the Sheriff's Department is looking for but cannot find. Maybe, viewers—just maybe—we can do better."

"Chuck, hi. Steve Giordano. Yes, I know, I'm sorry," Giordano said. "Look, I'm watching Channel Seven, the Richard Sanchez report? He's talking about profiling in the specific context of the case I am investigating down here. From what he's said so far, it's dollars to dogshit he's gotten hold of a copy of my profile—no, Chuck, I do *not* know how—and he's going to use it on air. I just thought you'd better know. Yes, yes, I'll tape it and call you later."

He banged down the phone. Kathryn stared at him. Steve lifted his chin toward the TV. Sanchez was again full-face solo on screen.

"In an earlier program we offered some hypotheses about the man who killed Barbara Gates," Sanchez said. "Tonight we go further. Deeper into the unknown. Into the horror."

He got up out of his chair and walked over to the outline figure on the back wall.

"Here he is. Here is the serial killer that Agent Giordano has dubbed 'the Gingerbread Man.' Yes, believe it or not, that's what they call him. Because they can't catch him, you see. Run, run, as fast as you can, you can't catch me, I'm the gingerbread man."

He paused to let that sink in. Love him, hate him, Kathryn thought, he was good. She looked at Steve.

"I was right," he said disgustedly. "The bastard's got our profile. But who the hell gave it to him?"

He didn't seem to want an answer, although it was a good

question, Kathryn thought; but since during the last week or so practically everyone above the rank of maintenance man had stopped into their office to ask about Dave Granz, they had a pretty wide field to choose from. She looked at Sanchez prowling in front of his silent audience like a panther. Although she was familiar with every phrase he uttered, the way he delivered them gave the words extra depth, a chilling gravity the printed page could never impart.

"Sources close to the district attorney's office state," he was saying, "that acting on the premise that any one of them might have been an attempt by the killer to abduct a victim, the DA's Special Investigation Unit, headed up by Assistant DA Kathryn Mackay and Agent Stephen A. Giordano of the Department of Justice, reexamined all reports of assaults on women made between the estimated date of the first murder and the present time. By a process of elimination, the total number of cases was reduced to seven, in each of which the victim was Hispanic and between fifteen and twenty-five."

He paused for dramatic effect. "In all seven cases the assailant was a man thought to be between thirty and forty, with dark hair, average height, average build. In two of the cases, he wore a tan windbreaker and dark slacks. In three cases, the most recent five nights ago in Marina Village, a tan or gold pickup was seen at or near the scene prior to the crime."

As the camera cut to Cliff Nagel filling in the details on the chart, Sanchez went back to his podium, picking up an official-looking file.

"All right, we've looked at the physical makeup of the killer. Now let me talk you through the psychological profile the investigators have compiled. Remember we spoke of a broken family, possible delinquency . . ." Sanchez stopped, frowning.

"One moment please, ladies and gentlemen," he said, bending his head forward to concentrate on the message coming through his earpiece. "I've just been told we've received a call from someone claiming to be the killer. We've got technicians setting up a link right this moment."

Kathryn tried to picture the pandemonium in the control box, intercoms ringing, the producer shouting instructions to his floor manager and the cameramen, every member of the production crew frantically trying to anticipate and cover the next contingency as the carefully timed shooting plan was abandoned. Sanchez picked up the telephone on his desk.

"This is Richard Sanchez." He nodded. "I'm putting you on the speakerphone. Go ahead."

As Sanchez spoke, Steve Giordano jumped to his feet again and went to the phone. He dialed a number and began talking rapidly. It sounded like he was giving someone orders. Kathryn shut out the sound of his voice, concentrating on the astonishing conversation going on in front of her.

"You're doing a lot of guessing, *cholo.*" The voice had a squawky, Donald-Duck quality: the caller was using some sort of voice distorter. It did nothing to conceal the contempt in his voice. "Why don't you just ask me whatever it is you wish to know?"

"Who are you?" Sanchez said. "What is your name?"

"I'm the man you're talking about," the disembodied voice replied. "I believe they call me the Gingerbread Man."

"How do we know you're who you say you are?"

"That's easy. I'll tell you something, something only the cops know. Listen carefully. I sign my work, *cholo.* So they'll be in no doubt it's me. You can ask them, if you like."

"What ... what do you do?"

"I wash them, *cholo.* Every time. All over. With Ivory soap. Ask the cops, *cholo.* They won't deny it. They can't."

"My God," Kathryn breathed. "Did you hear that? Steve, Steve!"

He made a signal, yes, I heard. He was still on the phone, waiting, watching the TV at the same time.

"Why are you telling us this?" Sanchez asked, staring at the screen.

"The last time you talked about me, you said I was stupid," the unearthly voice quacked, bulldozing the question. "You and the Mackay woman from the DA's office. If I'm as stupid as you tried to make me look, how come they haven't caught me?"

The electronic tone of a severed connection indicated the caller had hung up. Richard Sanchez put down the telephone and faced the camera, running his hands through his hair. He paused to collect his thoughts, clearly winging it.

"Ladies and gentlemen, you just heard the voice of a man

who claims to be the murderer of Barbara Gates and at least two other women. What truth there is in his claims we can only guess, although, of course, we will seek immediate confirmation from Sheriff Jake Gylam's office."

He paused again, either for an effect he didn't need, or to get instructions from his producer via the earpiece. He leaned forward, hands clasped together, looking directly into camera. Exactly the way he looked at me that day in Patrón's, Kathryn thought.

"Let us return to our examination of the killer," he said. "What kind of urges drive this madman? And more importantly, what makes him so savagely mutilate the bodies of his victims? The answer is in the psychological profile the investigators have constructed. The victim represents someone he kills again and again, and will go on killing. The ... scalping is a way of keeping score of how many times he has inflicted that revenge. It is also possible that he has begun enjoying himself, and now it's not just the revenge but also the *game* he enjoys: finding a victim, stalking her, ripping her out of her environment like someone ripping a page out of a book. That's part of his pornography, the power."

He stopped, swiveled to face the other camera in close-up. Here comes the big finale, Kathryn thought.

"Who is he, this mad dog they've nicknamed the Gingerbread Man? Let's recap. He's a fairly well-educated man between thirty and forty, dark-haired, white or Hispanic, who lives with a sister or a relative in a perfectly ordinary Santa Rita suburb. He's between five-six and five-eleven, average build. He has a pleasant voice and an ingratiating manner. He sometimes wears a tan windbreaker and dark slacks. He may drive or own a tan or gold pickup. Do you know him? Is he your neighbor, someone you know at work, a guy you see on the bus every day? Can you put a face to him? If you can, call me. Don't wait. Don't hesitate. If you think you know this man, stop him before he can kill again."

He stopped speaking, eyes looking upward as he listened to the voices in his earpiece.

"Ladies and gentlemen," he said softly, "we have another call from the same man. Yes, yes, I'm ready, put him on." He picked up the phone again. "Hello, who is this?"

"You know who it is."

In spite of the distortion, it was clear the speaker was angry; the voice was breathy, as if the man had just run upstairs.

"I was watching when you talked about their stupid profile. You tell them they're wrong, *cholo*. Wrong, wrong, wrong!"

"If that's the case, why don't you tell us—?"

"I'm telling you. You and all those so-called *experts*. I've read all the books and the psychological journals, the *FBI Law Enforcement Bulletin* and the *Journal of Forensic Sciences* and the rest. And do you know what they taught me? All these so-called *experts* know nothing. *Nothing!* There's only one person who really knows anything about it, and that's me. Me, *cholo*. I know myself better than all the experts in the country put together."

"Then tell us. Tell us now: What makes you tick? Why do you kill?"

There was a silence.

"You call me *cholo*," Sanchez said into it. "That's a term of contempt in my language."

"I know," the man said, compounding the insult. Sanchez refused to be rattled by it.

"You only kill Hispanic women. Is there a reason for that?"

"We know the truth not only by the reason, *cholo*."

"I don't understand."

"It's not necessary that you do."

"I ask you again," Sanchez said, letting his anger show. "Answer me! Why are you killing these defenseless women?"

"Are you angry, *cholo?*"

"Of course I'm angry!" Sanchez said. "We're all angry. You abduct innocent women, you defile and mutilate their bodies—and you expect us not to be?"

The sound of the caller's chuckle was macabre. "I can't help myself, *cholo*. I do it for revenge, remember?"

"Where do you take them?" Sanchez said. There was a sheen of sweat on his forehead. "Tell us—"

"No more questions. Just tell your experts they'll be hearing from me. Soon."

Once again there was the unmistakable sound of a broken connection. Sanchez put down the telephone. He listened again in his earpiece, nodded.

"Ladies and gentlemen, the clock on the wall tells me we have overrun our time slot, but I know you'll agree with me that it was worth it. With that astonishing conversation with the man who claims to be the Santa Rita serial killer, we end this edition of *Here and Now*. Tune in again Wednesday, when we will again bring you the truths no other program dares to face. I'm Richard Sanchez. Good night . . . and *Vaya con Dios*."

Kathryn switched off the TV as the credits rolled; that same moment her telephone rang. Steve Giordano jumped to his feet and snatched it off the cradle.

"Damn!" he said. "Damn, damn, damn!"

"What happened?"

"I called Earheart. I thought if he could get a tech team over to the studio they might be able to trace the call," he told her.

"You're wasting your time," Kathryn said brusquely. "He's too smart to be caught like that. Get ahold of Sanchez, the number's on the pad there, tell him we want broadcast-quality tapes of the program, like yesterday. I want to get them to a psycholinguist, fast."

She went over to the VCR and switched it off, extracting the tape. She stared at it for a moment, shaking her head a trifle ruefully.

"That was why he called me about the profile, that snake," she said, as much to herself as anyone. "He wanted to make absolutely sure he had an exclusive."

Steve made no reply; he was standing by the window, looking out at the ocean, a deep frown of concentration furrowing his brow.

"What is it?" Kathryn said. "You still trying to figure out how Sanchez got the profile?"

Steve shook his head. "I'll probably get my ass fried over that, but I can live with that. No, it's the killer, the way he was talking, what he said. He wants to punish us. *Us*, Kathryn. The authors of his shame. You heard him. There was rage in that voice. Deep, burning anger. He's going to show us just how stupid we are, and just how clever he is. He's ready to kill again."

31

On Monday morning the call-in from the serial killer on the Sanchez program was practically the sole topic of conversation on the second and third floors of the County Building. As soon as work commenced, Jake Gylam, making no attempt to conceal the fact that he was in a foul mood, called a quickie meeting to review the situation. It had to be a quickie, he said: every available person in his office was engaged in damage control. By ten A.M. practically every TV station and newspaper editor within a hundred miles had called to complain about his office giving Sanchez the inside track on such a story. His protestations that he'd had nothing to do with it, and that the profile had been stolen, had met with derision.

"I don't mind that it's not our finest hour," Gylam complained. "What I do mind is this whole thing makes me look like a dickhead."

No one commented on that, although one or two people in the room exchanged glances.

"That's the party line?" Giordano asked into the pause. "You're telling the media we had a break-in?"

"Come up with something better and we'll use that," Gylam rumbled. "Meanwhile, that's our story and we're sticking with it."

"Fine," Giordano said. "As long as you understand it doesn't change what actually happened."

Gylam's face got red. "You think I don't know the goddamn scuttlebutt around here? I've been hearing it for months: Sanchez has got a line into this office. Well, this time, I'm going to run it down."

"How do you propose to do that?" Giordano asked mildly.

"I want a list from you of everyone who got a copy of the profile," Gylam said. "Anyone who can't produce his copy better have a goddamn good excuse ready."

266

"Oh, come on, Sheriff," Steve said. "Haven't you ever heard of a thing called a photocopier?"

"Or a fax?" Kathryn chimed in. "Anyone up here or downstairs could have faxed a copy over to Sanchez in what, three minutes? And there'd be no record of it anywhere."

"I know, goddamn it, but I am not going to just ignore this thing," Gylam replied stubbornly.

"Nobody's asking you to, Sheriff," Kathryn said placatingly, "but more to the point right now, how badly has it hurt us? Does the leak in any way prejudice the investigation?"

"It sticks in my craw to say it, but Sanchez probably did us a favor," Steve replied. "He brought the killer out from under his rock."

"Are we going to get anything off the videotape?" Earheart wanted to know.

"Steve, you've couriered the tape to DOJ in Sacramento?"

"I'm waiting to hear from them," Steve replied. He didn't sound like he was looking forward to it.

"We've also sent copies to Abraham Mellish at Syracuse University and Sam Lepell at U-Cal," Kathryn reported. "Dr. Mellish is the top psycholinguist in the country. The FBI uses his services a lot. We sent him copies of the coded notes as well. He's going to run them through the computer. You know how it works."

The science of psycholinguistics was often used to identify anonymous letter writers or persons who made written or spoken threats. A "threat dictionary" was composed, and each word assigned by computer to a specific category. Words as used in the threat messages were then compared with the same words as used in ordinary speech or writing. The vocabulary usage could sometimes yield "signature" words unique to the offender, establishing that several letters had been written by the same person and at the same time offering insights into his background and psychology.

"What about the other guy, Lepell? He's the linguistics expert at the university, right?"

"I called him just before I came in here," Kathryn told the sheriff. "He says he hasn't had enough time to study the tape in detail, but he doesn't think he'll get much from it because of the voice distorter. All he can say for sure is the voice is undoubtedly male adult. And although he wouldn't swear to it in court, he's pretty sure the guy isn't Hispanic—he can't detect any trace of an accent or Hispanic speech patterns. He particularly draws our attention to the phraseology, which he says is more grammatically correct than is usual. 'Whatever it is you wish to know'—not 'want to know.' 'It's not necessary that you do,' instead of 'It doesn't matter if,' and so on."

"So our killer is nicely spoken," Jake Gylam said sarcastically. "Big deal. That it?"

Kathryn looked at Steve; he made a rueful face. Gylam had never made any secret of his feelings about profiling and what he called the other mumbo jumbo.

"Kathryn?" Earheart asked.

"I've got nothing else."

"Okay, people, thanks for coming," Gylam said. "Let's get back to work. And nobody talks to the press or TV without clearing it with my office, okay?"

Lee had no morning classes, so he stayed in his den and watched the Sanchez program on video. He was pleased; he had trashed their stupid profile and served them notice: *Tell your experts they'll be hearing from me. Soon.* And they would. He shut down the VCR, switched everything off, and came out, locking the door behind him. He could smell coffee in the kitchen.

"I'll get it," Carol said as he went across to the stove.

"I think I can manage," he told her, putting sarcasm into it.

"Do you want anything to eat?"

"I don't want anything, Carol," he said, measuring out the words. She took her lower lip between her teeth and wrapped the terry cloth robe more tightly around herself. Without makeup, her hair uncombed, she looked drawn and careworn.

"You look terrible," he said unsympathetically. "Didn't you sleep well?"

"I was . . . you were out. You didn't see it. Richard Sanchez had a program about . . . the murders. It upset me. I couldn't sleep."

"I've told you not to watch things like that. Why are you so stupid? Why don't you listen to me?"

"I . . . just had it on. I didn't know he was going to . . ."

"Don't argue," he snapped. She fell silent instantly, like a cowed dog. Then she surprised him.

"Where did you go last night?" she said. He stared at her stonily and she quailed again. She had broken the rule: *Never question me.*

"What?"

"I can't bear it, Lee. Wondering . . ."

"Then don't. Don't wonder. Don't think. Don't anything."

"It's started again, hasn't it?" she said. "Oh, God, it's started again."

He got up and banged his cup down on the table so hard she jumped visibly.

"Don't make me angry, Carol," he said. His voice was very soft. He stretched out his hand and she flinched. He stroked her hair, taking it back away from her face. Her eyes were wide with apprehension. That pleased him.

"I'm sorry," she whispered. "I won't do it again."

"Of course you won't," he said. "Because you know what will happen if you do, don't you?"

She nodded. She knew.

He had killed the girl in Burlingame on a Tuesday.

They were living in Redwood City. He told Carol he was going fishing, but instead he drove north to a bar called Mamacita's on El Camino Real. He'd heard one of his Hispanic students telling a buddy lots of girls from the local college went there looking for action. He parked in back of the place and went inside. A blast of noise and cigarette smoke and sweat and spilled beer hit him simultaneously. The place was done up like a Bavarian beer hall, with carved wooden booths and round tables covered with checkered tablecloths. He got a draft beer at the bar and stood there watching. There wasn't an unattached girl in the place as far as he could see. That didn't mean a thing: it was how they left that mattered.

He went back to the pickup and waited. Fifteen, twenty minutes went by. Half an hour. He thought about leaving, and then he saw a girl come out of the bar with two guys. She looked about nineteen, slim, tan, with long dark hair. One of the guys made as if to grab her, but she dodged him, laughing. The two guys got into a Chevy and roared out of the parking lot, tires squealing. The girl waved as they went by, then went across to her own car, a VW Beetle. Lee eased the pickup out behind her, following her through the dark suburban streets. They were somewhere down near the San Mateo golf course; he got an occasional glimpse of the toll bridge. She lived in a nice neighborhood, a big ranch-style home with a two-car garage set back on a neat plot under trees. He made a note of the address and drove away. Next night he was waiting for her in the dark as she got out of the car and he took her off the street like a pike taking a duckling.

It was all over the papers three days later when they found the body in a culvert up near the Crystal Spring Dam, with hourly updates on TV and radio. He consumed the news avidly. The body being brought down from the mountains. The grieving parents. The detective in charge of the investigation asking for any witnesses to come forward. The spot on *Crime Stoppers* that highlighted the lack of clues or witnesses. He especially enjoyed that.

"Why do you always watch these awful programs?" Carol asked him.

"They amuse me," he said.

"How can you find something so tragic amusing?"

"I have a warped sense of humor," he said. "Surely you must have noticed?"

"It's something else," she said. "You actually enjoy it."

"Don't talk nonsense."

"It's in your eyes. There's a look . . ."

Her mouth fell open. Her eyes suddenly filled with astonished knowledge.

"Oh, God, no," she whispered. "No."

"Stop this," he said, angrily.

"You said you were fishing. You said you cut yourself. That was why there was blood. On your clothes. Blood."

"I said stop it."

"It was on TV. She'd been to some bar. You had matches from there. Mamacita's. I found them in your jacket."

He stared at her. It wasn't possible. It couldn't be. She was too stupid to have put it all together. Yet there it was in her eyes. She knew, without knowing how she knew. Options flickered through his mind; anger began to bubble inside him.

"You're mad," he said. "Crazy. Do you know what you're saying?"

"It's . . . it was you," she said, staring, staring. "You."

"Stop this, I said. That's enough."

"What did you do? Oh, God, Lee, what did you do to that poor innocent child?"

Women were never prepared for violence. Never. He hit her in the face with his fist. She careered backwards, blood spraying from her nose and spattering the wall. She collapsed on the floor, one leg askew, her eyes clouded. He stood over her, rage throbbing through him. But not the rage he felt with the others, with them. This was a cold fury. This was a punishing anger.

"You want to know, do you?" he shouted. "All right, I'll show you. I'll show you!"

He grabbed her long blond hair and wound it around his fist, yanking her upright screaming. The wild roaring filled his head and the red mist floated behind his eyes. He dragged her by the hair, twisting and screaming along the hallway into the bedroom. When he let go of her hair she tried to cower away from him, but he grabbed her leg and pulled her back toward him and hit her low in the belly. She bent over, retching. Formless shouts of rage boiled out of him. He grabbed her arm and hurled her against the wall. Her legs buckled and she slid to the floor, half-conscious. He ripped off her blouse, tore off her skirt. She tried to get up and he hit her again, slipping on the blood spattered on the floor.

"Do what I tell you!" he shouted. "Do what I tell you now!"

He tore off her underclothes. She hunched naked, whimpering. Blood dripped on the floor.

"Face down, on the bed!" he yelled. "Now, you pathetic bitch!"

He tied her hands and feet to the bedposts. She lay face down, her body heaving with harsh, dry sobs. He went into his study and got the scalpel. Then he came back and looked down at her, his body still heaving with rage. He wanted to kill her but that was madness. Everything else, though. Everything else.

"Are you afraid, Carol?" he asked, his voice soft now and

to her infinitely more frightening than his rage. She moved her head dumbly to signify assent.

"You made me very angry, Carol. You have to learn never to question me, ever. And never to speak of this again. Never. Not to anyone. Do you understand?"

"Yes," she managed. The pillow under her face was soaked with blood. Her lips were already swollen to twice their normal size.

"Good," he said, almost jovially. "Because if you do, I will kill you. Do you understand that?"

"Oh, God," she whispered. "Oh, God, please."

"They all say that," he told her. "At the beginning. But in the end they do anything I want. Anything. I have a way of making them. Look."

She buried her bloody face in the pillow, sobbing, afraid to look.

"First, their hair," he said. "I cut their hair off. Like this."

He took a hank of her blond hair in his hand and sliced through it with the razor-sharp blade.

"No," his wife sobbed. "Oh, God, no please don't. Don't."

He sat astride her naked buttocks, humming the lullaby, cutting the long tresses of hair and dropping them on the floor beside the bed. When he was done, he knelt down beside her, grabbed her cropped head, and made her look at him. He held the blade in front of her eyes.

"Do you see it?" he hissed. "Do you know what it is?"

She nodded dumbly. He touched the blade against her buttock, moved it until a bead of blood popped up on the skin. She drew in a hissed breath of pain.

"See how sharp," he said. "You hardly felt it."

"Don't," she managed. "Don't hurt me. Lee, please."

"They all say that, too," he said, smiling.

He unfastened her bindings. She did not move.

"Turn over," he said.

She turned over and lay absolutely still, staring with fixed terror at the familiar ceiling of her own bedroom. Her face was a mess. He sat down beside her on the bed. She cringed at his contact.

"Do exactly what I tell you to do," he said. "Like a slave. Do you understand?"

"Please," she said. "Please. I'm sorry. I'll never . . . Lee. For God's sake, I'm your wife."

He slapped her, hard. *"Cholo,"* he hissed. "You call me *cholo."*

"Cholo," she faltered.

And then her nightmare began.

Back in their office, Kathryn and Steve replayed the videotape again and again. They were so familiar with it now they could almost repeat the exchanges between Sanchez and the killer word for word.

"I was right about one thing," Kathryn observed. "He doesn't like anyone saying or thinking he's stupid."

Steve nodded thoughtfully. "It's part of the pattern. You, me, Sanchez, the cops, we're all dorks. He's the only one with any brains."

"You think he really is that smart?"

"Intelligent, sure. Cunning. Devious. But ultimately, not smart. If he was smart he wouldn't be playing games like this."

"He's probably enjoying watching us squirm."

Giordano made an impatient gesture. "Go back to the first part of the second call. There's a phrase he uses in there that keeps bothering me."

Kathryn rewound the tape, stopped it, switched to PLAY. The now-familiar conversation replayed through the speakers.

"What is all that *cholo* business?" she asked Steve.

"It's Spanish street talk. It means, you know, the guy's a real ladies' man, a stud."

"Sanchez said it was an insult."

"If a white man says it to an Hispanic, it is. Like calling someone a spic or a wop."

"So the killer is probably white?"

"If you want my opinion, yes," Steve said. "But only partly because of that. What interests me much more is what he said when Sanchez asked him why he does it. He said, 'We know the truth not only by the reason.' What is that?"

"It doesn't ring any bells with me," Kathryn said, switching off the machine. "Could it be some kind of a quotation?"

She swiveled her chair around and lifted down her copy of *Bartlett's Familiar Quotations,* flicking through the index.

"Truth . . . reason," she muttered, turning back through the book. *"Pensées,* by Blaise Pascal. French theologian, seventeenth century. 'We know the truth, not only by the reason, but by the heart.' Does it mean anything to you?"

Steve shrugged. "Not to me. It obviously has some special resonance for him, though."

"I don't imagine many people read Blaise Pascal."

"I don't imagine all that many people even know who he is."

"So does that tell us anything? Maybe this guy reads theology?"

"Or *Bartlett,"* Steve pointed out. His conditioned reflex, she thought; no absolutes. "To misquote Doc Nelson, some wild herrings are nothing but red geese."

The phone rang and Kathryn picked it up. She pulled a face and held it out to Steve.

"Chuck Whitby."

Steve took the phone and listened to what his boss had to say, nodding once in a while, saying Sure, Chuck, a couple of times. Then he put the phone down.

"I have to go to Sacramento. Now."

"Trouble?"

"Right here in River City," he said soberly. "I think I am going to get my ass fried."

"That's not fair," Kathryn said. "It's not your fault."

He smiled ruefully. "I'll tell Chuck you said so." He pecked her on the cheek and headed for the door. Kathryn looked at the clock. It was a little after eleven. She felt as if she had already done a day's work. With a sigh, she pressed the PLAY command on the video recorder.

The telephone rang just after noon. The female voice that spoke her name was faint and hesitant; her first impulse was to switch the caller over to one of the secretaries, but something stopped her.

"Yes, I'm Kathryn Mackay," she said. "Who is this?"

"I don't want to give my name," the woman said. "It's about those women who have been killed. It was on TV last night."

"Go on," Kathryn said, suddenly aware of her heart pounding.

"I know who he is," the woman said. Her voice was hollow, haunted. "The man who did it."

"How do you know this?"

"I just know."

"All right. Tell me his name."

"His name . . ." There was a long silence.

"Are you still there?"

"Yes. I . . . if I tell you his name, will you arrest him? Will you put him in jail?"

"If he killed those women, I promise you he will go to prison for the rest of his life. But first you have to tell me who he is."

"The detective came to see him," the woman said. "The one whose picture was in the paper. I think . . . Lee tried to kill him."

"Did you say Lee?"

She felt the woman's panicked reaction to the question as surely as if they had been in the same room.

"No, no, I said he, *he* tried to kill him."

"He attacked Inspector Granz? How do you know?"

"That night, when he came . . . He had scratches on his face."

"Are you saying the same man who attacked Inspector Granz is the one who killed Barbara Gates and the other women?"

"He . . . must be."

"Please, please, tell me his name."

"I can't. If he . . . he'd kill me if he knew I was calling you."

"What is your relationship to him?"

"You've got to stop him. He won't ever stop, and I can't . . ." the woman whispered, her voice trembling with tension. "Someone is coming. I have to go."

"Please, tell me your name, or at least tell me how I can contact you again," Kathryn pleaded. The connection broke. She put down the telephone and discovered she was trembling. She caught a glimpse of her own face in the mirror on the wall. She looked like she had just seen a ghost.

"Lee," she muttered. "Lee." She flicked on her PC, accessed the database, and called up Granz's lists. Tapping the

keys eagerly, she instituted a search for the name *Lee*. She
leaned back in her chair and waited as the machine blinked
and buzzed, and the data started to scroll. After a few seconds the screen blinked:

>*No match found. Going to next record.*

"Damn," Kathryn muttered. "Okay, let's try all surnames
beginning with *L.*"
After a few seconds, the screen blinked again and three
lines of type appeared:

David D. Larson, 479, Seacliff Drive,
Laguna del Mar.
Charles P. Lewis, Jr., 335b, Jade
Street, Espanola.
Stephen J. Lord, 158, Escalona Drive,
Espanola.

Christian names next. Once again, there were only three.

Lawrence G. Murphy, 2228, Espanola Road,
Cliffside Park.
Leland C. Prewitt, 874, Ranchero Drive, Ala-
meda Heights.
Leslie N. Stagg, 662, Wyndham Street,
Santa Rita.

"Leland C. Prewitt," she said to herself. "Lee for short,
maybe?" Okay, it looked like there was only one candidate
there. The next step was to look at names with the initial *L.*
She tapped in another command. Once again the computer
hummed, whirred, and gave its warning blip, and then lines
of information ran across the screen.

Harry L. Branch, 1144, Cable Avenue, Harbor Park.
L. Parker Brownlow, 529, Garden Drive, Espanola.
Diego L. Cruces, 3167, Eastridge Drive, Santa Rita.
Charles L. Eberhart, 2022, Emerald Road, Cliffside
Park.
Dennis L. Gonzales, 1658, Toledo Drive, Laguna
del Mar.

Eduardo L. Jimenez, 4112, Clarendon Ave., Alameda.
Leonard L. Merrill, 2820, Broadstone Road, Santa Rita.
Albert L. Parks, 244, Kinsley Drive, Alameda Heights.
James L. Russell, 3324, Pacheco Drive, Outlook Heights.

She stared at the screen. One of those names is the killer, she thought. She tapped in the print command, waited while the printer buzzed and zipped. She tore off the sheet and laid it on her desk. Then she dialed Walt Earheart's number.

32

"SONOFABITCH," WALT EARHEART SAID SOFTLY, LEANING back in his chair. "Kathryn, I think we've finally got something."

They had run a check through the DMV printouts on the names Kathryn's computer search had turned up. Out of all the names, four were possibles: Leland Charles Prewitt of Alameda Heights; Charles Leroy Eberhart of Cliffside Park; Eduardo Leandro Jimenez of Alameda; and James Leland Russell, who lived in Outlook Heights. All were between twenty-five and forty, and all fitted the physical profile.

"What we need to do now is run a check on each of these guys, find out his marital status, what he does for a living, anything that might tie him more closely to our killer. Kathryn, run what your mystery woman said by me again, will you?"

Kathryn repeated her conversation with the anonymous caller as accurately as she could.

"She said he had scratches on his face?"

"That's right."

"CSI found traces of blood and skin under Dave's fingernails. That means once we arrest this guy, we might be able to get a DNA match. What else?"

"I think she's a relative. Mother, sister, lover, wife. She lives with him."

"Why?"

"She said, 'He had scratches on his face when he came ...' and then she stopped, caught herself before she could say the rest."

"You mean, like, when he came home."

"Or in, or back."

"Maybe, but she could just as easily have been going to say, When he came up to, or down to, or over to my place," Earheart interjected. "We can't draw any firm conclusions from something she didn't say."

"She also said he'd kill her if he knew she was calling me. I read that to mean she lives with him."

"At roll call, we'll check if anyone remembers talking to a guy with a scratched face," Earheart said. "Meanwhile I'll put a team on each of these four names here, try to get a picture of each of them. What's your next move?"

"I'm going to take a ride up to County Hospital and try these names out on Dave Granz," Kathryn said. "That's if he's strong enough to talk."

"He's sitting up and taking nourishment. Through a straw, but he's taking it. He'll be out of there before long."

"Has he come up with anything on his attacker?"

"No, he's still blank. He keeps saying he has this feeling he knows something important, but he can't remember what it is. It's bothering the hell out of him."

"Maybe the names will trigger something."

"From your lips to God's ears," Earheart said. "Dammit, we *deserve* a break. We've tried everything with this case except having Disney make a movie of it."

After stopping to tell Marcia where she was going and that she didn't know when she'd be back, Kathryn got into her car and headed for Mission Heights. All the way up to County Hospital she could feel the excitement building. Could this at last be the break they had all been praying for? She wished she could talk to Steve about it, but that would have to wait till he got back from Sacramento.

Granz was sitting in a wicker chair in the dayroom, looking out of the window across the neat, landscaped grounds sloping down toward town and the red roofs of the houses below. The lower half of his face and his hands were still bandaged, and he wore a green surgical hat over the cap of dressings on his head. Kathryn went over and kissed him on top of the hat.

"Hey," she said. "How's my best inspector?"

Dave turned his bandaged head so he could see her.

"More or less . . . in one piece," he croaked, and the laugh lines at the corners of his eyes crinkled.

Kathryn made a face so he could see it. "You always did have a bizarre sense of humor," she said. "Did you see the Sanchez report last night?"

He moved a bandaged hand. "Haven't stopped thinking about it since," he said. "What's the feeling downtown? You guys . . . think it was the killer?"

"We're pretty sure it must have been. No one else could know about the bath soap. Look, I know he used a voice distorter, but was there anything about his voice, anything at all about the way he talked or what he said that struck you as . . . you know, familiar?"

Dave made a movement that might have been the beginning of a head shake, then froze, inhaling sharply. "Doc Nelson warned me . . . not to . . . do that," he said. "Everything . . . goes twang. What was the question?"

"I asked you if the way he talked or anything he said sounded familiar."

"He sounded like . . . Donald Duck," Dave replied. "Is it . . . important?"

Kathryn nodded. "We think we may have a lead."

Granz's attitude changed completely. The indolence disappeared, and his pale blue eyes glinted with sharpened attention. She could hear the tension in his voice when he spoke.

"What kind of lead?"

"A little while ago I got an anonymous call," Kathryn said. "A woman. She claimed the killer is the same guy who attacked you, and that you talked to him."

He looked away, concentrating. "Now I get it. No idea who . . . she is?"

"No idea. My feeling is maybe a sister, a relation. That would fit the profile. Someone close enough to be frightened, desperate enough to make an anonymous call asking us to stop him before he does it again."

"Goddammit, if I could just . . . remember," Dave said, and there was anger in his voice. "It's driving me crazy,

Kathryn . . . I keep reaching, but I can't quite . . . I keep having this feeling I saw or I heard something . . . significant. Only I can't remember . . . what."

"Why the hell didn't you keep notes?"

"I did at first. But I . . . didn't really know . . . what I was looking for. And so much of the stuff was . . . immaterial. I knew I'd remember anything . . . important. Good joke, huh?"

"Does the name Lee mean anything to you?"

"Lee?"

"I'm not sure about this, but I thought the woman who called said his name, Lee. There are no Lees on your lists. Nobody with the first name Lee. We've got four names of men who might be known as Lee. I want you to take a look at them, see if anything hits you."

He stared at the four names and addresses on the sheet of paper for perhaps two minutes. "Lee," he said softly. "Lee, Lee, Lee." Then he made an exasperated sound.

"Dave, try!" Kathryn urged. "The woman said he came home the night you were attacked with scratches on his face. Did you scratch him, or hit him, can you remember?"

"For Chrissake, Kathryn, don't you think I . . . want to?" he said, angrily, and she saw his eyes close with pain.

"Dave, I'm sorry, don't . . . you mustn't shout, you'll hurt your throat."

"Tell me . . . about it," he said, his breathing ragged. "It's . . . okay. I'll be . . . okay in a . . . minute."

He stared furiously out of the window as if his angry eyes could somehow or other conjure the answer to his questions onto the glass in front of him. After a while his breathing returned to normal.

"I'm sorry, Kathryn," he said. "I get so damned . . . mad at myself. It's like . . . driving in fog. Once in a while you see . . . a flash of something, but mostly it's . . . just a gray blur." He gestured toward his throat. "Voice . . . runs out after . . . a while, too."

Kathryn put a gentle hand on his arm.

"Take it easy," she said. "I'll come back tomorrow, we'll talk some more. Is there anything I can bring you?"

"You can't see it, but I'm . . . smiling," Dave told her. "They won't let me . . . have booze. I can't smoke . . . if I coughed I'd . . . tear everything loose. I'm in no shape to meet . . . pretty girls right now. What do you . . . suggest?"

"How about a couple of hard sets of tennis?" Kathryn said.

The corner of Dave's eyes crinkled again and he held up his bandaged hands. "Sorry," he said. "Listen, say hello . . . to Giordano."

"He's in Sacramento."

"They going to . . . chew him out over Sanchez?"

"I guess so. We've all had to take some flak. Jake Gylam is mad enough to bite a grizzly bear. He's telling the media we had a break-in."

"I heard it . . . on the radio," Dave said. "Hell, Kathryn, that was no . . . break-in. Most people wouldn't know a CIA . . . if it bit them . . . in the leg. Sanchez has got to have . . . someone inside. Bet on it."

"I know. I just hate to think it's true. That it's someone we know."

"Sometimes people . . . you don't . . . expect. Things . . . happen to them, they . . . make bad choices."

Who was he thinking about? she wondered. Himself? The two of them? Someone else? He interrupted her thoughts with a question.

"You and Giordano . . . get along well?" It was a throw-away line but she knew he wanted more than a throw-away reply.

"A lot better than that, Dave."

She could see only his eyes. They did not change. "I didn't think he was . . . your type. Still don't. You think . . . it's going to be permanent?"

"I don't know," Kathryn said, realizing as she said it that she was ducking the question. "Listen, study the names on that list, will you? Concentrate. See if you can't remember something, anything. Call me if you do. Otherwise we'll talk tomorrow. You sure there isn't anything I can bring you?"

"Look at me," Granz said. "What could I need?"

"Okay, let's run through this stuff together," Walt Earheart began. This Tuesday morning they were in the sheriff's conference room again, the SO detectives sitting in the same shell chairs they had occupied when Steve Giordano outlined the CIA for them.

"We got lucky on a couple of things. I'll explain as I go along. Okay, first, Leland Charles Prewitt. Thirty-seven years of age, married, four children. He's five-nine, a hundred and sixty pounds, with brown hair, brown eyes. No criminal record, works as a computer programmer for Silent Systems, a consultant firm on Union Street. Joe, you want to tell us what you and Martin came up with in your neighborhood survey?"

Lanky and slow moving, Joe Coughlin had a deceptively casual air that concealed a sharp and agile mind. He and his partner Detective Martin Silvero were one of SO's best teams.

"If this guy's our man, I'm Chief Crazy Horse," he said to Earheart. "Everybody speaks well of him. No criminal record, not even a parking ticket. Drives a four-year-old Volkswagen Rabbit. Works hard, never takes a day off, loves his wife and kids, stays home nights except when he plays squash twice a week or goes to PTA meetings, takes care of his elderly mother-in-law . . . You want my opinion, which I know you do not, we can scratch him now."

"Steve?" Earheart said. Giordano was sitting next to Kathryn near the door. He hadn't said a word about what happened in Sacramento, and no one had asked.

"Normalcy is often a characteristic of the serial killer," he said, "but I think Joe's right, this guy sounds too much like Mr. Clean to be our guy. We need someone with a little more irregularity in his life-style. How tall is he?"

Coughlin checked his notebook. "Five-eleven, dark hair, green eyes. Why do you ask?"

"We believe our killer is also the guy who attacked Dave Granz," Steve said. "By extrapolation from the injuries Dave sustained, we've amplified the profile slightly. To begin with, we know he's right-handed; the knife wounds were delivered from right to left. The angle of the head injuries is consistent with their having been inflicted by a right-handed man quite a bit shorter than Granz. Dave's a shade under six feet, which means our guy has to be around five-seven. That would appear to let Prewitt out. Let's put him on the back burner and look at the others first."

"Okay, we'll move on," Earheart said. "Who covered Eberhart?"

"That was me and Mike, Walt," Hank Schiller said. He'd

teamed up with Detective Mike Curran to run a check on the Cliffside Park suspect, Charles Leroy Eberhart, thirty-eight, married with two children, a former employee of the Santa Rita County Conference and Visitors' Center. It was a waste of time; Eberhart was suffering from terminal cancer.

"No way he could be our man, Chief," Curran added. "The guy's only got months to live. He can't weigh more than a hundred pounds. It's all he can do to pick up a newspaper."

"That leaves Jimenez and Russell," Kathryn said. "What have we got on them?"

"Jimenez looks promising," Henry Chu said. Henry was short and solidly built; he was particular about the way he looked and was a bit of a fashion plate, but a reliable and conscientious investigator. His partner on the A-Team was Tom Ney, a transplanted Nebraskan whose family claimed descent from the Napoleonic marshal.

"Give us a rundown," Earheart said.

"Eduardo Leandro Jimenez," Henry Chu read from his notebook. "Known to his friends as Lee. Twenty-nine, five-foot-eight, a hundred and fifty pounds, black hair, brown eyes. Single, lives with his widowed mother and two sisters. Born in New Mexico, moved out here five years ago. Works as a fruit packer at Valley Foods in Catalina. And get this: he drives a pickup. Wrong color, admittedly—black—but he's got one. He's got a poor work record, takes time off and drops out of sight for a couple of days at a time."

"This is looking good," Earheart said. "This guy might have access to a cold facility someplace. Anything else?"

"He's got a record," Tom Ney said. "ADW, 1985, Albuquerque, New Mexico. He went after a girlfriend with a knife, claimed she was two-timing him. He got a suspended sentence. We accessed NCIC to be on the safe side, but that appears to be it."

"What do you say, Steve?" Earheart asked Giordano, who had been silent throughout the meeting. "He sound promising?"

"Was he one of the ones who said they'd talked to Granz?"

"Yes."

"Do we know anything about his educational background?"

"No," Henry Chu said. "But he doesn't come over as any genius, if that's what we're talking about."

"He certainly comes close to the profile. I think we ought to see what else we can come up with on this guy, Walt. Run some checks in New Mexico, find out anything we can about his background."

"Okay, done," Earheart said with a nod. "That leaves Russell. Ed?"

Ed Black was sitting by the window, his chair tipped back on its rear legs, his feet crossed in front of him, his hands folded across his sizable paunch. The oldest and longest-serving detective in SO, he had the dead eyes and disappointed expression of a man who has spent a lifetime listening to lies.

"You think Jimenez is promising, wait till you hear about this guy, Steve," he said to Giordano.

"Skip the buildup," Earheart said impatiently. "Get to the story."

"James Leland Russell, forty-three, married, no children. Teaches English at Cabrillo Park High School." Ed Black smiled with satisfaction at the reaction this information got.

"That might explain . . ." Steve said, as if thinking out loud. His voice tailed off. Everyone looked at him expectantly. After a moment, he blinked.

"Sorry," he said. "If this is our man, it might explain why he was more careful about the way he put the Gates girl's body down the inspection pit. He wanted to remember how she looked, anytime he might go in there, later, when all the fuss had died down. These guys get it off revisiting places associated with their crimes."

"You think that's good, wait," Ed Black said, "it gets better. Russell is five-seven, weighs around a hundred and forty. He's got dark brown hair and brown eyes. He's lived at the Outlook Heights address for about three years; came down here from Redwood City. He goes fishing, according to neighbors, two or three days at a time, sometimes midweek, no apparent pattern. Neighbors also say they don't socialize; we got the feeling there are marital problems."

"Okay, this guy looks like a definite possibility," Earheart said, "but he still doesn't match anything as well as Jimenez."

"Tell him, Merv," Black said to his partner Merv Phy.

"One of the neighbors told us Russell had Hispanic relatives," Merv said, shifting his footballer's shoulders into a more comfortable position against the wall he was leaning on. "Stepmother and stepsister. Apparently they died in an apartment-house fire in Chicago."

"Anything else?"

"Yeah," Merv drawled. "He collects trout flies. Ties them himself. Got a couple of hundred of them, apparently."

"What does he drive?" Kathryn asked.

"Honda Civic two-door sedan," Ed Black said, referring to his notes. "And no, he doesn't own a pickup."

"Had he talked to Granz?"

"He was down as a no."

"What about his name? Does he go by Lee?"

Ed Black and Merv Phy exchanged looks.

"No, everyone calls him James," Ed said. "Not Jim. James."

"Except his wife," Merv added meaningfully. "She calls him Lee."

Kathryn's heart bumped. She turned toward Steve, surprised to see he had a faraway look in his eyes. "Steve?"

"Uh? Oh, sorry, I was thinking."

"Yes? And?"

"Jimenez sounds good, although he doesn't sound like someone who might read the *Journal of Forensic Sciences*. He's also Hispanic, and all our assault witnesses said the assailant was white. Russell, on the other hand, fits all our requirements, but he's married and—if he's telling the truth—he never met Granz. I like him a lot, but Jimenez sounds good too. Walt, I think we need to know a lot more about both these men."

"Okay, here's what we do," Earheart said. "Mike, Hank, you team up with Henry and Merv on Jimenez. Get in touch with the New Mexico state police in Albuquerque, determine whether he had any other police contacts there or elsewhere."

"While you're at it, ask them if they can give us any information on him, schools, employers, anything, get the details. We'll have to get court orders or search warrants, but if he's our guy I'm sure we can come up with probable cause enough to convince a judge," Kathryn said.

"Run him through the Department of Justice in Sacramento, the National Crime Information Center in Washington, and anything else you can think of," Earheart continued. "I want a complete picture of this guy's life so far. Joe, Martin, you work with Ed and Hank on the other one, Russell. Same deal. One of you talk to his colleagues at Cabrillo Park High, only keep it low key, we don't want to alert him. Check out prior addresses, employers, military service, anything, everything. Any questions? Right, let's do it."

33

AS THEY LEFT THE MEETING KATHRYN SUGGESTED TO STEVE that they drive up to County Hospital and talk to Dave Granz again. They went down to the parking lot and got into her car; before she started the engine, Kathryn used the phone to let the office know where they would be.

"You haven't said a word about Sacramento," she said, as she pulled out onto Pacific and headed north.

Steve looked out of the side window. "Do we have to talk about it?" he said.

Kathryn was taken aback. "No we don't. I thought you might want to."

"Look," he said wearily, "it went exactly like I thought it would go. I got reamed out by the assistant director. End of story. Okay?"

"Well, excuse me," she said, her own mettle rising. "For living."

He turned in the seat to look at her. "Don't be angry," he said. "I just didn't want to get into it right now, that's all."

"Fine," she said briskly, staring straight ahead.

"Don't be mad, Kathryn."

"I'm not," she said.

Steve shook his head. "I didn't want to tell you like this. There's something else. They're calling me back in, Kathryn."

"What?"

"After he got through blasting me for not maintaining an appropriate degree of security, and telling me if it hadn't been for the killer calling in I'd be in a lot worse trouble, the AD said my presence in Santa Rita is redundant. The analysis is completed, the investigation is moving to a conclusion . . . so they want me back in Sacramento. Like, immediately."

"I see," Kathryn said, as they turned into the driveway of the County Hospital. "What do you want me to say?"

"I could ask you the same question."

"We haven't got much time to talk."

"You know it."

She parked the car and they went inside.

"I want to say hello to Morgan first," Kathryn said. "Okay?"

Giordano shrugged and joined her in the elevator down to the basement, the familiar flat odors of the cutting rooms and the morgue enveloping them as the doors slid open. The pathologist was hunched over a microscope; he looked around irritably when Kathryn knocked, his expression changing when he saw who his visitors were.

"Katie, come in!" he said. "I was thinking about you."

"Something on that slide remind you of me?"

He smiled. "Hello, Steve. To what do I owe this pleasure?"

"We're on our way to see Dave Granz," Kathryn said. "Thought we'd say hello to you first."

"They told me you were here yesterday. How did he seem to you?"

"Fine," Kathryn said. "We talked about the case. He told me he can't wait to get out of here."

"He didn't tell you anything . . . else?"

Kathryn frowned. "Like what?"

Nelson moved a shoulder, looked away. "He's got a lot of adjusting to do. The next stage will be hard for him."

"You mean when the bandages come off?"

"I mean after the bandages come off."

"Is . . . is he badly scarred?"

"He'll need plastic surgery, but it could have been a lot worse. Speaking comparatively, the facial scarring is slight. There was some damage to the muscles which will make him look a little . . . lopsided, maybe, and he won't smile exactly the way he used to, but there was nothing they couldn't handle. Except . . ." His voice trailed off.

Kathryn felt a chill of dread creeping over her body. "Except what, Doc?"

"Why don't you talk to the surgeon? Dr. Pelligrini. She'll explain it to you."

"The hell with Dr. Pelligrini. You explain it to me."

Morgan sighed. "It's his right hand. They did their best, but there was radical damage to the transverse carpal ligament, the flexors and abductors and—"

"Could you put it into English, Doc?" Steve intervened.

Morgan grinned apologetically. "Sorry, force of habit. Simply put, there was severe damage to the ropes and pulleys that work the hand. With treatment he may get some of the mobility back. But ..."

He shrugged, as much as to say, That's all.

"How much of the mobility?" Steve asked.

"The prognosis is he won't regain more than about thirty percent use of the hand."

"Thirty percent?" Kathryn said, horrified.

Morgan nodded. "Looks that way. From what Pelligrini tells me, he won't be able to make a fist. Write a report. Or more to the point ... fire a pistol."

"But that means ..." Steve didn't finish the sentence.

"I know what it means," Morgan said.

"Who's going to tell him?"

"He already knows, Katie. Dr. Pelligrini told him yesterday morning. That was why I asked you if he'd said anything."

"You mean he knew about all this ... before I talked to him?"

"He knew."

"Well, goddammit, Doc, what is it with all these strong silent men, anyway?" Kathryn said, her vision blurring as tears filled her eyes. "Why does everyone have to act so damned tough all the time?"

Morgan abruptly shook his head, a warning signal. They turned to see Dave Granz shuffle in through the door wearing a bathrobe with mandarin sleeves that accommodated his bandaged arms, and carpet slippers that looked about two sizes too big.

"Hey, Kathryn," he said, his voice a hoarse whisper. "One of the nurses told me ... you were here. Hi, Steve. What brings you ... to the funny farm?"

"Need I tell you?" Steve said, covering for Kathryn, who was still staring at the wall, blinking back her tears. "We were just talking about you."

"Price of . . . fame," Granz said. "Thought I'd . . . come get some of that . . . coffee you promised me, Doc."

"Grab a chair," Morgan said. "Same as usual?"

"Just as it comes," Dave said. "So, what were you . . . talking about?"

Morgan concentrated on the job of pouring the coffee. Steve watched him doing it as if it was the most fascinating thing he had ever seen. Dave caught the atmosphere and turned his head so he was looking directly at Kathryn.

"What?" he said.

"We were saying it was about time you got out of here," Kathryn said. Too bright, dammit, too bright.

"Can't be too soon . . . for me," Granz said, without moving his eyes from Kathryn. "I can't wait to get back . . . in harness."

She looked at Morgan as he put the coffee on the desk in front of Dave and stuck a glass straw in it.

"Grab a chair," Morgan said.

Dave sat down with the chair turned so he could see all three of them. Nobody spoke.

"For Chrissake, what?" Dave said, catching the silence. "What is it?"

"Doc just told us, Dave," Kathryn said. "About your hand."

His eyes were as expressionless as pennies in the slit between the bandages. "I see," he said. "And?"

"I . . . I don't know what to say."

"Then don't . . . say anything," Dave said.

"Dave, you don't have to be alone in this," Morgan said. "We want to help any way we can."

"How?" Dave said harshly. "You going to be a . . . hand donor, Doc?"

The room was very silent.

"That was pretty rough, Dave," Kathryn said.

"Yeah." The tone was apologetic but the eyes remained defiant. "It was. Sorry, Doc. I'm touchy. Not like me, I know, but . . . there you go."

"It's okay," Morgan said. "You don't want to talk about it, we don't talk about it. Let's get off the subject."

"Fine," Dave said. "I didn't come down here . . . looking for . . . sympathy."

"Dave," Kathryn said softly. "We're your friends. Don't shut us out."

She thought for a moment she saw the glint of tears in his eyes, but it might only have been a trick of the light.

"I've got to . . . come to terms with it, Kathryn," he said, speaking more softly. "Just . . . you guys just give me a . . . little time, okay? Till I can . . . handle it."

There was another silence, but this time it was not unpleasant. Dave leaned forward and took a slurp of his coffee.

"You want us to go?" Steve said. "Or do you want to talk?"

"Talk," Dave said. "Yeah. I suppose I'm still good for that."

"We need you to use your head, not your hand," Steve said, putting an edge on it. "What about that list Kathryn left with you yesterday? Did it trigger anything in there?"

Granz regarded him levelly for a moment. Something close to a smile touched the corners of his eyes. "All right, Giordano," he said softly. "All right. The answer to your question is, No. I stared at it until my eyes crossed. And I got nothing."

"We just came from the Sheriff's office," Steve told him. "They've whittled it down to two suspects. A guy named Jimenez, and another named Russell."

Granz leaned forward, his bandaged arms on his knees, his eyes fixed on Steve's. "Go ahead."

"Eduardo Leandro Jimenez," Steve said. "Known to his friends as Lee. Lives on Clarendon Avenue in Alameda. You know that area, it's low to middle income, most of the people are manual or unskilled workers. Jimenez is twenty-nine, five-eight, a hundred and fifty pounds, black hair, brown eyes. He lives with his mother and two younger sisters. He's down as one of the people you talked to."

Squeezing his eyes shut, Granz drew in his breath, let it out in an angry rush. "Nothing's happening," he said. "I'm still fucking brain dead. Excuse me, Kathryn."

"This guy's from New Mexico," Steve continued. "He moved out here five years ago, works as a fruit packer in Catalina. He's got a rap sheet: tried to knife a girlfriend in Albuquerque in 1985."

"And you like him for our guy?"

"He's a definite maybe," Steve said.

"What about the other guy, Russell?"

"James Leland Russell, lives on Pacheco Drive in Outlook Heights. He teaches English at Cabrillo Park High School."

"Where they found . . . Barbara Gates," Granz said softly.

"Russell is forty-three, married, with no children. He's five-seven, weighs around a hundred and forty, dark brown hair, brown eyes. Been in Santa Rita about three years, came down here from Redwood City."

"Why do you like him?"

"Well, for one thing, opportunity: he goes fishing two or three days at a time, sometimes midweek. And for another, although he's known to everyone else as James, his wife calls him Lee."

"That it?"

"There's more. Turns out Russell also had a Hispanic stepmother and stepsister," Kathryn said.

Granz wasn't looking at her. Following his gaze, she saw he was staring at something lying on Morgan's desk, a flat blue and silver foil vacuum pack maybe three and a half inches long and an inch wide. On it was the brand name: *Miltex by Kai* in blue letters on silver, *Carbon Steel Sterile Surgical Blade* in silver on blue.

"What is that thing, Doc?" Dave asked, his voice suddenly tight with tension.

Morgan frowned. "It's just a scalpel blade pack," he said, puzzled by Granz's intensity.

"Hold it up so I can see it."

Morgan held the slim pack up. Granz stared at it for what seemed like long minutes, his eyes glittering. Then he let out his breath with a long, soft sigh of almost sexual satisfaction.

"Sonofabitch," he muttered. "Sonofa-goddamn-bitch."

"What is it, Dave?" Kathryn said. For some reason she couldn't understand, she was as tense as he had been when he first saw the silver and blue pack.

"Let me ask you another question, Doc," Granz said, ignoring her question. "The guy who did all this to me"—he made a clumsy gesture with his bandaged hands—"were you ever able to figure out what kind of knife he used?"

"It's impossible to say, Dave," Morgan said. "It could have been any one of a dozen different weapons."

"And the women. The mutilations. You had the same problem there, right?"

"You know that. All I could say for sure was that the wounds were inflicted with a very sharp blade, probably pointed, not very big."

"Like that thing?" Granz said. "Open it up, Doc. Let me take a look at it."

Morgan opened the pack and took out the blade; it shone with inanimate menace.

"Well, Doc? What do you say? The wounds on the Shelter Island victim, the one in Sedgewick Park, Barbara Gates." Granz's voice was harsh, angry. He made the clumsy gesture with his hands again. "And this? Could it have been done with a scalpel?"

Morgan frowned, pinned to his seat by the intensity of Granz's voice. "I told you, I couldn't say with any certainty what kind of blade the injuries were caused by. But yes, they would certainly be consistent with a scalpel."

"Why, Dave?" Kathryn asked urgently. "Why is it important?"

"Chicago," Dave said, turning to Steve, his eyes alight with fierce excitement. "Chicago, right?"

"You mean Russell? Yes, he was born in—"

"No, the stepmother. And her daughter. They died in an apartment-house fire in Chicago."

"You remember?" Kathryn said breathlessly. "You remember him?"

"I interviewed him. His wife called him Lee. He collects trout flies. Am I right?"

"That's right."

"Goddammit, goddammit, it's him, I tell you, it's him!" Dave said, getting up off the chair and pacing about in excitement. "He had a book on tanning leather, claimed it wasn't his. I remember sitting talking to him, and thinking, sonofabitch, he fits. He fits. He goes off alone on fishing trips. He collects trout flies. And now this."

"Now what?" Steve frowned.

"Lee Russell," Granz said. "The sonofabitch had a scalpel blade pack just like that one there. On his desk."

When they got back to the County Building, Kathryn went straight up to Walt Earheart's office on the third floor. The big man was in his shirtsleeves, hunched over a file on his desk. He looked up as she came in, and a smile replaced the frown.

"I've been waiting for you," he said.

"You talked to Dave Granz?"

Earheart waved a hand at the file he had been studying. "I had a detective interview him," he told her.

"What do you think?"

"I think it makes Russell our killer," Earheart said. "And I think I want to go out and bust the sonofabitch."

"Not so fast, Chief," Kathryn said. "It's still only circumstantial. We need more than that for an arrest warrant."

"You didn't come in here to ruin my day," the big man said. "What do you have in mind?"

"I'm convinced now it was Russell's wife who made that anonymous call. Which means she believes—or maybe even knows—her husband killed those girls."

"Even if she does, the law says she can't testify against her husband."

"She can if she waives her privilege."

"We'd still have the problem of marital communication."

"Let's worry about that when the time comes. What we need to know now is, what does she actually know? What was it convinced her he's the killer?"

"And how do we find that out?"

"I called Cabrillo Park High School. Russell is at work; he'll be there all day. I want you to interview the wife. Don't give her any warning, just turn up on her doorstep and tell her we know she made that phone call."

"What, just like that? Aren't you afraid it might freak her?"

"I don't much care if it does," Kathryn said bluntly. "Finer feelings don't count here. I want this bastard off the streets, and if giving Carol Russell a hard time is a way of doing it, I'm not about to lose any sleep over that."

"How would you feel about going up there with me?"

Kathryn shook her head. "I'm a prosecutor, Walt, not an investigator. I leave asking the questions to you guys."

"I know, and generally speaking I'd agree. But this one is different, Kathryn. If Carol Russell really believes her husband's the killer, she's got to be in a highly emotional state. She sees two gorillas on her doorstep, who knows which way she'll jump? Whereas if you're there . . . I've seen you in court, trying rape cases. You're real good with victims. And the way I see it, this woman could be as much a victim as any you've ever talked to."

She couldn't argue with that. She went down to his car with him and they drove up to Outlook Heights. Earheart pulled to a stop half a block down from the Russells' modest house.

"Ready?" Kathryn said. "You know what to do?"

"I hit her right between the eyes, tell her we know she made the call and that we want her to come in for an interview."

"And if she denies it?"

"Then you step in, explain to her, sort of hypothetically if you like, that although we know he's the guy we want, we can't lay a finger on him unless whoever it was made that phone call helps us."

Kathryn nodded. "Okay, let's give it a try."

Carol Russell was a faded blonde who looked every one of her forty-eight years. Her skin was sallow and she wore no makeup. She combed her straggly hair away from her face with her fingers, her eyes shifting from Kathryn to Walt Earheart, standing behind her on the front porch, then back to Kathryn again.

"What is it?" she said, nervously bunching the front of her dress in her hands. "What do you want?"

"Mrs. Russell? Mrs. Carol Russell? I'm Lieutenant Walter Earheart, ma'am, chief of detectives, Santa Rita Sheriff's Department. This lady is Assistant District Attorney Kathryn Mackay."

"My husband is not here. He—"

"Actually, it's you we want to talk to, if you can spare a few minutes."

"Me? Oh, no, I . . . I was just . . . going out." Carol Russell's movements were almost spastic. She swallowed noisily. "Yes. That's it. If you could come back . . . some other time. I . . ."

"This won't take long, Mrs. Russell," Earheart said, moving forward purposefully. "Wouldn't it be better if we talked inside? Where your neighbors can't see?"

Her washed-out blue eyes flickered nervously as she looked up and down the street. She unlatched the screen door and pushed it open. A long hall that smelled of Pledge ran from the front door to the rear of the house. The carpet was thin and worn. Carol Russell opened a door to her right and sunlight streamed in, millions of dust motes dancing in the beams.

"We can ... in here," she said, with a vague gesture.

The living room was square, with a patio door that looked out onto a small neat backyard with variegated shrubs and a lawn. The windows had white interior shutters that needed painting. Somewhere the metronomic tock of a quartz clock counted the seconds.

"Nice place you have here, Mrs. Russell," Earheart said. "Your husband's at work, I take it?"

They saw her gather herself together. "Yes, he's at school. Sit down, please. I'll make some ... would you like tea?"

"Nothing, thank you," Earheart said pleasantly. "I'm sure you know why we're here?"

Carol Russell's pathetic attempt at self-possession evaporated in an instant. She stared at him as if she was hypnotized. Her lips moved, stopped.

"It's in connection with the call you made to the district attorney's office on Monday, Mrs. Russell," Earheart said, hitting her with it like a fist. She paled and went across to a chair, almost collapsing into it.

"I . . . don't know what . . . what you mean," she whispered, avoiding their eyes.

"Last Monday, at about eleven-twenty, you called the district attorney's office. You spoke to this lady here, Kathryn Mackay."

Carol Russell shook her head. "No," she said. "No."

"Are you saying you didn't make that call, Mrs. Russell?"

Again the woman shook her head, still not meeting their gaze. Earheart looked at Kathryn and shrugged.

"Well, someone called me, Mrs. Russell," Kathryn said. "Someone who accused your husband of brutally murdering and mutilating three young Hispanic women in Santa Rita. Can you think of any reason anyone would do a thing like that?"

"No," Carol Russell whispered. "It's a mistake."

"Does your husband have any enemies, Mrs. Russell?"

"No ... no, none that I know of."

"You don't know anyone who would want to harm him or get him into trouble?"

She put her hand to her forehead; a gesture almost of despair, Kathryn thought. "I don't ... think so."

"Then why do you suppose that person called me, Mrs. Russell?" Kathryn said softly. "Do you have any idea?"

"I . . . she might have thought . . . she might want someone . . . to stop him. If it's true."

"Do you think it could be true, Mrs. Russell?" Earheart asked softly.

"I don't know," she said piteously. There was a pleading tone in her voice, a trace of tears in the lackluster eyes. What agonies was this woman going through? Kathryn wondered. What agonies had she already gone through? There was something haunted about her, as though she knew unbearable things.

"Let's suppose you're right," Kathryn said, cuing Earheart. "And the reason she called was, she wants us to stop him."

"You see, Mrs. Russell, it's not quite that simple," the big man said. "The only way we can stop this man is to arrest him and bring him to trial. That would mean you . . . that would mean whoever made the call would have to testify against him."

"Suppose . . . she can't?" Carol Russell said, her voice almost inaudible. "This woman. Whoever she is. Suppose she just can't?"

"You mean she might be afraid? She doesn't have to be. We'd protect her, Mrs. Russell."

"It might not . . . she might have some other reason."

Earheart looked at Kathryn and raised his eyebrows. Over to you.

"What other reason could there be?"

"Maybe she . . . maybe she knows . . . things."

"What kind of things?"

"Things . . . she can't tell." The pale blue eyes were wide and empty, as if she was staring at pictures beyond comprehension.

"Is that what it is?"

The woman moved her head, not quite a negative.

"Do you love him, Carol?" Kathryn said quietly.

Carol Russell put her head into her hands and wept without shame. "Oh, I can't," she said, through her sobs. "I can't, I can't."

Kathryn watched her weep, wrenched with pity. So many victimized women believed they loved their abuser, locked into a cycle of unending hurt by the fear that aloneness was worse. But you couldn't tell them. You couldn't ever say it. They saw it as betrayal, not deliverance.

"You know he's going to kill again, don't you?" Kathryn said.

Carol Russell's head came up. She stared at Kathryn wide-eyed, her mouth an *O* of shock. Shivering visibly, she wrapped her arms around herself, got up off the chair, and walked across to the patio door to stare out at the featureless little backyard.

"You know, don't you?" Kathryn insisted.

Carol Russell turned to face them, lifting her tear-streaked face and combing away her wet hair with her fingers. Her eyes had the look of someone who has witnessed a terrible accident and doesn't know what to do. She took a crumpled tissue from the sleeve of her dress and wiped her eyes and nose.

"Yes," she whispered again.

"He has to be stopped, Mrs. Russell," Earheart said urgently. "Please, help us. Tell us what you know."

Kathryn lifted her hand slightly, a signal to the big man: let me.

"Why did you make the call, Carol?" she asked.

"It was when he said that detective, the one who was nearly killed—"

"Granz?"

"He said Granz hadn't been here. And he had. He had. And then I knew. I knew it must be him. Why else would he have lied?"

"You know someone attacked the inspector? Someone who fractured his skull and cut him to pieces with a knife?"

"It was in the paper. I . . . he . . . I think it was him."

Kathryn's eyes met Earheart's.

"You mean your husband?" he asked. "You think your husband tried to kill Granz?"

"That night, the night it happened, he came in late. He had scratches on his face. He said he'd walked into a tree in the dark, but I knew it was . . . something else. Something worse. The next day I read about the detective being . . . being cut . . ."

She turned away, her balled fists pressed against her face.

"Would you tell the judge what you just told us, Mrs.

Russell?" Earheart said. She shook her head, not turning around.

"I couldn't ... say it. Not with him ... looking at me," she said, her voice trembling. "Don't you understand? All the things ... I couldn't."

"Suppose we found another way?" Kathryn said. "So that you could tell us without anyone else being there, just you and me and the judge and jury? Would you do it then?"

Carol Russell shook her head slowly from side to side, not looking at them.

"What about the girls?" Earheart asked. "Do you think he killed them, too?"

"You don't understand," she said, her voice a monotone. "It would ... everything would be over. Everything."

"There's more, isn't there?" Kathryn said quietly. "Much more than you've told us."

Carol Russell did not reply.

"Where does he go, Carol?"

Again, silence. Earheart looked at Kathryn and stood up. She followed suit; there was nothing to be gained by trying to bully the woman into cooperating. She crossed the room and put her hand on Carol Russell's thin shoulder. The woman flinched as she felt the contact.

"I wish there was some way I could help you," Kathryn said. "I think I know how desperately afraid and alone you must feel."

"Nobody can," Carol Russell whispered. "Nobody."

"Remember—don't be afraid," Kathryn said. "I'll leave you my home number. If you need someone to talk to, if there's any way I can help you, anytime—call me."

Carol Russell remained where she was, staring out of the window, not turning around as they left. Earheart led the way out into the sunny street. They got into the car and drove down the hill. The big detective didn't speak until they were passing Outlook Heights Junior High on Alameda.

"Well, that does it for me," he said. "Russell's our man. And if I was a gambler, I'd stake my pension his wife knows enough to put him in the gas chamber."

"No bet," Kathryn said. "But unless we can get her to testify, we don't have squat."

"Goddammit, you think I don't know that?" Earheart said angrily.

34

AT THE THURSDAY MEETING WHEN KATHRYN AND WALT EAR-
heart reported their conversation with Carol Russell, Benton's reaction was first disbelief, then frustrated anger.

"God damn it, there must be some way we can persuade
her to testify," he said, his tone aggrieved. "Tell her we'll
arrange for DOJ to put her into a witness protection
program."

"Hal, she's scared of him even finding out we talked to
her," Kathryn said. "We can't force her to waive her
privilege."

"Even if we did, it doesn't mean she'd talk. I'm telling
you, this is one freaked-out lady. You guys saw the police
interviews with her neighbors. Like a ghost in her own
house, low self-esteem, suffers from migraine headaches,
jumps out of her skin if Russell so much as looks sideways
at her. If I'm any judge of character, she knows a hell of a
lot more than she's telling. Maybe a lot more than she ever
will tell."

"There must be some way," Benton said. "We need her,
Walt. We've got to get this bastard off the streets before he
finds himself another victim."

"Fine, Hal, we all feel the same way," Earheart said, letting his own impatience show a little. "Just tell us how we
do it."

"What about putting Russell under round-the-clock surveillance?" George Tannenbaum said. "Watch every move
he makes. Bug his phones at home and work, put a homing
device on his car, fiber-optic cameras in his house and office,
really get on his case?"

"Always supposing we could get the court orders without
probable cause, always supposing we could spare the manpower, where would it get us?" Podnoretz said. "How long
before he kills again? A week, two weeks, a month? How
long could we tie up all our resources in that kind of
operation?"

"Norm's right, Hal," Earheart said ruefully. "You know how many men it takes to keep someone under surveillance twenty-four hours a day?"

"I bet you're going to tell me."

"If he's on foot, a minimum of two men every four hours. If he's driving, a minimum of two cars every trip, also in shifts. Two-man teams on the phones, same deal. You're talking eight to ten men, six times a day, seven days a week. And if the bastard spots the surveillance, twice that many."

"All right, all right, it was just an idea. We can't just sit here and do nothing, for Chrissake."

"We need probable cause, Hal," Kathryn said. "We need something to tie him in with the attack on Dave, or with one of the murder victims. If the wife would cooperate, we might be able to get it. Without her . . ."

She shrugged; the sentence didn't need finishing.

"Anything else?"

"Doc Nelson sent over the results of the electrophoretic tests on the blood samples from Dave Granz's clothes and fingernail scrapings. They contain different PGM characteristics, which means one of them is probably Russell's—his wife said he came home with scratches on his face the night Granz was attacked."

"But they're no damned use to us at all without a sample of his blood for comparison," Podnoretz said. "What if I get one of the boys to mug the bastard and take a swab from him?"

"Let's be serious, here, people," Benton said, amid laughter. "What else have we got, Walt?"

"Steve Giordano is moving mountains for us in Sacramento," Earheart reported. Since Dave Granz had clinched the ID, the pace and character of the investigation had changed. Now every facet of James Leland Russell's life was being reexamined, backtracked, sifted. "He's got half the CIRT team checking our boy."

Steve had left on Tuesday night, planning to come back Saturday and spend the weekend. It had been a strange parting, temporary, yet feeling oddly permanent, happening, but strangely unreal.

"I think you know what I want, Kathryn," he told her before he left. "Now you have to decide if you want the same things."

"You want me to come to Sacramento."

"I talked to Barclay Hanwell in the DA's office. He said they'd jump at the chance to have you up there."

"Why couldn't you move here?"

"What I do, I do there. If I moved here, I'd have to take a step down the career ladder."

So would I, she thought, but didn't say it. "Would that be so bad? We wouldn't have any money problems."

"I told you right at the start I'm old-fashioned, Kathryn," he said. "I have old-fashioned ideas about being the bread-winner, too."

"I should have known better than get mixed up with an Italian," she said, lightening it up. But the problem remained, like a cloud on the horizon gradually coming nearer. As if that were not enough, come Sunday Jack was supposed to come up for his regular visit with Emma. This was one weekend Kathryn was resolutely not thinking about until it arrived.

"When did you talk to Giordano?" she heard Podnoretz ask.

"Just before we came in here. He said the Department of Justice team got on to the cops in Chicago, they're doing some digging to see if they can come up with something on Russell there. They'll fax through anything they locate. Same applies to Redwood City. We asked a few questions up at Cabrillo Park High, found out Russell taught at an all-girls' school before he came down here. Also that he served in Nam. The DOJ team will get his service record from St. Louis. We're going to have our hands full just processing all this information."

"Information, information," Benton said impatiently. "I want evidence, dammit, something I can take to a judge and get a warrant."

"It'll come, Hal," Podnoretz said.

"Yeah, yeah, okay," Benton said. "Move along, Walt."

"We're also checking out all missing persons reports," Earheart told them. "We've currently got seven. Three of them are Hispanic. Maria Hirano, twenty-four, lives in Catalina, missing since Saturday. Rafaelita Medina, fifteen, dropped out of sight ten days ago, we're working on that with the Espanola PD. The third one is Terry, that's short for Teresa, Resquerdo, nineteen, from Harbor Park, reported missing Sunday night. Any one of them might be a victim."

"Let's just pray none of them is," Benton said. "Okay, let's break this up. But stay on it, all of you. By the way, how's Dave Granz? Anyone been up there to see him?"

"I looked in this morning," Kathryn said. "Doc Nelson tells me they're going to take off the bandages tomorrow."

"Will he be able to . . . you know, come back to work?" Podnoretz asked.

"You heard about his hand, Norm," Earheart said. "What do you think?"

"I think, one hand or two, he's still one of the best men I've got," Podnoretz said angrily. "And I'm ready to fight for him if I have to."

"Hell, sure, we all are," Benton said.

The four men gathered up their papers, still talking about Granz as they went out into the hallway. Kathryn looked up as Marcia came in past them carrying a brown six-by-nine envelope sealed with a metal clasp.

"This just came by hand," she said. "It's marked urgent."

Kathryn took the envelope. The words FOR THE URGENT PERSONAL ATTENTION OF KATHRYN MACKAY were written in ballpoint capitals on the front. She slit the envelope with her letter opener. Inside was a single piece of paper; she could see printed capitals. Her entire body went cold.

"Marcia!" she snapped, "get everyone back in here! Fast!"

The rasp in Kathryn's voice made Marcia flinch. Eyes wide, she ran out into the hallway calling Benton's name as Kathryn, holding it with a pair of eyebrow tweezers she had taken from her purse, moved the envelope to one side, extracted the note, and laid it flat on the desk so she could read it.

"What the hell happened?" Benton said as he came back into her office with the others close behind him. "They declare World War Three or something?"

"I just got this," she said. "Look."

Earheart stifled a curse and snatched up the phone, punching the numbers as if he hated them.

"Who's this?" he snapped. "Garfunkel? Earheart. I'm with Kathryn Mackay, DA's office. Get John Kazanowski up here on the double. I don't care what he's doing, I want him up here now. Got it? *Now!*" He banged down the phone and looked up. "Kazanowski's our puzzle freak. He'll break this in ten minutes."

"Okay, make a copy of the message," Podnoretz said. "Bag the original, Kathryn, and I'll get it to Sacramento."

"You'll be wasting your time," Earheart rumbled. "Look at it. It's the same as all the others. Cheap legal pad paper, printed in ballpoint, block letters. Why would he make it easy for us?"

"Okay, I've made a copy," Kathryn said. "It's yours, Norm."

Podnoretz picked up the paper with Kathryn's tweezers and dropped it into a transparent plastic evidence bag; then he did the same with the envelope. He strode out of the office to arrange for its immediate transmission to DOJ in Sacramento. The others stared at the printed message Kathryn had copied in large felt-pen letters on her legal pad.

F TXOKBA VLR
ILLH LRQPFAB
YXV 32
L = O

"It looks pretty simple," Benton said. "*L* equals *O*. That would make the fourth word something like *book*, or *look*, or *cook*."

"Or *hood*, or *good*, or *mood*, or *food*, or *wood*," Jack Burrows offered. "Forget it, Hal, we could be here for a week. Where the hell is Kazanowski?"

As if in reply to his question, a young deputy appeared at the door, wearing the khaki uniform of the Santa Rita County Sheriff's Department. He was young, tall, strongly built, with close-cropped black hair and dark eyes.

"Sir?" he said.

"Get over here, Kazanowski," Earheart growled. "We've got a puzzle for you to solve."

"Sir?" Kazanowski said again, frowning.

Earheart went to the door, took the young deputy by the elbow, and led him to the chair Kathryn had just vacated.

"Just sit down and do it, John," the chief of detectives said. Kazanowski's eyes widened. He sat down and stared at the cryptogram.

"Is this what I think it is, Lieutenant?"

"Never mind that, can you decipher it?" Benton asked.

Kazanowski shrugged. "Let's try the easy way first," he said. He picked up a pencil and wrote out the alphabet. Beneath the letter *O* he wrote the letter *L,* and continued the alphabet to the letter *Z,* ending with *W.* Beneath the letter *A* he wrote *X,* and continued until he reached *K.* When he was finished he had:

ABCD EFGH IJKL MNOP
QRST UVWX YZ
xyza bcde fghi jklm nopq rstu vw

"Okay," he said. "Let's see what we've got here." He frowned as he printed out the letters. "I . . . warned . . . you. Look . . . outside. Bay . . . 32."

"Jesus H. Christ!" Earheart said. "Kazanowski, with me, fast!"

The big detective almost knocked Hal Benton over as he ran for the door, with Kazanowski close behind him. Norm Podnoretz appeared in the doorway, stepping aside open-mouthed as the two men charged past him.

"Now what?" he asked.

"My office!" Benton snapped, and pushed past Podnoretz into the corridor. Kathryn ran through the office after him, Podnoretz close behind, ignoring the astonished faces of the secretaries. In Benton's office they crowded together by the window overlooking the parking lot. Down below, they could see Earheart and Deputy Kazanowski running between the parked cars.

Bay 32 was halfway along the double row of visitor spaces on the central tier of the lot. As they watched, Earheart bent down to peer inside a green Chevy Nova, its windshield and rear windows blanked by cardboard sun shields; the one in front had the word HELP printed in giant capitals on it. They saw the big detective recoil, then snap an order at Kazanowski. The young deputy ran flat out for the main entrance, holding his pistol against his hip. Down below, Earheart looked up and saw them at the window. He lifted his chin and drew a forefinger across his throat.

35

THE VICTIM WAS RAFAELITA MEDINA OF ESPANOLA. DARK, pretty, and Hispanic. And fifteen years old. She lay naked in the back of the Nova, curled up on the rear seat as if she was asleep. The first crime scene investigator who opened up the car took one look and came out fast, gagging; he staggered behind a nearby car vomiting helplessly. The girl had been savagely beaten; her face was half destroyed. The lower half of her body was a mass of wounded flesh, and the semicircular contusions of bite marks stood out in livid contrast on the waxy skin of her belly and inner thighs.

From the moment the news of her death broke, the County Building was under media siege. No one from the DA's office or the SO could leave the building without having to fight his or her way through a clamoring pack of reporters.

Inside the building, even clerical staff in the county admin offices and the Environmental Health Department were caught up in the tension as Kathryn sent teams of investigators out to talk to anyone and everyone who had ever known or might have talked to the dead girl: family, friends, schoolteachers, doctors, dentists, storekeepers in Little Mexico. A pedestrian and vehicle survey was set up in Espanola and passersby were shown photographs and asked if they might have seen Rafaelita either alone or in company with a dark-haired man of maybe thirty-five, possibly wearing a tan windbreaker and dark slacks. At the County Morgue, Morgan Nelson concluded the sad, grim ritual of establishing the cause of death.

"No question about it being our man?" Giordano asked him. He had driven down from Sacramento as soon as he heard the news of Rafaelita Medina's death.

"You saw the body."

They were in Morgan Nelson's cluttered office. Steve was sitting on a shell chair, his legs crossed at the knees and a manila folder on his lap. He was in shirtsleeves, his hands jammed into his pants pockets. There were dark smudges beneath his eyes. He had spent most of the morning going through the crime scene video and photographs, taking notes, and talking to Earheart and Burrows.

"The immediate cause of death was manual strangulation," Morgan said. He shook his head reflectively. "He may not have even intended to kill her. There's no indication of a violent, sustained throttling. He may have been just trying to stop her screaming when he ... It seems almost irrelevant. In view of the rest of it."

The physical trauma inflicted on the defenseless, childlike body of the girl was more extensive than anything they had seen before, he added. "What beats me is, why would he take one of her eyes?"

Steve Giordano's face remained thoughtful, almost impassive.

"The escalation is significant," he said. "Almost as if this time he's saying, See what I will do."

"You said that," Kathryn recalled. "You knew, didn't you?"

"You can't *know* with people like this, Kathryn. They don't know themselves. But ... I could hear the rage in his voice. And I knew that in a way it was directed at law enforcement. Us."

"You think some of this was done ... for you?" Morgan said. He could not keep the disbelief from his voice.

"No. I don't think that. What he's doing ... it's more complicated than that. The victim's pain, her distress ... he wants her to feel that, to know he knows she is feeling it. That's an integral part of his fantasy. But if he thinks it distresses us, as well, that's like ... a bonus. A new dimension."

"And does it? Kathryn?"

"It makes me angry," she said. "We could have prevented this. We know who is doing it, at least we think we know."

"He'd already abducted the girl, Kathryn," Steve pointed out. "Ten days ago. Long before we put it together."

"Okay, okay. But he's still out there."

"Not for much longer," Steve said.

They got back to the County Building in time for Benton's daily update meeting, held during the lunch hour so they could talk without being interrupted. Everybody grabbed something to eat and drink and congregated in the conference room, where Kathryn opened the proceedings by laying out the crime scene photographs in numerical sequence, then reading Morgan's preliminary findings and his enumeration of the injuries inflicted on the body. No one spoke when she was finished. No one asked any questions.

"Run what you've got by us, Jack," Benton said. "Just hit the high spots."

"The family lives in a two-bedroom apartment on Dulcinea Street, Harbor Park," he said. "Rafaelita left the building around four-thirty in the afternoon. This is a week ago last Sunday, first of the month. She said she was going down to the beach to meet the crowd, kids she hung out with. That was it. When she didn't come home, the parents called it in. Sheriff's Department sent a unit down there to check, you know how it is, they have to be sure the kid's not a runaway before they give it full MP status."

"I thought we told them to suspend that?" Podnoretz said.

Burrows shrugged. "Somebody fouled up, who knows what happened? Maybe they had a rookie on the desk, maybe someone forgot. Any way you look at it, it wouldn't have made much difference. The kid just disappeared somewhere between there and the beach at Espanola."

"Anyone talk to her friends?"

"I put Curran and Schiller on that. They talked to as many of them as they could find. All of 'em said pretty much the same, they're just, you know, kids. Mostly Hispanic. They go to the beach every weekend. Same spot every time, same barbecue pit, everything."

"They didn't think it strange when she never arrived?"

"It's not, it wasn't, you know, formal. You turn up, you turn up. You got a date, something else to do, you don't."

"What about the pedestrian and vehicle survey at Espanola?"

Earheart spread his hands. "We had a team out asking questions. They didn't get anything useful. We'll do another at the weekend, but I'm not hopeful. You know what it's like down there on a Sunday, Kathryn. Wall-to-wall people. She'd be just another kid in a tank top and shorts."

"What about the family?" Podnoretz asked.

"Father's a car mechanic, works in a repair shop on Espanola Road," Burrows reported, reading from a notebook.

"Mother works in a grocery store. There's three other children, all younger."

"She had no boyfriends?"

"The father was pretty strict. She could go out with a crowd, you know, mixed boys and girls. But she wasn't allowed on dates yet."

"How are they coping?" Kathryn asked.

"How do you think they're coping, with reporters and TV crews camping on their doorstep round the clock? They had to shut off the phone, couldn't deal with the calls they were getting. Every newspaper and TV station in California has picked up on it. Not to mention every religious freak, psychic healer, and certifiable nut between here and Oregon."

"Tell me about it," Kathryn said feelingly. "My phone's been ringing off the hook ever since Walt found her out there."

"What about the car?" Benton asked, taking a chunk out of his smoked ham and Swiss on rye.

"Stolen from the parking lot in the Linda Vista Mall about three hours before we found it," Earheart told him. "Belonged to a guy named Duffy. He was on his way home from night shift work, stopped off to buy some breakfast at seven-thirty A.M. When he came out the car was gone."

"Did the Crime Scene team get anything from it?"

"They got enough fingerprints to start a new file cabinet," Burrows said, disgustedly. "Duffy has two sons, both of whom borrow the car regularly. The wife also drives it. Add to that all their friends and relatives . . ."

He shook his head and took a swig of coffee from the cup he was carrying. Kathryn wondered how much of the stuff he actually drank; she couldn't recall ever seeing Jack without a cup in his hand.

"So, where does that leave us?" Benton asked. "He picked her up someplace between Little Mexico and Espanola last Sunday—are we checking all along that route? Jack? Yes? Okay, he picked her up, took her somewhere, killed her. Then yesterday he stole a car, put her in it, drove it down to our parking lot, and walked away. And nobody saw a goddamned thing. Is that about it?"

"That or something like it," Burrows said. "I've got a couple of deputies checking Russell's movements the last ten days. Should hear from them before long."

"If we're so sure we know who the guy is, why the hell don't we just haul him in for questioning?" Harry DiStefano said.

"You think that isn't bugging the hell out of everyone in the department?" Earheart said. "We all want this bastard, Harry, not just you. But we can't lay a glove on him. We don't have any physical evidence linking him directly to any of the victims, we don't have a damned thing more concrete than Giordano's profile and some circumstantial evidence."

"What about the wife? What about the phone call? Isn't that enough?"

"It's enough to bring him in for questioning, all right," Jack said. "But we couldn't hold him. Any kid straight out of law school could have him back on the streets before we could read him his rights. And anyway, Steve's advice is hold off, don't move yet."

"Steve?"

Steve, who had been sitting way in back of the room listening carefully to everything that was said, put down his sandwich and stood up. The men in front half-turned in their chairs to hear what he had to say. He'd fitted in well, Kathryn thought, never perceived as an interloper, always carefully deferential in offering his opinions.

"Everything we know about Russell tells me not to stampede him," Steve said. "The danger is, if we tip our hand too soon, he'll destroy whatever physical evidence might exist. He might even stop killing, wait us out. Or worse still, he might take a hike. If he moved away ..."

He didn't need to say the rest. The possibility that the killer might drop out of sight, change his name, start over in some completely unsuspecting environment where his presence might not be detected until he killed again, was a nightmare nobody wanted to have.

The session went on for over an hour, some of the detectives taking notes, one or two asking Giordano questions. They took a coffee break and then came back to it, going over each of the killings again in detail, with Giordano walking them through the changes in what the murderer was doing to his victims, and why he might be doing it.

"Okay," Benton said, looking at the wall clock. "That would seem to about cover it for today. Anyone got anything else?"

"Let me ask you this, Steve," Burrows said. "Suppose we go see Carol Russell again, hit her with the details of how this kid was killed?"

Benton said, "You think that might persuade her to testify against him?"

"I don't know. Maybe, if we leaned on her hard enough."

Earheart shook his head. "We can't, Jack. We don't dare. If we so much as go near her, those damned reporters waiting outside will follow us to her door and splash her all over the news."

"So what do we do?" Burrows wanted to know. "Sit on our butts and wait for something to happen?"

"Unless you've got a better idea," Benton told him.

"Shit," Burrows said.

It was pleasantly warm in the bedroom, and Kathryn sighed as Steve ran his hand down the center of her naked back, drawing her closer to him. She felt the familiar sensation of slow surrender, the aroused readiness of her own body.

The telephone rang.

"No," she said, pulling Steve closer. "Let it ring."

The tape came on. "Hi, this is Kathryn. I can't take your call right now, but if you have a message for me or Emma, please leave it after the tone and we'll get back to you as soon as possible."

"Hello? This is Carol Russell. I wanted . . . I thought you might be home. I need . . . I'll try to call again."

Kathryn was off the bed in a flash of naked limbs, picking up the telephone in one hand, slipping into her robe with the other. Steve rolled onto his back and stared at the ceiling.

"Mrs. Russell, I'm here, go ahead," Kathryn said breathlessly. Don't hang up, don't hang up, she pleaded silently.

"It's about . . . you know," her caller said. Her voice was breathy, apprehensive. "You said . . . if I needed to talk to someone."

"Yes. Do you want me to come over?"

"No!" The response was panicked, fearful. "Don't come near the house whatever you do! He'd—"

"It's all right, Mrs. Russell, calm down," Kathryn said, her mind working fast.

"I'm sorry," the woman said. "It's my fault, isn't it?"

"What's your fault?"

"That poor little girl. It's my fault he killed her."

"Do you know for a fact he did?"

"Can you meet me somewhere? He's out. He said he wouldn't be back till late. Can you?"

Kathryn looked at the digital clock beside her bed. Ten forty-five.

"Where?"

A slight pause. "You know the restaurant in Cabrillo Park?"

"Won't it be closed?"

"I'll be outside. Don't bring ... anyone."

"Give me fifteen minutes," Kathryn said and put down the telephone. She started to dress. Steve was already putting on his clothes.

"I'm sorry," she said, touching his face. "I wanted us to have this time together."

"So did I," he said, not meeting her eyes.

"We haven't made any decisions."

"Maybe not," he said, his tone ambiguous. "You're going to meet her?"

"I have to, Steve."

"Then I'm coming with you."

Kathryn shook her head. "She said come alone. If I bring someone along, it might scare her off."

"You're not afraid she might be setting you up for him?"

A small chill touched her innermost being, like a feather; the thought had never even occurred to her.

"No," she said, hoping she sounded more convincing than she felt. She put on her jacket and picked up her purse. As an afterthought she went across to the chest of drawers against the wall. In the top drawer, beneath her sweatshirts, was the SIG-Sauer P226 9mm Parabellum automatic Dave Granz had bought for her a couple of years ago, when a serial rapist had threatened to kill her and her daughter if he was convicted.

She kept the pistol wrapped in a soft polishing cloth; a neat, deadly little weapon, seven inches long, weighing less than two pounds loaded, it smelled of oil and the promise of death. She slid in the fifteen-shot magazine and hit it home with the palm of her hand.

"Can you use that thing?" Steve asked her as she put the gun into her purse.

"Yes," Kathryn said.

She was aware that he was watching her. The overhead light accentuated the age lines around his eyes and mouth; he looked older, sad. She went to the door, sensed something, paused.

"What?" she said.

"Something wrong here," he said. "The beautiful lady goes out alone into the night. The big tough special agent stays home to babysit."

She blew him a kiss and headed for the elevator. Along Beach Avenue the ocean mist was rolling in like special effects from a Stephen King movie. Her headlights cut sharply etched tunnels through the swirling vapor. Although it was Saturday, there was hardly any traffic on the suburban streets; the whole drive up to Cabrillo Park had a dreamlike quality about it. She came to a stop in the parking lot of the restaurant and killed the engine. When she switched off her lights, it was almost pitch dark. The sound of the slamming car door was like a shot.

The beam of Kathryn's flashlight bounced off the windows of the circular restaurant building. She walked toward it, her hand on the automatic in her purse. The blue and white umbrellas were folded down, the white chairs stacked upside down on the tables. The crunch of her feet on the gravel sounded loud and invasive.

"I'm here." Kathryn jumped involuntarily at the sound of the woman's voice. She ranged the flashlight beam right and left, saw Carol Russell sitting at a table beneath a tree. She went toward her.

"Mrs. Russell?"

"Please," the woman said. "The light."

Kathryn doused the flash. The darkness seemed blacker. Tendrils of mist moved across the open ground; their dampness touched her skin like passing ghosts.

"He mustn't ever know," Carol Russell said. Her voice was tense, edgy. She sat on the edge of her chair as if poised for flight. "Will you promise?"

"You're talking about your husband? What mustn't he ever know?"

"About . . . this. That it was me."

"I can't promise that, Mrs. Russell. But I'll do my best to protect you, of course."

"Carol. Call me Carol."

"All right. I'll try, Carol."

"You must think that I'm quite crazy."

"No," Kathryn said softly. "I don't think that at all."

"I never really had any women friends. All these years . . ." Carol Russell's voice was remote, as if she were talking to herself. She made a sound that might have been a mirthless laugh. Or one of self-contempt, Kathryn thought with a flash of insight. "I taught art, you know. I was a good teacher. He was . . . nice. Considerate. For a long time. I used to read to him. Beautiful things . . ."

Her voice dwindled and died as she listened to the silent echoes of her own yesterdays. Kathryn strained to see her face clearly but could not.

"Blaise Pascal?" she asked softly.

"That was his favorite," the woman said almost inaudibly. " 'We know the truth not only by the reason, but by the heart.' "

"When was this?" Kathryn said into the empty night, shivering slightly as she spoke. Her face and the backs of her hands were damp and she could feel the moisture settling on her hair, her clothes. Carol Russell made an impatient gesture, banishing beautiful things.

"He told me, a long time later. I think he enjoyed it. He said he never would have married me. He had to, it was an all-girls' school. There was talk . . . the parents didn't like the idea of an unmarried man teaching teenagers. So . . ."

She made another movement. It might have been a shrug.

"Why did you ask me to meet you, Carol?"

"He has a den," Carol Russell said. "At home. Like an office. The holy of holies, he calls it. I'm not allowed to go in there."

Kathryn waited patiently. Carol Russell needed to get to whatever it was she wanted to tell her in her own time, her own way. The best interrogators knew how to let silence work for them.

"Then this poor little girl, what was her name? Rafaelita . . ."

"Medina," Kathryn said. "She was fifteen."

"He killed her, didn't he?"

"Yes," Kathryn said.

"Did he . . . hurt her? Like the others?"

"Worse than the others, Carol. Much worse."

Kathryn heard the woman on the other side of the table draw in a long, deep, ragged breath. "Oh, God. And it's my fault. My fault."

"It's nobody's fault."

The words were empty and she knew it; they wouldn't help Carol Russell but they were all she had to give her. How many years of physical and mental abuse did it take to condition someone to live in silent knowledge of such horrors for so long? And what sympathy or understanding could you possibly offer someone who had?

"All these years . . . He told me never to ask where he went. What he did. I never . . . disobeyed. Never. All these years . . ." Her voice was a monotone, as if she was speaking a soliloquy. She stopped, took something from her purse. "These were in there. In his desk drawer."

She pushed a plastic bag across the table. Kathryn flicked on her flashlight. Inside the bag were four or five pairs of panties. They were grubby, stained; some were cut or torn. One pair had what looked like a bloodstain on it.

"Whose are these?" Kathryn whispered.

"Not mine. Is that what you mean?"

"Whose, then?"

"I think they must have been . . . theirs."

"You found them in your husband's desk?" She sensed, rather than saw, Carol Russell nod. "And you'll swear to that in court?"

"Do I . . . can't you do it . . . some other way? Without me?"

"Carol," Kathryn said. "You know I can't. You have to be there."

"Oh, God," she said. She drew in a deep, quavering breath. "Oh, God, oh, God, I can't."

"You must, Carol," Kathryn said. The silence closed in; it seemed to last a long time.

"All right," Carol Russell said. "All right."

Got you, you sonofabitch!

36

A LITTLE AFTER DARK ON SUNDAY NIGHT, SEPTEMBER 15, Lieutenant Walt Earheart brought James Leland Russell down to "Mission Dolores," the County Jail. On the sidewalk by the entrance on Alameda, it was like the premiere of *Gone With the Wind*, lit as brightly as day by the sunguns of the TV crews and the flickering chain lightning of a hundred flashguns; it seemed as if every TV and newspaper reporter in California was out there. Handcuffed to two big SO deputies, dead-eyed and disheveled, Russell stared at them stonily through the window of the patrol car as it slid past. One or two of the photographers ran alongside the car, firing off frame after frame at random, hoping just one of them might catch the face of the suspect, until they were stopped by the line of deputies guarding the entrance.

All vehicles approaching the jail passed sensors that recorded their arrival, while CCTV cameras filmed everything that happened below. In normal arrests, officers stopped to report what they had aboard via a mike link to the jail interior; tonight everyone knew who was coming in.

Within minutes of Russell being arrested, Kathryn headed downtown to be present at the booking process. Meanwhile, Jack Burrows would take Carol Russell into protective custody. The house on Pacheco was secured and a guard of two deputies posted to keep it that way; as soon as she was through at the jail, Kathryn would take Carol Russell in front of a magistrate and obtain a Skelton search warrant.

Flashguns flickered, and reporters clamored around her car as she turned in to the entrance of the jail, banging on the windows, shouting questions. A deputy raised the barrier and let her in. The jail complex was fronted by a long, low administration building, with Courtroom E adjacent to the entrance. Inside it was like all jails everywhere. Prisoners— hands cuffed behind them, no exceptions, ever—came into a covered receiving port. A bulletin board carried a typed list of the names of every prisoner coming through. A camera for mug shots was positioned just across from two large inkpads for fingerprinting. There was a desk with a computer unit; a radio played "Leavin' on a Jet Plane" in the background.

"Hi, Cyndie," Kathryn said.

Receiving Officer Cyndie Donato was a tall woman with moussed red-blond hair. She looked more like your average mom than a woman whose job it was to pat down killers, rapists, and thieves. Looks were deceptive. Most of the time prisoners were no trouble, but if they were, Cyndie could handle it.

"Your man's already in the tank," she said. "Cell Four. You want to go through?"

"Nothing on the computer, I suppose?" Kathryn asked. A prisoner's personal statistics were taken and entered on a national networking computer. Cyndie shook her head.

"He say anything?"

"Yeah," Cyndie replied. "He said, 'Have a nice evening.'"

She opened the security door and let Kathryn in the small, padded room in which prisoners were patted down, asked questions about their health, and asked to complete documentation—thus securing a sample of their handwriting for comparison if needed. On the far side of the room was another door, which led to the holding tanks. Drunks went into one, first-timers another, known gang members another. Anyone out of control was put in what they called the "quiet room," which had bare, soundproofed walls. CCTV cameras monitored each cell.

The largest holding cell contained maybe eight or ten prisoners waiting to hear their semi-immediate fate. Within the next five or six hours they'd either be bailed out, released on OR—their own recognizance—or join the jail population to await trial. Some of them pressed their faces against the cell's glass door, yelling things Kathryn couldn't hear.

She ignored them and went to the door of Cell Four, looking in through the inspection window. Inside were a burly deputy, the jail nurse, and Russell. It was Kathryn's first good look at the suspect. Why was it the monsters never looked like monsters? Medium height, straight dark hair parted on the left, slightly pudgy features—James Leland Russell, just another face in the crowd. He was getting undressed, preparatory to undergoing the series of tests and checks—the suspect kit, as they called it—which the jail nurse would now conduct. As he took off each item of clothing, the deputy bagged it for forensic examination, noting its condition.

Kathryn tapped on the door. The deputy looked up sharply, then smiled and let her in. Naked, Russell looked uneasy and helpless. He stared at her, hate in his eyes. The jail nurse smiled.

"I'm Sally Katz," she said. "And you're . . . ?"

"Kathryn Mackay, DA's office."

"This one of yours?"

"As of now," Kathryn said.

"All right, let's get started."

The routine was just that, routine. Sally Katz's expression remained impassive as one by one she briskly carried out her tasks. Finger-, palm-, and foot-printing had already been done. This was followed by a blood draw for typing and comparison. Then she carefully collected and bagged scrapings from beneath each of Russell's fingernails. Next, his entire body was scanned with a Wood's lamp for secretions or foreign materials. As the nurse worked, his eyes met Kathryn's over her bent body.

"Enjoying yourself?" he said.

"No," Kathryn said, making it hostile. Russell smiled.

The nurse had Russell sit down while she examined his mouth and took two oral swabs; from these, two dry-mount slides would be prepared. Next, his external genitalia were scanned with the Wood's lamp, and his penis and scrotum swabbed—one urethral swab, one from the glans and shaft. The nurse worked efficiently, clinically, combing Russell's pubic hair for foreign matter, and taking fifteen or twenty hair samples. Throughout the examination Russell never took his eyes off Kathryn. She met his gaze unflinchingly as Nurse Katz took further hair samples from his head and body, teeth impressions for comparison with the bite marks.

With all these, the DOJ criminalists would now be able to complete the DNA tests that would establish whether or not the semen found on the panties that Carol Russell had given her was Russell's.

"That's it?" Russell said.

"That's it," Nurse Katz said, straightening up. "Put your clothes on."

The jail supplied clean underwear, socks, laceless slip-on shoes, and the standard orange prisoner jumpsuits. Russell put them on, stood up.

"All yours, Harry," the nurse said to the deputy.

"You have anything else, Ms. Mackay?" he asked. Kathryn shook her head. "Okay, sir," he said to the prisoner. "You want to come with me?"

"One minute," Russell said. He turned to face Kathryn. "It was Carol, wasn't it? You turned her against me."

"I didn't need to," Kathryn said. "You did that by yourself."

"You won't find anything else," he told her. "At the house. There's nothing there."

"Let's go, Mr. Russell," the deputy said. He put his hand on Russell's shoulder and steered him toward the door. As he opened it, Russell twisted around.

"One last thing," he said, and although his voice was very soft, she could see the anger in his eyes. "I want you to know I'm very angry with you, Kathryn. Very angry indeed."

"Get him out of here," Kathryn said to the deputy, losing her patience. The heavy door swung shut. Sally Katz looked at Kathryn and shook her head, Can you believe it?

"Thanks, Sally," Kathryn said. "You'll get that stuff to the lab right away, won't you?"

"What did he mean, he's angry with you?"

"He means he'd like to kill me for what I've done," Kathryn said. "So you guys take real good care of him."

"Bet on it," Sally Katz said.

Kathryn got back into her car and drove out fast before the huddle of reporters could block her exit. She drove straight around to the deserted parking area in front of the Courts Building where she knew Jack Burrows and Carol Russell were waiting for her. The next item on the agenda was the search warrant that would enable them to take Russell's house apart. The paperwork was already done; all they had to do was put Carol in front of the magistrate and have her tell her story. Kathryn felt confident, eager again. She hadn't realized how much she missed this part of her life.

"Will ... will it take long?" Carol Russell asked as Kathryn walked in.

"Don't worry," she said reassuringly. "The judge just wants to hear what you have to say. You're not on trial."

"I'm nervous."

"Don't be," Kathryn said, and squeezed her hand.

Judge Blackmer, who had been apprized of their coming, was already in his chambers; with him was the court reporter Janie Welsh. She was already seated at the table, feeding a fresh pack of layered transcription paper into the machine.

Kathryn, Burrows, and Carol sat on one side of a long bench table, the judge and the court reporter on the other. Blackmer began the proceedings by swearing Burrows and Carol Russell. He was a short, thickset man with a square, fleshy face and large, stubby-fingered hands that he splayed on the table in front of him. His hair was gray and curling, cut very short. He wore half-frame bifocals perched on the end of his nose; every time he leaned forward to look at Kathryn he had to dip his head to peer over them.

"Are we ready, Ms. Mackay?"

"Yes, Your Honor."

"Very well," the judge said. "Now, Mrs. Russell, we're going to go nice and steady here. Don't be in a hurry to answer my questions, take your time. This is a legal proceeding, but I'm not going to be judgmental. If you have any problems, we can always stop. You understand?"

Carol Russell nodded wordlessly. Blackmer smiled and began.

"Please state your full name and spell it."

Carol did as she was bidden, and then in response to further questions gave her age, address, and employment. She stated that she did not have a criminal history.

"Mrs. Russell, you're here because you have some information which you've discussed with the investigating officers in this case, is that correct?"

"Yes, it is."

"What is your relationship to James Leland Russell?"

"He is my husband."

"I show you a photograph. Please identify it."

"This is a photograph of my husband."

"I show you another photograph. Please identify it."

"It's my home. Thirty-three twenty-four Pacheco Drive, Outlook Heights."

"That's in Santa Rita."

"Correct."

"Will you now please tell the court, in your own words, what you know about your husband's part in the murder of Barbara Gates and the attempted murder of David Granz."

"I believe he committed those crimes."

"Mrs. Russell," the judge said, "you're only to refer here to matters of which you have personal knowledge."

"I'm sorry. I ... My husband was visited by a detective named David Granz. He said he was investigating the murders of these women. Two nights later, the detective was attacked and left for dead in Laguna del Mar."

"Be specific about the date, please."

"The detective came to our house on a Thursday. I believe it was August fifteenth."

"And did you notice anything out of the ordinary about your husband that night, Mrs. Russell?" Kathryn asked.

"He went out, came back late. He had scratches on his face."

"Did you connect them with the attack on the inspector?"

"Not then. We had a call from the Sheriff's office. They asked if Granz had called on us. My husband told them no."

"But you knew he was lying."

"I was there. Mr. Granz talked to my husband for more than half an hour."

"Why did you think your husband lied about it?"

"I could only think of one reason. He must be hiding something. It was then I began to wonder if ... am I allowed to say this?"

"Go ahead, Mrs. Russell," the judge said. "I'll tell you if you go astray."

"I began to think ... maybe he had something to do with the murders ... And then I started thinking, maybe Lee had attacked the detective, too."

"By Lee, you are referring to your husband, James Leland Russell?"

"That's right."

"And what did you do then?"

"I telephoned you."

"Let the record show that Mrs. Russell is referring to

Assistant District Attorney Kathryn Mackay," the judge said.

"And what did you say?"

"I said I knew the murderer of those women . . . all those women."

"But you refused to give your own name, isn't that correct?"

"Yes."

"Did you receive a visit from a lieutenant of detectives named Walter Earheart and myself on the afternoon of September tenth?"

"Yes."

"And did you tell us on that occasion you believed your husband was the killer?"

"Not in those words. But, yes."

"And when we asked you if you would testify to that effect in court, what did you say?"

"I said I couldn't do it."

"Why was that?"

"I was . . . I'm frightened," she said, her voice little more than a whisper. She looked at Kathryn, then away.

"All right, all right, Mrs. Russell," Blackmer said, "please don't distress yourself." He glanced at Kathryn as he spoke.

"Would you like to stop for a moment, Carol?" she asked.

"It's . . . no, I want to tell you."

"Very well," Kathryn said. "I'd like you to tell us now what happened on the night of Saturday, September fourteenth. Just tell it in your own words."

"After that little girl was killed I . . ."

"You are referring to Rafaelita Medina, who was killed September twelfth, is that correct?"

"Yes, the little girl. I couldn't . . ." She looked at the judge and smiled apologetically. "What I'm trying to say . . . I didn't want to believe it was true."

"But?"

"On Saturday he went out. He—"

"That's Saturday, September fourteenth?" Kathryn interposed.

"Yes, that's right. He has a study, he always keeps it locked. The holy of holies, he calls it. He would never let me go in there, not even to clean."

"You had a room in your own home you had never once

been in, Mrs. Russell?" Blackmer said, unable to conceal his surprise. "How long had you lived there?"

"Since 1988," she replied.

"And you didn't insist on seeing it?"

She frowned, as if the question made no sense. "He ... said never to go in there. Never."

"But on this particular Saturday you decided to go into that room anyway," Kathryn prompted.

"I thought . . . maybe . . . maybe while he's out. I can find something, once and for all. That would prove . . . it was him."

"And what did you find?"

"I looked in all the cupboards, everywhere. There was nothing. Then I looked in his desk drawer. The middle one. It had a key in it, but it wasn't locked."

"And what did you find in the drawer?"

"Panties."

"How many pairs of panties?"

"Five."

"All the same?"

She shook her head. "Different colors. Different sizes."

"And what did you do with them?"

"That was when I telephoned you. At your house. I asked you to meet me."

"And when we met, what did you do?"

"I gave the panties to you. In a plastic bag."

"The garments were shown to the parents of one of the victims, Barbara Gates, Your Honor," Kathryn said. "They identified one pair as having belonged to their daughter. I have their declaration here."

She pushed the papers across the table; Blackmer looked at them, checked the signatures, nodded.

"I have to ask you a couple of other questions, Mrs. Russell, then we'll be done," he said. "These have to do with your motivation. Okay?"

She nodded.

"Why are you cooperating with law enforcement in this matter?"

"I couldn't bear ..." Her chin came up, her voice got a little stronger. "I wanted it to stop. I want them to stop him."

"And is the information you have provided here tonight offered in confidence?"

"I'm sorry?"

"Would you be doing this if you thought your husband was going to know?"

Her shoulders drew in, and she shook her head like a small child, not answering.

"Do you believe he might physically harm you?" Blackmer asked.

"Yes," she whispered.

Blackmer nodded, finality in the gesture. "Ms. Mackay?"

"Your Honor, I request you make a factual finding regarding the credibility of the witness based on her testimony and the statements contained in the affidavit."

"I'm convinced, Ms. Mackay. Accepted."

"Thank you, Your Honor. I now request the court to rule on probable cause."

"Probable cause to issue a search warrant is found," Blackmer said. "Anything else, Ms. Mackay?"

"That's all I have, Your Honor."

Blackmer nodded, drew the papers in front of him, and scribbled his signature and the date on the affidavit and the warrant.

"That's it," he said. "Where will Mrs. Russell go from here?"

"Mrs. Russell is being taken to a safe location, Your Honor," Kathryn told him. "Where she'll be protected."

"Fine," Blackmer said. "Have you got enough to put him away?"

"Yes, Your Honor."

"Good luck."

Kathryn turned to say something to Jack Burrows. He was already gone; they found him outside at the bank of phones in the atrium, passing the word to SO that they had the warrant. He looked up as Kathryn tapped on the window.

"Take Mrs. Russell to the apartment, Jack," she told him.

"What about you?"

"I'm going up to the house. I want to see what's happening up there."

She stood watching as Carol Russell got into Burrows's car and they drove off. Across Alameda knots of reporters were still hanging around hopefully, waiting for something to happen. Kathryn got into her own car and headed for Outlook Heights.

By the time she got to Pacheco Drive, a team of crime scene investigators had already descended upon the Russells' two-bedroom house. The Honda Civic was already gone, impounded and taken down to the storage garage to be stripped down by investigators. She went inside the house. One of the criminologists was vacuuming; as he finished each room, the contents of the bag were sifted before being sent to the lab to be analyzed. The rest of the team was taking the house apart, inch by inch. In one room all the carpets had already been taken up and were rolled to one side; an investigator was prizing up the floorboards. She went into the den. The holy of holies, Carol Russell had called it. A leather reclining chair, a desk, a portable TV on a swivel table, some bookshelf units. The banality of evil.

"Hi, Kathryn." The deputy grinned as she came in. He was a big, burly guy of about thirty with blond hair and a sunny smile. His nameplate said MAZZINI. "Come to give us a hand here?"

He was taking the drawers out of the desk and checking every piece of paper, every notepad, every envelope: the fact that Russell had kept mementos of his victims promised there might be more.

"Find anything in the desk, Billy?" she asked.

"Some maps. I'll send them for electrophoretic testing."

"That all?"

"We just got started. Long way to go yet."

One investigator was taking the books off the shelves one at a time, carefully riffling through the pages, looking for photos or documents that might show the names of victims, addresses, telephone numbers. They would search for legal pads, envelopes, pens that might have been used for the coded notes. They would look for news clippings, videos, feature articles that might refer to the murders or the killer. They would also search for trinkets, souvenirs, anything that might have been taken from the victims before or after the murders. And most of all, a scalpel ...

Kathryn went outside. Two deputies were digging up the garden, foot by foot, carefully turning the earth; another was scanning it with a metal detector. Two officers were searching the garage, shelf by shelf, inch by inch. Suddenly Kathryn felt very tired. She looked at her watch; it was already nearly ten and she had been running on sheer adrenaline for the past four hours.

"I need a sandwich," she said to the nearest cop, a brawny guy with a nameplate that said ZANDUSKY.

"There's a twenty-four-hour Mexican place a couple of blocks over on Pompano," he said helpfully. "They do good quesadillas."

"Think I'll head for the barn," Kathryn said. "You guys can manage without me."

"Be tough," Zandusky grinned, "but we'll try."

She drove down toward Alameda, leaving the bright oasis of lights around the Russell home behind her. She found herself yawning as she turned east onto Alameda, and decided to skip the sandwich. What she really needed was a good night's sleep.

The first item on her agenda tomorrow would be Russell's arraignment: once arrested the defendant must be brought before a magistrate within forty-eight hours. By the time that arraignment took place, it was Kathryn's job to have reviewed all the police reports and filed charges. At the arraignment the judge would inform the defendant of his rights, which included the right to a preliminary hearing within ten court—working—days, unless he "waived time." If he did not, the prosecutor had exactly that number of days to put together a case; ten if she went to prelim, probably less if she convened the grand jury.

Either way, she thought as she turned into her own driveway, it was going to be a three-ring circus.

She looked up as Walt Earheart appeared in the doorway of her office.

"You looked pleased with yourself," he said.

"So do you, Lieutenant. How's it going up at Pacheco?"

"They're still digging," Earheart told her. "You went up there last night."

"It was on my way home after the booking."

"It's good knowing we've got that bastard locked up," he said. "Have you people decided what you're going to do after the arraignment?"

"I've got a meeting with Hal in about five minutes to discuss it," Kathryn said. "Why don't you sit in?"

"Might just do that." Earheart lowered himself into one of Kathryn's white wicker chairs, which noisily acknowledged his bulk. "Got to stop eating so many of those damned chili burgers," he said.

"You know we're alleging a number of special circumstances on each of the murders?"

"I heard. You ought to be able to prove up what, two, three?"

"Probably two. We'll allege kidnapping; we might have trouble proving the sexual assaults. But one is enough to get us the LWOP or the death penalty."

"And on Granz?"

"Attempted murder."

"Sounds good," Earheart said. "Have you met with the wife again?"

"A couple of times. Why?"

"She bothers me, Kathryn. Every time I talk to her, I get the feeling she's holding back, that there's something she either won't tell us or is afraid to tell us. The trouble is, I can't lean on her any harder in case she backs off altogether and changes her mind about testifying."

"What else could she know?"

"That's what I can't figure out. If I had some idea, we could ask her some questions that might open her up. As it is . . ."

"I'll have to prep her before she testifies. Maybe she'll open up to me." She looked at her watch. "Time for my meeting."

They went through to McCaskill's office. Earheart said his hellos and settled massively on a chair near the window.

"Okay, let's get to it," Mac said. "Arraignment's Wednesday, eight-thirty in Muni B, Judge Cross." He looked at Kathryn. "Russell hired himself a lawyer."

"Who?"

"Leonard Wurzelman."

Wurzelman was one of the most controversial attorneys in central California. The more sensational the case, the better. Handsome, flamboyant, Wurzelman claimed the courtroom was a stage where life's more tragic scripts were played out. He was that kind of lawyer.

"Where is Russell getting that kind of money?" Kathryn asked. "The Wurzelmans of this world don't come cheap."

"Hell, he's probably doing it free," Earheart said. "You know how Leonard loves grabbing the headlines."

"Wurzelman has offered us a deal," Mac told her. "He reckons we haven't got enough evidence to get the death penalty. He'll take life without parole."

"LWOP on this? Does he think we're crazy?"

"He thinks, Kathryn, and he is doing it out loud right now in front of the TV cameras, that if we go to trial, it will be a long and costly proceeding, and with that I cannot argue. He says, and I believe him, that he'll fight us every inch of the way. He calculates that this case could tie us up in court for five, six months, and cost the taxpayer what, add it up, half, three-quarters of a million. If the jury rejects the death penalty for LWOP—and they could, Kathryn, they could—that's money down the toilet. That's what he thinks."

"Mac, this bastard has killed four women, not to mention committing God alone knows what other crimes we don't know about. On a scale of redeeming qualities, he's a minus. And you talk about cutting a deal for him?"

"I'm just telling you what Wurzelman said to me," Mac replied calmly. "And what they'll be saying on TV Wednesday. Quote, This case could be settled immediately with no threat to the public safety, yet the district attorney persists in pursuing the death penalty. When the community is clamoring for better police and fire protection, for improved roads and schools, surely there has to be a better use for the money than to secure the needless execution of a man who has already volunteered to plead guilty and be incarcerated without parole for the rest of his natural life. Unquote."

"We can't go down that road, Mac, and you know it," Kathryn said angrily. "What are you going to do next time, when you're looking for LWOP and the defense offers you twenty-five to life because it will save you money? The people voted for the death penalty. If they want to revoke it, let them do it at the ballot box. Till they do, we're obligated to pursue it."

"There's more. Wurzelman's writing to newspapers all over the state expressing his 'concern' for jurors and other 'innocent people' who will be forced to hear gruesome testimony about these killings for weeks on end, making them the ultimate victims of Russell's crimes. Why, he asks, are we spending all this money to create even more victims? Here, he brought me a copy, you want to read it?"

"No, I don't," Kathryn said. "It's garbage. No deals, Mac. Either we go for broke, or Hal can find himself another prosecutor."

"All right, let me ask you this: do we have enough to indict Russell on the special circumstances?"

"It depends what you mean by enough."

"Run it by me once more."

She outlined the physical evidence she would introduce. Most of it was circumstantial: a pair of panties identified by Barbara Gates's parents; a criminalist's testimony linking the bloodstain on the second pair of panties to a second victim.

"We're waiting for the lab tests on everything else."

"What about Sam Lepell's spectrograms? Didn't he say that the Sanchez voice samples contained marked similarities to the ones we took from Russell?" Earheart asked.

"He did," Kathryn said, "but we can't use it. Voiceprint evidence is inadmissible: *People* versus *King,* 1968."

"Anything at all at the house?" Mac asked.

"They're still working up there," Earheart reported. "But so far they haven't come up with anything that directly links Russell to any of the victims. We felt sure we'd find enough up there to nail his coffin lid down. Instead of which, two bags filled with dust balls. Apart from the fact that he had a copy of Pascal's *Pensées* in his den, and that he owns scalpels of a kind which might have produced the wounds on the victims and Granz, it looks like the place is clean."

"I'll tell you the truth, Mac, if we didn't have Carol Russell, we wouldn't have enough to indict," Kathryn said.

McCaskill pinched his chin between forefinger and thumb and stuck out his lips, considering the pros and cons of the choice before them.

"I take it you don't want to go to prelim, right?"

"Carol Russell is terrified of even being in the same courtroom as her husband as it is. If we give him the chance at a prelim, Wurzelman gets to jump all over her. You've seen him in court, Mac, Billy Graham one minute and Dracula the next. With the media eating her up as well, she'd probably fall apart," Kathryn said. "I'd like to keep her away from all of that as long as possible."

"Okay, we take the case to the grand jury," Mac said. A prelim was a minitrial at which witnesses appeared and were examined by both the prosecutor and the defense. At a grand jury hearing, the prosecutor had to present evidence that a crime had been committed and that there was a reasonable suspicion the defendant had committed that crime, presenting the same evidence he or she would have presented at a prelim. Since neither the defendant nor his attorney was permitted to appear, this would have the additional advantage of limiting Carol Russell's exposure to the adversary trial process.

"At least we'll be able to protect the wife and keep the pretrial publicity to a minimum," Kathryn said. "Maybe even save ourselves a change of venue."

"That would be good," Benton said. "The arraignment alone is going to be a media circus. The court's already received a dozen requests for permission to film."

"That probably explains why Richard Sanchez keeps calling me," Kathryn said.

"And everyone else from the governor on down," Benton said. "You didn't talk to him, did you?"

"You're kidding, of course."

"Are you going to object to letting the TV people film, Hal?" Earheart wanted to know. "Don't forget, there might still be witnesses out there who could ID Russell. If he goes on TV, they won't be worth squat."

"I know. It's a pretty safe bet Wurzelman won't want cameras in the courtroom, either," Benton said. "He doesn't want Russell's picture on every TV screen in California."

"There's only one thing worrying me about this, Kathryn," Mac said. "Testimony before the grand jury isn't admissible at trial. If between now and then the wife develops 'amnesia' or gets scared off and disappears, we'll be in trouble."

"I expect to have the DNA results in by the time we go to trial," Kathryn said. "In fact, we may have them much faster. There's been a new breakthrough by some British company: they call it REMS, Random Elimination Mass Screening. They're already using it over there. The makers claim they can get a comparison genetic fingerprint from a blood sample in under twenty-four hours, and it only costs about sixty dollars. When you get a match, they work it up into a full presentation for prosecution purposes. They're evaluating it right now at the Department of Justice in Sacramento."

"Sounds too good to be true," Earheart said. DNA tests usually took between four and eight weeks, and could cost thousands of dollars. "Is it for real?"

"Doc Nelson is getting some literature sent down. I'll let you know what he says."

"I still don't like it that the indictment hinges entirely on the wife's testimony," Mac said. "If she doesn't come across as credible, the grand jury might let this bastard off the hook."

"I'll work with her, Mac," Kathryn promised, hoping she sounded more confident than she felt. "She'll come through."

37

WITH FUNDS FROM THE DEPARTMENT OF JUSTICE'S WITNESS Protection Program, Carol Russell was installed in a rented furnished apartment on West Bayshore Drive near Seal Point Park. Regular checks by telephone monitored her safety and her anonymity. She had a panic-button phone number for immediate response on a twenty-four-hour basis. The number of people who knew her whereabouts was restricted to an absolute minimum.

There was no question in Kathryn's mind now that Carol Russell was an abused wife. All the symptoms were there: the fear, the ambivalence about testifying, the self-blame, the protective attitude toward her persecutor. Perhaps she would be able to gain her confidence, break down the barrier that Earheart had perceived, and persuade her to tell them everything she knew. It was essential to convince her first of all that it was not her fault she was a victim, and second that it was not her responsibility to decide what should happen to her husband.

Kathryn called to say she was on her way: Carol had been instructed not to leave the apartment or open her door to anyone who had not previously advised her he or she was coming. When she got to the apartment, Kathryn found Carol watching a repeat of *Knots Landing*. She told her they had decided to go before the grand jury and that Lee Russell would be arraigned in Municipal Court B the following day.

"Do I have to be there?" Carol asked, switching off the TV as if she was reluctant to leave the comfortable troubles of the soap opera world for the grimmer realities of her own.

"No, you don't. The whole thing will only take about five minutes. They bring him in, the judge reads the charges and explains his legal rights."

"When you . . . how long will he go to prison for?"

Kathryn frowned. "Carol, we will be seeking the death penalty in this case," she said. "Surely you knew that?"

Carol Russell just stared at her, her washed-out blue eyes wide and empty. Was it possible she still hadn't realized her testimony could send her husband to the gas chamber?

"Carol, whatever happens now, you mustn't feel guilty," Kathryn said. "As far as I am concerned, you are a victim just as much as any of the dead women. I want you to understand it's the system that's in charge of punishing Lee now, not you. It's been taken out of your hands. Even if you were to ask me, beg me not to proceed against your husband, I would say no. Do you understand?"

Carol nodded mutely. Her passivity was another indication of what she had suffered, Kathryn thought. Women learned that dependent behavior made the abuser feel strong and in control, and adapted accordingly. Accepting the blame for their situation somehow helped them combat their sense of despair and helplessness.

"What will it be like, in court?" she asked now.

"There's nothing to be afraid of," Kathryn said reassuringly. "Appearing before the grand jury is very simple. The only people allowed into the courtroom are the jurors, a court reporter, the district attorney—in this case, me—and you. There is no judge. Just you and me and the jury."

"What about . . . him? Lee? Won't he be there, too?"

Kathryn shook her head. "He won't be anywhere near the place. He'll be in his jail cell the whole time."

"I thought if there was a trial, he would have to be there."

"This is a hearing, not a trial, Carol," Kathryn told her. "We're just presenting the evidence to the grand jury. What we do is, we subpoena the witnesses who are appearing for the prosecution to appear at a certain date and time. They all wait outside the courtroom until they are called, one at a time. We'll arrange things so you are called first."

"What happens inside?"

"The foreperson of the jury will ask you to go to the podium to be sworn. Then you'll take the witness stand, give your name and occupation. I will then ask you questions. When we get through, you will be warned not to disclose what you have told the grand jury under penalty of law. And that's it."

"It sounds very ... perfunctory."

Kathryn smiled. "You won't be the only witness, Carol. I'll be calling deputies, detectives, criminologists, and doctors. Inspector Granz will testify, too."

"How long will it take?"

"The whole presentation? One, maybe two, days. But you'll only be there for a couple of hours."

"They don't let people in to watch?"

"No. No audience. It's nothing like TV, where there's always a crowded courtroom. Most of the time courtrooms are empty anyway, except for witnesses and lawyers and other people who have to be there. In the case of the grand jury, that's the law."

"And you're sure ... about Lee?"

"Quite sure," Kathryn said. "Would you like some tea before we get to work?"

"Work?"

"I want to go through what we're going to talk about when you take the stand."

"You mean, like a rehearsal?"

"Sort of," Kathryn said. "Except I don't want you to think you've got to learn anything. Just relax and be natural and answer my questions. If I ask you anything you don't understand, say so. Say, I don't understand the question."

"Yes."

"It may well be when you appear that for technical reasons I'll ask you a question that seems dumb to you, like, Is your house in Santa Rita County, or Does the front door of your house open inward or outward? Even if the answer to the question seems obvious to anyone with eyes, just go ahead and answer and trust me; I know why I'm asking. Now, have you got any questions?"

Carol Russell shook her head, her eyes apprehensive.

"Let's have that tea," Kathryn said. "Then we'll begin."

Her thoughts were busy as she went automatically through the routine of making the tea, pouring it, slicing lemon. She had read and reread over and over again the transcripts of Carol Russell's statements to Walt Earheart's detectives. She had sat alone for hours watching the videotapes of the interviews, noting the woman's hesitations, highlighting the transcripts to cue them in her own memory when the time came, outlining her own direct examination as she went along. This little run-through would give her a chance to put her conclusions to the test.

"Carol, we'll assume you've already been sworn. That means you'd have given your oath to tell the truth, the whole truth, and nothing but the truth. You know about that, don't you?"

"Yes."

"Okay, we'll begin. Don't be afraid. Just answer the best you can. I'll call you Carol now, but it will be Mrs. Russell on the stand, is that clear?"

"Yes."

"All right, let's begin. You are the wife of James Leland Russell, is that correct?"

"Yes."

"And you live with your husband at thirty-three twenty-four Pacheco Drive in Outlook Heights, Santa Rita."

"Yes."

"If this were a courtroom, Carol, I might say something to you here like, Mrs. Russell, I'm not sure if the jury can hear you properly, and ask you to speak a little louder. Don't worry about it now, but it's important in court that the jury hears everything you say. Okay, let's go on. Mrs. Russell, how long have you been married to James Leland Russell?"

"Since 1982."

"You were married in Redwood City, is that correct?"

"Yes."

"And how long did you live there?"

"Until 1988. Then we moved here. To Santa Rita."

"Is your marriage happy?"

"Do I have to answer?"

Kathryn nodded.

"It was at first."

"But not now? Can you tell us when it changed?"

"It started after we'd been married about . . . two years, maybe a little longer. He . . . we didn't sleep together anymore."

"Was that arrangement of your choosing, Mrs. Russell?"

"No, it was . . . He said he hated my body."

"He said those words, 'I hate your body'?"

"He said women . . . use their bodies. To trap men into marrying them."

"Did he mean that was what you did?"

"Not . . . not really. He . . . do I have to say all this?"

"You don't have to now if you don't want to."

"He always . . . had trouble. He said it was my fault. I didn't excite him."

"You're saying your husband had trouble maintaining an erection, is that correct?"

Carol Russell turned away to look out of the window. "Yes," she said, almost inaudibly.

"Are you and your husband the same age?"

"No. Lee is forty-three. I am forty-eight."

"Did this age difference have anything to do with your husband's attitude toward you?"

"He always said that was why he . . . couldn't do it. He kept telling me I was ugly. Old. He called me names. The old crow. The old hag. In front of our friends. When we went anywhere. He made fun of me all the time, cruel, cruel fun. He . . . seemed to enjoy hurting me. Do we . . . do we have to talk about this anymore?"

She looked imploringly at Kathryn, entreaty in her eyes.

"All right, let's take a little break," Kathryn said, turning away. She wasn't sure whether she wanted to go on with this anyway. To give Carol more time, she looked around. The apartment had no personality. Everything about it had a transient feeling, as if no one had ever lived here for any length of time; the furniture looked as if it had been bought at a bargain price from a window display in a furniture mart. Kathryn poured herself some tea and sipped it, waiting until the older woman composed herself.

"All right," she said. "Let's move on to the day you made the anonymous call to my office. You remember that?"

"Yes. It was a Monday. After Labor Day."

"Can you remember why you called?"

"A detective had come to the house to talk to Lee." Carol

Russell turned around and came back to sit down facing Kathryn.

"Here I'd show you a photograph of Inspector Granz and ask you if he was the man who came to your house. Okay, go on, what happened then?"

"I read a couple of days later in the paper that he had been attacked and was in intensive care. I asked Lee about it and he said something like that sort of thing happens to cops all the time, that's what they get paid for."

"And you didn't think any more about it at that time?"

"Not until someone telephoned from the Sheriff's office to ask if the detective had been to see us. And I heard Lee tell them no, he hadn't."

"But you had seen Inspector Granz at the house, is that correct?"

"I opened the door, let him in."

"And why did you think your husband lied?"

"I remembered that the night the detective was attacked, Lee came home with scratches on his face. And all at once, I realized he must have been the one who'd done it."

"And did you know why he had attacked Inspector Granz?"

"Not then. It was later. There had been a program on TV about the murders. And a man called the station and said he was the killer. And Richard Sanchez said, 'If you know this man call me.' "

"But you didn't call him."

"I didn't want ... it would have been on TV. Then the papers. I didn't want that. People coming to the house."

"So you called me. Why?"

"It said in the paper you were in charge. Of the investigation."

"Can you remember what you said?"

"I told you I knew who the killer was."

"But you wouldn't tell me his name. Or yours."

"That's right."

"Why not?"

"I didn't know whether it would be ... my name would be kept secret. I was afraid."

"Because you thought your husband was the killer?"

"Yes."

"Why?"

"It was ... all of it. The detective and the scratches on

Lee's face. The way he called Sanchez *cholo*. And then what he said. When they found the dead girl at his school."

"You mean Barbara Gates?"

"He said the strangest things about her. How beautiful she was."

"When was this?"

"After he came home. The day they found her."

"Why did you find it strange he thought she was beautiful?"

"I thought, He couldn't have seen her then. I saw it on the news. They brought her out in a trolley thing. And then I began to wonder ... could he have seen her before?"

"And do you think he could have?" Kathryn asked, carefully keeping her voice very even, very unemphatic. The whole tenor of the conversation had changed. It was as if the woman was in a self-induced trance, remembering things she had kept buried for a long, long time.

"I know he did."

"How do you know that?"

Carol Russell's eyes flooded with alarm, like a child who realizes how dangerously close to a fire it has gone. There was something else there, Kathryn thought. Some experience, some hurt so traumatic Carol Russell could not bear to bring herself to think about, much less put into words. But what? *What?* She repeated her question.

"I ... just know," Carol said.

"Carol, you'll be under oath on the witness stand. You'll have to answer."

"They can't make me."

"If you don't answer, you'll be in contempt of court. They could send you to jail."

"I don't care," she said. The confessional tone was gone. Whatever she had been on the brink of revealing, she had buried again, perhaps even deeper than before.

"Do you remember I came to see you at your house with Lieutenant Earheart?"

"Yes. Last week."

"We talked about the woman who had called, and you said she might know things she couldn't tell. Is that what you meant a moment ago?"

Carol Russell shook her head, her breast heaving. "It's ... haven't I told you enough?" she pleaded.

"It's all right, Carol," Kathryn said reassuringly. "You're not the one who's on trial. But remember, we're asking you these things so we can make sure Lee never gets the chance to hurt you or anyone else again, ever. So if you know anything that will help us to do that, we need to know it, too."

"Can I ask you a question?"

"Go ahead."

"Is ... are your parents still alive?"

"My mother is. My father died when I was fourteen."

"Do you still see her? Your mother?"

"She lives in Kansas City. We visit with her a couple of times a year."

"Is she proud of you?"

Kathryn smiled. "I think she's more surprised than proud. But we get along. Why do you ask?"

"This," Carol Russell said, her gesture including the apartment and the events that were to come. "It's going to be in all the papers. About Lee. Everything."

"I don't think my mother follows my cases."

"My father ... he's seventy-eight," Carol said. "He's very frail. If I have to tell everything ..."

"About you and Lee, you mean?"

"Not just that," Carol said, with a hint of impatience in her voice that said *you really don't understand.* What did it mean?

"You're afraid it will distress your father? Reading about Lee?"

Carol shook her head; again, Kathryn sensed impatience. *It's more than that.*

"Do you mean because of what he did to you?"

Carol Russell stared at her wide-eyed. "You know?"

"I know you said he never physically abused you. But that wasn't the truth, was it?"

"No."

"He hurt you, didn't he? Do you want to tell me about it?"

"I ... I can't."

"Try, Carol. There's nothing so bad you can't tell me about it."

"You don't know," Carol said. "You don't know."

"Carol, you don't have to feel guilty because you were a victim."

"Is this . . . what you're going to ask me, in court?"

"I may have to. To show the jury why you decided to testify."

"You don't know," Carol said again. "It was . . . One time . . . when it got very bad, I said . . . I wanted to go home. He said if I ever . . . he said he would follow me. If I tried to leave. He said he'd find me no matter where I went and . . . do terrible things to me."

"What sort of terrible things?"

"He had a book about forensic pathology. It had . . . awful pictures in it. Dead people. And he would make me look at them, and then he'd say, 'That's what you'll look like with your throat cut,' or 'That's what you'll look like if you're strangled.'"

"Go on."

"Once he . . ." She shook her head; her breathing became ragged, distressed again. "He went out at night a lot. There were things . . . happening. I asked him where he went all the time. He said I'd made him angry. Very angry. He made me lie face down on the bed and he, he . . ."

"Go on."

"He tied my hands. My feet. And he cut . . . he cut . . ."

She thrust her fingers into her hair, an unexpected gesture that seemed completely out of place. Kathryn frowned.

"He cut you? With a knife?"

Carol Russell shook her head, the dull flaxen hair swinging. "He said it was . . . punishment. He said, 'Never ask me questions again.' I . . . he . . ."

"You said there were things happening. What things?"

"No," Carol said. "It's too . . . it's . . . I should have told someone . . . before. But now it's too late." She stopped, her body racked by dry sobs. After a while they stopped.

"I'm sorry," she said, her face averted.

"You don't need to apologize, Carol," Kathryn said. "I just want to say one thing to you. Don't be afraid. Whatever happened, whatever it was, it's not too late. It's never too late."

Carol Russell got up and went across to the window, staring out at the ocean.

"Did they have long hair?" she asked without turning around. "The girls who were killed?"

It was Kathryn's turn to be surprised. In her mind's eye she saw the photographs she and Steve had studied so intently and for so long. The girl on Shelter Island, upside down, arms and legs extended to form an *X,* her dark hair cropped short; the fish-belly gray body with the milk-white eyes found by the bums in Sedgewick Park, hair plastered like a dark black cap against her skull; the childlike corpse of Rafaelita Medina, huddled in the backseat of the Chevy Nova, her hair as short as a boy's.

"Only one," she said. "Barbara Gates had long hair. Why do you ask?"

Carol Russell continued staring stolidly out of the window.

"Carol? Is there something significant about the girls' hair?" Kathryn persisted. She thought she saw a slight shake of the head. Anything else she might have been going to say was interrupted by the telephone. Kathryn picked it up.

"Who is this?"

"Mrs. Russell?" The voice was female, unfamiliar. "Am I speaking to Carol Russell?"

"Who is this?" Kathryn repeated. The caller hung up and Kathryn replaced the phone, frowning. Outside the sheriff's and her own office, no one had this number or knew Carol's location. She dialed the Sheriff's Department and asked for Walt Earheart.

"Kathryn?"

"Walt, I'm with Carol Russell," she said. "Could you check whether anyone in your office just called the apartment?"

"Hold on." She heard him put down the phone and waited a couple of minutes, tapping her fingers impatiently on the table, until she heard the rattle of Earheart picking up at the other end.

"Nobody from here," the big man told her. "What's the problem?"

"No problem yet, I hope," Kathryn said. "Thanks, Walt."

She redialed, this time getting through to McCaskill, asking him the same question she'd asked Earheart. A few minutes later Mac gave her the same answer. No one in the DA's office had called the apartment.

She stared at the silent telephone. Who could have tracked Carol to this apartment? And how? She picked up the phone again. Maybe it would be smart to move their witness before whoever had phoned came looking for her in person.

38

FOR A WHILE, RAGE CONSUMED HIM. HE SAT IN HIS CELL, STARing at the wall, and the rage grew stronger, fiercer, like a volcano stirring to life. When the lawyer told him, he hadn't believed it. But it was true: his own wife had betrayed him. The cretinous crone. The stupid bitch. If it hadn't been for her, they would never have found him. Even now, even here in a jail cell, he could not altogether believe it. All these years, and now this. It was unbelievable, and yet she had done it.

After a while, the hate drained away, leaving him exhausted and despondent, playing over and over in his head the gray scenario that lay ahead: arraignment and trial and sentencing and . . . It wasn't fair. He'd done everything right, everything. Now if they put Carol on the witness stand, if she told them . . . he had no chance. God damn her treacherous soul. If he ever got out of here . . .

The thought of escape did not occur to him at first. But after a while he became aware of his surroundings. He began to watch, to listen. He quickly learned where each door, each passageway, led. After a few days, he could have drawn a map of the place. It wasn't that difficult: it wasn't that big. The jail unit had been built to hold about two hundred prisoners; four hundred were regularly crammed into it. In the dayrooms, bunks were stacked three high, and mattresses were spread out on the floors to cope with the overflow.

Most of the prisoners were petty offenders. Bums with medical problems got themselves arrested so they could get taken care of. The hospitals handed over mentally disturbed patients they couldn't handle. The druggies, the winos, the drifters, came and went. Fights among inmates were common; the gangs bullied lesser inmates into surrendering turf. As a result, inmates like Lee, who would normally have received special supervision, didn't always get it, because to do so would have compromised overall security.

The reason more prisoners didn't escape, Lee decided, was because most of them were cretins, only slightly more cretinous than the men who guarded them. And once the realization dawned on him that he could escape, he became obsessed with the idea. All he needed was to find a weak spot. That one existed could not be in doubt. Something, somewhere. The hope grew to certainty.

Every chance he got, Lee watched how prisoners were moved from their cells to see their attorneys, or probation officers, or family, or the chaplain, or—most importantly—between the jail facility and the courtrooms. Since there was no underground tunnel or walkway along which the prisoners could be led to make court appearances, it meant they had to be loaded into vans in manacled daisy chains of six or twelve and driven from the jail to the courtrooms. Most days it was chaos; at peak periods, the Santa Rita jail facility was about as secure as a downtown bar.

For now Lee was a model prisoner. Already the guards—they called themselves detention officers to make what they did sound more important—were treating him with a sort of tolerant contempt. They said sit, he sat; they said stand, he stood. He called everyone sir. He didn't roll his eyes and talk in a haunted whisper like a movie serial killer. He spoke only when he was spoken to. That was fine: he had nothing to say to any of these dumbasses anyway. He would watch and wait. And if a chance came, he'd take it.

By ten the arraignment in Muni B was over. It was normally a simple, routine procedure, but not this morning. The courtroom was like all the others, a little simpler perhaps, but the same blond wood, the same Great Seal, the same bench and flags and bookcases. What was different was the atmosphere. Hal Benton had won his little fight against allowing the TV cameras into court, but that didn't keep the media out. The place was bedlam, every bench jammed with reporters, feature writers, sketch artists who arrived at the crack of dawn to get seats, all jostling for elbow room, with more standing in back in direct violation of the fire regs.

Judge Cross was a short, gray-haired man in his early fifties. He regarded the noisy courtroom over the rims of his bifocals and banged the gavel hard, three times. There was immediate silence. Judge Cross read the complaint, asked the defendant if he understood the charges. He might have been talking to a fourteen-year-old.

Leonard Wurzelman, wearing a beautifully cut dark suit and a blow-dried razor cut, gravely asked that his client be released on his own recognizance; with only the faintest trace of a smile, Judge Cross as gravely refused his request.

"Defense requests bail hearing be set for Friday, Your Honor," Wurzelman continued. "And requests permission for my client to dress out for all court appearances."

"So ordered," Judge Cross replied. "Do you wish to waive time, Mr. Wurzelman?"

"No, Your Honor," Wurzelman said. "Defense refuses to waive time."

Cross looked at Kathryn over his glasses.

"Very well," Cross said. "Bail hearing is set for Friday morning, ten A.M."—he looked at his calendar—"preliminary hearing set for Tuesday, October first."

His words were almost drowned in the noise of the reporters pushing and shoving to get out of the courtroom to a telephone. He shook his head sadly and signaled to the bailiff to take Russell back down, and the comparatively calm, everyday bustle of the courts resumed. After stopping off in one of the rest rooms to duck the more persistent of the reporters and to freshen up, Kathryn made her way back to her office and sat staring at the calendar on the wall.

October first. Hal Benton had to assemble the grand jury by then or the ten–court day deadline beat them. She sifted through her message slips. Two more calls from Sanchez. A couple of others that would have to wait and one that simply could not: a please-call-immediately from Steve Giordano.

Steve. She hadn't had time to even think about him since he'd left on the Sunday following her Saturday-night meeting with Carol Russell.

"I thought . . . I'd hoped we'd have longer," she had said as he got into his car.

"It's not like I was going to China."

The smile touched his lips but not his eyes. She had wanted to say, Yes it is, but she said nothing, pushing tomorrow out of her mind and thinking, One of these days I am going to have to stop pushing tomorrow out of my mind. She picked up the phone and dialed his direct number. It was good to hear his voice.

"How did your arraignment go?"

"Quietly in court. A five-ring circus afterwards."

"You're taking it to the grand jury?"

"That's the plan. Wish me luck."

"You don't need it. How's Emma?"

"She's okay. I think she'd gotten used to my being around, so it's been a bit tough for her to go back to the old routine. How's your research coming along?"

"We're building quite a file on your boy. It's going to surprise you."

"Tell me more."

"You'll have it by the end of the week. We've been pulling all the stops out up here. How's Dave, by the way?"

"I heard he's coming into the office later."

"Say hello for me. He deserves whatever credit there is for our getting Russell. Dave's one of the good guys, Kathryn."

"I always knew that."

"How are you doing with Carol Russell?"

"Walt Earheart still thinks she's holding out on us, and I agree."

She related how Carol Russell had shied away from confronting whatever it was in her past that so distressed her.

"She was so specific about how old her father was, as if it had a special relevance. What do you think, Steve, is there something significant in her trying to keep this from him?"

"All I can do is guess. It could be simply she's afraid it will distress him. Then again, it may not be anything as overt as that. It may be something much more subtle, something Russell told her, something he made her do. Something that made her part of or party to his fantasy and that she simply couldn't bear her father knowing she had done. Remember you said she's just as much a victim as the murdered women. This is all about power, control, domination. That applies to her just as much as any of the others. When do you go before the grand jury, do you know?"

"It's got to be by the first of the month. I'm working up my case right now."

"Can I ask you something else?"

"Go ahead."

"Why are we talking about all this, instead of about us?"

"I don't think we can do that on the phone, can we?"

"You're probably right. So would it be okay if I come see you this Saturday?"

"Will you stay over?"

"No, I have to get back. I'm seeing the kids Sunday. But we'll still be able to have some quality time together. Okay?"

"Wonderful."

He hung up and she sat staring at the telephone for a few minutes. *We know each other so well, and yet we don't know each other at all. We've never said, I love you. Never once.*

And then, as if someone had suddenly switched on a strong light, she thought, *We know the truth not only by the reason, but by the heart.*

Kathryn was immersed in preparations for the grand jury hearing when Walt Earheart called.

"Kathryn? It's Walt Earheart. I've got Dave Granz over here. A bundle of stuff on Russell just came in by courier from Steve Giordano in Sacramento. I think you'll want to take a look at it."

The scars on Dave's face and hands were still covered by light dressings; no one outside the hospital staff had yet seen him without them. He had a strap sling on his right arm. He looked up as Kathryn came in.

"I'll say one thing for your friend Giordano, he can kick ass," he said. "He's pulled a hell of a lot of stuff together in a week."

"Turns out he's a big fan of yours, too," Kathryn said. "He said there's no question you're the one who got Russell."

"Maybe I did and maybe I didn't," Dave said sourly. "But he sure as hell got me."

Earheart let that one go by him, swiveling around in his chair to lift a thick bundle of files out of a box on his rear table and put them in a pile on the desk in front of him.

"All this already?" Kathryn said. "That's astonishing."

"Like Dave said, Giordano did wonders in Sacramento," Walt said, opening a file. "Okay, here we go, James Leland Russell, born Chicago, October third, 1952. Mother died when he was a kid. The Chicago cops checked juvenile records, came up with a file on him. From that they ran down which school he went to. Seems he was in trouble a lot; at one point it got so bad they threatened to throw him out. There's a whole list of things, fights, truancy, some girl who claimed he was a peeper, a kid who said Russell poisoned his rabbits. The school counselors put some of it down to his home life. His father had remarried, a Hispanic woman with a daughter about the same age as the boy. According to a social worker's report, the daughter wasn't any better than she had to be."

"How did he end up in juvenile court?"

"Vandalism. Breaking windows, slashing tires on a neighbor's car."

"Is the father still alive?"

"You remember Russell told me his parents died in a fire? They checked newspaper files in Chicago and came up with the story: Donald Russell, his wife, and stepdaughter died in an apartment-house fire, August 1968. Cause of death was asphyxiation—carbon monoxide poisoning. It was established the seat of the fire was some trash ignited by a cigarette butt: apparently the wife was a heavy smoker, the fire inspectors figured that had to be what started it. Put it another way: they couldn't come up with anything to indicate otherwise."

"You mean they suspected something?"

"Reading between the lines."

"Where was Russell when all this happened?"

"College. His freshman year."

"In August?"

"Nobody really checked," Earheart said. "Why would they?"

"What did he do after his parents died?"

"Lived with an aunt in Broadmoor, south of San Francisco, went to college up there. The Department of Justice team contacted the college. He was an adequate student, didn't stand out."

He paused, letting her think about it, and she did. "What about girls? Did he have any relationships?"

Dave shook his head. "Nothing on that. All we know is, he got through college and went on to grad school."

"What was his major?"

"English."

"You're not going to tell me it was Blaise Pascal?"

"No such luck. But get this: his master's thesis was 'Themes of emasculation in *Hamlet*.' "

"Wait till the shrinks get hold of that," Kathryn said. "Did he go straight into teaching?"

"Yeah, got credentialed, taught for a couple of years at Upper River High School in Marin County," Walt told her. "Then in seventy-four he was drafted, went to Nam. He served in the Office of Military Information in Saigon till the end, never heard a shot fired in anger. After he was discharged, he went back to Upper River. Stayed there three years, then quit to teach at Canyon Heights High, a girls' school in Redwood City. That's where he met his wife: Carol Woodley, as she was then."

"That's it?"

"That's just the beginning, Kathryn," Earheart said, his voice grim. "We opened up a real can of worms with this one. Steve got the DOJ team to check San Francisco and San Mateo County homicide files for the period Russell lived in San Francisco, concentrating on any unsolved murders involving Hispanic women between sixteen and twenty-five. They came up with three. All in the Bay Area, all hookers. Ages nineteen, twenty-four, and twenty. Cops up there thought it was probably the same guy did all of them. They never found him."

"How were they killed?"

"One strangled, one suffocated. The third one was stabbed to death. They'd all been beaten pretty badly."

"Sexually assaulted?"

"Forensics found no traces of semen, no fresh vaginal or anal trauma."

"What about mutilations?"

Earheart shook his head. "First thing DOJ looked for. No, there was nothing like that."

"One thing I remember Steve saying about serial killers, Walt. He said, 'Don't expect them to be doing the same things when they're forty they might have done when they were twenty-five.' It's progressive, like cancer. Were there any other similarities?"

"Nothing that matches our guy."

"But?"

Earheart frowned. "The reason they thought it was the

same guy. All the victims had long hair. He chopped it off, probably with a knife."

"He said I'd made him angry. Very angry. He made me lie face down on the bed and he, he . . ."

"Go on."

"He tied my hands. My feet. And he cut . . . he cut . . ."

She thrust her fingers into her hair, an unexpected gesture that seemed completely out of place.

"The hair," she breathed. "Of course. That's what it was."

"What?"

"Sorry, Walt. Something just occurred to me. Finish what you were saying about Russell. What about Redwood City?"

"Yeah, while Russell was teaching there, two murders were committed nearby, one in Burlingame, the other in San Bruno. In both cases the MO bore some similarities to the San Francisco killings, but the Redwood City cops never put them together. They did establish that the perpetrator had probably removed the bodies from the primary crime scene, dumped them where they were found. One victim was left in a storm drain, the second in an alley behind a shopping mall."

"Hispanic girls again?"

"One eighteen and the other twenty."

"Hookers?"

"No. One worked in a supermarket, the other was in college."

"Hair cut off?"

"One was. The other not."

"What about coded notes? Anything like that anywhere?"

"Nothing recorded."

"And no one apprehended?"

"The cases are still open."

"It could still be nothing but coincidence," Kathryn said.

"We thought that, too."

"Until what?"

"Until this," Walt said and laid a file in front of her.

"United States Army Criminal Investigative Command, Saigon," she read. "What's all this about?"

"Tell her, Walt," Dave said.

"We got it almost by accident. What happened was, I went up to see Dave at the hospital, because I promised to keep him posted on developments. Doc Nelson was there, and when I was telling Dave about the way the hair was cut off, Doc got real thoughtful, you know?"

"I asked him what was bothering him," Dave said, "and he told us it was something he remembered from when he was in Nam. You knew Doc was over there with the Army, didn't you?"

"Yes, I did. Go on."

"He said he vaguely remembered doing an autopsy on a Vietnamese girl who'd been found badly beaten and sexually assaulted. She'd had her hair cut off like that, crudely, like the guy used a knife. And I said, I wonder if Russell was in Nam, too?"

"We called Steve," Walt put in, "and he told us Russell's service files were as clean as a whistle. So on the off chance, I told him what Doc had said and asked him if they could check the Army Criminal Investigation Division's files at Fort Holabird. And there it was. During the year Russell was in Saigon, they had a couple of unsolved murders of B-girls. CID got into it because each of them had last been seen with a soldier. They were both killed the same way, tied up, hair cut off, badly beaten and sexually assaulted."

"We all just assumed the victims had short hair," Kathryn said. "Even Doc. We had no reason to think otherwise. But they . . . it was him, wasn't it?"

Earheart nodded. "Is that what you meant earlier?"

Kathryn nodded as the picture of Carol Russell staring out of the window in the depersonalized little apartment reappeared in her mind.

"Did they have long hair?" she asked.

"Only one," she said. "Barbara Gates had long hair. Why do you ask?"

Carol Russell made no reply, but continued staring stolidly out of the window.

"Carol? Is there something significant about the length of the girls' hair?"

She let her breath out slowly. "I think I've got it, Walt."

He frowned at her uncomprehendingly. "Got what?"

"The key to Carol Russell's locked door."

"Do you want to tell us what you're talking about?"

"You said yourself you had the feeling she was holding out on us. That she knows something she won't tell. Or maybe can't tell."

"And?"

"I think she knew, Walt. I think she knew."

Earheart stared at her. "You mean, about . . . the others?"

Kathryn told them quickly the relevant part of her conversation with Carol.

"Steve said the reason she was holding back might be because of something Russell had done, something that forced her to be part of his fantasy."

"And so?"

"I'm guessing now. But it would explain why he did it."

"Go on."

"She guessed, or she put it all together, it doesn't make any difference how. She confronted him and he did it to her. Remember he said it was a punishment. For asking too many questions. He did everything except actually kill her, tied her up, probably stripped her naked first. Maybe he beat her, maybe he even cut her. That's why she's so terrified of him. And why she's too ashamed to tell us. She knows he did the other killings. She's known all these years."

"Jesus, Kathryn, if we can get her to talk . . ." Dave said.

"Maybe we can. It's worth trying."

"Look, I know I'm probably being slow here," Earheart said, "but does one of you want to explain this hair-cutting thing to me?"

"Punishment, Walt," Dave said. "If they didn't fit the fantasy, he punished them. Cutting off their hair was part of it."

"Then why didn't he do it to Barbara Gates?"

"A guess?" Kathryn said. "Maybe she was more compliant, maybe she got nearer to fulfilling the fantasy than any of the others. We'll probably never know."

Walt looked at her, then at Dave, who pointed a finger-and-thumb pistol at the telephone and fired it. Earheart checked his book for the number of the apartment to which they'd moved Carol Russell, then picked up the telephone and dialed. They could hear the phone ringing. Slowly the big man's expression changed, becoming a frown of concern. After twenty rings, he put the telephone down with a decisive bang and stood up, reaching for his jacket.

"She doesn't answer," he said urgently. "We'd better get over there."

39

LOOSE ENDS BOTHERED KATHRYN, AND THERE WERE ALTO-gether too many of them in the disappearance of Carol Russell; for the moment, however, there wasn't much else she could do but voice her unease and leave Walt Earheart and his detectives to do what they were best at.

The mystery phone call that she had taken at the West Bayshore Drive apartment was still just that, a mystery—as was the reason for Carol's disappearance from the second apartment they'd moved her to. She had vanished completely; every available detective was assiduously trying to establish her whereabouts because without Carol Russell, Kathryn had no case. Visited by the Redwood City PD, Carol's seventy-eight-year-old father, George Woodley, confirmed his daughter was not with him at his home, and had not been in contact. There was a sister in Oregon; a call was put in to the police department at Boring, who reported back that Mrs. Patricia Bundy was on vacation in Canada and the house was closed up.

Other leads being pursued included a list of the names of friends and fellow teachers with whom Carol Russell had worked when she lived in Redwood City. Each of them would be located and checked out. But that was going to take a lot of time; and they were running out of that.

"Where does that leave the case against Russell?" Steve asked her. He'd arrived from Sacramento in time for brunch, and they drove down to a fish restaurant called The Captain's Table on the wharf at Espanola. Emma was spending the day with her friend Julie.

"Up the well-known creek," Kathryn said. "I hate to even think about Russell walking away from this, much less put it into words: but it's a possibility."

"Hang in there," he said, smiling. "There's still a good chance they'll find her, Kathryn. And you'll get your indictment."

"I hope you're right," she said. "What are you working on now?"

"That's one of the things I have to tell you. I've been assigned to a case up in Susanville. I'm going to be there for a while."

"So we won't see each other."

"That's the way it looks. I was hoping you'd . . ." He stopped, holding her gaze. Kathryn shook her head.

"I thought about it," she said. "I thought about it till my brain ached. And the answer is no. I don't think Sacramento is what I want, Steve."

He didn't speak for what seemed a long time.

"I think I always knew you were going to say that," he said, regret in his voice. "I even think I understand why. But I'm still disappointed."

"What do you mean, why?"

"Why you made the decision you did. You need to be in control, don't you? You see us, being part of a couple, as some sort of surrender you're not sure you want to make. Am I making any sort of sense?"

"That's not the me I see in the mirror," Kathryn said. "But perhaps it's the me you see. Perhaps it's the me everyone sees. If it is, I can't change it."

"Do you remember the day we took Emma to San Francisco? We talked that night, about working together. Close, warm, as lovers. And you said something about not being able to imagine yourself as a fifty-year-old prosecutor."

"I still can't."

"Then you said, I guess I'll just have to wait and see. And I realized as you said it that you'd excluded me from that future—without even thinking about it."

And I heard the sadness in his voice and wondered why, she thought. Neither of them spoke for a little while.

"We could still see each other," he said.

"No. I want to be honest with you, Steve. I looked in my heart and you weren't there."

"That's honest," he said. Whatever he was feeling, nothing showed on his face. "Not to say brutal."

He got the check and they walked down to the end of the wharf, staring out at the ocean. Just a little while ago they hadn't needed to talk, Kathryn thought; now there were so many things they needed to say, and there was no way to say any of them. After a while Steve straightened up, nodded.

"I'll drive you home," he said.

"No, Steve," Kathryn replied. "If you don't mind, I think I'd like to stay here for a while. I can walk back."

He stood irresolutely for a moment, then the faint smile she knew so well now touched the corners of his mouth.

"I want you to regret this," he said.

She smiled in return, no less sadly. "Maybe I already do," she said softly.

"You're quite a lady, Kathryn," he said. "I'm going to miss you."

"I'll miss you too."

Steve shook his head slowly, the faint smile fading.

"I doubt that," he said. He kissed her quickly on the lips, then walked away. She watched until his broad back disappeared in the crowd, then went across to the balustrade at the end of the wharf. She stared at the water for what seemed a long time. Gulls and pelicans wheeled above. Down below, a sea otter slid silently through the water. She watched it till it swam out of sight, then turned and made her way along the wharf. Emma would be waiting. Time to go home.

Sunday night, Richard Sanchez revealed exclusively on his evening broadcast that the investigation of the background of James Leland Russell, accused of the murder of four women in Santa Rita, had been extended to include the deaths of a number of other young women in the San Francisco and Redwood City areas. He went into enough detail for it to be quite apparent that he knew what he was talking about.

Once again, as Norm Podnoretz resignedly observed, the manure hit the air-conditioning. And once again Sheriff Jake Gylam angrily called a Monday meeting to bang heads on the subject of how the hell Sanchez had gotten hold of the information. Since nobody had the remotest idea, it was pretty much a waste of time, and the meeting broke up without anything having been conclusively established other than that Jake Gylam was not a happy camper. Which, as Hal Benton remarked in an aside to Kathryn as they rode down in the elevator, was of considerably less import than the fact that whoever was passing the information to Sanchez was being very selective about what they gave him.

"All the material is confidential, of course, and whoever is doing it knows they'll get their ass fired out of here the second we find out who it is, but they haven't done anything actually criminal," he observed. "The more I think about that, the more I wonder whether the leak is in our office rather than Jake's."

"Let's hope for all our sakes you're wrong," Kathryn said, but the thought, once planted, remained stubbornly difficult to uproot.

Tuesday morning Dave Granz appeared in her doorway.

"What are you doing here?" Kathryn asked him. "I thought you were still on leave?"

"I got bored sitting around," he said. "So I dropped in to see Walt. Listen, I hate to do this, but I've got some bad news for you, Kathryn."

"Seems like the only kind I get these days," Kathryn said. "What is it this time?"

"Walt was going to call, but I said I'd tell you. The San Francisco police found Carol Russell. She's dead."

She just stared at him, too surprised to speak. Then she managed a one-word question.

"How?" Dave echoed. "She drowned. Her body was washed up on Angel Island yesterday morning. Positive ID, looks like suicide, as far as they can tell. Coroner estimated she'd been dead a couple of days."

"Why?" Kathryn whispered.

"Why are there more questions than answers, Grandpa?" Dave said, sitting down in one of the wicker chairs. "Why wouldn't she tell us what was bothering her? Why did she take off like that? Who's feeding all our secrets to your friend Sanchez?"

"Dammit, Dave, he's not my friend."

"It's still a good question."

"I know. I keep looking at everyone in the office and wondering ... could it be you? Or you?"

"At least you know it's not me," he said. "I wouldn't tell Sanchez the time if I owned Bulova. Incidentally, how's your case looking?"

"As of this moment, it doesn't look as if I have one,"

Kathryn said. "Without Carol Russell I'm dead in the water."

"You can still get him with the forensic evidence, can't you?"

"If it gets here in time," she said gloomily.

"Cheer up," he said. "You can come to my unveiling."

"What?"

"Thursday," he said, gesturing with his left hand at the dressings on his face. "My unveiling. The world sees for the first time the lovely new me. Hey, I've got an idea. How about we celebrate Friday? Pick Emma up from school and get pizza. Like the old days?"

"You never change, do you?"

"Wrong," he said emphatically. "I learned something when . . . this happened. Life's now. The past is just that, the past. And tomorrow is not guaranteed. There's no time for grudges."

I could change.

That'll be the day.

"Since you say that, let me ask you a serious question," Kathryn said. "How do you feel about Russell?"

"That sick bastard? If I had my way I'd drag him out of the County Jail, stick him up against a wall, and shoot him."

"No time for grudges, huh?" Kathryn smiled. "Don't worry, he'll end up in the gas chamber sooner or later."

"That's what worries me," Granz said thoughtfully. "Justice always takes the long way around. Even if you get the death penalty, it might easily be ten years before they gas him. A bullet draws a straight line."

"You're not talking about justice," Kathryn told him. "You're talking about revenge."

"You forget," Dave said. "I'm a victim. Now, about that pizza?"

The detention officers who ferried the prisoners to and from the County Jail to the Courts Building never stopped bitching about the job. This morning, DO Eddie Burkholder was in charge. He was about thirty, with thinning fair hair, bright blue eyes, and the beginning of a beer gut.

"People don't realize how stressful this job is," he said to his partner as they rode across. "Four twelve-hour shifts a week. I'm telling you, I worked four years as a reserve, I never was uptight the way I am now."

"Yeah, I know what you mean," the second DO said. He was a thin man in his mid-forties, with bony shoulders and a long angular face. His ID nameplate said SCHELL. "I reckon it's because you got to watch yourself the whole time. Every day, taking what, a hundred custodies across to the court, bringing them back. That's one fourth of the jail population. People don't realize."

"You know how many we got back in there right now?" Burkholder said. "Three hundred ninety-one. Three hundred ninety-one prisoners in a facility was built to take what, two hundred?"

"Two thirty," Schell said. "Shit, that's nothing. You know how many people we processed in and out last year? Forty thousand, man. Forty thousand. That's the same as the population of the city."

"You guys do a great job considering the difficulties," Lee said. "It must be tough working in conditions like that."

The two officers looked at him as if they had been surprised by his ability to talk.

"Listen, you prisoners don't know the half of it," Schell said. "Just getting toilet paper to everyone is bad enough. You think about it, we never stop, moving prisoners back and forth to see their attorneys, standing by while the doc makes his rounds, or the chaplain, or the probation officers or whoever."

"What I can't figure is why the fuck the county can't build a tunnel underneath Alameda, save us all this hassle," Burkholder said.

"They don't have money to build a bigger jail, they sure as hell can't put no tunnel in," Schell told him.

"I understand it was also because the jail is too close to the floodplain of the river," Lee said.

"That right?" Burkholder said.

"How long have you been a detention officer?" Lee asked him.

"Just coming up for two years," Burkholder said. "What you going across for today?"

"Bail hearing," Lee said.

"Who's your lawyer?" Burkholder asked.

"Leonard Wurzelman," Lee said. "You ever hear of him?"

"I just realized who you are," the DO said. "You shut your fucking mouth, I don't want to talk to you."

Most of the prisoners in the van—only one or two wearing civilian clothes—were appearing in court and would be there all morning; Lee's bail hearing took only half an hour, after which he was brought back to the Alameda Street facility shackled to another man, a surly, dark-haired Hispanic whose case had been continued. DO Schell brought them in from the van and shepherded them to one side while he talked to the woman desk officer at the receiving unit.

"Returning twenty-two twenty-eight Enriquez, general facility, forty-four thirty-nine Russell, special supervision," he said.

"Put them in number eight, Harve," the female DO at the desk told him.

"They put a plate on that lock in there yet?" the DO asked, as if the two prisoners were in another room. The female DO flashed an angry look at him.

"Goddammit, Harve, you ought to know better than that!" she snapped.

Schell looked over his shoulder at his prisoners. Enriquez was sitting with shoulders slumped, staring at the floor. Lee stared stolidly at the wall as he had done since he came into the facility.

"Ah, shit, they don't know what the hell we're talkin' about, Lacey," the DO said. "Let me have the key."

He took them along the corridor and put them into the holding cell, taking off the leg manacles holding the two men together. Then he locked the door and went away. Lee turned to the Hispanic man.

"You!" he snapped. "You speak English?"

"¿Que?" the man said.

"For Christ's sake! Have you got a comb? A nail file? Something thin, hard?"

"¿Que?" the man said again, staring at him with dumb astonishment.

"¿Un peine? ¿Alguna cosa delgada?"

The Hispanic man's face brightened. He dug into the pocket of his jumpsuit and produced a comb. Lee snatched it off him and went across to the door. Squatting on his haunches, he found he could see the cam in the lock. He broke off the teeth of the comb and stuck the spine into the space, levering it between the lock and the doorjamb. He felt something give; the cam moved back and the door opened.

He bent low and eased his head out until he could see into the corridor. Anyone looking would not expect to see a head or foot off the floor. It was empty. To the left was the door leading into the reception facility. To the right was a large sally-port garage door: it was open. He could see cars going by on the street outside. He eased out into the corridor, his heart pounding like a drum.

"Hey, hombre, espera!" Enriquez said hoarsely behind him. Lee shut the door firmly and walked toward the garage door. He was trembling with fear, tension, excitement, disbelief. A deputy standing by a patrol car looked at him incuriously as he walked out onto the street.

Jesus, he thought. I'm out.

Fifty yards west on Alameda he came to the bridge across the river. He went down the steps on the far side then up the hill. His heart was hammering and he fought the urge to run, expecting any moment to hear the sound of police sirens behind him at the jail. He came out of the park in back of the post office building; veering left, he emerged on Mercado Street, checking parked cars as he went.

A dozen or so cars later he came upon an Olds Cutlass Supreme standing outside a one-hour photo facility, keys in the ignition. He looked around quickly, saw no one, got in, and sped north up Mercado, heading for the Alvarado Highway. He tuned the radio to the news channel; they had to have discovered his escape by now, but there was nothing on the news. He kept going north, across the interchange and on through dark stands of redwood up the winding mountain road that led to Mountain View.

The town looked like a set for a western. He slowed down and wound down the window. Loud country music came from the open doors of the bars along the single street. Lee parked the car in a space between two pickups. A trio dressed in mountain man uniform—baseball cap, tank top, jeans, cowboy boots—was drinking canned beer on a bench on the sidewalk outside a place called Larry's. Lee got out, leaving the keys in the dash, smiling at them.

"Hi, guys," he said. "Can you tell me where the post office is?"

"Two blocks down, one block over," one of them said. "Just passin' through?"

"I'm from Carmel," Lee said. "Let me ask you something, will my car be safe if I leave it here overnight?"

"Sure," one of them said. "We'll keep an eye on it for you. Right, you guys?"

"Right," another said. "Asshole."

They all laughed. Lee smiled. Those good ole boys would probably be out joyriding in that Cutlass before he even got where he was going. Wherever the cops found it, it wouldn't be in Mountain View. He started walking. A long hike lay ahead of him, but at the end of it he would be safe. He looked back over his shoulder, smiling now.

Run, run, as fast as you can . . .

As soon as he got the news of Russell's escape, a little after midday, Hal Benton called Kathryn to his office. He looked distracted, like a man who has problems coming at him from every point of the compass.

"I just talked to Jake Gylam," he told Kathryn. "If he had any more egg on his face he'd be *huevos rancheros.*"

"I heard his statement to the media," she said. "I still don't believe it."

Benton shrugged. "All we know so far is, a detention officer took Russell and another man back from the Courts Building and put them in a holding cell on the Perry Street side of the jail. When he came back to take them to their cell blocks, Russell was gone. The other man, Enriquez, said he used a comb to pick the lock."

"A comb?"

"The lock on the door of the holding cell was faulty. They were waiting for metal plates to be fitted."

"How did Russell find that out?"

Benton shrugged again. "Nobody knows. They've got a series of one-way doors and locks over there nobody could get through in the normal course of events, even if they were armed with riot guns."

"Yet Russell just walked out. One of the damned deputies even saw him go. They better not let him get away, that's all."

"Gylam's got everybody on the street except the Texas Rangers. There's a statewide alert," Benton said. "Russell can't get far. No car, no money. Don't worry, Jake says they'll pick him up real fast."

"Is that supposed to reassure us?"

"We'll get him," Benton said grimly. "We have to. Or Richard Sanchez and the rest of the media are going to crucify us."

"Is there anything I can do?"

"You might try praying," Benton said grimly.

Kathryn went back to her own office, looking at the piles of material she had gathered for the grand jury hearing next Tuesday. She let out her breath in a rueful sigh. As she sat down behind her desk, Marcia came in. She was wearing a tunic dress with a blue and white polka-dot blouse underneath it. Her long black hair was shampoo-shiny.

"You look spiffy," Kathryn said.

"All compliments gratefully received." Marcia grinned. She handed Kathryn a small mailer. "Special delivery. Just came."

Kathryn took it from her. The return address in San Francisco meant nothing to her, nor did the name of the sender, Sylvia Bannerman. She ripped open the envelope. A bunch of keys with a plastic tag fell onto the desk. Inside was a one-page letter and a sealed envelope with Kathryn's name on it. The single-page letter was from Sylvia Bannerman. She and Carol Russell, she wrote, had been old friends; they had taught school together in Redwood City. Carol had stayed with her for a few days before she killed herself. One of her last requests was to ask her, if anything should happen to her, to send the enclosed envelope and the keys to Kathryn.

Kathryn slit open the envelope.

Dear Kathryn,

I am sorry I ran away but I had no choice. It was because of Richard Sanchez, the man who does those TV programs. I don't know how he knew where I was, but he called me at the apartment. He wanted an exclusive interview for his show and said if I didn't agree, he would give my phone number and address to the newspapers. He said they would make my life a living hell. He didn't know that it already is.

I am staying with a friend. She will send this to you. I found the keys the same night I found the panties. I think I always knew there was somewhere Lee went, and if this is the place it may hold the answer to all your questions, and many that you have never asked. I want you to know I tried so hard to do what you wanted me to do. I think if we had talked some more, I might have had the courage to go through with it. But the knowledge of what my husband has done is too much for me to bear.

Good-bye,
Carol Russell

The key tag read MARCUS REALTY CO., 221 Boulder, Mountain View. She picked up the telephone and dialed Walt Earheart's number. Fifteen minutes later a squad of detectives was on its way up into the mountains with the set of keys and a sheaf of photographs of James Leland Russell. Less than an hour later, Kathryn's phone rang.

"Bingo," Earheart said without preamble. "My men spoke to Charles Marcus, a realtor up in Mountain View, showed him the photograph of Russell and the keys. He ID'd Russell as a man he knows as Bernard Niemand, says he rented him a cabin way up in the hills about eighteen months ago. Niemand—Russell—paid six months in advance, comes in and pays cash when the rent falls due. You like the alias?"

"Niemand?"

"It's German for 'nobody,'" Earheart said. "The creep has a sense of humor. Marcus says the place is a big old wood-and-concrete cabin, hidden way on back in the brush, miles from anyplace."

"You think Russell might be there?"

"I'm sending in a team right now. If he's in there, we've got his ass."

"Aren't you worried you'll tip him off if you show up in force?"

"No chance," Earheart said. "It's down a single-lane dirt road, two, three miles off the main highway. If he's in there, no way can he get out."

"And if he's not?"

"We'll stake the place out and wait for him. Kathryn, you know what I wish? I wish I could send Dave Granz up there. If he knew about this, his teeth would bleed."

"Listen, Walt, I go to the grand jury Tuesday. I need what's in that cabin."

"Take the advice of my sainted old mother," Earheart said. "Hope and pray."

"Either way, you're going to need a search warrant." She looked at the clock. She would probably be able to find one of the judges in his chambers around midday. "Who's going to swear the affidavit?"

"I'll do it."

"Fine, come on down. There are a couple of other things I want to talk to you about anyway."

"Like what?"

"Like I think I know how to flush out the snitch who's been passing information to Sanchez."

"By God, Kathryn," Earheart said. "If you can swing that, Jake Gylam will be your friend for life."

"Wow," Kathryn said, smiling. "Imagine."

40

THE STAKEOUT WAS METICULOUSLY PLANNED. ONCE RECON-naissance had established that the cabin was unoccupied, seven unmarked units—all observing radio silence and communicating only by cellular phone in case Russell had a scanner to check police channels—were strategically placed. The car code-named Alpha, parked a little distance off the highway, covered the entrance to the unmarked road that led to the cabin; in it sat detectives Joe Coughlin and Martin Silvero. Two more units were on the highway about five hundred yards farther on, ready to join them in sealing off the road behind Russell the minute he turned off the highway. That accomplished, the two units stationed near the cabin would move uphill to meet him, while the other two, concealed below the sight line on his flanks, would also close in. Once Russell was in, there was no way out.

Jack Burrows, Earheart's team leader, had his units in place before noon, the detectives and deputies sweating in their flak jackets. A few minutes after one the team leader's cellular phone burred and he picked it up.

"Alpha, Jack. We have a problem. A TV remote van entering the restricted area. What do we do?"

"A what?" Burrows's voice squeaked with disbelief.

"I'm telling you a fucking KKSU remote is on its way in there, Jack," Martin Silvero snapped. "You want us to let him roll or what?"

Burrows thought quickly. "Stay put. Let him roll. I'll intercept." He tapped George Tannenbaum on the shoulder and pointed up the hill. "Up there. Fast!"

"You got it," Tannenbaum said, and gunned the car out of the yard and up the dirt track.

"Can you believe this?" Jack gritted as they slewed up the hill. "That sonofabitch Sanchez has turned up. With a goddamned film crew!"

Tannenbaum shrugged; not my problem, his expression said. He pulled the car around the long uphill left-hand bend and they saw the KKSU-TV van with its satellite dish skewed across the road. A videocamera operator was already taking establishing shots. Burrows got out of the car. He was clearly having trouble controlling himself, but he managed it.

"I am going to give you and your people exactly thirty seconds to get out of here," he said, his voice all the more menacing because there was no menace in it. "No discussions, nothing. Out, or I arrest the whole damned lot of you for obstruction of justice and anything else I can think of."

"What's in that house down there?" Sanchez asked, ignoring the threat.

"If you know enough to come up here, you know the rest."

"I'm going down there. You can't stop me."

"No, you're not. You're getting out of here now. Don't argue, just do it."

"It's a stakeout, isn't it? You think Russell will come here, don't you? Well, I'm not moving. And you know you can't make me."

"Twenty seconds," Burrows said. Inside his car the cellular phone burred. Tannenbaum picked it up.

"Jack," he said, his voice urgent.

"What?" Burrows snapped angrily into the phone. His voice changed. "What? Oh, shit. Yes, move in. Fast, dammit!" He threw the phone into the car. "You, Sanchez! Get that fucking truck around behind this boulder."

It was too late. Up on the crest of the hill they saw a pickup come to a sudden halt. A moment later a man got out and ran into the woods.

"Jesus Christ, are you getting it?" Sanchez shouted at the videocamera operator, who waved a hand, shut up, yes.

Burrows was already in the Jeep. It roared off up the hill toward the abandoned pickup. At almost the same moment it reached the truck, the three units that had come up from the highway rocked to a dust-raising stop behind it.

"Spread out, the bastard ran into the woods!" Burrows shouted, spilling out of the car. "That way, over there, over there!" He banged on the car roof. "George, get on the radio, Code Three. Tell 'em we want a chopper up here, fast!"

Within twenty minutes, by any standards an admirable response time, four green-and-whites had arrived and a helicopter was circling the area. After three hours, the search was abandoned. Russell had got clean away.

"You going to call Earheart?" Tannenbaum asked Burrows.

"You want to do it for me?"

"Thanks a lot, but no thanks," George said. "You want my advice?"

"Go ahead."

"See the chaplain," the fat man said. "Get yourself a TS slip."

"What the fuck is a TS slip?" Burrows asked angrily.

"Tough shit," Tannenbaum said.

The side road was not posted; even with Earheart's detailed directions, Kathryn very nearly missed it. She swung off the highway and shifted into low gear to negotiate the steep, twisting, single-lane road that led upward into the trees, turning on itself like a snake every two hundred yards. As she negotiated a tight right-hand bend, she saw a shack down at the bottom of the slope that looked like something out of *Tobacco Road.* As she passed, two huge black Rottweilers hurled themselves at the gate, baying with fury. Even inside the car she felt the chill of fear. What sort of people lived like this?

A little farther up the hill the surface changed to dirt. On the right was a painted sign that said USE THIS ROAD AT YOUR OWN RISK. Thick brush crowded the sides of the dirt road, scratching the sides of the car. The trail led up to the top of the hill and over, into a stand of pine that kept out the light of the sun. Then she came out of the timber into open countryside, sloping away in front of her. Off the track a tow truck was hitching a chain to a pickup; she identified it automatically, a Dodge Adventurer Club Cab 100. Russell's pickup. This must be where he had seen the TV van down below, she thought.

She could still hear the disbelief in Walt Earheart's voice.

"We had the bastard, Kathryn, we had him," he said wearily. "And Sanchez screwed it up."

Way on down ahead she could see a rooftop surrounded by tall trees. The track bent to the right, around a huge boulder, maybe twenty feet high. As she came past it, two deputies materialized from nowhere. Both were armed with pump-action shotguns. She wound down her window and held out her ID.

"Hi, guys," she said. "You made me jump."

"That's about the general idea," one of them said with a grin. "Go on ahead, Ms. Mackay, they told us you were coming."

As she approached the old house, another deputy waved her over to park under the trees that shaded it. She got out of the car and stood looking at it. Single story, concrete block base and foundations, wood shingle sidings and roof, sash windows. Transplant it to Laguna del Mar and you could put a quarter-of-a-million-dollar price tag on it. Up here in the boonies, you'd be lucky to get a third of that.

There were SO green and white police cars everywhere, the usual electronic noise that was a characteristic of crime scenes coming out of their open windows. She signed the log and went inside. A hallway ran from the front to the back of the house. Two large rooms at the front, one a bedroom, the other a living room sparsely but comfortably furnished, lots of wood paneling, big stone open fireplaces. Each had its complement of technicians.

In back to the right was a big, old-fashioned kitchen; three of the Crime Scene team were taking it apart inch by inch. To the left were two more doors, one leading into a bathroom that contained an old clawfoot steel bath, a hand basin, and a toilet with an overhead cistern and chain pull. The second door was open; stairs led down to the cellar. She looked down and saw Walt Earheart.

"Come into my parlor," he said, his voice flat and tired.

She went down the steep wooden stairs into a big stone-walled, stone-floored cellar that appeared to run the entire length of the house, starkly lit by the photographic lamps and auxiliary lighting. Over at one end of the cellar was a huge stainless steel drainboard and sluice sink, as big as, perhaps bigger than, anything she had ever seen at the morgue. On it were glass jars full of scalpels, every conceivable shape and configuration. Other jars, contents as yet undetermined, were being carefully examined and identified by investigators prior to being taken back to the lab for full forensic examination. In the center of the concrete floor was a drainage sluice. Another investigator was kneeling beside it, scraping the sides with a long-handled implement and depositing what he found in specimen cases.

Two huge wall-mounted air conditioners kept the temperature just a few degrees above freezing; but even had it not been bone cold in the cellar, Kathryn would still have shivered. Ranged like trophies along one wall in front of her, tanned, cured, and stretched on circular basketry hoops, like the insane craft work of some unimaginable tribe, were seven triangles of pubis.

"Oh, Jesus, Walt," she said faintly, turning away. "Seven?"

"This is where he brought them," Earheart said. "There's a sort of room in back. Nothing much in there, a table, a bed. It's still got the supplier's plastic cover on it. We found ropes, handcuffs, blood, semen stains, God knows how many different kinds of female hair. The place is like Bluebeard's castle. Did you go into the bedroom?"

"Not yet."

"It's incredible. Every inch of the walls lined with Polaroids. You look at it and you can't believe what you're seeing. Closeups of things . . . like a nightmare. Some of them are the Santa Rita victims. There are others, God knows how many. It looks like he also made videotapes. Insanity. We've found drawers stuffed full of women's clothing, shoes, underwear, right next to shelves of books and magazines about psychiatry and psychology. And down here . . . It's like a goddamn butcher shop. If I wasn't so goddamned angry, I'd be sick to my stomach."

"So Russell was here?"

"Probably came straight up here," Earheart told her. "We were that close."

"Don't beat your brains out. You did the best you could."

"At least it wasn't a complete loss," the big man said venomously. "Richard Sanchez got his thirty seconds of videotape."

"I have really had it with that guy," Kathryn said. "You want to help me screw him, Walt? And get his snitch at the same time?"

Earheart grinned.

"You saw Carol Russell's note. She said Sanchez telephoned her at the apartment, remember? Probably got the number from his snitch, right?"

Earheart nodded. "And?"

"Suppose we arrest him for intimidating a witness?"

"Tell me more," Earheart said. "Is this what you were talking about last night?"

"Here's the plan. We arrest him, offer him a deal, immunity from prosecution in return for the name of the snitch and a guarantee that he'll testify against him at trial. You know Sanchez. He'll go after it like a barracuda after a herring. The media will do the rest. You know how much they love a reporter who reveals his source."

"About as much as a cop who sells out his snitch."

"Okay, let's talk to Hal about it," Kathryn said, grinning. "How about tomorrow?"

"What's tomorrow, Thursday? Fine."

Kathryn looked around at the toiling crime scene investigators. "Who's the investigating officer up here?" she asked.

"Mike Harkins," Earheart said. "You want to talk to him?"

"No, I was just wondering how long it would be before they get through."

"You're thinking about your grand jury. They'll probably be done with the grunt work by tomorrow night. But it's going to take days just to inventory all this stuff. And God alone knows how long to complete all the forensic tests."

"Lieutenant, telephone!" someone called.

Kathryn followed Earheart back upstairs, not unhappy to leave behind the nightmarish atmosphere of the cellar. Earheart was in the lobby, a cellular phone to his ear.

"Hold on," he said to the caller. "You heading back?"

"I've got a few things to do at the office. Then I have to pick up Emma."

"Okay, see you tomorrow," Earheart said.

It was a little after five by the time Kathryn got back to the County Building. She felt drained, exhausted by the day's events and the things she had seen in the cabin at Mountain View. No matter how hard she tried to block it from her mind, she couldn't help but think about how those young women might have felt, lying bound and gagged in that cold, bare room on the sweating plastic mattress cover, waiting ... waiting ...

At the end of the day she piled her things into her briefcase, said good night to her colleagues, and went down to the parking lot, beginning the daily metamorphosis that was as much a part of her routine as setting the alarm. She drove almost automatically, so used to the movements of the traffic and the route she was traveling that she hardly needed to think about it.

"Mommy, hooray, you're early," Emma shouted when she saw her. "We won't be late for swim class."

"Maybe we can even stop off for a frozen yogurt on the way home," said Kathryn, grinning. "Come on, get in the car."

The swim class was held in the children's pool in back of a leisure complex in Catalina, about a fifteen-minute drive away. It was relaxing to just sit in a shell chair and empty her brain, another mother among the dozens all around, their children shouting, splashing, crying, running by. When the lesson was over, they drove back up the freeway and took the exit for Laguna del Mar, where they stopped at the Fancy Freeze and had their frozen yogurt before heading down the hill for home.

Half-listening to Emma chattering away like a starling as they took the elevator up from the garage and walked along the corridor to the condo, Kathryn rummaged in her purse for the keys, frowning as she saw the note pinned to the door. Then she saw what else was there.

"Emma!" she shouted, and snatched her daughter into her arms, running like a deer back along the corridor and down the stairs. She hammered on Ruth's door, her heart pounding so hard she thought it would burst, her breathing harsh and ragged. Ruth opened the door and they fell inside, Emma crying hysterically.

"Need the phone," Kathryn said, pushing past Ruth and dialing 911. She mastered her breathing, doing her best to speak slowly and distinctly so the dispatcher would make no errors.

"What the hell is going on?" Ruth said, her eyes wide, arms around the weeping child.

"I'm sorry, I thought something bad had happened," Kathryn said, giving Ruth a signal with her eyes. "Emma, you stay here with Ruth for a few minutes, okay? I'll be right back."

"No, no, don't go out there, I'm scared, I'm scared!" Emma whimpered. "Stay here, stay here."

"There's nothing to be afraid of," Kathryn said reassuringly. She went out and back up the stairs. After a little while she heard the deputies pounding up the stairs. She didn't know either of them. The older one's nameplate said GUZMAN. The young blond one was called ESTERHAUS. Kathryn identified herself and went along the corridor to her door with them.

"Jesus Christ, what is *that?*" Esterhaus said, his voice thick with disgust.

"It's an eye," Guzman said matter-of-factly. He leaned closer. A burst of radio traffic squawked from his transceiver. He ignored it. "Can you read what this note says, ma'am?"

"It's in code," Kathryn said. "But I know who it's from."

After the deputies left, Kathryn went back to Ruth's condo and told her what had happened. Ruth suggested it might be a good idea if both she and Emma slept over, but Kathryn assured her it was not necessary.

"Em, how about if you sleep over with Ruth tonight?" she asked her daughter. "I have to go back downtown to talk to the detectives awhile. All right?"

Emma nodded. "Okay. But why is it always you, Mommy? Why doesn't someone else do the work sometimes?"

"They don't have anyone else as good as me," Kathryn told her, smiling reassuringly. "You're not frightened anymore, are you?"

"Not now," Emma said gravely. "But in the hallway I was. You scared me right out of my lungs."

"Don't worry, Ruth," Kathryn told her friend. "There are two detectives from SO out there. They'll be staking the building out all night."

"What time will you be back?"

"About ten, I'd guess. Don't wait up."

She went down to the garage and got into her car. As she drove out, she saw the unmarked sedan parked unobtrusively against the curb near the front entrance of the building; Ed Black and Mervin Phy gave no sign of having seen her as she drove by.

Walt Earheart was waiting for her in his office, his eyes bleary with fatigue, sipping coffee. Detectives Henry Chu and Tom Ney looked up as Kathryn came in.

"Quite a day," Henry observed. "How do you feel?"

"I feel like I want this creep pulled in before he frightens the wits out of me like that again."

"He may have something a bit more permanent than that in mind," Earheart rumbled. "We ran the note past Kazanowski, Kathryn. It wasn't such an easy one this time, but he worked it out."

He pushed a piece of paper across the desk. She turned it around and looked at it.

18/ 16/ 16
25/ 22
8/ 22/ 22/ 18/ 13/ 20
2/ 12/ 6

Underneath the coded message was Kazanowski's translation:

ILL
BE
SEEING
YOU

"This shithead's sure got a twisted sense of humor," Tom Ney said, reading the message over her shoulder. "Signed it like always."

"Yeah, the little gingerbread man. Not that he needed to. His prints were all over it," Earheart said to Kathryn.

"And the eye?"

"I hate to tell you."

"Go ahead."

"I sent it up to Doc Nelson. He says he can't be sure, but it looks like it may have belonged to the Medina kid."

"This is one sick bastard we're dealing with here, Kathryn," Henry Chu observed. "Don't you think maybe you ought to take a little vacation till we get him off the streets for good?"

"I might send Emma to stay with her father for a week or two," Kathryn said. "But I can't just take off, Henry. I've got the grand jury next week."

"We've got Kathryn's condo staked out in case Russell comes back," Earheart said, stifling a huge yawn. "Ed Black and Merv Phy have the swing, Joe Byrne and Bill Larson are taking the graveyard shift, Mike Curran and Hank Schiller will relieve them in the morning. I've briefed Patrol Division to keep a lookout. You guys hit the streets, talk to your snitches, see if you can come up with anything. Russell's out there somewhere."

"Okay, I'm out of here," Henry said, buttoning his immaculately pressed jacket. "Tom?"

"Yo."

The two detectives went out of the office, leaving Kathryn alone with Earheart. He yawned again and rubbed his eyes.

"If I drink any more coffee, I'm not going to be able to sleep until Christmas," he said. "Kathryn, you okay?"

"I'm all right, Walt."

"You want me to drive you home?"

"From the way you look, maybe I should be making you that offer. Thanks, but it's not necessary. Tell me, did you see Dave Granz today?"

"No, I didn't. You want to talk to him? He's probably home."

"He was having his . . . he called it his unveiling. They were taking off his bandages."

"Aha," Earheart said, as if that explained something that had been bothering him.

"What does 'aha' mean?"

"I tried to call him a couple of times, got his answering machine. It had a new message on the tape. It said, 'Dave Granz has gone out with a strange man. He'll be back as soon as they get used to each other.'"

Kathryn shook her head. "He's probably sitting in a bar someplace charming the socks off some impressionable young woman." She stood up and stretched. "I'd better be going. See you tomorrow, Walt."

"I'll walk down to the car with you," the big man said.

"That would be nice." Kathryn smiled. It was Walt's way of looking after her, and to tell the truth, she didn't mind if she had company as she crossed the empty parking lot in the dark.

"Good night, Kathryn," he said as she unlocked her car. "And don't forget: tomorrow is Screw Sanchez Day."

"A-men." Kathryn smiled and got in the car. She smelled the alien presence immediately and opened her mouth to scream. A hard hand clamped itself over her face, stifling her.

"I'm very angry with you, Kathryn." Russell's voice was a papery whisper. He laid the cold blade of the scalpel against her neck. "Very angry indeed."

41

FIRST HE MADE HER CLIMB OVER INTO THE PASSENGER SEAT. From behind he roughly gagged her, then handcuffed her hands behind her back. Then he came around the car and bound her feet together so tightly that she cried out with pain, the sound stifled by the gag. He tilted the passenger seat back so that she was practically lying flat and no one who drew up alongside the car would be able to see her. Then he got into the driver's seat and pulled out of the parking lot, heading north. As he drove he hummed a familiar tune, a nursery rhyme, but Kathryn could not remember what it was called.

Her mind was racing, trying to decide how to defend herself, what approach might work with this madman, when they got to wherever they were going. She tried desperately to remember everything she knew about him, as much to keep at bay the icy fear that kept trying to blank her mind as to think of some way to save herself.

She had no idea where they were, but it did not seem very long until she felt the car slow as he braked and pulled in somewhere. She thought of the automatic in her purse. Useless. It was pitch dark; she could see nothing through the car windows. What time was it? If she didn't get back to her condo, would Ruth call the police? She recalled despairingly that her last admonition to her friend had been that she should not wait up. Unless there was a good late movie on TV, Ruth was probably already in bed. What about the stakeout deputies? They would change over at midnight, quite possibly neither team realizing the other did not know she wasn't back.

He opened the passenger door. The smell of grass and cool evening air filled the car. A park?

"Clever Kathryn," he said, almost as if he was talking to himself. "You made her tell, didn't you? All her pathetic little secrets."

He took hold of the front of her jacket and hauled her to her feet, hitting her flat-handed across the face, hard, hurting blows.

"Bitch," he said conversationally each time he hit her. "Bitch, bitch, bitch."

She felt her lips split and the trickle of blood from her nose. As she teetered on the edge of consciousness, he turned and hurled her to the ground. She fell hard on her shoulder, felt the brittle slipping click of a bone breaking somewhere, and lost consciousness for a moment.

She swam up through blackness. Someone was doing something to her clothes. She opened her eyes and saw the flickering glitter of the scalpel blade in his hand as he cut away her clothing. *Dear sweet God in Heaven no!* Making frantic noises, she thrashed from side to side, trying desperately to get away from him.

"I ... told ... you ... bitch. Don't ... make ... me ... angry," he panted.

She screamed and screamed but nothing got past the stifling gag except a thick choked gurgle. As if in some ghastly nightmare, she recognized where she was: this was the open-air café at the entrance to Cabrillo Park where she had sat and talked to Carol Russell. The blue and white umbrellas towered above her head like ghostly steeples. She felt cool air on her thighs and knew he had cut away her skirt. He kneeled on her legs so she could not move, and she felt him fumbling with her panties. She arched her back, but she could not dislodge him.

"Ah," Russell said, and her soul shriveled as he touched her. Then something moved off to her right and Dave Granz came out of the night. In the strange diffused glow from the street-lights on the highway, his scarred face looked misshapen, like a gargoyle's. Russell saw him too, and sprang to his feet, retreating from the advancing inspector.

"Keep back!" he hissed, brandishing the scalpel.

"Kathryn?" Dave said, never taking his eyes off Russell. "If you're all right, nod your head."

She managed to move her head. He stepped past her toward Russell, who edged back, the scalpel still in his hand.

"Put the knife down, Lee," Dave said softly.

"Why aren't you dead?" Russell shouted. "Why aren't you dead?"

"Last warning. Put the scalpel down."

Russell shook his head and took a step forward. Without hesitation Dave raised his left arm straight out and shot him three times, the slugs from the Bodyguard Airweight .38 Smith & Wesson pistol all grouped in an area the size of a half dollar immediately below the breastbone. Russell collapsed to his knees, a surprised expression on his face. Then as he folded to the ground, Dave stepped light-footedly forward and kicked the scalpel away from the dying man's outstretched fingers. Not five feet away, Kathryn saw Lee Russell's lips move, heard him sigh a single word as the light went out of his eyes.

Then she felt Dave's strong hands lifting her to her feet, cutting the rope binding her feet, taking the gag from her mouth. She tried to say something but her tongue would not function.

"Wait," he said. He went across to the body of Lee Russell and checked the dead man's pockets until he found the handcuff keys. He unlocked them and threw them into the car. Then he put his arms around her and held her tightly as she shivered uncontrollably.

After a while the sheriff-deputies arrived.

Hal Benton insisted on sending her to a spa up in the mountains with strict orders to do nothing but sleep and eat and then sleep and eat some more. After a couple of days of doing nothing, Kathryn started taking bicycle rides, saunas, whirlpool baths, long lazy swims in the heated outdoor pool. She picked up magazines, put them down. Tried to read a detective story, couldn't. By the fourth day, she was bored stiff. She called Hal.

"I want to come back to work," she said without preamble.

"You're supposed to be taking a week off," he said. "What's the matter with you, can't you relax?"

"Maybe if I had a prefrontal lobotomy," she said. "Come on, Hal. I feel fine. Besides, I promised Walt Earheart I'd file on Sanchez."

"Don't you read the papers up there?" Benton said. "Sanchez quit KKSU."

"When was this?"

"The day you were due to appear before the grand jury. The official line is he intends to pursue other career goals."

"And the truth?"

"Walt told me your idea. We all liked it a lot. So Mac issued a warrant for Sanchez's arrest."

"Aw, Hal, that's dirty pool," Kathryn protested. "I wanted to shove it to Sanchez myself."

"No more than the rest of us did. Kathryn, forgive me. I wasn't sure how long you might be . . . away. And I wanted that door shut. Tight. Anyway, Sanchez-wise, you can take my word for it, it's been shoved. All the way."

"I just wish I'd been there to see it. Tell me what happened."

"Sanchez turned himself in. After about fifteen minutes he gave us the name of his snitch. You want to make a guess who it was?"

"Greta Brotherton?"

There was a momentary silence. "Come on, Kathryn, you're kidding, right? No, no one in our office. It was one of the senior detectives, George Tannenbaum."

"I always wondered how he could afford to wear so much gold."

"He was greedy. Turns out Sanchez didn't even have to approach him, he went to Sanchez. Told him he'd pass him inside information on a retainer basis, three hundred bucks a week. Sanchez couldn't believe his luck. That was chicken feed for the kind of stuff he was getting."

"What will happen to him?"

"Tannenbaum? It already happened. Jake Gylam bounced him out of SO like a big rubber ball."

"You still stole my thunder, Hal. That means you owe me."

"So I owe you. So what do you want?"

"First of all, I want you to go out and buy a case of Wild Turkey. Have them send it to Dave Granz. Put a card in it that says, uh, wait a minute . . ."

"He's right here, do you want to talk to him?"

"What's he doing there?"

"Talking about coming back to work, what do you think? He's as crazy as you are."

"What about his hand?"

"We talked it through. He thinks he can cut it and so does Norm Podnoretz. After all, Dave's been trained to shoot left-handed as well as right. He did okay the other night, right? And the prognosis on his injuries is better than we first thought."

"I'll talk to him in a minute. But the whiskey, Hal."

"I'm waiting to hear what goes on the card."

" 'You Were Never Lovelier.' "

"I like it. Anything else?"

"Yes. I want to come back to work."

"Sure. As soon as you're—"

"Tomorrow."

"You know what? You're nuts," Benton said. "But you're my kind of nuts."

"Does that mean yes?"

"Of course it means yes," he told her. "Okay, here's Dave."

"Kathryn?"

"I never got a chance to thank you properly."

"Hell, you don't have to thank me. I had a score to settle myself."

"I still haven't figured out how you managed to turn up like that. How did you know where I was?"

"Pure accident. I heard about what happened at your condo from Rafe Guzman, one of the deputies who responded. He said you were going in to the office, so I came down there to meet you. Got there just as Walt Earheart was getting into his car. He said you'd just left, you were going home. I saw you pull out, but then your car turned north on Pacific. It didn't make sense. So I followed. Simple as that."

"He would have killed me." She shuddered as she remembered the twisted face staring down at her, the glimmering flicker of the scalpel blade.

"Forget that. Remember what I said the other day? Yesterday's gone, tomorrow never comes?"

"I remember. Thank you, Dave."

"Listen, what's this about you're planning to come back to work?"

"I want to. Correction: I need to."

"I know that feeling." There was a pause. "Kathryn?"

"Yes?"

"Russell said something, didn't he? Just before he died?"

"Kim," Kathryn told him. "He said, Kim."

"I wonder who the hell she was?" Dave said.